Artifice

Nights of Shadow

Lianne Miller

Edited by: Christina M. Frey, Page Two Editing
Cover Design by: Suzie Safi, SuzieDesigns
Book Layout ©2013 BookDesignTemplates.com

Artifice–Nights of Shadow (Book One)/ Lianne Miller — 1st ed.
ISBN 978-0-9963768-1-5
ISBN 099637681X

Dedication

For all kindred and tortured spirits enduring challenges and surviving the darkest night of the soul.

Blank Slate

Her eyes flutter open, struggling to focus on her surroundings. The blurred images of three people sharpen into
two men—one tall, the other short—and a woman standing
before her. *Who are these people?* She doesn't know them.
She doesn't know herself. Terrifyingly, there is nothing to
reference, not a single memory, as if she didn't exist until
this moment. *Who am I? Who are they? Why am I here?*

The woman makes eye contact with her and begins to
speak. She doesn't know the foreign language, but the woman's accent seems familiar, and she doesn't know why. The
woman mutters several incomprehensible words and leaves
the room with the shorter man. With an oddly triumphant
smile he glances back at the tall man before exiting the room.

After the door closes behind the others, the tall man steps
forward and motions for her to sit in one of the two chairs
facing each other. Seated, he looks at her as if studying her
face. He seems vaguely familiar, yet she cannot recall seeing
him before. Surely she'd remember him, wouldn't she? Aside
from his towering eight inches over her, he is a man that

people, especially women, don't forget.

His deep-brown, almost-black hair hangs long over his brow and ears. She watches as he raises a strong hand with long fingers and slowly rakes them through his hair twice, pausing at the crown to keep his bangs from falling. When he lowers the hand, his bangs slide down past his eyebrows again and slightly brush his long eyelashes when he glances up at them. His dark-brown eyes settle on her again, seeming to suggest he is trying to decide where to begin.

Waiting for him to speak, but enjoying the chance to observe him in silence, she examines his features. The man's face reflects strength, with high cheekbones and a straight nose that is not too wide, thin, long, or short. His lips are full, well balanced but not fat; in her estimation, perfect like his nose. His dark eyes are penetrating, smoldering—eyes she would gladly burn hours watching.

Sweeping her gaze over his lean, well-toned body, she notices he is wearing a pair of blue jeans and a short-sleeved red T-shirt that fit him well. Desire to touch him—to see whether he is real—propels her hand forward as she reaches for him. Her arm stops midway, dropping to her lap when he abruptly speaks.

His natural pitch is deep, smooth, and melodious. She notices the English words are tinged with a slight accent as he speaks:

"Hear me. You will do as I command. Your name is Eliza Ross. You were born twenty-three years ago in Bozeman, Montana, and you live there now. I am going to tell you about your life, and you will believe these details as your thoughts and memories.

"You will not remember me when you become self-aware, beyond obeying any commands I give you. When I snap my fingers, you will remain in an altered state of consciousness, perceiving and interacting with its reality. You will not achieve self-awareness until I fully release you from my control. Do you understand me?"

"Yes." She doesn't recognize the sound of her voice but knows it's hers, although the American accent seems off somehow. *This isn't right, or is it? Why did I expect Italian? Wait, how do I know the difference between accents?* It occurs to her that the woman's accent was Irish, but this man's accent is Bulgarian. She is clueless how she knows this, but she does.

With unanswerable questions threatening to overwhelm her mind, she refocuses her attention on the man sitting before her. The emotions flickering in his eyes seem to bury one in particular behind the others, making it stand out more—profound pain. She feels a strong urge to please him, and to ease whatever burden he's carrying.

His eyes never waver from hers, as if he's giving her time to absorb what he said, before he speaks again. "What is your name?"

"Eliza Ross."

"How old are you?"

"I'm twenty-three."

Trying to gauge whether her answers please him, she misses the next question, and he repeats it. "Where do you live?"

"Bozeman, Montana." It occurs to her to add, "I was born here."

"Yes." A faint smile creases the corners of his mouth. "Good. I am going to tell you about your thoughts, your memories. You will always remember them after I release you from my control when you become self-aware. Do you understand?"

"Yes, I understand."

In the next moment, she finds herself lying in bed in an apartment—her apartment, she realizes. She sits up and looks around, feeling confused. Climbing off the bed, accepting that the strange encounter was a dream, she wanders through the tiny apartment and finds she is alone. *I live alone. I've always been alone.*

No one wants her; there is no family, and she doesn't have any friends. Sighing, she accepts that life has always been this way.

TABLE OF CONTENTS

TABLE OF CONTENTS (continued)

CHAPTER 1: ELIZA

Intruder

The phone on the other end is ringing. *Pick up, pick up, pick up!*

On the third ring someone finally answers. "9-1-1, please state your name and the location and nature of the emergency."

Terrified, Eliza chokes out the words in a hushed whisper. "There's a stranger in my apartment."

The detached voice of the woman asks, "What's your name and address, please?"

"Eliza Ross, 1245 Broken Willow Drive, Apartment 3B." The words rush forward, tripping and strangling one another into a murmur. There are moments, like now, when she wishes this apartment were within the city limits instead of being on the rural outskirts; it always delays an emergency response.

The woman sounds professionally aloof and bored. "I'm sorry, Miss Ross, I can barely hear you. Please restate your address."

"1245 Broken Willow Drive, Apartment 3B." Frustrated, her voice is sharper than she intended. *Too loud, he's going to hear me.*

"Thank you. Is the intruder still inside your home?"

"Yes, I think so. I don't know." The stranger disappeared from the bedroom the second she picked up the phone, but she can't shake the feeling that he's still in the apartment somewhere.

The operator's obviously scripted directions carry no emotion. "We have sheriff deputies en route. Please stay on the line with me until they arrive. Where are you in the apartment?"

Eliza crouches with her back pressing against the wall. Holding a hand over her mouth and the phone, she speaks in a shaky voice. "In the bedroom closet. Can you please hurry? I'm afraid."

"The deputies will be there within five minutes. I need you to remain calm and stay on the line with me. Do you understand?"

Through the slats in the closet door, Eliza watches in terror as the intruder's shadow appears and stops on the other side of the thin barrier between them. A breath catches in her throat and her heart thumps wildly. Convinced her body is betraying its presence, she retreats further into the corner behind a garment bag and struggles to swallow the bile that is rising, choking her.

"Eliza, do you understand?" There's a hint of impatience in the woman's voice.

The shadow doesn't move. Her racing mind tunes out the

operator. *Who is this man? Why is he stalking me?* This incident is the fifth time in under a month that she's awakened to find him standing near the foot of her bed, staring at her. *Why? What does he want from me?*

Afraid to speak—fearing the stalker will hear—she presses a button on the phone, hoping the operator will understand. The intruder's shadow moves closer to the closet door, and the doorknob slowly starts turning. A violent shudder surges through her, almost releasing the scream lodged in her throat. *He's going to find me—he's going to find me. I have no way out.*

"Eliza, I'm still here, and I assume that you cannot speak. Please don't push any buttons on the phone. I don't want the call accidentally cut off. The sheriff deputies are ninety seconds away. I will not hang up. I am here. I will remain on the line with you until they arrive."

She leans forward, peering around the garment bag, and watches as the shadowy man begins to open the closet door. The hinges creak as the intruder steps to the left of the door to look inside. Body trembling, Eliza retreats further, pressing back once more against the wall. She stops breathing for so long that her lungs begin to ache. *I must breathe. God, don't let him hear me, don't let him find me.* As quietly as possible, she draws a long, deep breath and raggedly exhales.

"The sheriff deputies are at the apartment complex and should be at your door in a minute. Is the intruder still in your apartment?"

Wide-eyed, Eliza listens to the operator as the stalker shoves the hanging clothes toward her. The garment bag drapes over her crouched frame. Her eyes shift up to the closet rod; she sees the man's hand slide the clothes to the opposite side. The steady reassurances from the operator fall away as time begins to run out. Instinctually, she changes position and balances on the balls of her feet, ready to spring past the man.

She startles at a sudden loud knock on the apartment door. *They're here ... they're here.* The man steps back and his shadow wafts away. *Has he left? Is he lying in wait for me to poke my head out? Do I stay put until they find me?*

"Eliza, the deputies are at your door. Can you open the door?" To gain her attention, the operator's voice rises in pitch and repeats the question.

A shattering crack resounds from the other room, followed by a loud bang as the apartment door thumps violently against the wall. Eliza flinches at the sound. *What if he's still in the room? Will they catch him before he can grab me?* Eliza knows the deputies are in the apartment; but terrified that he is standing there, waiting, she struggles to put her body in motion. She sucks in a deep breath and leans forward to look around the garment bag, through the open door, and into the bedroom. No one is there.

Quickly springing to her feet, Eliza bolts from the closet and runs headlong from the bedroom through the short hallway without looking back. Relief resonates in every inch of her body as she bursts into the living room. *I made it. I made it. Thank God, they're here.* She sees the deputies, and a huge smile spreads across her face but falters when her mind registers their threatening reaction.

"Stop, or I'll shoot!" the officers are shouting, guns drawn and pointed at her chest.

CHAPTER 2: ELIZA

Interrogation

Blinking at their repeated commands, Eliza at first fears the intruder has followed her. Afraid to look behind, but not knowing whether she's within his reach, she takes another couple steps forward.

Then she sees the nearest officer's eyes narrow and his shoulders tense, preparing to fire.

"Lie down on the ground and lace your fingers behind your head," the shorter of the two deputies is hollering.

The taller officer is shouting, "Get on the ground, get on the ground. Now!"

Confused, Eliza stares at them until it finally registers that their demanding, gruff voices are directed at her. Dropping to the floor, she begins moving her hands over the back of her head to comply with the deputies' commands. A knee slamming into her back causes abrupt pain, knocking the breath out of her. She attempts to look over her shoulder, but before she can see the officer's face, he slams her head against the floor.

Her eyes dart wildly around the room. The shorter deputy is standing over her, pistol aimed at her head, while the other deputy wrenches her arms down and behind her back.

"I'm Eliza Ross. I live here." A whimpering groan escapes from her as the cold metal cuffs tighten around her wrists. "I'm Eliza Ross! I live here!"

The deputy standing over her says, "Is there anyone else in the apartment?" His eyes scan the room and look beyond, toward the empty hallway.

"I live alone. The intruder was in my bedroom as you busted through the door."

"Don't move." The second deputy rises to his feet.

Immediate relief sweeps over Eliza as the pressure of the deputy's knee leaves her back. She watches both officers cautiously approach the short hallway leading to the bedroom. One after the other disappears around the corner. Pulse pounding—afraid of what may await them—Eliza holds her breath. Anxiety and fear threaten to explode her heart.

Minutes impersonating hours pass before she hears the second deputy call out, "Clear."

Moments later the deputies return to the living room, and one pulls Eliza roughly to her feet. Spinning her around, nearly knocking her off balance, he removes the cuffs. The other officer directs Eliza to take a seat in the nearest recliner. Shaken, she quickly complies and rubs at the red welts encircling her wrists.

"We've searched the entire apartment, Miss Ross, and we're not finding any signs of an intruder," the shorter deputy says.

Eliza's eyes roam over the officers' name badges.

"Are you certain someone was in here tonight?" he continues.

The absurd question is infuriating. "Yes, absolutely. I live here alone and was sleeping, but a man standing at the foot of my bed woke me."

"Your door was locked and secured when we arrived." The taller deputy, Rasmussen, sounds skeptical. "Your windows and sliding glass door are locked, and we're not seeing any signs of a break-in here."

"I know what I saw." She scowls and bites back the nasty retort that is balanced on the edge of her tongue.

After a moment Deputy Rasmussen continues. "Does anyone else have a key to your apartment? A friend, a boyfriend, a family member, perhaps?"

Great, here we go. Her head shakes from side to side. "I'm the only one with a key, aside from the apartment manager. A man was in my bedroom."

The first deputy, Kline, punches a number into his phone and steps past the broken door into the third-floor hall of the apartment building. His voice is muffled, making it difficult for Eliza to hear precisely what he is saying.

Deputy Rasmussen continues asking questions, but his expression grows increasingly dubious each time Eliza tries convincing him that a stranger was in the apartment when they arrived. *Why doesn't he believe me?*

"Are you certain that you've never given a key to anyone, or that someone didn't have access to obtain a key?" he asks for the fourth time.

Deputy Kline returns, and Eliza arches an eyebrow as he strides across the room and whispers in the other man's ear. Together they look at her, disbelief written plainly across their faces.

"Will you excuse us a moment, Miss Ross? We'll be right back."

They leave her sitting alone and feeling perplexed. She tunes out her other senses, her keen hearing isolating their voices as she listens to their conversation. They are trying to decide what to do and obviously think she has made a prank call to get attention. Her would-be rescuers are standing in the hallway, doubting every word she said. Disgusted, she replays the night's events in her mind.

That evening she went to bed around ten o'clock, an early bedtime for her, but she was planning to attend an astronomy lab before regular classes in the morning. She fell asleep around midnight, and then something—not a sound or a touch but another's presence, watching her—jolted her awake. When her eyes opened, she saw the dark figure of a man standing at the foot of the bed. He was just staring at her, no movement or sound. She recoiled into a sitting position against the headboard and stared back, unable to breathe as she took in his features in the dim light. For several seconds she felt frozen in place, captured by his penetrating gaze.

The man was tall and clean shaven, with dark hair falling past his brows and into his eyes. His deep, dark eyes bored into her, and a shiver ran up her spine. Her heart pounded in her ears. Fear choked her as she fumbled for the cell phone on the bedside table. Not finding it, she averted her eyes barely long enough to snatch up the phone from the floor. She had no idea how it had gotten there. When she looked back, the man was gone.

Where did he go? Wildly she looked around at the shadows along the walls and near the furniture. Her ragged breaths sparred for room, with one rushing out and another racing to get in. Her mind pleaded with her trembling body to move. *Run. Run. Run. Hide. Run. Hide.*

Eliza sprang off the bed and jerked the closet door open, closing it quietly behind her. *I hope he didn't hear that.* The shoes on the floor tripped her as she moved to the side near the long garment bags with formal gowns she never wore. She sank to her knees and struggled to control her shaking hands.

Fumbling fingers pushed 9-9-1. *Damn it, get it right!* Freaking out, she sucked in and blew out a deep breath to steady her hands as she dialed a second time. Fingers hit the right keys and her fear dropped a notch as the operator answered the call.

Lost in a tangle of thoughts, Eliza startles when Deputy Kline clears his throat, and she looks up to see him standing right in front of her. "Miss Ross, our department shows that this is your fifth call this month about an intruder in your apartment. Each time we've responded we've found no one, and your doors and windows are always securely locked. Are you sure you're not having a dream or imagining this event?"

Sometimes I hate it when I'm right. Exhaling a snort, Eliza says, "You're kidding me, right?"

Deputy Kline's tone is unequivocal. "No ma'am, we're quite serious."

"I am not imagining this, nor have I dreamed it up. A man is stalking me and somehow he keeps getting into my apartment in the middle of the night."

Deputy Rasmussen starts to say something, but stops and instead asks if Eliza will answer a series of other questions. He claims it will help him and his partner determine what is going on, but she knows better—it will be a waste of time. The conversation the deputies had in the hall, combined with their body language now, tells her their minds are made up.

His face is stern as he asks, "Are you on any medications? Sleeping pills or antidepressants?"

"What? No. I don't take any drugs." *Yep, now they think I'm some flaky attention-starved wacko chick.*

"How long have you lived alone?"

"I've lived in this apartment for four years. I moved here after my first year of college."

"Have you ever had any roommates or boyfriends that may have had access to your key?"

"No." Eliza's cheeks flush and she looks down at her battered wrists. Embarrassingly, she's about to admit there has never been a boyfriend, ever. "I've lived alone since I left the college dormitory, and I don't date."

The deputies persist, grilling Eliza about her life. Who are her friends—she doesn't have any. What about family— she doesn't have any. Their disbelieving tones imply there must be family, friends, boyfriends, or lovers, something, someone. After the fifth time they repeat their line of questions, her mind mockingly screams the circumstances of her life. *I. Don't. Have. Anybody. There's. Never. Been. Anyone. In. My. Life.*

She has lived a life of isolation, routinely discarded and dismissed by others. Abandoned to the state as a baby, she was transferred once or twice a year from one foster family to another. When she turned eighteen and graduated high school, it was a relief being free from those who never really wanted her. The last set of foster parents barely contained their joy the day she moved out.

Bouncing from home to home wasn't ideal for forming friendships with her peers. Eliza never attended the same school long enough to make friends. In college, she expected that to change, but quickly discovered that people shy away from her. They are polite, yet remain distant; she has no idea why.

Because I'm a freak. A freaking unwanted reject.

Pathetically, at age twenty-three she's now admitting to these officers that she has never dated—ever. She briefly recalls a few good-looking young men she has daydreamed about and hoped ... and still hopes. They sit with her in the same classroom, but they never notice her enough to look twice, and rarely speak to her beyond social courtesy.

The officers glance over her slender build and lithe figure, their manner shouting disbelief. She's five foot seven with long dark-brown hair that reaches the small of her back. Matching deep-brown eyes set off her creamy yet pale complexion—a reflection she's seen enough to know that while not stunning, she's not ugly either. Her shoulders slump as her body pulls in on itself. She knows they'll reject her like everyone else does.

Eliza finally raises her eyes and Deputy Rasmussen cringes and shudders as her gaze meets his. He blinks and squints as if trying to remove an unwanted image from his mind. She ponders his reaction; she has seen it before with others and still has no idea what causes their revulsion. She knows how to be charming and witty, but people hardly give her the chance to show that side of herself. If someone, anyone, ever took a moment to talk with her, they would find out she's intelligent and considerate too. A defiant anger swells inside her. *I'm not going to allow them to tear me down. I'm not crazy.*

"Miss Ross, it's not that we don't believe you, but it is getting increasingly difficult to conceive the possibility that someone is routinely breaking into your apartment."

Deputy Kline's smug contradiction firms her resolve. Taking two steadying breaths, she says, "I don't know what to tell you. I know someone is getting in here. I don't know how he's doing it or why, but I know he's been here several times."

The deputies exchange a look, and Deputy Rasmussen says, "We'll keep extra patrol in the area tonight and will have our shift sergeant call you in the morning. Meanwhile, you'll want to let your apartment manager know that your door needs to be repaired, and you may want to install new locks. To secure the apartment after we leave—given that we broke the doorjamb—lodge a kitchen chair under the door handle until it can be fixed."

Dejected, Eliza nods, thanking them as they leave. After cleaning the broken doorframe debris off the floor, she wedges a chair under the doorknob. She is physically drained, but her mind whirls with a dozen cascading thoughts.

Who is the man stalking me? How is he getting in? Why is he watching me? Why does he keep coming back, and why does he care when no one else does? Didn't he get the memo that I'm to be shunned and outcast by the whole of society? She smiles deprecatingly at her own joke.

CHAPTER 3: ELIZA

Déjà vu

Eliza makes one more trek through the apartment, double-checking the locks on the windows and sliding glass door. In the bedroom, she peers under the bed and in the closet for the mysterious intruder. A sigh whispers past her lips as she slides under the covers on the bed. She knows she is acting like a five-year-old looking for monsters.

Ready to hit redial if *he* returns, she clutches the cell phone under the blankets. She doesn't want to sleep. She's afraid to because of what, no, whom she may see when she wakes. Hours slay minutes as Eliza lies in the dark. Something buried deep in her brain keeps nagging, a thought or a memory, and she cannot bring it forward enough to evaluate it. A strong sense that something is wrong, abhorrently wrong, with her fills her with dread. Even the deputies' comments suggested something is not right. *Am I losing my mind?*

Eventually Eliza starts to doze. Her eyes fly open, jarring her awake, and she looks around the room. Nothing. Eyelids grow heavy, close again, and she drifts off only to startle awake again moments later. Peering around the room, she still finds nothing. Three hours and a dozen checks later, she finally drifts into a deep sleep.

He's watching. He's watching me. HE'S WATCHING ME. Subconscious thoughts jolt Eliza awake. Her eyes immediately settle on the man standing at the foot of her bed, and her pulse races. *He's back.* He's staring, watching, not moving or saying a word. *What is wrong with him? Why is he here?*

Her trembling finger moves toward the touch screen of her phone, trying, needing to hit the redial square. Faintly she hears a ringing sound. Relief fades when she realizes the man hears it too. For a split second, he glances toward the hand under the covers, then back to her face. He is unnaturally still—his lack of sound and movement almost unhinges her—and her gaze locks on him. She becomes lost in the depths of his penetrating eyes. *I know those eyes ...*

Spellbound, she cannot pry her focus away. Eliza searches the strong lines of his face for a clue. He's perfect—so perfect, the angles and planes too perfect. Every feature is handsome, proportional, a balance of strength and character. His straight nose, slightly parted full lips, square jaw, rounded chin, and the dark, shaggy hair hanging over his brows and past his ears are exquisite. Then she notices his bottom lip quivering and the pain flickering through his eyes. Her breath catches, forcing her to gulp and dislodge it from her throat.

He's been so still for so long that Eliza recoils when he

raises a hand to sweep the hair away from his face. His hand rakes through a second time, remains at the crown of his head, and his eyes trap hers. There's something ... the way he's standing there, looking at her, is hauntingly familiar. *I know him. How do I know him?*

Fear seizes her throat. "W-who ... who are you?"

Several long minutes pass. Neither moves, and the stranger doesn't answer. The silence suddenly shatters into raised voices and fists pounding against the apartment door. The man glances furtively past the open bedroom door toward the commotion coming from the other room. Eliza's eyes remain locked on him.

Dropping the hand from his head, he turns back, and his deep voice fills with anguish before it fades. "Elizabetta, don't s—"

Then he disappears, leaving Eliza gaping. Her mind can't process it; he didn't turn, walk, or run away, but just vanished as if he were never there. She wonders whether her eyes and mind really are deceiving her.

The deputies enter the apartment, calling her name. Incapable of responding at first, she keeps staring beyond the foot of the bed. Then, shaking and panting for air, she musters enough sense to call out. "I'm in here."

Flashlights pan around the room as the deputies rush in and find her with wide, terrified eyes riveted on the spot where the stranger stood mere seconds before. "H-h-he was—was—was right there, right there ... h-he just disappeared."

"Are you all right?" One of the deputies reaches for her

arm. She doesn't resist as he pulls her to the edge of the bed.

Eliza is trembling uncontrollably. "He ... he—"

"Are you hurt? Did he touch you?"

This makes no sense. How am I going to explain this? "He ... he ..." *People cannot simply vanish into nothingness.* "That man was back."

"Where is he now?" Another deputy looks around the room, his posture tense.

Glancing up at the officer, Eliza blinks several times and lowers her gaze to the floor. She whispers, "I ... d-don't know."

This time four officers are present, including Deputies Kline and Rasmussen. They seat her in a chair in the living room again. Then the questions start, questions she cannot possibly answer. Finally they ask one she can.

"He's tall, maybe six two or six three, with a lean build. He's white. Dark-brown or black hair that isn't short or long, but kind of shaggy like he needs a haircut. Dark eyes, maybe brown. No beard or moustache."

"Can you tell us what he's wearing?" Deputy Rasmussen is asking the questions now.

When she doesn't respond, he rephrases it. "Eliza, can you describe the clothes he had on?"

I have no idea. She realizes that after becoming trapped in his gaze, her eyes saw nothing else. The heat of blush prickles her skin at the thoughts flickering ahead of her response. *He could have been standing there stark naked for all I know. Why didn't I notice? Wow, what if he's been naked each time he's been here?* She's unsure which is more disturbing, the possibility he was undressed or that she didn't notice. "I don't know."

"Did he have any identifying marks, scars, or tattoos?"

"I don't know." *Why can't I get beyond his eyes?*

"Are you certain you were awake and not dreaming?"

"I was awake. This was no dream." *I know him. Why can't I place him? Is he in one of my classes?*

"Did this man say or do anything?"

Eliza's head tilts in confusion, eyes squinting as she tries to make sense of what the intruder said. "Not really. He mostly just stood there. The only thing he said was 'Elizabetta, don't s—'" *Don't what? Scream, say, start, shout? Shinola—shit.* "I don't know what he meant. His voice faded right before he disappeared."

"Is Elizabetta your full first name?"

"No, Eliza is my full name."

"Do you have any idea why he would call you that?"

"No."

"Are you taking any kind of medication?" The dubious look on Deputy Rasmussen's face matches his incredulous tone.

Infuriated, Eliza snarls, "What?"

"Are you taking any medication at bedtime that may produce hallucinations or vivid dreams?"

"No." Disgust drips off each letter.

"Have you had any recent illnesses or injuries to your head?"

Seriously? She blinks a few times and stares at the deputy for a long moment. "No. That man was here, and at the foot of my bed as you pounded down the door."

"Ma'am, your bedroom window and balcony door are locked. If there was a man in your room, where did he go? He never came past us."

"He ... it was like he ..." *They're not going to believe me.* "He just vanished, disappeared."

"What, like into thin air, just poof?"

"Yes."

Another deputy suppresses a laugh, and Eliza gives him a scornful look. Exasperated, she adds, "I don't know how he did it, I only know that he did."

Silently exchanging skeptical looks, they excuse themselves to talk privately in the hallway. A few minutes later, they return. A tinge of concern is in Deputy Rasmussen's voice. "Would you consent to a medical evaluation?"

"What?"

"We'd like to take you to the emergency room and have you evaluated. Will you consent to going?"

"Look"—anger explodes to the surface—"I'm not crazy. I know what I saw. I'm not on any drugs, and I don't have an injury or illness. I don't see the point in it."

Kline, who seems less empathetic than the other deputies, counters. "You're saying a man vanished, and that he is the same man you now claim has broken into this apartment six times this month—the last two times just tonight. We really need to eliminate all possibilities. So will you please come with us willingly? It is best for you to cooperate." At her hesitation, his eyes narrow. "If we have to remove you against your will, it will result in a seventy-two-hour medical hold rather than a quick medical review to ensure that you are okay."

Eliza's eyes flash with anger at his threat. *I know I sound crazy, but I'm not freaking nuts!* She shakes the thought away, still trying to form a reply, but she's unable to let go of a nagging doubt. *Am I?* She notes the looks on each of the four faces before her—concern, skepticism, annoyance, and determination—and she knows they will give her no choice if she refuses to comply. Grudgingly, she nods in consent.

They allow her to change out of the pajamas she's wearing and into street clothes, and within minutes she is sitting in the backseat of a patrol unit. A blur of images race past—she is too lost within her mind to notice—as they transport her to the hospital. *What is wrong with me? Is there something wrong with me?*

Closing her eyes, she vividly recalls the stranger's expression just before he vanished. The anguished tone in his voice—when he said that name, Elizabetta—carried or implied something, but what? Her eyes fly open. Aside from familiar, his voice sounded, no, felt as if it curled around and caressed the name in a tender embrace. *Why?*

Eliza's mind drifts over her past encounters with him. The deputies know of the last six visits, but in truth, she has now seen him almost a dozen times. At first she believed it was a dream or imagination; if she blinked or looked away he was gone when she looked back. It wasn't until the night he lingered that she realized he was real.

A shiver crawls up her spine as it replays in her mind. She woke and found him standing at the foot of the bed. Expecting he'd disappear when she looked away, she rolled out of bed to get a glass of water. He turned to follow her. Determined her mind was playing tricks, she dismissed it, but when she turned away from the sink, he was standing in the archway, watching, staring at her. The glass slipped from her hand and struck the floor, shattering into a dozen pieces as it splattered water everywhere.

She stumbled back, uncertain and dizzy, and slid down the front of the cabinet. Eyes clenched shut, she rested her head against her knees. *He's not real, not real, not here.* When Eliza lifted her head, he was gone. She cleaned up the broken glass and water before she filled a second glass. Her hands shook as she gulped and half choked on the water. It took her a moment to loosen her grip and leave the glass on the counter.

Barely past the threshold of the bedroom door, her arm brushed against someone in the dark. She dived across the bed, grabbed the phone, and dialed 9-1-1. He was gone before the deputies arrived. The other nights after that encounter she never hesitated, but called the moment he appeared. Each time the officers responded, checked the apartment, and took a statement, she was deeply rattled and unable to describe the intruder.

Ironically, this time Eliza finally recalled details of this man, and met complete disbelief from the deputies. *They think I'm nuts. I'm not crazy. He was there.*

CHAPTER 4: DMITRI
Torment of Tantalus

I hate this, every rotting last minute of it.

Shashenka Belyakov has deliberately imposed this duty on Dmitri, knowing what it will do to him, knowing the price he will pay for either success or failure. Dmitri's nostrils flare as the cops' SUVs pull away from the front of the apartment building. *This is not good. If they knew we are beyond their imaginable fears, they'd let her go and never come back.*

Tugging keys from his jeans' front pocket, he unlocks his car and starts the engine. Traffic is light this late and Dmitri quickly catches up to the patrol units, then slows to allow space between them. The patrol unit following the SUV Elizabetta is in turns in another direction halfway through town. Dmitri, tailing the first vehicle at a discreet distance, watches as it parks in front of the emergency room doors. His mind rushes over ways to snatch her from the cops, but he cannot seem to form a solid plan. Short of killing two deputies, for the moment it's impossible.

Walking in through the emergency room entrance, he notices the waiting area on the right, and on the left, the admissions window next to a long hallway with examination rooms. Elizabetta is sitting with the admitting clerk, both deputies standing nearby. Not expecting to see her mere feet away, and fearing her reaction should she see him, he turns and rushes for the exit. The doors are closing behind him when an uncomfortable prickling sensation crawls up his neck. He tenses suddenly at the thought of allowing her out of his sight, turns back, and slips unnoticed into the waiting area again. Taking a seat that allows a view of the opposite corridor, he sighs. *I need to get her out of here. It'd be so much easier if I could just walk up to her.*

Dmitri thumbs through a magazine, pretending to read the articles, occasionally glancing at the wall clock. He wonders when the chance to grab Elizabetta will present itself. Hope fades when one officer takes up guard near the door of the exam room she went in. Each passing minute increases his tension, and nervous panic sets in when Dmitri sees the troubled expression on the nurse exiting the room. *This was not supposed to happen.*

Surreptitiously he snaps a photograph of the nurse and deputies with his cell phone. He repeats the action when the first doctor, and then a second doctor go into the room. When he succeeds in removing Elizabetta, these others will need their memories of her erased. Destroying the hospital records will be the easy part. Hunting down and then wiping the minds of those involved will be more difficult. He watches a lab technician enter after the second doctor leaves, and waits patiently to take a photograph of the young man. That makes nine people he needs to find after he rescues Elizabetta.

Almost an hour later, the second doctor reenters the exam room. Her posture is tense. The deputies are still standing by, and their body language also hints at the growing medical concern. Doubtless they are yet unaware of what the problem is, but perceptibly understand that Elizabetta is not normal. Hiding the telltale markers of her true nature is impossible. He needs to plan her escape and stop this before it goes too far.

Dmitri stands, stretches, and walks back to the hallway intersection and through the main hall. Although he would prefer to spirit Elizabetta away and take her through the closest exit, it's more prudent to find an alternate route out of the hospital. And that offers no quick solution. Several areas are locked for the night; it takes him at least fifteen minutes of careful searching to find another exit, one that won't trigger an alarm.

After grabbing Elizabetta, Dmitri will whisk her down the halls to a corner stairwell. They'll go into the basement, past the storage rooms and morgue, and leave through the doors next to the unloading dock. Given the parking available, he decides to pull the car around before they make their run. He'll need to throw the deputies off their trail and leave no opportunity for them to see the make and model of his car.

Their escape is ready. Dmitri returns to the emergency room but freezes when he discovers the deputies are gone. He rushes outside and finds an ambulance parked where the patrol unit had been. Pushing fingers through his hair, he grips the top of his skull and squeezes his eyes shut. *Will this un-mitigated catastrophe ever end?* He's not thinking clearly and is about to lose control. If Shashenka has to send the others to help him clean up this mess, it will bring trouble. The only way to minimize Shashenka's certain wrath is to find Elizabetta and bring her back into his control before he has to report his folly.

Dmitri runs to the car and drives wildly back to the apartment. Disappointment staggers him for several minutes when he finds it empty. *Think, damn it, think. Is it possible that she's still at the hospital?* When he didn't see the deputies standing guard at the door, he assumed they had left with her. Perhaps they returned to duty if the doctors kept Elizabetta because of the medical mystery he knows she presents.

After racing across town and reentering the hospital, Dmitri steals a lab coat from an employee locker before going to the emergency room. His steps falter as he registers the condition of the examination room. No one is on the bed. It's been remade.

Turning, he smiles at a young woman behind the counter of the nurses' station. His body releases an attractant phero-mone as his eyes lock on hers, and immediately he notices the fluctuation in her pupils; it signals she is resistant to mind control. A very small percentage of the human population is fully immune, but some, like this woman, have natural inhibitors that hinder the effectiveness of his defenses and charms. "Excuse me, can you help me?"

The woman reacts the way he expects; she pauses, takes in

his features, and returns a smile. She says with a suggestive expression, "That depends on what kind of help you're looking for."

"I'm new here. This is my first night, in fact, and I'm not finding the patient I'm supposed to do a blood draw on." Dmitri is standing close enough to the counter that she won't notice he lacks a lab kit.

The woman's brows crease as she feigns a pout. "Oh, I was hoping ..." She sighs without finishing the obvious thought. "What's the patient's name?"

"Eliza Ross. She's supposed to be in exam room three, but it's empty."

The woman looks across the hall. "I must have been examining the patient in room five. I didn't know she'd left."

"Do you know where she went?"

He waits patiently while the woman reviews the log.

"Very strange. We always log a patient in and out, noting their disposition."

Dmitri forces a soft, teasing chuckle. "Seems I'm not alone in losing track of patients tonight." His tone turns sardonic. "Makes me feel so much better."

"But it is totally against protocol. The last item in the system is Miss Ross's intake. There's nothing showing where she went."

Panic turns into anger, and he irrationally wants to destroy the woman. Fearing that he's about to lose control, Dmitri glances down the hall. His mind is on fire. Frantically he pulls against the rage and tries to restore composure. *Shit, shit, shit. Not good, fight it, think.*

He grips the edge of the counter to prevent his hands from ripping her throat out, and snarls, "Well, can't you ask someone what happened to her?"

The nurse scowls, acting more disturbed by the protocol violation than by the missing patient or the underlying threat in his tone. "Rhonda was the nurse attending her. Doctors Carlson and Shelby did her examination. Rhonda and Dr. Shelby are in Trauma Two with an auto accident victim with multiple injuries. I won't be able to interrupt them and don't know when they'll have the patient stabilized. I think Dr. Carlson went home. He was only on call tonight."

When he doesn't respond, the nurse says, "Perhaps you should return to the lab and I can call you there later. Until either the record of her visit is logged, or Dr. Shelby and Rhonda come out of the trauma room, there is little we can do to find her."

Nodding, Dmitri turns to leave the emergency room. He has to use every trick he's learned as a Druzhina not to go on a murderous rampage. *I've got to get her back. I can't lose her now.* For several long minutes he sits in the car as he forces logic and reason past his primal urge for bloodlust. He decides to return to the apartment, where he can finish calming down and start planning the search for Elizabetta.

Except that once there, the more he plans and paces, the more worked up he becomes. He can't hide her disappearance; it's only a matter of time before others discover his failure. Unlike the programming setbacks, this is far worse than a missed deadline.

Elizabetta was supposed to be ready within three to four

months of the start, but her resistance to the mind reset and lapses of self-awareness have repeatedly pushed back the completion date. Over the last eleven months, it has brought suspicion that Dmitri is deliberately stalling. He's not. This isn't the first time he's programmed someone's mind, but he's never experienced this level of difficulty before and has no idea why it's not going well. There were only a couple of elements left to plant in her mind; he was optimistic of finishing on time. It likely won't happen now, and there is no way to keep the others from finding out.

Shashenka routinely sends others to check on his progress, and Dmitri expects another visit from one of them within the next few days. Desperate, he hopes it will be anyone but Alexander Kozlov, especially with this latest development. *Let it be anyone but him.*

Dmitri's thoughts linger on Alexander for a moment, and he stops pacing and looks at the living room wall. The last time they met, Dmitri put a fist clean through the wall in Elizabetta's apartment. There is no sign of the damage now, but his anger, which even the thought of Alexander provokes in him, still ripples near the surface. Dmitri's fists clench and unclench as he recalls their last encounter.

Alexander's face was smug as he said, "Shashenka's getting nervous, you know."

"Yes, I know. Tell Master that I am doing my job."

A boisterous laugh filled the room. "I hope for your sake that you don't cross him again. To watch him kill you because of her would be a shame."

"You're a sick, sadistic bastard," Dmitri growled as his

hand clamped around Alexander's throat and slammed him into a wall.

Amusement danced in Alexander's eyes. Dmitri's grip tightened and the other man choked out, "You have no one to blame but yourself."

That comment signaled that their conversation would go nowhere. Dmitri released him. "Just leave, Alexander. I don't need your reminders. Leave now."

Alexander straightened his shirt. "I wonder"—he paused—"are you going to make the same mistake twice?"

Dmitri's hands curled into fists. "It wasn't a mistake," he mumbled under his breath.

Laughter thundered from Alexander before he continued. "Of course it was a mistake, dear brother, of course it was. You promised the same last time, and you reneged on the deal. Why do you think Shashenka gave you this shit detail?"

"What was a mistake? You know it's beyond any one of us when it happens. And who could have done it?"

"Then you never should have promised anything about her to begin with. You should have merely taken her and been done with it, and you wouldn't be in the position you're in now."

Dmitri knew that—knows that still—and didn't need reminders, especially from Alexander. That broken promise links inextricably his worst regret and deepest remorse. His jaw flexes at the memories.

His reply was terse as he told Alexander, "There'll be no mistakes this time."

"Good." Alexander's hand clasped his shoulder. "I will

hold you to that, for your sake. It'd be a shame to watch Shashenka destroy you. I've enjoyed your company far too much never to see you again."

Alexander left and Dmitri's pent-up rage exploded to the surface. That's when he punched the wall.

Thinking back, Dmitri sighs. It hasn't always been this way between them. Ironically, they got along very well when Dmitri first joined the Druzhina; he even teamed with Alexander on numerous missions over the years. They were effective, worked well together, and dare he admit, even liked one another. That changed when Dmitri brought Elizabetta into their fold.

Immediately smitten with her, Alexander boldly sought her affection. He went out of his way to go on assignment with her, under the guise of training her, even though Dmitri was the one tasked to do so. Alexander claimed seniority in order to spend time with Elizabetta and ignored her repeated rebuffs of his advances. That's where the animosity began between the two men. Alexander didn't relent in his pursuit; instead of respecting her decision, he blamed Dmitri for costing him a chance he never really had from the start.

For years Dmitri has dodged Alexander's many attempts to harm his standing with the Druzhina, and he has put up with the petty jealousy games ever since. If he had not, Alexander might have succeeded in destroying him long ago.

Dmitri glances again at the wall where the hole once was; she never knew it was ever there. The hidden reminder of where it was echoes the truth of the many details he's either taken or planted in her mind about this false reality she's living. He has no such luxury—his life is a nightmare, not a lie.

Endless remorse smothers the last of the rage inside him. *Shashenka has destroyed all that was good in my miserable life. This punishment is killing me ... my punishment ... my ... torment of Tantalus. All this I suffer for failing to uphold my promise of her recruitment to him, for failing her.*

A sad resignation settles over him as he realizes that he may not be able to find Elizabetta in time. The situation will be far worse if one of the others, especially Alexander, arrives and her whereabouts are unknown. There's only one way he can avoid the consequences of her disappearance—he must report this debacle to Shashenka now. Finding her first is no longer an option.

CHAPTER 5: ELIZA

Medical Enigma

The deputies transport Eliza to Trinity Hospital and leave her sitting in an exam room with an officer outside the door. *Why am I here? Is there really something wrong with me? Why won't the cops leave? Sheesh, they act as if I robbed a bank.* She looks down at what she's wearing. She's feeling like a criminal—a vulnerable one, sitting there in a hospital gown—and she shifts uncomfortably as cool air seeps through the openings of the gown. Perhaps if she plays their game, this will all be over in the next couple of hours.

A nurse enters the room to take her vitals. She asks the basic questions, but confusion turns her face into a perplexed mask while she jots the details on the patient forms. She drops Eliza's wrist twice while trying to take her pulse. Sounding disoriented, she directs Eliza to wait for the doctor to come in, and scurries out of the room.

Eliza sits on the edge of the bed, rubbing her feet one against the other in a feeble attempt to exhaust her nervous energy. She keeps glancing up, watching the clock. Almost forty minutes pass before the doctor arrives. Nothing makes sense—from the deputies' disbelief to the nurse's even stranger behavior. The woman seemed rather unsettled and stopped looking her in the eye. She wouldn't answer Eliza's questions, either, and was noticeably trembling and swallowing hard by the time she left the room. A foreboding feeling swells inside Eliza, and she is unable to understand why the nurse was so upset.

"Hello, Miss Ross, I'm Dr. Carlson, and I'm the on-call psychiatrist tonight."

I'm not crazy. The glare she gives him is all the greeting he's going to get.

After a long moment, he seems to figure that out and launches into a litany of questions about her diet, health, work, school, and exercise routines. Dr. Carlson says that another medical doctor will evaluate her physical health soon, but for his own reference he will need to know whether she's had any recent illnesses or past head injuries.

I already told the nurse—didn't you read the notes? "I've never been sick or needed medical treatment of any kind." Eliza's tone is icy.

"Ever?" Dr. Carlson sounds incredulous.

"Never." She eyes him coldly. "Is this absolutely necessary?"

He nods. "Yes, I'm sorry, it is. Are you certain that you've never had any illnesses or injuries?"

Why do they keep asking that? It's normal for someone my age, isn't it? "None."

"Hmm. Okay." His gaze narrows as he studies her. "What

I'd like to do, Miss Ross, is have Dr. Shelby finish the physical exam, and then decide our next step."

She finds it disconcerting the way he says "next step"; something tells her that she won't want to take it. Her stomach twists into a knot, but she nods and looks down at the floor. *Why do I need to see another doctor? Am I losing my mind? Is that how the man that is there, but isn't, keeps appearing and disappearing—because he doesn't exist?*

Dr. Carlson leaves, and another twenty minutes pass before Dr. Shelby enters the room. She takes Eliza's vitals again, frowning with apparent concern. "I thought the nurse was mistaken or had used faulty devices, yet I'm seeing the same results with mine. I'm stumped by the presentation of your vitals."

Eliza's stomach does backflips as she stares at the doctor. "What do you mean?"

Tilting her head, Dr. Shelby replies, "You feel cold to the touch, and the thermometers consistently record your body temperature far below normal. I cannot feel a pulse, and my stethoscope is not detecting your heartbeat or breaths."

Loud alarms ring in Eliza's ears, nearly drowning out what the doctor says next.

Dr. Shelby waves her hand. "I'm sure there's a logical explanation. Must be our night for faulty devices."

Then her questions mirror what the others have asked repeatedly, and Eliza numbly answers each. She focuses on a speck in the floor tile.

Think. Think. Am I going crazy? Have I lost my mind? Why don't I feel chilled? If I'm asking those questions, doesn't that prove I'm sane? Then she remembers why she's here. *I swear, if I ever get my hands on that man, I will kill him for putting me through this.*

"And are you certain that you've never had any medical care in the past?" Dr. Shelby asks for the umpteenth time. "What about routine physicals and well-care checks? Is there a family doctor or a family member we could inquire with regarding your medical history?"

What is wrong with these people? Have they never seen a healthy young adult? "No. I've never seen a doctor for any reason." The pent-up frustration comes forth as a ragged sigh. "I highly doubt my past foster families would provide information. The longest I spent with any of them was just under a year, and they all acted relieved when I moved on to the next family."

"I'm sorry to hear that, Eliza." Dr. Shelby looks empathetic. "I'll order your lab work and see whether everything is normal before I give my recommendation to Dr. Carlson, if that's all right with you?" Her tone is clinical.

Does it matter if it's not? "Yes, that's fine." Eliza doesn't look up.

After the doctor steps out of the room, the minutes tick by more slowly, and Eliza finds herself watching the clock. The sun will be up in a couple of hours; at this rate she will miss the astronomy lab, and possibly her first class. *Go to the hospital, they said. It is just a quick evaluation, they said. At this rate I'll be in my thirties before they're done with me.*

Eliza's irritation starts to give way to doubt. *What if something is wrong with me?* She places a hand over her heart and feels a slow, regular thump. *I can't be imagining it. Is it possible these professionals are wrong? The cops don't believe me about the man in my room. The doctors don't believe my medical history. Is everything I believe a lie? Is this a dream? Am I dead? Damn, get a grip. I'm stronger, better than this. They are wrong.*

Knowing she's normal and healthy doesn't assuage her runaway fears. *Am I oblivious of reality?* She wonders whether this mystery is why various foster families always seemed relieved to be rid of her, or why fellow students are reluctant to accept her attempts at friendship. *Is this why no guy has ever shown the slightest interest? Am I a colossal freak of nature?*

Eliza's thoughts are in an enormous tangle when the lab technician walks into the room. She notices that he's in his mid- to late twenties and above average in looks. The timid smile she gives goes unseen as he sets the tray aside and prepares the items needed for the blood draw. He barely looks at her arm—never her face—frowns when he touches her cold skin, and speaks only when his job demands it. The familiar pang of rejection strikes her heart. *Why am I so invisible and unwanted?* She sulks as he fills three vials of blood and leaves the room.

It's a quarter after five when the doctor comes back. The way Dr. Shelby's brows draw together quickly blunts Eliza's relief.

"Eliza, I know you've been abundantly patient since you were brought in, but I'm afraid that we'll need to redo your labs."

Worry and dread take root, writhing through her body and claiming every cell they touch. "Is there something wrong with me?" There's an odd relief in saying it aloud.

"Something is wrong with your lab results—I cannot tell if it is a lab error or something indicative of your health. I don't know what to make of it."

Puzzled, Eliza stares at the woman as if she isn't speaking English.

"It's an anomaly that I've never seen before. Apart from your temperature, parts of your CBC—your complete blood count—defy explanation. We're still waiting for the full results."

Eliza's voice pitches up in fear. "What does that mean?"

Dr. Shelby chuckles nervously. "Well, if these counts are accurate, it means that you're dead." She smiles, seemingly amused by the brash and incomprehensible comment.

That's so not funny. Eliza gulps. "Excuse me?"

"That's the anomaly. Plainly, you are sitting here, breathing, talking, and moving, yet your red cell count is too low to sustain life. Your white cell count is typical for someone with a high-grade fever. Your hemoglobin is devoid of any oxygen, and your platelet counts are contrary to the red cell count in a manner that is impossible. We can't even discern your blood type. The conclusions defy logic."

The only part of Eliza's body still working are her eyelids. Her vocal cords and mouth have gone on strike. She blinks and blinks again, unable to make her brain send any words to her eagerly waiting tongue.

Dr. Shelby says, "I'd like to rerun the lab panels and see

whether we can get true results. However, we'll probably transfer you to Mercy first and then order the blood workup from there."

"Mercy?" Her body is trembling, and a chill that wasn't there moments ago is seeping through her bones.

"Yes, Mercy Medical Center. It's a specialized medical hospital with a psychiatric wing."

Great, I'm not only crazy, but now I'm sick too? "Why there?"

Dr. Shelby places a hand on Eliza's shoulder. "Dr. Carlson feels a seventy-two hour evaluation is necessary to resolve the reason for your various 9-1-1 calls. Given recent events, and now this ... with your blood results and physical examination, I think it's best if we move you there until we have answers for both mysteries."

"I'm not crazy." Eliza's voice is flat.

Dr. Shelby grimaces. "I'm sorry, Eliza, it is an involuntary hold and you must comply with Dr. Carlson's orders. Myself, I am more concerned with your lab results and whether there may be an underlying medical condition causing what is happening to you."

Eliza's eyes dart toward the door and see two officers now standing guard. They'd probably tackle and Taser her before she got twenty feet out the door. "What happens when the seventy-two hours is up?"

"If everything checks out, and the labs reveal you're healthy, then we will release you."

"I don't have any choice in this, do I?"

"No, I'm sorry, you don't."

Dr. Shelby leaves moments later and an orderly enters with a wheelchair. Eliza scowls at him as he explains it is protocol. Reluctantly she moves off the exam table and sits in the chair. The orderly wheels Eliza to the waiting patrol unit as Deputy Kline appears and walks ahead to open the doors. Deputy Rasmussen is already behind the wheel, waiting. When they reach the cruiser, Kline opens a rear door and motions for her to get in. His smug look tells her that he is even more skeptical now than when he first came to her apartment. Irrational fear swamps her senses and she refuses to move; the orderly and deputy lift her unwilling body out of the wheelchair and place her on the backseat of the patrol unit. She flinches as the officer buckles her seat belt and slams the door.

Ten minutes after leaving Trinity Hospital, they arrive at Mercy Medical Center, where Dr. Carlson is waiting in admissions with a warm smile. He actually looks eager to see her. Eliza feels sick to her stomach. *I can't do this, shouldn't be here.* The officers flank either side of her and escort her forward, making escape impossible.

CHAPTER 6: DMITRI

I am Dead

I am dead. I am so damn dead. Dmitri steps out of the apartment and gets in the car before he places the call. As the phone begins ringing, he almost hangs up. Closing his eyes, he summons the courage needed to face the wrath about to befall him.

"Hello, Dmitri." Shashenka's tone is polite, a dangerous sign. "Tell me you have good news today."

The parched lining of his throat and mouth prevents swallowing. His voice cracks. "We have a complication, Master."

A long pause is never good. "What do you mean by a complication?"

"Something happened. Elizabetta reached a moment of self-awareness between sleep and programming."

"Surely that's not a difficulty for you, Dmitri. Why are you bothering me with this trivial detail?" Shashenka's words drip animosity.

It shouldn't be difficult. Something isn't right; she's like a corrupted computer program. Dmitri looks up at the apartment before answering. "Before I could lull her into a trance, she called 9-1-1 and the cops arrived."

"What?" The voice thunders through the phone.

"She told them that I was an intruder." He adds quickly, "They never saw me, of course, but the problem is that they ..." He deliberately omits the number of times they've been called. "They now think she's sick or crazy and took her to a local hospital for evaluation."

Shashenka doubtless understands the implication. "You must remove her now."

"That, Master, is the complication."

Heavy rapid breaths and another long pause. "What do you mean?"

Ignoring the lump in his throat, Dmitri explains, "I left to recon the layout of the hospital, looking for the best way to remove her. When I returned to the examination room, she was gone."

Shashenka roars in disbelief, demanding to know how this is possible. A shiver rockets through Dmitri's body. A long minute passes as his mind struggles between remnants of past torture and the need to answer the question now being shouted at him. *Yep, I am so dead.* He swallows hard and clears his throat. "Gone, Master. No longer in the emergency room, and she hasn't returned to the apartment. I don't know where she is."

"This is intolerable. How dare you fail me again, Dmitri. I am sending six of the Druzhinas to help you find her and fix this mess. When you find her, you will undo any damage from this blunder of yours."

"Yes, Master."

"You will wipe the memories of every cop, doctor, and nurse in contact with her. Do you understand me?"

"Yes, Master."

"You'd better be clear on this point, Dmitri. If you leave one sliver of proof of her existence or fail to find her, I will make your death excruciatingly painful and slow. I will make sure you endure a hundred years of daily torture before I take pity and end your life. Are you grasping that?"

"Yes, Master, I'm clear on what needs to be done." Even though he is not standing before Shashenka, Dmitri bows his head and adds, "I am sorry, Master."

The call cuts off.

I'm dead—my body just doesn't know it yet. Dmitri closes his eyes, leans back against the seat, and takes another deep breath. He needs to think, to develop a plan. At best he has fewer than twelve hours to search for, perhaps find Elizabetta before the others arrive.

Returning to the hospital, Dmitri moves stealthily through the corridors until he spots an unstaffed computer terminal. Within a few minutes he finds the intake record for Eliza Ross. The file contains no other notes or status of admittance or discharge. He searches system-wide for any other files. He looks again. Nothing ... nothing. *Where the hell is she?*

About to delete the file, Dmitri thinks better of it; if Elizabetta is still under medical control, someone will create a document trail. First he must find her. He can destroy the records afterward.

It takes three hours to look in every room of the ten-floor hospital. Elizabetta is nowhere to be found. Discouraged, he wonders whether he missed so much as a broom closet, but knows he hasn't. Not once in all his years as a Druzhina has he ever failed to locate a target. *I will find her.* Finding another unstaffed terminal, Dmitri accesses the patient files again; there's still nothing beyond her intake records. *She is somewhere, damn it.*

He doubles back to the apartment, in case she has returned there. She hasn't. Looking at his watch, Dmitri knows the others will arrive before midnight, and he's running out of time. A wild thought sends him rushing out the door. *What if the doctors didn't look too closely, discharged her, and the deputies have her at the station?* He decides it is worth a look.

Using caution, Dmitri slips into the sheriff's department building; it takes under an hour to search the basement and the two floors above ground. She's not there, either. He crosses the street to the courthouse on the slight possibility they've taken her there—nothing. He returns to the last place he saw her, the hospital. It doesn't take long to find an open computer terminal and perform a third search for her records. Still nothing.

"When does this damn place input patient information?" he grumbles aloud, then closes the screen and slams his palms against the keyboard, splintering it into dozens of pieces. *Shit. Shit, shit, shit.* Dmitri unplugs it, gathering all the broken parts. After placing them in the nearby trash can, he takes the bag out of the receptacle. He knows not to leave evidence behind, and a missing keyboard raises fewer suspicions than one inexplicably pulverized.

After leaving the hospital again, he detours to a shopping mall on the other side of town and disposes of the garbage bag in an outdoor food court trash can. At times like this, Dmitri is grateful for the ability to go unnoticed.

There is nothing left to do but return to the apartment to wait for the others. Once there he slumps onto a recliner, rests his elbows on his knees, and laces his fingers across the back of his head. The silence wraps him in a suffocating shroud. Dmitri finds it takes extra effort to keep his mind off past events. It's not the recent past but ancient past gnawing and nagging, as it has been the closer Elizabetta's reset nears completion. He wants to restore something, anything, go outside the boundaries and leave some original personality or trait intact. He'd choose her confident smile, or perhaps the mischievous glint that always sparked in her eyes right before she did something daring and breathtaking. Maybe it should be her self-assuredness, or her ...

Grimacing at the truth—she will never be that way again—Dmitri knows he'd fully restore her if given the chance. The fractured, cringing shell she is now is disgusting to watch. It doesn't make any sense to him to take Elizabetta to this extreme. *What is Shashenka going to do with her in this broken state?* They've left her intelligence alone, yet dumbed her down to a stupefied idiot. Still, the question nags at him.

The ringing phone disrupts his thoughts; the others are a

few blocks away and will arrive soon. Minutes later Dmitri answers their knock and sees a mixture of expressions on the faces before him. After years of serving together, he knows each of them well and is not surprised by their demeanor.

Married to his best friend, Vladimir Jagr, Anna Kachida often stands in silent support of both of them and is equally unhappy about the changes in Elizabetta. Her long black hair is hanging loosely down her back and her short, spritelike figure barely contains her happiness to see him. Smiling warmly, she glides forward to give him a hug. "It's good to find you well, Dmitri. We'll find her. Everything will be all right." She places a hand against Dmitri's cheek, her almond eyes conveying silent reassurance.

Vladimir's face is set in a fierce scowl; but as he comes through the door behind Anna, he pauses, clasping Dmitri's shoulder before nodding curtly and going into the room. His displeasure is for their mission. They've spoken privately many times about Elizabetta's reset, and the circumstances for it have never sat well with Vladimir. Unfortunately he is as powerless as Dmitri is to stop it.

Stephan Vasilou and Kees De Haan look uncomfortable, making it obvious that they'd rather be elsewhere— something they share in common with him. Dmitri nods at them as they walk into the room.

Shaking her head—no greeting or words, only a sigh to let him know she's looking out for him—Katherine Zervas walks through the doorway, her blond curls bouncing. Her features are similar to those of her mate, Kees, but their temperaments are opposite; she's outspoken action and he's quiet analysis. Katherine has bailed Dmitri out of a few scrapes before, and it's a relief to see her now. She's always been vocal with her displeasure over Shashenka's punishments for failure. Dmitri knows that she'll do everything possible to bring success to their mission.

The last to enter is Alexander. His quick smile, sandy-brown hair, and gray eyes are deceptive; Dmitri knows he's relishing the prospect of this debacle turning out for the worst. Doubtless he's eager for it to result in punishment for Dmitri.

For Alexander this current fiasco is merely another round in the game of rivalry between them—a game that Dmitri stopped playing long ago. Unfortunately his refusal to engage in this twisted pastime has never stopped Alexander from continuing his side of it, because there are moments, like now, when Dmitri is forced to play along.

Dmitri closes the door, thinking about those Shashenka didn't send—Maria D'Arcy, Sofia Castillo, Victoria Edwards, and Justin Walker. He is particularly disappointed that Maria isn't on the rescue team. Her talents, given the self-awareness Elizabetta is displaying, would swiftly restore his control over the situation.

Katherine is the first to speak. "Okay, Dmitri, bring us up to speed. What are we dealing with here? What are your theories?"

"Yes. Tell us, dear brother, how did you possibly lose her?" Alexander laughs.

Glaring, Dmitri answers Katherine's question. "As I told Shashenka, there's been a problem with Elizabetta reaching

self-awareness when transitioning from sleep to programming state. The foundation seems intact—she believes the
backstory of her life and she has accepted the false memories
and thinks she is a college student. But during a transition
she thought I was an intruder and called the cops." He omits
once again the fact that it was the sixth time she had called
them. "They took her to the hospital, and while I was scout-
ing for the best exit, they moved her."

"Moved her?" Anna raises one eyebrow.

Katherine asks, "Are you certain that she wasn't admitted?"

"I've checked the entire hospital and she is not there."

"How much ground and how many sites do we need to
cover?" Kees's question signals that his analytical mind is
ready to calculate the odds of success or failure and find the
flaws in their plans.

"It's clear that Elizabetta's not here and hasn't returned
since they took her. We're far enough along in her"—Dmitri
pauses over the word he detests— "reprogramming that if
she were free of them, she'd come here. I've checked the
hospital, sheriff's department, and courthouse, with no
success. Considering the circumstances, I think she will
remain in either police or medical custody—both are within a
ten-mile radius of this location."

Dmitri looks at them, knowing their preferences; they
usually split into the same teams when on assignment.
"There are seven of us—we can either work in groups of two
or three. I will remain the odd man out because I know the
territory."

Everyone approves with little discussion among them. Vladimir, Anna, and Alexander will form the group surveilling and searching the sheriff's department. Stephan, Katherine, and Kees will take the hospital. Dmitri will watch the apartment and provide skills to both groups as needed.

There is no need to assign individual tasks; after years of working together, each knows the skills and roles the others will perform. Proficiency, perfection, efficiency, and speed are traits of the Druzhina. Their successes are legendary, with no failed missions among any of them, Dmitri included, until these setbacks with Elizabetta.

Dmitri is hoping they'll find and return Elizabetta to the apartment by sunrise. Given who she is, failure to secure her would bring more than just embarrassment to the Druzhina; it could cause their downfall.

CHAPTER 7: ELIZA

Seventy-two Hours

When the intake paperwork is complete, Dr. Carlson leads Eliza through a series of brightly lit hallways to an elevator, taking them to the seventh floor. The unease raging inside her threatens to become manic as the doors open. *Are they keeping insanity out or creating it inside these walls?* Reinforced mesh–laced glass protects the nurses on the other side of the counter. Heavy steel doors with security-style locks are on either side of the short hall. Looking up, she notices security cameras mounted in various locations, vigilantly watching the halls.

A nurse hands Dr. Carlson a paper through a concave slot in the center window. When he hands it back with his signature, she nods to a coworker, then steps toward the locked door near the end of the counter and waits until the buzzer sounds before joining those waiting in the hall. The deputies follow Dr. Carlson and Eliza while the nurse leads the way. Her voice is overly cheerful as she says, "Right this way. Your room is in the isolation sector at the end of the west wing."

Eliza suddenly envisions permanently removing the smile from the woman's face by gouging her eyes out and shredding the flesh from her cheeks. Almost as quickly she shakes her head to dismiss the violent thought. *What is wrong with me?*

They pass through one of the heavy steel doors into a common area filled with tables, chairs, two couches, and a flat-screen television mounted on a wall. Next they walk past windowed wards, many with curtains drawn around individual beds. Still more have curtains open, exposing people too dazed or drugged to react. A few try looking in Eliza's direction, but she doubts their minds register what they see. Others lie with eyes closed, or staring blankly at the ceiling. A foreboding fear pervades Eliza's body and triggers an internal alarm. *Am I going to end up like them?*

A series of doors along the hallway lead to smaller rooms; private patient rooms, Eliza speculates. Near the end of the hallway is another forbidding steel-reinforced door. The nurse swipes a card through a reader to unlock the door, and the small group continues forward.

This area looks and feels different from the previous section; it's more impenetrable, severe, and ominous. A shiver runs up Eliza's spine. *I'm never going to get out of this place.* Twice as many cameras line the corridor, and above each door is a motion detector with a blinking green light that turns red as they pass. Each door has a small, square glass window at face level.

Eliza's instincts scream that she cannot do this, must not be here. "I don't understand. Why am I here?"

A smile starts to spread across the nurse's face, but it falters as she seems to notice the rising panic and confusion in Eliza's expression. "The isolation wing of our mental health facility serves two purposes—protecting patients posing a high-risk threat to themselves or others and providing quarantine for patients diagnosed with a communicable disease."

I'm the one being stalked by some madman, and suddenly I'm the threat? Scowling because no one is listening to her, she argues, "I'm not sick, and I know I'm not crazy."

Dr. Carlson smiles as if she's a daft child. "We've yet to determine the full state of your mental health. It's your lab and physical results requiring the need for an isolation room."

"But Dr. Shelby said the tests are an anomaly and their results impossible."

"I understand that, but until we know the source of the lab error or a true result on your blood work, we must remain cautious."

Mouth gaping, Eliza struggles to find words. Arguing will only make this worse. Maybe if she plays along, this seventy-two hour hold will end and she can add this to her long list of bad memories.

"Um ..." Her mouth overrides what her brain is shouting. "Okay."

Dispirited, she follows the nurse to a room at the end of the hall. The nurse swipes a card and enters a code on the keypad before the door unlocks and swings open. The number painted on the center of the gray steel door, above the window, simply reads ISO-7G.

The stark emptiness of the room sends another shudder through Eliza's body. The room is white, with padded walls, and the single exterior window is a long, narrow solid pane of glass near the top of the wall. There is no furniture beyond a thin plastic mattress with no bedding, and in one corner is a bedpan. Two security cameras are perched near the high ceiling in opposite corners, focusing on the room below.

Dr. Carlson turns to the deputies, thanks them for the escort, and instructs the nurse to lead them out. He promises to tell their department, at the end of the required hold, the results of the evaluation. Eliza watches as they leave, a sinking feeling growing inside.

I need out. I need out now. I can't be here, I can't ... they'll never let me go. She runs a hand under her hair, tugging at the nape of her neck. *There's something wrong with me. I know there's something wrong with me.*

Now Dr. Carlson's tone is abrupt. "I have to do my rounds now, but I'll make sure the nurse takes care of the labs Dr. Shelby requested. I'll have my secretary tell the nurse of your appointment time, and will see you later this morning or this afternoon."

Nausea grips her as he leaves the room. Eliza wraps her arms across her churning stomach, unsure what to say. "Thank you" seems inappropriate—she is neither thankful nor eager to be inside this room. Instead she nods because it's the single motion she can muster.

The middle-aged nurse reenters a few minutes later and scans the patient tag on Eliza's wrist into a small handheld device. She taps briefly on the keypad before putting it in her pocket. Because of the isolation standards, she explains, they will serve all meals directly to her in this room, under the continuously watching cameras. Because Eliza missed breakfast, the nurse promises to check with the kitchen for a late meal or snack and have it delivered to the room. Before she leaves, she confirms that a lab technician will arrive shortly for the blood draw Dr. Shelby ordered.

Eliza flinches at the sound of the automatic lock engaging as the nurse leaves. She moves slowly to the middle of the room, turns in a deliberate, slow circle to look for a way out, and, examining its details, finds none. Feeling dazed and drained, mind overloaded, she lowers herself onto the mattress in the corner and pulls her knees against her chest. With chin resting on them, she rocks and waits.

I am not crazy ... I am not crazy ... crazy ... I am ... I am crazy. No, I am not crazy. Her mind shuts down, leaving silence in its deafening wake as she stares at the door.

The seventy-two hour hold becomes a blur. Doctors, lab technicians, nurses, and other staff frequently enter and leave the room. The buzz of excitement among them adds to Eliza's confusion. They are repeatedly asking questions, always the same questions. They poke, prod, and draw blood once, twice, three times. They take turns feeling for a pulse they cannot find and listening to the supposed silence of her heart and lungs.

Finally left alone for a few moments, Eliza scowls at the IV in her arm. It is there for two reasons: first, to give easy access for more blood draws, and second, to provide fluids since she's now unexpectedly developed difficulty eating. Since arriving here her rebel stomach has decided to revolt, rejecting every meal they bring. Still, they deliver food trays and encourage her to try eating. Now she looks across at the latest tray of untouched food. No point in trying; the unappetizing food won't stay down regardless.

The door opens and someone steps into the room, wearing a protective suit. Everyone entering her room wears one now; they proclaim it is something to do with the unknown reasons for her blood test results. They don't know if she's contagious. It makes them look alien, every inch of their body hidden from view but their eyes, visible through the clear pane of plastic. This current visitor is Dr. Shelby.

"How are you doing today, Eliza?"

"I'm fine." *At least I will be if you let me go.*

"As I told you yesterday, I've sent your lab results on to a doctor specializing in blood serum analysis. He's recommending pooling the resources of his department and the CDC to further explore the anomaly of your blood."

What is wrong with me? "I honestly don't feel sick. I feel healthy. Is it possible that this is normal for me?"

Dr. Shelby winces. "It shouldn't be normal or healthy for anyone. I think Dr. Jacoby's analogy is the best I've heard." Her eyes look sympathetic. "Understand it's quite a mystery—he means no offense by it. He said he's seen corpses with better blood screens. Whatever is going on defies logic and medical science."

Eliza closes her gaping mouth. *Real funny, laugh at the*

walking dead girl. Shaking her head, trying to clear it—none of this makes sense—she replies, "I don't understand."

"Neither do we, and we're working diligently to find answers."

Eliza stares numbly at the door after she leaves. She's still staring at it when another hooded figure enters the room. It's Dr. Carlson, and the grave concern in his eyes makes her inwardly cringe.

He looks at her, looks away, and then toward her again. "Please sit down, Eliza." He motions to a chair—one of two they've since brought to this barren room.

Complying, she sits, not taking her eyes from him. "You don't look happy."

Dr. Carlson inhales deeply through his nose. "The results of your psychological test aren't as baffling as what Dr. Shelby's team is dealing with, but they cause me some concern."

Well, of course. "Why?" Eliza is blunt. No matter what Dr. Carlson says, there is nothing wrong with her mind.

"The tests are intentionally redundant. They're meant to ferret out true emotion and the psychological scope of a person's thought and mental processes. Someone answering consistently but presenting contrary to those answers may be exhibiting symptoms of one or more disorders."

Translation: I'm screwed. "Disorders?"

Dr. Carlson nods. "Because your tests reveal that you're mentally competent, or at the least functional, they give a foundation for a diagnosis that we'll work with."

When Eliza frowns and says nothing, he continues, "I'm diagnosing you with low latent inhibition, or LLI. It's an overstimulation of senses that can lead to antisocial behavior and personality disorders. It explains your hypersensitive and acute simultaneous awareness to all stimuli. LLI people often struggle to, or cannot singularly focus."

He pauses. "It may explain your isolation from society. Going by these results, I'm inclined to think that because of LLI you may be in the early or a dormant phase of dissociative identity disorder, or DID."

I'm not antisocial, and my ability to focus isn't why society shuns me.

He doesn't react to Eliza's body tensing as it begins to tremble.

"DID is a newer term for multiple personality disorder, or MPD. Your test results may imply one dominant and one or more suppressed personalities. If we rule those out, we need to look at the possibility of paranoia or schizophrenia."

"What?" Eliza nearly shouts. "That's not possible. I'm fine. I know I'm fine, and there's nothing wrong with my mind." *This is bullshit.*

"I'm sorry Eliza, but you're not fine." He seems to consider her response. "You are claiming to see a man who doesn't seem to exist. With proper mental health care management and medication, though, you can still lead a nearly normal life—with some supervision, of course."

"Proper mental health care?" Her heart is pounding—she can feel it, regardless if they claim it's not there—and the sound of it reverberating in her ears threatens to drown the next words he says.

"Yes." Dr. Carlson's face is a mask of professional calm.

"We can do a lot to stabilize and manage your conditions through counseling therapies and medications. Regrettably, until Dr. Shelby figures out the nature of your blood disorder, I'm hesitant to start any medication that may further aggravate that unknown condition."

There is something wrong with these people. It's not me. "No, no, no. The tests are wrong. This can't be right. There's nothing wrong with me."

"Eliza, denial is a normal part of this process, and we'll help you cope and get through it. I will conference with Dr. Shelby as her team continues treating your blood disorder and general health."

Rage is building; her chest is heaving and nostrils are flaring with each word that tumbles out of his mouth. He's either oblivious or ignoring it.

"Then we'll start you on the appropriate medication to treat your condition. Meanwhile, until we start your medication, I will get you started with the counseling right away."

Eliza jumps to her feet and takes a step toward him. She wants to cut him to shreds and tear his eyes and tongue out. Briefly she pictures doing just that, and the potential for destroying the man horrifies her. Eyes clenched shut, she forces the gruesome images from her mind. "What if I don't want your or Dr. Shelby's treatments?"

Dr. Carlson shakes his head. "That is not an option, Eliza. Now please sit down. It's in your best interests to allow and follow our treatment plans. Even healthy, until you're able to resume eating meals and keep them down, we wouldn't release you."

The world is imploding in pandemonium, and her chest constricts against its pressure. She slumps into the chair. *Seventy-two-hour hold.* The verdict—in Eliza's mind—is indefinite involuntary medical detention. She listens numbly as Dr. Carlson details the circumstances and conditions of her continued stay.

Hers is a complicated case, he explains. They don't know whether her blood disorder is contagious, fatal, or both. They cannot figure out why it's impossible to detect a pulse, heartbeat, or air moving through her lungs, and won't take her word for it that she can feel those signs of life. They are consulting other experts about the eating disorder. They are going to poke, prod, question, report, and test and fail, and start again. They will perform MRIs, CAT scans, sonograms, and other procedures to unlock her mysteries. Some tests must wait until they know whether her condition is contagious. Until they know more, they will not let her go; she is to remain in this isolation room as Dr. Shelby's team tries solving the physical health mysteries. Dr. Carlson and his staff will treat the LLI daily while testing her for DID, paranoia, schizophrenia, or some combination of the lot.

She doesn't feel paranoid about anything, other than being kept in this place. Raking through memories of the stalker, Eliza wonders again if the man exists. She knows he does. *If I ever get my hands on him, he's dead meat.* The whole ordeal is threatening her sanity—if she wasn't a lunatic before, she surely will be when they finish with her. She is powerless to stop this madness.

They finally allow her a blanket and pillow for the thin

mattress on the floor. They also deliver a small table, several magazines, a pocket calendar, a journal, and a single pen for her to use. After Dr. Carlson leaves, Eliza sits at the table with the journal open before her. Hours pass as her mind replays the events leading to the present. Her thoughts keep coming back to the strange man at the foot of her bed. This started with him; she knows it. *He is real. He is not a dream, a delusion. He exists, and I should know him.* Finally she takes the pen and writes three words: "Who are you?"

CHAPTER 8: DMITRI

More Complications

Four days pass before Dmitri's team catches a break in locating Elizabetta. Katherine's monitoring of the hospital records alerts them to the transfer. The hospital staff seemingly delayed entry of the records because of a seventy-two-hour medical hold, but now that a decision has been made, someone finally has added the data. The news brings little relief; the Druzhinas know time is running out. If one person makes the connection to what Elizabetta is, the upheaval in their world will have lasting ramifications. There will be no way to undo the damage such knowledge will cause—no way to avoid the mass hysteria and chaos that will ensue.

Stephan makes the call to Dmitri. "We know where she went. They transferred her to Mercy Medical Center; we're trying to learn whether she's still there or if they released her."

Is it another dead end, or do we have her this time? Dmitri looks around the apartment, trying to squelch the hope soaring in his chest. "Don't destroy the records there until we are

77

certain where she is. She's not here, so I'm assuming they still have her at Mercy."

As soon as Stephan hangs up, Dmitri quickly places a call to Anna. "We may know where she is." *Elizabetta is finally within my reach.* His tone is urgent. "I'm on my way to get you three, and we'll pick up the others at Trinity. We'll all go to Mercy together and hopefully find her there."

"It's about time," Anna exclaims with a loud exhaled breath. "Shashenka is becoming impatient with our lack of progress."

Dmitri snaps, "I know that." He's uncomfortably aware of their master's growing anger and disappointment. If the team fails, Dmitri's life is over. "I'll see you soon."

Minutes later he's picked up both groups and they're heading to Mercy Medical Center. They park in the underground garage, where Dmitri recaps the plan to find Elizabetta.

Anna and Stephan will access the computers, search for Elizabetta's records, and stand by to delete them. Dmitri and Vladimir will try to reach Elizabetta's room and get her out of the hospital.

"Perhaps we can enter her room as visitors," Dmitri says. "Katherine, Kees, and Alexander, see if you can find any scrubs, lab coats, or other garb we may need to remove her."

Alexander scoffs. "I don't see why that's necessary when we have the ability to hide our presence from them."

"Yes, *we* do, but it will cause an unnecessary commotion if someone raises an alarm at seeing Elizabetta leave without a medical professional escorting her. She's in no condition to make herself invisible to them."

Dmitri snaps his teeth in a hiss as Alexander continues, "We're going to alter their minds anyway. What difference does it make if they see her walking out alone?"

It's obvious why Shashenka never uses Alexander when moving a live target. "The difference is the growing list of minds we need to scrub after we get her back," Dmitri says. "It's one hurdle finding and removing memories of those directly involved—it's quite another, hunting down an unknown number of others to discern what they may know."

"Oh." Alexander concedes with a dismissive wave of his hand. "You may have a point."

Dmitri glares at him before addressing the rest of the group. "Let's get this done."

They take the elevator up to the ground floor and go in separate directions from there. All but Vladimir and Dmitri veil their presence by using their speed and releasing a pheromone that blocks others from registering in their mind what their eyes see. One of their kind could be standing right next to an unsuspecting person, and that person would still insist that no one is there.

The patient information desk is in the lobby across from the main entrance. The older woman behind the counter smiles up at them as they approach. Dmitri cringes as Vladimir stumbles over Elizabetta's name, but the woman seemingly ignores it, and he's unable to stop a low growl rumbling in his chest when Vladimir claims to be her brother and Dmitri, her boyfriend; it is too close, and yet too far from the truth. When the woman remains reluctant to give out Elizabetta's room number, Vladimir takes her hand and uses his touch to influence her.

A blank expression settles on her face. "She is in ISO-7G, seventh floor."

Dmitri's nerves are dancing as if he's holding on to a live wire; he can hardly wait to have Elizabetta out of here. He struggles to rein in his impatience as Vladimir wipes the woman's memory of their encounter. After Vladimir releases her hand, she returns the patient directory to its search entry screen and stares past them as they turn to walk away.

They take the elevator to the seventh floor, and when the doors open they immediately realize that they have another problem. The nurses' station across from the elevator is glassed in from the countertop to the ceiling, with a rectangular slot for passing papers or other small objects through; it hinders their use of pheromones and prevents touch influence. Heavy steel doors with No Unauthorized Entry signs block the hallways of this floor, and a similar door is at one end of the nurses' station. The entry keycard boxes and security cameras near the doors indicate that movement is strictly controlled.

With caution, they approach the partitioned nurses' station. A nurse greets them. "May I help you?"

Dmitri tenses for a moment, undecided how to proceed. When the nurse repeats the question, he replies, "Yes—we are conducting an internal audit of the hospital patient security protocols, and the director sent us to speak with the charge nurse."

Uncertainty spreads across the woman's face. "I'm sorry,

no one told us to expect you. I am Bonnie, and I am the charge nurse."

"Nice to meet you, Bonnie." Dmitri smiles while using his gaze to influence her mind. "I'm Eric Richards, and this is my associate, Jim Brown." When he sees her pupils dilate, he knows it is working. "This will only take a moment of your time. We are here to verify that patient security and confidentiality standards are being followed."

Bonnie stares blankly and nods.

He continues, "What are the rules for patient visitors on this floor?"

Her voice is monotone. "In the general ward, visitors are allowed if they are on the patient's list of approved family or friends and have a valid photo ID. The isolation ward is stricter, with fewer visitors permitted, and then only with an escort by authorized medical staff."

Dmitri exchanges a knowing look with Vladimir. "Good. How are these visitors otherwise controlled or monitored?"

"In the general ward, visitors must stay in the common areas, where they are under video surveillance. A staff member will escort them in, get the patient, and monitor the visit, but only as the patient's medical schedule allows. The isolation ward, again more limited, requires medical personnel to remain with the visitor while in the patient's room, and visits are restricted to fifteen minutes. All visitors must sign in, receive a badge, and adhere to patient safety compliance—no sharp objects, belts, shoelaces, medication, or weapons. All data is retained for one year following a patient's release."

For the love of God, can this possibly get any worse?

Dmitri plunges both hands through his hair, his fingers digging into his scalp. *If we can't get her out soon, I am going to need a room here myself. This is driving me out of my mind.*

Vladimir notices Dmitri shaking his head, and speaks up. "Just one more question, Bonnie. Are these protocols faithfully followed by all personnel, and what measures are in place to make sure they are properly enforced?"

"Yes, we follow them to the letter. All personnel must log in and out every time they arrive on or leave the floor. Whenever a badge is used for patient medication and interaction or for hallway or room access, it is recorded. Each badge is a unique identifier for the person it's issued to." She points to a sign on the wall behind the nurses' station. It reads "No ID, no signature, no badge, no entry."

It confirms what they suspect: Elizabetta is in a quarantined medical lockdown, and only authorized medical personnel have access to her room. The security on this floor will further complicate their mission, and they are unprepared to address it at this moment. Realizing there is little they can do, they blank the nurse's mind and return to the ground-floor lobby to regroup.

Vladimir goes to retrieve Katherine, Alexander, and Kees, while Dmitri finds Anna and Stephan in the records room. The grave look Anna gives Dmitri tells him that whatever she's learned about Elizabetta's stay isn't good, and the thought settles like a brick in his stomach. Given the risk of discussing it here, they close the records and head for the underground garage.

The others are waiting near the car. "Get in," Dmitri

growls as he unlocks the doors. "We need a new plan."

Stephan offers to call in the update to Shashenka.

"Let's get our plan in place first. You may make the call then." Frustration colors every word. Dmitri can see and feel these setbacks spiraling out of control. Each downward spin only brings him another notch closer to dire consequences—he's now playing Russian roulette, and Shashenka is pulling the trigger.

When they return to the apartment, Anna explains what they encountered. "This hospital is faster at updating their records, and we learned a lot about her case." She looks toward Stephan.

"Her case," Stephan spits out, "will be complicated to contain and scrub. It's not a matter of getting her, destroying local records, and wiping a few minds. They've sent her blood to other institutions around the country. Reports flow daily to a Dr. Shelby at the other hospital."

Alexander's booming laugh draws everyone's attention. "You've exceedingly screwed up this time, dear brother ... it will be remarkable if Master leaves any hide on your body."

Anger floods Dmitri. "Why are you here, Alexander? Is it to ensure my failure? Is it to gloat over the price I'm paying for mistakes I made? Is it possible for you to do your job and keep your mouth shut? Why, why are you here?"

Alexander exaggerates a shrug. "Relax, brother. I'm here to help, but alas, you know that I cannot help enjoying this."

In the next instant, Dmitri lunges and starts pummeling him as they crash to the floor. His fists land blow after blow on Alexander's face, but the man displays a smug smile for a few seconds before explosively reacting. Alexander leaps to his feet and his hands shoot forward, catching Dmitri squarely in the chest. As Dmitri's body sails through the air toward the opposite wall, Stephan, Kees, and Vladimir step between the pair. Vladimir and Stephan restrain Alexander as he scrambles forward. Kees pounces on Dmitri, pinning him to the floor.

"Just stay down," Kees warns, tightening the choke hold as his legs wrap around Dmitri.

It's never going to stop. I have to end him. "Let me up," Dmitri bellows. "I'm going to kill him. Let me go. I'm going to kill that son of a bitch."

Kees growls and adjusts his hold on Dmitri's writhing body. "You know we can't let you do that. Now stay down and let us end this fight."

Katherine crouches near Kees. "He's right, Dmitri. This fight must stop—now. We have bigger issues to attend to."

"Oh, let him go. It's about time we settled the score." Alexander writhes against the hands restraining him and tries to wrestle away from Vladimir and Stephan.

Vladimir grabs him by the neck, pinning him against the wall. "Alexander, I don't give a rat's ass about this endless dispute between you two. I will not, however, permit you to keep agitating him. Leave him the hell alone until this mess is cleaned up, or I will gladly kill you myself."

Nostrils flaring, Dmitri locks gazes with Alexander. The smile fades from Alexander's face. He knows he has pushed too far. Grimacing, he jerks loose from Stephan and Vladimir and sneers. "Fine. I'll be on my best behavior."

Anna tries to refocus everyone's attention. "Back to business, boys. We need to resolve the problem and get Elizabetta back."

Dmitri and Alexander exchange fearsome glares. With the unfolding debacle of Elizabetta's reset, it is clear to Dmitri that Alexander will take advantage of every opportunity to bring him down. It plays right into Shashenka's hands and makes Dmitri's job all the more difficult. *It's gone on far too long. Once this matter with Elizabetta is settled, this will have to stop, even if it means killing him.*

Realizing the discussion has moved on without him, Dmitri clenches his eyes shut and refocuses his attention on what the others are saying. Together the team works out a plan. Dmitri will find a way to enter Elizabetta's room, stabilize her, and after determining the best way to extract her, remove her from the hospital. They must minimize further damage to her reset. After the Druzhinas identify each person involved, and all locations storing any records, blood, or tissue samples, they will begin the purge of minds and files of those connected to Elizabetta's case. People will forget she ever existed.

They realize the rescue operation will not be a fast sneak and snatch; there are far too many people involved in Elizabetta's detention and so-called medical intervention. Notes and test results are kept in at least two hospitals and were sent to two other institutions and a half-dozen specialists.

The unknown setbacks may require extra reprogramming of Elizabetta's mind before they can fully extract her to the Belyakov compound. They don't know if the medical revelations have destroyed the barriers preventing Elizabetta's discovery of what she is, and this will create a bigger problem for Dmitri to solve. Time is running out. If she hasn't already learned the truth, she may figure it out soon, and that will leave only one solution—wipe her mind and begin again. Dmitri shudders at the thought; Shashenka will never tolerate starting over. It is imperative to remove her quickly and safely, but it may take days before they are ready to extract her from the hospital.

The manner in which Stephan is responding to Shashenka on the phone reveals that their latest news is ill received. Grateful that Stephan is making the call on his behalf, Dmitri tries to focus on the problem. He suspects what is coming, and his mind is shouting, not ready to face it.

I'm dead. I am so dead.

CHAPTER 9: ELIZA

Tribulation

Long, never-ending hours fill each day as Eliza sits in the solitary quiet of her room. She is feeling increasingly stir-crazy over the situation. She marks off each day on the calendar and has been trying to use the journal; Dr. Carlson thinks it will help her cope with the stress and aid his management of her care. For days, each entry is the same.

"Who are you?"

Then the entries change.

"Who am I? What am I? Who are you? Will this nightmare ever end? Will they ever let me go? I want to go home. I want to go home. I'm going insane and I want to go home."

Trying to think of something new to write, Eliza desperately grasps at words floating in her mind. Dr. Carlson has encouraged her to write positive thoughts about this experience. The idea is outrageous; she has nothing good to write. *Pluck a duck, this is stupid!* Disgusted, she scrawls, "I hate this place" and hastily closes the journal.

She stands and shoves the chair against the wall. Crossing

the small room, she walks onto the mattress and sits in the middle of it. It is time to open the pocket calendar and mark a diagonal line through today's date block—another day has ended. Staring at the days marked, she flips back a page and counts the crossed-out dates. *No, no, no, no, not real, not happening, not real.* She rocks back and forth, drowning in the ebb and flow of her mind. Tears welling in her eyes, she counts the days a second time. Seventeen days have passed, more than four hundred hours, almost six times longer than the involuntary stay she expected.

Frustration simmers inside her. Eliza has cooperated and done whatever they have asked or told her to do. She sleeps because they give her drugs to sleep. She has tried eating, but they have stopped bringing her food trays; she cannot keep the food down. It has presented a new mystery to solve and creates the need for another team of doctors. *Why didn't I have this eating problem before coming here?*

She should be losing weight and weakening from lack of nourishment, but she's not. They still cannot solve the riddle of her silent heartbeat or the lungs failing to draw and expel air. They cannot explain why her body temperature is so low, and find it impossible that she doesn't feel cold. They draw blood daily and get the same results, with no answers for the expanding riddles. The IV pumps a steady stream of antibiotics, but nothing changes the results of her blood tests.

Eliza knows it is taking a toll on her physical appearance; she sees it in the eyes of those who enter her room. They look at her as if they were staring at death. She laughs under her breath. *If only it were that simple, I'd be outta here.* She doesn't feel as if she's dying, and the mysteries are as confounding to her as they are to the experts.

Still, her hope is fading, and there are no answers as to whether they'll ever release her. The whole ordeal is unfathomable. Shouldn't she have felt something, anything, if she were that sick? It is illogical to her how living and engaging in life one moment can be completely derailed the next, just by calling 9-1-1 to report an intruder.

It leaves her wondering whether the doctors are doing this deliberately. Then she remembers Dr. Carlson's rebuke when she voiced that sentiment. "It's a sign of paranoia," he said as he scribbled notes on his writing pad.

Why don't I feel sick now? Instead she feels annoyed, angry, and tired, exhausted, really, because of the drugs they insist she take. *Yeah, let's throw more drugs at the problem, that'll fix everything.* She glances toward the now-darkened ceiling. They turn out the lights in her room every night, and now she's staring up where the light shone moments before. She can't keep her eyelids from drooping. Eliza curls up on her side, facing the wall. *Nothing will be different when I wake.* The drugs take her, kicking and fighting, into sleep.

Then a strange and familiar sensation prickles the hair on her arms and the back of her neck. A shiver bursts through her. Opening her eyes to the wall, Eliza slowly turns over. It takes a few seconds of blinking before a coherent thought registers in her foggy brain. *He's here. No freaking way.* Somehow, some way, the stalker has found her. He's standing right there, staring down at her.

He takes a step. Eliza struggles to sit up, fighting the effects of the drugs trying to pin her to the mattress. His lips are moving, but she hears no words. He's kneeling, reaching, and she's scrambling across the mattress. Her back slams into the wall. Now he's crawling on his knees toward her. *Oh shit, he's really here.* The moment his hand settles on her arm, she finds her voice and starts screaming.

The light in her room flickers on and the intruder glances toward the door. His lips are still moving with no sound coming forth. *What is he saying? Why can't I hear him?* Then suddenly he's gone. The electronic lock disengages, the door swings open, and the nurse comes in with a worried look on her face.

"Are you all right?"

Blinking, trying to comprehend what she just saw, Eliza squeezes her eyes shut. "He was here."

"Who was here?"

Her eyes fly open. *Do they pay you to be stupid?* "The man that's been stalking me."

The nurse gently places her hands on Eliza's shoulders and encourages her to lie down. "I think it was just a bad dream, honey. We're the only ones here. Everything's fine now. Relax."

Eliza shouts, "He was here, I saw him. He—he touched me."

The nurse tries for reassurance. "Hush now, it was just a dream. Just a bad dream, but it's over, and you're safe now."

Dream my ever-aching butt. "I've had it with you telling me it's my imagination or bad dreams! I know what I saw ... he is real."

"Eliza, you need—"

"I am not safe here. I need ... *have* to get out of here. Why won't you people let me go? I want to go home." She leaps to her feet and begins pacing the room, looking for a way out. Her attempt to stifle a guttural cry fails, and angry tears spill from her eyes.

The nurse utters a tsking sound and slips out of the room. A few minutes later she's back with two orderlies and a syringe. By now Eliza is sitting in the corner on the mattress, resting her shoulders against the two walls.

"This sedative will help you relax." Insisting she lie down, the nurse injects something into Eliza's hip. She continues in a soft voice, but the words are lost as the drug tugs Eliza into unwelcome sleep.

When her eyes open next, the lights are on and daylight is streaming through the narrow window high on the wall. Eliza feels groggy and rubs her hands over her face. Her head is pounding. She's still trying to wipe away the sleep and regain her wits, when the door opens. It's another nurse.

The cheerful sound of her voice grates on Eliza's nerves. "Good morning! Beautiful day out. I heard you had another unpleasant dream last night. How are you feeling now?"

Let me beat you to a pulp and then ask me. "Drugged," Eliza grumbles.

"The sedative Celine gave you is powerful and will take a while to wear off. I'm sure you'll feel better by the time Dr. Carlson arrives today."

Eliza watches as the nurse checks the IV and pulls out the digital thermometer to measure her body temperature. When the nurse finishes taking her vitals, she leaves the room. They no longer comment on her unnaturally low body temperature. She doesn't know if that's a relief or whether it increases the anxiety she feels.

The day passes in a blur of nurses, lab technicians, doctors, and assistants entering and leaving her room. Today there are new doctors, sent from WHO—the World Health Organization—and they have military escorts. It puzzles her. *Why do they need military guards just to see me?* They offer no explanation. All of them take turns poking and prodding. They take her blood, force her to eat food she cannot keep down, and exhaust her with never-ending tests and repetitive questions. They stare, scowl, frown, ponder, smile, and repeat the process.

When Dr. Carlson steps in, he seems well informed of the previous night's events and wastes no time in dismissing the whole thing as a symptom of her illnesses. Nothing she says dissuades his belief, so she stops arguing and stares at the door until he leaves.

It is as though she's a mutant spectacle in their sideshow. Obviously something is wrong with her, but she knows she's okay, or at the least, normal for her. She'd be better if they'd let her out of here. *It's them, not me. I'm a freak, and they need to get over it.*

Nighttime comes again and the nurse gives her a new cocktail of sedatives and sleeping medicine that knocks her out within seconds. The drugs work too quickly, denying Eliza the chance to feel relief that the day is over. Her mind is gone, body deadweight, and she's in the deepest, darkest recesses of sleep when suddenly she becomes aware that she's no longer alone in the void.

It takes a few minutes before she realizes there's a hand gently grabbing her shoulder. His touch should repulse her, but she feels drawn to it. A deep male voice speaks in a hushed tone that sounds melodic. Someone helps Eliza roll over, and she struggles to focus, unable to clear her vision and see him. If she could just see his majestic face, gaze in his mystical eyes, then perhaps this upside-down world would make sense again. He must be an angel. The angel can save her, take her away from this crazy place. *I had an angel once. Where have you been for so long? I need you.*

Her eyes finally focus ... recognition ... horror. She knows the man kneeling beside her, gripping her arms, and he's no knight in shining armor. Terror fills Eliza's mind, and she starts to scream. Before the sounds escape her throat, the man clamps a hand over her mouth. Moving blindingly fast— a blink of her eyes barely registers it—he is straddling her body. Strange tingles excite her where his hands and body make contact with hers. One of his hands remains over her mouth and the other is pushing against her chest, pinning her to the mattress.

"Shh!" The deep voice is now a melodic whisper. "Please, Elizabetta, be quiet and listen to me."

Eliza thrashes against his hold, but he's too powerful for her to wrest her body free. His hand remains pressed across her mouth and his eyes are pleading. Her eyes dart frantically across the room to the security cameras mounted near the ceiling. Surely someone will see him and come running soon.

Why aren't they coming?

He whispers, "I'll remove my hand if you don't scream. Listen to me."

It is incomprehensible that he is here—this is a locked room on a secure floor. It makes no logical sense. *Why can't they hear him?* The cameras have microphones, but he's too quiet. She has one choice: she needs to make some noise.

Eliza nods and the man slowly withdraws his hand. Sucking in a large breath of air, she screams, long and loud. The man's hand clamps harshly across her mouth again.

"Elizabetta, stop this." His tone drops in pitch, almost beseeching, and his hand squeezes her face. "We have to talk. I need you to be quiet and listen."

The sound of the electronic door lock releasing catches their attention. Defiantly, Eliza looks into the man's deep, dark eyes. *Ha! Gotcha this time.* He stares back, and conflicting emotions sweep across his face. The anger she expects, but the disappointed and wounded look in his eyes unsettles her. Shaking his head, he looks down as if in failure.

Then his eyes snap to hers. "Don't se—" he murmurs and is gone.

The nurse runs to where Eliza lies on the mattress. "Everything is okay. It's okay—I'm here. It was just another bad dream."

Bewildered, Eliza says, "D-d-didn't you see him?"

"See who?"

"That man ..." She gasps, sucking for air that won't fill her lungs. "The man ... there was a man ... in my room ... just now."

Looking around and then back at Eliza, the nurse shakes her head. "Honey, there is nobody in your room. We're the only ones here."

"No. No, no, no. He was here ... didn't you see him on the monitor?" She's panting now and finding it difficult to breathe. *Not crazy. Not crazy. Not crazy.*

"I was watching the monitor and heard you scream, but I haven't seen anyone but you in the room for the last few hours." The nurse shakes her head again. "I think, perhaps, you are confused. There's no one here and no one can get into this room without the right credentials. You're safe here. No one can hurt you."

Shock and disbelief flood Eliza. *Why are they lying to me?* He was here—she saw him. He spoke to her and she heard him. She remembers the firm touch of his hand on her mouth. Her mind whirls, seeking answers; it is too real to be a dream. "Do the cameras record?"

Clearly taken aback by the question, the nurse blinks a few times before answering. "Yes, we automatically record all patients in the isolation rooms."

"Please go look at the video. He was here."

The nurse gives a knowing nod. "I'll suggest it to Dr. Carlson when he comes on shift in the morning. Meanwhile, I'll stay right here until you get back to sleep."

Why won't they admit he was here? Am I hallucinating? What is happening to me?

Eliza doesn't want to sleep. The nurse watches her trying to resist but says nothing, and finally Eliza loses the battle against the powerful force of the drugs pulling her back into a stupor. Her eyes roll and blink as she struggles to keep them open. With the walls leaning in, folding over her, the heavy veil of sleep brings darkness.

Daylight is streaming through the small window at the top of the wall when her eyes flutter open. The brightness temporarily blinds her, making her head ache. A glance around the room reveals she is alone. She starts at the sudden thud of the automatic lock releasing.

Dr. Carlson steps into the room. "Good morning, Miss Ross." He peeks at the chart he is holding. "It appears you had a rough night. I see you were administered another sedative for a panic attack."

Let's stick a stalker in your bedroom and see if you panic. Eliza's jaw flexes at the analysis. Dr. Carlson looks at her as though waiting for a response. *He exists.* Her tone is belligerent: "I panicked because he is not a dream, and the nurse dragged her feet getting to my room."

The doctor gives a sympathetic smile. "I assure you, it was a dream. I reviewed the video from last night, and I promise you that no one was in your room aside from the nurse who checked on you."

How can that be? Her mind rushes to recall the times the man appeared in her apartment bedroom. At least twice he was present even as the deputies broke through the door. Surely no dream allows recognition or conscious thoughts and awareness of one's surroundings.

"How is it possible to be dreaming—see and hear an intruder—and actively, consciously dial 9-1-1 to seek help? How is it possible to know cops are busting down my door?"

"The mind is a phenomenal part of the body. In layman terms, if you were sleepwalking, it would be possible for you to interact with others. To recall doing so is the only remarkable facet of your experience, as people in a sleepwalking state do not typically remember anything they did or said during that period."

"You think I'm sleepwalking?" *I'm like a freaking zombie ... can barely move or think with the drugs you're poking down me.*

Dr. Carlson smiles, looking condescending. "It's a distinct possibility. Again, I reviewed the video of last night—and I assure you, you were alone in the room. That leads me to consider one potential explanation."

"One?" she asks, unsure she wants to hear more. "Do you mean there are others?"

"We would need to do a sleep study to be sure, but yes, there are other potential explanations if you were fully awake." His gaze is intense while he seemingly considers whether to continue. "Hearing or seeing people that do not exist are often signs of paranoia or schizophrenia. Both conditions can result from LLI."

Dr. Carlson waits for Eliza to react to his comment. She shakes her head back and forth, eyes darting about, searching for ... finding nothing. He seems to watch the range of emotions that cross her face; she knows they are a cocktail of confusion, doubt, fear, and disbelief, but she is powerless to stop them.

"I want to do a few additional tests and order a sleep study for you. It will help me diagnose the underlying condition that may be the cause of such manifestations and symptoms as you are displaying."

Eliza's thoughts keep tripping over the deep-seated feeling that something is wrong, and she is convinced that her mind isn't the problem. Compared with others, she doesn't lead a typical life, but she has always had a solitary existence. Still, she knows something is off about her, and somehow, by the way people shy away, she knows others have noticed it too. Answers to what and why are elusive.

She finally asks, "What if these tests are inconclusive or fail to diagnose what is happening to me?"

"That is highly unlikely." Dr. Carlson flips through the pages on the clipboard. "Your blood disorder may be altering the chemicals of your brain, distorting your thought processes. These tests are designed to find such anomalies."

Her fingers tremble as she tugs a loose thread on the hospital gown. "If the tests reveal something, will I ever be able to have a normal life and get out of here?"

"I'll order the tests and sleep study today. It may take a few days to complete and analyze them, but they will provide a basis for diagnosis and allow me to tailor a treatment plan for you." An encouraging smile spreads across his arrogant face. "Treatment alternatives with therapies, medication, and counseling are options that may allow some normalcy and a return to living a productive life."

Yep, quick evaluation—in and out. Not. They will never let me go. The thought of continuing psychological care and daily medication to control her mind nauseates her. The only nightmares and delusions are the waking hours she spends in this place. There doesn't seem to be an easy way out. Bewildered and scared, Eliza reluctantly submits. The only way back to a life away from here may be by doing what they demand.

CHAPTER 10: DMITRI

New Plan

Freeing Elizabetta from the hospital is proving more diffi-cult than expected. The team is standing by to complete the extraction. All people connected with her case have been identified and their addresses divided among the six mem-bers of Dmitri's team; it will take less than a full day to find them and wipe their minds. But Elizabetta's self-awareness is thwarting Dmitri's attempts to regain control, and has pre-vented the others from starting their assignments.

"Her medical treatment is interfering." Katherine pinches and rubs the bridge of her nose. "You're going to have to call Maria. She is the only one who can find a way around this and help return Elizabetta to your control."

Dmitri exhales slowly. He knows Katherine is right. Eliz-abetta shouldn't be this self-aware—especially with the programming incomplete—and the combination of drugs she's on is exacerbating the problem. Nodding, he places the call.

"Hello, Dmitri." Maria's soft voice belies the fiery Irish

spirit that makes her a formidable ally or foe. "I trust you have good news for me to pass on. Your master's anger is growing by the hour."

"I wish it were so, but there is only bad news to convey." Before she can respond, he adds, "Elizabetta's lapses into self-awareness are severe and made worse by whatever they are giving her. It is causing problems for us—well, for me, mostly. I can't invoke a programming state when her antics and screaming bring others running. Then they give her more drugs, which prevent her from waking at all."

"I see." Maria pauses. "These lapses, are they brief? She's not showing signs of programming failure?"

"I think the base programming is intact, but I'll need to fully assess that once we have her out of there."

"Allow me a little time, and send me her current medication list. I need to look closely to ensure whatever I choose will not adversely interact with what's in her system."

Dmitri ends the call and relays Maria's words to the others. It goes unsaid that all are hoping she'll have a solution to restore Dmitri's control over Elizabetta.

Thumbing through a stack of papers, Stephan punctures the tense silence. "I'll be glad when Elizabetta is back where she belongs." His gaze shifts to Dmitri. "If we get her out in the next few days, can you finish her programming by the deadline?"

Dmitri sweeps a hand through his hair, his brows furrowing. "Doubtful. I've lost over two weeks already, and I still need to reinstate her hunting and tracking skills. Until we get her out of there, I'll have no idea what or how many setbacks in the programming I'll need to overcome."

Anna grimaces. "We'll do our best to calm and distract Shashenka so you can quickly finish." Her gaze meets Dmitri's, and he reads the fear in her eyes. The same trepidation is gnawing at his bones. It's inevitable that Shashenka will tire of this at some point, and when he does, Dmitri will suffer a cruel punishment.

The room falls into silence again. Dmitri startles when the phone rings. Maria's number is displayed on the screen. "I didn't expect you to call back this soon."

"I explained the predicament to Shashenka," Maria says in an even tone. "He wants us to try a concoction first, and send me only if that fails."

Dmitri waits for her to go on. Finally she says, "Do you know whether you can get her to drink a potion?"

"I highly doubt it. She becomes hysterical the moment she sees me."

"I understand." Maria rambles aloud as she considers and rejects various potions. "Ah, I know ... yes, this should work. I'm going to send an overnight package to you. It will contain a vial of heaven's scent."

"Heaven's scent?"

"Yes. It's an injectable potion that enraptures the person under its influence. It will leave Elizabetta feeling euphoric and should give you the time necessary to bring her under your control."

Dmitri laughs. "So it's a feel-good drug."

"Not exactly. It's a hallucinogenic more than anything else. It's often used to bring unwilling or hostile victims into a pliant state. Although its effects are not permanent, it will put her in a trance for at least thirty minutes."

"How quickly does it take effect?"

Coughing as if to cover a laugh, Maria replies, "You'll notice an unmistakable and immediate shift in her mood. I should warn you, though, the reason it's called heaven's scent is that its potency causes the victim to see, hear, or smell divine beings and things that aren't there. Granted, it may be pleasant or even entertaining to watch, but you can't let Elizabetta's reaction to it distract you. You'll need to quiet her and bring her under control before it wears off."

A smile tugs at his lips as the image filters across his mind. How fitting, given that she used to call him her angel. "Okay."

"Have the team ready to go. If this works, then you'll need to move fast."

He's about to hang up when Maria suddenly says, "Dmitri ... weigh this as you will. I don't agree with what Shashenka is forcing on either of you. I never have."

Dmitri's jaw flexes at the reminder; under orders from Shashenka, she cast the spell that turned Elizabetta into a blank slate. She isn't the first to convey regret after Shashenka announced and began Elizabetta's punishment. Although Dmitri isn't certain where Sofia, Justin or Victoria stand, it is obvious that the Druzhinas present, aside from Alexander, feel the same way. *If so many are against Shashenka on this, why are we allowing it? Why have the others never tried to stop it?*

Without another word Dmitri leaves the living room, goes

into the bedroom, and stares at Elizabetta's empty bed. He cannot bear what they are doing to her. Her life is now illusion—an atrocious lie. But regardless of how desperately he wants to reveal the truth to her, he cannot do it without risking both their lives. Elizabetta is his charge, his punishment for his part in their botched rebellion, and it still strangles his heart.

When he first recruited her, he was the finest of the Druzhinas, but within a few short years she surpassed him. She became the best-skilled, smartest assassin they ever had; there's been no other like her since. In a mix of heartache and pride, Dmitri smiles as tears well in his eyes. The Elizabetta who led the effort to destroy Shashenka was the most beautiful and deadly woman Dmitri had ever known. He never expected her plan to fail. But it did fail, miserably and in spectacular fashion. It left them unprepared for the punishment Shashenka meted out afterward.

Their treachery nearly resulted in their deaths. Given the threat Elizabetta posed to Shashenka, wiping her mind was the only alternative to being executed; still, she fought against it, knowing that a mind reset would leave her never knowing herself again. She tried to hold on, but the bond she shared with Dmitri was irrevocably severed. Right or wrong, he was too selfish to let her go and assured her that they would find a way to recover what they were losing.

A lump forms in his throat as he wonders for the thousandth time if he was wrong.

The retribution against Elizabetta, while cruel, was designed to remove Dmitri from her heart and memories, but not inflict lasting pain. It will give her a new life with a weaker personality and strip her of the mental strength to ever challenge Shashenka again. It's supposed to leave her with just enough skill to continue as a low-level Druzhina.

Dmitri's punishment was far more sinister and cruel. After being held prisoner for a decade, he was tortured daily for another decade. His body still carries the scars from the many whippings and beatings inflicted on him by Shashenka or his lackeys. Whenever they brought him to the brink of death, Shashenka had Maria restore his health with potions or mending spells. The torture was meant to break Dmitri, force his full submission to Shashenka's will, and teach him a harsh lesson about going against his master.

A third decade passed in isolation, with Dmitri confined to the cells below the Belyakov estate. Then Shashenka inflicted another round of torture until Dmitri broke five years later. He had no fight or strength left to resist, and with great personal shame, he agreed to Shashenka's demands. When they finally let Dmitri out, Shashenka specifically assigned him to help Maria preserve Elizabetta's catatonic life. He attended to her minimal needs—feeding, bathing, grooming—for almost five hundred years, and Elizabetta will never know. There could have been no greater punishment than being close to the one he was forbidden to have, and knowing that any violation of that edict meant a gruesome end for them both.

To further humiliate Dmitri, Shashenka made him responsible for Elizabetta's reprehensible reprogramming. Under constant supervision of others, Dmitri has been flawlessly grafting and weaving the backstory of her supposed life. The biggest issue is her resistance to the procedures; her ability to do so is baffling. Regardless, she is not who or what she thinks she is. The memory wipe ensures that she will never remember who she once was, but the other blocks on her mind will eventually be removed to reveal her nature. Shashenka himself chose the details and methods of her programming, designing them to mold her personality and character into someone she'd never be of her own accord.

Blatant and continual threats ensure that Dmitri will forever bear this burden alone. He must endure the memories—see the constant reminders of all that is lost between him and Elizabetta. Everyone in the coven is expressly forbidden from revealing the truth to Elizabetta, and it would mean a slow, horrific death for her—a death that Dmitri would be forced to watch and live beyond—if she ever found out. It has left him enduring this miserable half life. His only consolation is that at least she's alive.

Dmitri's hand touches the pillow that once cradled her head. *I need her ... miss her.* A paradox, considering that for nearly a year now he has spent almost every minute of each day with her. On a few rare occasions he has even taken advantage of the situation and held her to chase away whatever bad dreams she was having. Stolen moments that she'll never remember or know about when this is done. Moments that are as lost in time as the years he spent helping Maria care for her at the Belyakov estates before her reprogramming.

Dmitri inhales sharply as he recalls the bittersweet memory of what Elizabetta used to be like. She was a strong, brave woman, passionate, vivacious, and daring. Now her quick wit, gentle smile, and easy laughter are gone. She is so introverted that it is sickening to watch. He sighs. She remains breathtakingly gorgeous to him. He finds her pale complexion stunning against her dark tresses and eyes. The shape of her curves is one alluring feature that enabled her to be a proficient killer; men foolishly trusted her because of her looks, and it led many marks to their deaths. Although her beauty is still there, he knows her capacities won't remain the same when they have finished remaking her.

God, she is—was—a remarkable woman. Will she ever truly know me again? Would she ever forgive me for what I'm doing to her?

A knock on the door disrupts Dmitri's reverie. "Come in."

Vladimir opens the door and steps inside. His eyes convey compassion. "I wanted to give you a few minutes, but we must know what Maria had to say."

Dmitri squeezes his eyes shut, drags a hand through his hair, and then motions Vladimir toward the other room.

Alexander scrutinizes his every move as they enter. Ignoring the proverbial thorn in his side, Dmitri tells the others about the drug Maria is sending. They outline the extraction plan, trusting that her potion will work.

All will go to the seventh floor, and while Dmitri is handling Elizabetta, the rest will begin wiping the minds of those working that shift. Then they will split into two teams, with Katherine, Kees, and Stephan purging the computer files and splicing random images into the videos, while Vladimir, Anna, and Alexander destroy all physical evidence. In the meantime, Dmitri must remove Elizabetta from the hospital while she is still under the influence of the potion. He will be on his own to regain control of her while the others carry out their tasks.

Too many days have passed to regain swift control of her mind, and there will be no time to bind her to a reprogramming state before they leave the hospital. Instead he will take her to a service elevator, leave through a restricted employee-only door, and drive her to an abandoned warehouse that Shashenka owns. It should provide the isolation and privacy needed in case Elizabetta panics or resists his attempts to retake her mind. Once she's under control, Dmitri will take her back to the apartment and evaluate the damage done to her programming. When that is known he will create a new timeline for extracting and delivering her to the Belyakov coven.

It doesn't take long for the team to agree on the locations each Druzhina will cover during the mop-up phase of their plan. After they finish at Mercy, they will scrub records at Trinity, the offices of Drs. Carlson and Shelby, and the sheriff's department. Proceeding separately, they will wipe the minds of anyone with knowledge of Elizabetta. They hope to have all evidence of her existence removed in twenty-four to thirty-six hours. Still, they will need to move fast to accomplish their goals.

Stephan looks over the papers scattered on the table. "When we finish everything at those city levels, we'll still need to send one of us to handle things in Los Angeles."

"I think Alexander should go there." Dmitri looks across

the table at the other man. "I don't need you here distracting me and causing problems."

Alexander sneers, his expression cold. "What, you don't trust your own abilities to complete the task with me watching over your shoulder? I'm so wounded."

"It is not my abilities I'm worried about," Dmitri growls. "I've already lost more than two weeks and will not meet the current extraction date to return Elizabetta to Shashenka. I don't need you here stirring up a shitstorm and complicating the problem."

"He's got a point." Vladimir levels his gaze at Alexander. "We all know that Dmitri is in enough trouble, and you, no doubt, would love to add to his problems with Master."

Alexander huffs. "Fine. I'll go to LA, but I will return here when I'm done there, whether you like it or not, Dmitri."

Katherine narrows her eyes as she leans back in her seat. "If I didn't know better, I'd swear you were relishing the idea of failure for this mission."

"Not true, my lovely sister. There's nothing I'd like more than to return Elizabetta to Shashenka." Alexander sneers at Dmitri again. "That's not to say that I don't relish Dmitri's discomfort over cleaning up the messes he makes."

The comment strikes a match, burning away Dmitri's resolve to remain quiet. "Stop goading me! I will make you this one promise: if this ends badly, I will take you out before Shashenka destroys me."

"Enough, both of you." Vladimir's fierce eyes dart between the two. "Your petty bullshit is going to stop right here, right now. It's not helping anyone complete this mission."

Several heads nod in agreement. Alexander glares at Dmitri for a moment before rising from the chair and leaving the apartment. A chorus of sighs settles the room into silence as Dmitri's chest continues rising and falling in heavy breaths. He is about to his limit for tolerating Alexander's antics. It is pure, raw jealousy driving the conflict, and Dmitri is powerless to stop it.

Stephan refocuses their attention on the logistical part of the plan. "Are we missing any other locations?"

"Someone needs to go to Geneva and scrub the records at WHO. Aside from that, provided they haven't sent her case forward to anyone else in the world, then yes, we have everything covered." Katherine smiles at Anna. "We've kept well apprised of the communications and have all the names and locations."

Stephan says, "Shashenka's in Prague and can get there more quickly than any of us can. Given the gravity of the mission, I'm sure he'll help at least that much."

Vladimir looks at each of them. He's one of the oldest Druzhinas, one of the first, and he knows their capabilities very well. "Can we still accomplish this in the time allotted?"

Kees, silent until now, trails a finger across the map on the wall. "Trusting Maria's potion to resolve the issue with Elizabetta, and barring any glitches in the plan, it should be doable. My biggest concern is intercepting any last-minute phone calls, file transfers, or biological samples."

Anna smiles. "If Justin, Sofia, Victoria, and Alexander are

sent forward to the outlying locations and able to catch late developments there, I think we can handle it."

"Then it's time to call Shashenka and have him send the others." Katherine studies Dmitri for a moment. "Do you want me to call him?"

Grateful for the offer, he nods. The group quiets while Katherine is on the phone. Dmitri infers, from her end of the conversation, that Shashenka is resisting sending the other three. Katherine debates the matter with him for a few minutes before disconnecting the call and exhaling in relief. "He's not happy, but he'll send them and do his part. He expects them to return to the estate when their tasks have finished, so if we have any unforeseen problems, it'll be up to us to handle it."

Dmitri massages the back of his neck. He understands the implication: Shashenka will not accept any more errors. It's crucial for them to succeed with the plan. If one more thing goes wrong or the attempt to extract Elizabetta fails, it may well be the end of him.

CHAPTER 11: DMITRI

Rescue

Dmitri's team arrives at Mercy, anxious to complete this mission. All are wearing the white lab coats they stole from the doctors' locker room. The phony name badges that Katherine created are clipped to their collars. To avoid setting off any alarms or panicking people they encounter, they will arrive on the seventh floor in two groups. The thick glass of the partition will hamper their ability to exert quick influence over the minds of those working on the other side of it; using the technique of touch is not an option. Because of that, they will rely on Anna's strong persuasion skills to fool the nurses and gain access.

The elevator door opens and Dmitri's group steps forward. A nurse sitting behind the partition looks up and smiles as they approach the counter. "Can I help you?"

"Yes." Anna's voice is professional, cool. "We're here to review the patient medical charts of Eliza Ross."

"I'm sorry, but we're restricted on giving out that information." The nurse cocks her head to the side and places a hand on her hip. "No one has notified us to expect anyone else, especially this time of night."

A flash of rage courses through Dmitri, and his jaw flexes. Ignoring him, Anna glances at her watch; it's a little past one in the morning. "It is awfully late, but I assure you that Dr. Shelby sent us to do this review to see if we can help with Miss Ross's case."

The nurse recognizes Dr. Shelby's name, but still appears uncertain. "Let me get the charge nurse."

She waves at a man using a terminal in the back of the room. "Adam, please come here. These doctors claim to be here for a patient review."

Dmitri's eyes wander over those working on the other side of the partition. Fewer people work this shift, and the intel suggests half are likely somewhere else on the floor. *This will work. It has to.*

Adam approaches the counter. "A review for whom?"

"Eliza Ross. They say Dr. Shelby sent them."

The charge nurse looks them over and then toward the clock on the wall. "This is highly unusual." He squints to read the name badge on Anna's coat. "We haven't received any notice for your access to this case, Dr. Yu."

Dmitri's pupils widen and then narrow as he captures Adam's gaze, fully using his ability to influence the man with his eyes. It gives the needed boost to Anna's voice persuasion. She says, "Yes, it was late afternoon when Dr. Shelby requested us. This is the first collective break we've had in our shifts to perform the review."

Adam scrutinizes them once more and then turns to the

nurse at the counter. "Go ahead and buzz them in."

When the buzzer sounds, they hear the click of the lock release on the door at the end of the partition. Dmitri's group steps into the nurses' station and springs into action. Moving at supernatural speeds, they bind the hands of the few nurses present and are seating them to bind their ankles when the elevator dings and the second group of Druzhinas steps out. The team quickly uses their skills to command quiet, and the stunned nurses watch in silence.

Kees, Katherine, and Alexander immediately move to search for any medical personnel working the floor. Dmitri unclips Adam's lanyard from his collar, taking the cards needed to gain access to Elizabetta's room. He sees Katherine in the hall of the common area. She's escorting two people to the nurses' station; their blank expressions indicate they are fully under her control. She wishes Dmitri luck as they pass one another.

Dmitri swipes the stolen access card in the key slot and enters Elizabetta's room silently; he doesn't want to wake her, not yet. Sliding the syringe with the heaven's scent out of his pocket, he kneels beside her. Gently he brushes her hair away from her face, places one hand on her head, and plunges the needle into her neck with the other.

She's heavily drugged and only begins to stir as the last of the purple liquid is injected. Dmitri gently rolls her onto her back. "Wake up! Come on, wake up, Elizabetta."

Her lashes flutter as she fights to open her eyes. *She is so beautiful, gorgeous.* "Come on, love, I need you to wake up now."

Elizabetta struggles to open her eyes, and he can see she's trying to focus, but it's as if her eyelids are too heavy to lift. She whispers, "Are you an angel?"

A smile spreads across Dmitri's face. Maria was right. The drug is a thunderbolt of speed. He notes the time; they only have half an hour. They can't afford to waste time here, so Elizabetta will have to change out of the hospital gown at the warehouse. Bending his head toward her ear, he says, "No. Now come on, we need to get you on your feet."

"You look like an angel."

She giggles, and Dmitri chuckles in response. "I'm here to take you home."

"Home." A pucker creases the space between her brows. "What do you mean by home? Is that my place or yours?"

He looks down at her, and his heart constricts when the truth drenches his thoughts. She will never go home—their home—again. Swallowing the lump in his throat, he says, "Yours, love."

He lifts Elizabetta to her feet. She staggers and nearly falls, but he catches her around the waist and pulls her to his side. Tugging her forward, he asks, "Can you walk?"

She swats at his arm around her waist. "I'd much rather fly. You look strong ... can we use your wings to fly home?"

"I don't have wings, love. Can you walk?"

"Yes, you do," she counters with a pout. "All angels have wings."

"I'm not an angel. Come on." He pulls her into the hallway. The others are already in place and waiting for him to bring her out.

"Yes, you are." She grins and punches his ribs playfully. "If you're not an angel, then you must be a fairy, and you're too big to be a fairy."

Her giddiness and faltering steps are costing them precious time. Dmitri effortlessly scoops her into his arms. "I'm not a fairy either, love."

"Why do you call me love? Who are you?"

"I'm Dmitri."

"Dmitri." She slowly sounds out the name as if it's foreign on her tongue. Then she frowns. "That's a funny name for an angel. Are you sure that's your name? Isn't it Michael or Gabriel or Raphael or something ... divine?"

"My name is Dmitri," he says as they enter the area near the nurses' station.

He looks toward his six comrades, quickly counting; they've rounded up and are restraining thirteen people. Seven sit on the floor, wrists and ankles bound. The Druzhinas hold the other six by their arms, ready to wipe their minds. Dmitri sets Elizabetta on her feet and tosses Adam's lanyard to Vladimir. Before he can say anything, Elizabetta starts laughing hysterically. Everyone looks toward her.

"Do you see them?" she hisses, pointing at the group behind the partition. "Seriously, do you see them?"

Hesitantly he replies, "Yes ..."

"They look like you. Do all angels radiate light? Where are your halos?" She strains to look closer as they pass the nurses' station. "If you're not an angel or a fairy, and they aren't either, what are you? No, no, don't tell me. You're cherubs. Right? Aren't all of you supposed to be naked or something?"

Elizabetta howls with laughter and his team members look on with amusement. The captured medical staff's faces and body language display fright and concern. Dmitri shakes his head and feels slightly embarrassed by her imbecilic ramblings. He knows that if her mind weren't altered by programming or drugs, she'd be mortified by such undignified outbursts.

When Dmitri doesn't respond, she cups a hand to his face. "I know you. I've seen you before."

Dmitri sees surprise register on some of the Druzhinas' faces, and quickly he looks away. "Yes, you know me." Lifting her back into his arms, he whispers in her ear as they approach the service elevator, "We know each other."

"I don't know any angels. Unless I count you, but you're not real, are you? That mean nurse is going to come and tell me this is a dream. They think I'm crazy—do you know that? I'm not crazy, am I?"

Elizabetta prattles on between bursts of giggles as they leave the hospital. Dmitri tries to ignore and quiet her, clamping a hand over her mouth to muffle her outbursts and laughter. When they reach the car, she suddenly grabs the collar of his shirt and pulls his head closer.

"I remember you! You've always been my angel. You went away. Where have you been? Don't leave me again. Please, please, *amore*, tell me that you'll stay with me always. Please tell me that you'll always be my angel." She's not laughing anymore, and her eyes convey urgency.

Dmitri freezes and studies her face. The sober tone in her

voice is unnerving. Is she hallucinating or actually remembering their past? There was a time when she called him her angel and *amore*, but her memories were taken long ago. *How can she know this? How is it possible?* Her self-awareness is far worse than he expected, and they are running out of time.

She resumes babbling, but Dmitri ignores her as much as possible while they drive to the warehouse. He has never heard her drone on before; it's giving him little time to think. It infuriates him that Shashenka has done this to her. While she's blissfully ignorant, Dmitri is ashamed and humiliated enough for them both.

When they arrive at the warehouse, he pulls the car inside and shuts the outer door. Returning to the car, he finds Elizabetta leaning forward and staring up through the windshield. He opens the passenger door to help her out of the car.

"I hate to tell you this," she whispers, "but your palace is drab. Celestial palaces are lovely and white ... white everywhere, with gold and purple. This place is dreary." She sniggers. "Maybe you should talk with the big man and ask for an upgrade."

Dmitri leads her to a room in the corner of the building. He hands Elizabetta a bag with undergarments, a pair of jeans, a T-shirt, and running shoes. Certain she will comply in putting them on, he steps out of the room to give her privacy while she dresses. Several minutes later, he pushes the door open to see whether she's ready.

His breath catches in his throat at the sight before him.

Elizabetta is lying on her back with her knees bent and feet on the floor, and she is wearing a single article of clothing—a pair of panties. She has strewn the remaining clothing and shoes about the room.

Rocking her knees side to side, she sings, "Oh, yesterday upon the stairs I saw a man, but he was not there. He was not there again today—oh, how I wish he'd go away. I'm a nut, you bet, I'm a nut."

He recognizes it as a variation on an old song. Dmitri's eyes roam over her figure, a familiar ache and longing building inside him. *It's been so long.* Taking a calming breath, he steps into the room. The smile Elizabetta flashes is nearly his undoing. He smothers the desires rising in him and gathers the scattered clothing. It's a welcome distraction that doesn't last long enough. Then he pulls her to a sitting position and kneels to help her dress. His fingers tremble while fastening the bra clasp between her breasts. It's a struggle for him to stay focused. She's uncooperative and tries to push the shirt away while he's tugging it over her head.

"I don't want to wear clothes," she whines.

"You have to get dressed, love."

Her flailing legs make it nearly impossible to slide her jeans up. When she refuses to lift her backside off the floor, he hauls her to her feet and tugs the jeans over her hips. His fingers linger briefly between the material and her skin. *I want her so much.* He sighs. Hitching the jeans' flap together, he deftly zips and buttons the pants.

Dmitri softly asks her to sit on the chair, but she starts twirling around the room instead. He grabs Elizabetta's hand

and leads her to the chair again. He is trying to seat her when she suddenly wraps her arms around his neck.

"May I hug you? It's not wrong to hug an angel, is it?"

His jaw drops open. Logically, he knows it's the heaven's scent, but a part of him is yearning for what he has needed so very long—to hold her. Knowing it's not helpful to her reset, Dmitri tries to pull her arms away from his neck. He would rather wrap her in his arms forever. He shakes his head to refocus; it's becoming difficult to remember why they are here.

She whimpers as he holds her wrists. "Please. Please hold me."

He looks down at her face, her pleading eyes. *I've missed those eyes knowing me.* He searches for another spark of true recognition. A brief flash lights her eyes and undoes his resolve to remain distant. It's wrong, deadly wrong, and he knows that, but he pulls her into his arms. With one arm wrapped around her waist, he presses her head against his chest with the other hand. Dmitri closes his eyes, welcoming the sensation of her body molded against his.

Elizabetta purrs, "I like the way you hug. It's exquisite." Words burst past her lips in a rush. "You smell terrific. Do you taste as sweet? I want to taste you—is that okay? May I? It's okay to kiss an angel, isn't it?"

Tenderly hooking his thumbs under her jaw, Dmitri tilts her face up—he gives no thought to the minutes devouring the dwindling time remaining to bring her under his control. Instead his head lowers and he brushes a chaste kiss against her lips. Her mouth presses closer as she parts his lips with her tongue for a deeper kiss.

Breathless, Elizabetta pulls back, smiling. "Wow, you taste wonderful." Then she places a hand on his neck and pulls him in for another fervent kiss. Her lips trail kisses to the corners of his mouth, then across his jaw and down his neck. The way his breath catches and strangles the moan in his throat seems to cause her to pull back and look up.

"Do you know that I've always loved you?" she says.

Purpose flees, abandoning the illegitimacy of her mind reset to undeniable truth. "*Elizabetta ... ti amerò per sempre.*"

The lucid moment passes as she withdraws from his embrace, laughing. "Of course you do. You're my angel and you have to love me, silly."

Her comments are enough to jar Dmitri back to reality. *Oh God, what am I doing? I'm going to ruin everything and get her killed.*

Settling her in a chair, Dmitri slides the other chair in front of her and sits. Her delicate fingers stroke his hair while he puts the socks and shoes on her feet and ties the laces. She's making it difficult for him to concentrate. He gathers the remaining shreds of his willpower to push past her distractions.

Leaning forward, elbows on his knees, he takes her hands in his. "Elizabetta, I need you to listen. Hear me."

She ignores his command with a smile. "Are we going to play a game?"

Dmitri flexes his jaw and inhales deeply, closing his eyes as he exhales. "Elizabetta, please, you need to focus. I need you to hear me."

"My name's Eliza. And I'm not deaf." Her head tips to the side. "The lilt in your voice is extraordinary, musical. Do all angels sound like you? Sing for me, Dmitri."

Ignoring the absurd banter, he curls a finger beneath her chin and waits for her to look at him. "Hear me! You will do as I say."

She blinks. Dmitri gauges her response—her eyes are blank. "You will submit to my control. Now tell me who you are."

Looking perplexed, she scowls. "You're not a very nice angel. I don't think I like you after all ..."

He groans and starts again; the heaven's scent drug is more powerful than Maria told him. Each time the trance starts, Elizabetta resurfaces in a delirious diatribe. Dmitri drops her hands, rises, and starts pacing the room. If he didn't know better, he'd believe she has the same immunity as some humans. He looks at his watch; forty-five minutes have passed since the injection. It should've worn off by now. He wonders whether the other drugs in her system are causing it to linger.

Unsure when she'll come to her senses, he returns to his seat and keeps trying. "Elizabetta, be quiet and focus. I command you to hear me."

"I'm not going to listen to you if you keep calling me that name."

"Fine, Eliza," he growls. "Now focus, love. Hear me."

"Why are you being so mean to me?"

She shouldn't be so resistant. It's not the programming. Maria may need to reinforce the baseline again. "Hear me."

"I'll listen if you kiss me again ... I like you better when you're good."

Dmitri leans forward and quickly pecks her lips.

"That's not a kiss. I want a real kiss ... you have to mean it."

Dropping her hands, he cups her face. Her arms reach up and pull him closer. Her lips press tightly to his as the kiss becomes insistent, hungry. Then she freezes.

Dmitri's eyes fly open, meeting the horrified look in her eyes. Elizabetta shoves him, toppling his chair backward and dumping him on the floor. She jumps out of the chair, legs scrambling, and runs from the room before he can get to his feet.

Damn it! I am so dead.

CHAPTER 12: ELIZA

Escape

One sweet kiss follows another. She relishes the sensation of those lips on hers; something about it seems so right, perfect, hungry. Their lips part, tongues each sliding past the other and greedily seeking refuge in the moment. It ignites something deep inside Eliza—a spark spreading a fire throughout her body, burning her addled thoughts away.

Then suddenly the mouth on hers is real, and it shouldn't be there. Her body freezes. She forces her eyes open and gasps. *It's him. Oh my God, he is kissing me!* Scrambling to her feet, she knocks him over and bolts through the door of the small room. She is almost at the outer door before he catches her.

"Let me go!" Screaming, she tries to wrench free of the man's strong grasp.

He drags her back toward the little room as fear wells inside her. *Who is this man? Is he going to kill me? Why was he kissing me?*

She kicks his legs and claws at his arms, but his grip

around her torso is like a vise. Back inside the little room, he slams her into a chair and immediately straddles her lap. Strong hands push down on her shoulders, pinning her to the chair.

"Stop fighting me. I need you to be still." His voice is terse and there is a determined look on his face.

Terror seizes Eliza and she struggles to catch the words free-falling from her mind and past her tongue. "Who are ... why are ... where ..." *Can't breathe ... can't think. Breathe, just breathe.*

"Elizabetta, please calm down. I need you to hear me."

I am hearing you, and you said the same stupid crap earlier. A rush of recent memories flood her mind. The waking horror as each day brought more rounds of tests and questions. A dreamlike stupor caused by the cocktail of drugs, which clouded her thoughts or kept her asleep. Then there are the lost chunks of time and the mystifying appearances by this man nearly every night over the last week. Her increased anger toward him and the way she considered inflicting grave bodily harm on him, only to be too terrified to act on her plans whenever he appeared.

Her hand touches the spot where she remembers someone injecting something. By the tenderness in her neck, she knows it was real and not a dream. Clenching her eyes shut, she recalls the sense of warmth and ecstasy that replaced her fear and confusion. Images of a shadowy figure and an ethereal glow of light fill her mind. She remembers a deep, soothing voice.

His voice? An angel's voice? Angel, my ass ... probably a

demon ... his voice!

Someone carried her through halls and rooms she didn't recognize. Snapshots of white, gold, purple, and other people or angels fell away as a fresh, redolent air overwhelmed her senses. Even now, she smells a hint of it in the air. Her skin prickles as she recalls the sensation of hands on her skin, someone dressing her. There's an echo of touching short, silky strands of hair; her fingertips tingle at the memory. Then the blood pulses in her lips, remembering a kiss and the familiarity of those lips ... of a long, lean body pressed into hers.

Disjointed thoughts bubble up. *I know him. I love him ... I think.* Her eyes fly open and her breath catches in her throat. *No ... no, I don't know him.*

There's a pleading look on his face. "Elizabetta, hear me."

"My name is not Elizabetta!"

He seems taken aback by her outrage and blinks several times.

"Who are you? Why are you doing this to me?"

She watches the frustrated look on his face; he just stares as if he's trying to solve a complicated riddle. Finally, anger flashes in his eyes and he responds, "It's not important who I am."

His gaze locks on her as his hands slide down and grip her arms. Panic overwhelms her, leaving her speechless and rasping for breath. *I'm in a secure hospital. This is a delusion, my imagination, a bad dream. This is not real. Oh snap, I am going crazy. I've totally lost my mind.*

His deep-brown eyes penetrate hers, mesmerizing her for

a moment, but she shakes her head to break free of his control. "I'm losing my mind. This isn't real. You don't exist." She mumbles to herself, "I've freaking lost it ... they'll never let me go."

He says softly, "Trust me, love—I exist and this is happening."

"No. No, it isn't, and the nurse will come in any second now and put me back to sleep."

Holding her arms firmly to her sides, he shakes his head. "Yes it is, Elizabetta, and you're no longer in the hospital. Please stop struggling. Don't fight me. I need you to look at me."

Their eyes meet again.

"Good, now hear me." There's a hint of desperation in his voice.

"What is wrong with you?" Eliza bellows. "I am hearing you. What is your problem? Why are you doing this to me?"

The man squeezes his eyes shut. He roughly rakes a hand through his hair twice before he swipes the hand down his face. "Damn it, this shouldn't be happening."

"Oh, you've got that right, and you need to let me go. Now!"

"I can't do that, love."

They stare at each other in silence for a long minute. His hands move back to grip her shoulders. His eyes seem to convey an urgent desperation, and for a moment it looks as if he wants to shake her into understanding something only he knows. *If he's right and I'm no longer in the hospital, I need to try something else ... somehow divert his attention. I need to escape.*

"If you get off me and tell me who you are, where we are, and why you're doing this to me, I'll cooperate with you."

A low growl rumbles from his throat. "My name is Dmitri. We're in a warehouse not far from your apartment, and I'm tasked with ... preparing and returning you to Shashenka Belyakov."

Truth drips from every word, she knows it, and it unsettles her. Eliza searches his eyes. "Dmitri." She pauses and a sick feeling twists her stomach. Her voice quivers. "What do you mean by 'preparing'?"

"I cannot tell you." He changes the subject. "If I stand, will you promise not to run?"

His remark stuns her. *Cannot tell me? What the hell?* She nods in spite of herself. Slowly he rises and releases the iron grip on her shoulders. He steps back, eyes not wavering from hers, and reaches for the chair lying toppled on its side. Righting the chair, he sits across from her once more.

"Elizabetta—"

She cuts him off. "Why do you keep calling me that? My name is Eliza."

He swallows, clearing his throat. "Eliza ... there are many things I am forbidden to tell you, questions I cannot answer. After everything you've been through these last several weeks, I know it's difficult, but you need to trust me. I will never hurt you."

Anger boils inside her at the reminder of how his direct involvement in all that has happened has derailed her life. "Why? Why? Why? God, why are you doing this to me?" She is shouting now.

Dmitri looks toward the pale night sky, illuminated in the moonlight shining through the skylight of the ceiling. "I cannot say, Elizabe—Eliza. You know that."

She stands, folds her arms across her chest, and irrationally stamps a foot on the floor like a child. "No, I don't know that. I don't know who or what you are, or why you're tormenting me this way. I don't see the point in your nightly visits and I can't fathom any good reason for you to be here. You're making my life a living hell, jackwagon!"

A pained frown pulls his lips into a tight line. "I'm sorry, love, we have no choice and must—"

"Do you even listen to yourself and these ridiculous statements you make? And stop calling me 'love.' I am not your love or anyone else's, for that matter. This entire ordeal is asinine and cruel, and you know it."

Her words hit their mark; Dmitri winces and sits back in the chair, looking away from her. His voice is suddenly soft. "Excuse me, love. I need to make a call."

Eliza watches as he leaves and closes the door behind him. This may be her only chance to escape. Her heart speeds up as the thought sends a burst of adrenaline through her. Scanning the room for another way out, she sees a vent below the ceiling on the exterior wall. Her attention focuses on it as she considers its size; it may be just large enough for her to crawl through and escape.

As the muffled sounds of Dmitri's deep voice come through the other side of the door, she quietly moves a chair under the vent. Standing on the chair, she grabs at the sides of the grate and tries prying it off. It doesn't budge; rusted screws hold it firmly in place.

I've got to get out of here. She quickly looks around the room for anything she can use to pry the grate loose. A beat-up metal cabinet is in one corner; she rushes over to it and jerks it open. The warped door screeches as she opens it. Her heart thumps wildly as she holds her breath, waiting to see whether Dmitri responds to the noise, but he's still talking with someone on the phone and doesn't seem to have heard her.

The inside of the cabinet is empty. In disbelief she reaches in and swipes her hands over dust-filled shelves. *I've got to get out ... get out now.* Her attention returns to the grate. *Shit. It's that or the door.* She dashes across the room and leaps onto the chair, wedging her fingers between the mesh squares of the grate and hooking her fingers around the screen, her thumbs pressed against the outside of the frame. She tugs. A screw head breaks off; she pulls harder. When it abruptly gives way, she tumbles to the floor and jumps to her feet again.

He's still talking on the phone. *I can't believe he didn't hear that.* Standing again on the chair, she looks back over her shoulder at the closed door. Then she leaps up, throwing her hands through the open space and slamming her palms against the tin plate covering the outside of the vent. It takes a few jumps and hits before the plate dislodges and clatters as it hits the pavement outside.

Reaching through the vent, Eliza grabs the exterior wall and hefts her body up. Her shoulders squeeze into the narrow hole and she wriggles forward, pumping her legs and bracing her elbows against the outside wall. Eliza is so focused on the struggle to climb through the tight opening that she almost misses the obvious, but then it registers. *I'm going to fall on my freaking head.* Dangling by the waist, she rapidly assesses her options. Then she spots an electrical conduit within arm's reach on the side of the building. Her left hand grasps it, and she pulls as her legs continue kicking. Her hips move free, her body twists, and she grabs the conduit with her other hand as her legs pull clear of the vent. Then she drops to the ground. Her feet find traction on the pavement and she starts running. *See ya, creep.*

She never gave thought to where she would go—she only knew that she needed to escape. Now that she's free, there are few choices available. It's too risky to return to her apartment, and she doesn't have any friends or family who will take her in. Somehow Dmitri found her after she was admitted to the hospital, despite the security there. Keeping him from finding her again is paramount.

Just go, run. Run. RUN.

Looking up at the street sign on the corner to get her bearings, Eliza starts running. She turns left at the next intersection and heads for the south edge of town. Near the railroad tracks, the industrial section ends and undeveloped lots begin. Beyond them lies a buffer of trees and the highway. Not slowing—it's the middle of the night and traffic is minimal—she darts across the road.

Eliza has never been beyond the highway but can see the ridgeline of the mountains in the distance against the night sky. *Ha! Let him try to find me there.* Sprinting through the trees, she dodges low branches and feels them snag and tear at her hair and clothes. When she breaks free of the small patch of woods, she stops and surveys the long, grassy field before her. On the other side of the field she can make out the shape of more trees that stand like silent sentinels in front of the towering mountains. She starts running again. Her sole focus is putting as much distance between her and Dmitri as possible. When she reaches the base of the mountain, she slows her pace a little, jogging up the slope where she can, and stopping to climb where she must.

Near the ridgeline, she looks back toward town. The lights of the cityscape are a few miles behind her; ahead, the mountains continue past the horizon. She has no idea what they contain or how far it is to the next town, but the pull of freedom is too strong, and she makes an impromptu decision to keep going. Smiling at her successful escape, she looks once more at the life she is leaving behind. *So long, Bozeman. I don't think I'm going to miss you!*

CHAPTER 13: DMITRI

Prices Paid

Pacing in front of the closed door, Dmitri updates Maria on the problem. "She's too self-aware. I can't influence her. I think you need to reinforce the baseline."

"Did you try after the heaven's scent wore off?"

"Yes, and the effects lasted almost an hour. While Elizabetta was under it, she was giddy and uncooperative. When it wore off, she rebuffed every attempt I made to gain control."

Maria blows out a breath. "I was afraid that might happen. That's not good. Where is she now?"

"We're in the warehouse. I took her there in case she started screaming and attracted unwanted attention."

"You're right—I'll need to reinforce the original spell. I'll let Shashenka know." Maria mutters curses and clears her throat. "Give me a few minutes and I'll call you back."

Shoving the phone in his pocket, Dmitri grabs the doorknob, but pauses before going into the room. He was hoping that Maria would have advice to help him regain control now, not later; his only course of action is to keep Elizabetta re-strained. He pushes the door open and his jaw drops. The room is empty; he sees a chair against a wall, and the vent cover is lying on the floor.

Oh hell, no.

He is stunned by the ways Elizabetta keeps thwarting him. One side of his mind can't accept she's escaped, but the other side knows she's always been able to avoid being trapped or hunted. Immediately he turns and runs out of the room to the warehouse exit. He has to find her before she gets too far. When he reaches the place below the vent, he anxiously scans the streets and alley. Elizabetta is nowhere in sight.

Damn it, this can't be happening. He punches the wall, cracking a cinder block and splitting open his knuckles. *Shit, shit, shit.* He shakes out his wounded hand.

I can't catch a single break. He should have known that even dormant, Elizabetta's skills are exceptional and her mind too strong for the programming necessary for this re-set. Then he realizes the precarious position this puts him in. Scrubbing a hand over his face, he slumps against the wall, takes out his phone, and sinks to the ground.

It takes a moment after Vladimir answers before Dmitri finds the ability to speak. "Vlad ..." His voice falters, chokes. "I'm a dead man. He's going to kill her."

"What are you talking about?"

The words rush out. "We've lost control ... I couldn't take control of her. I stepped out of the room to call Maria, and when I returned, she was gone." He chuckles darkly. "She escaped through a damn vent in the wall, she's nowhere in sight, and I don't even know where to start looking."

"*Sakra!*" Vladimir curses in his native Slovak language, a sign of his increasing frustration with this mission. "Go to the apartment. Maybe she's gone back there. If she's not, call me before you alert Shashenka."

Dmitri flinches. He hasn't even considered calling their master yet. *It will be the end of me.* He jumps up and runs for the car. He must find Elizabetta. As he drives the few blocks to her apartment, his mind is in turmoil. What-ifs lead to dead ends. There is only one way out that is favorable for their survival—capture Elizabetta before Shashenka learns of this latest escape.

At the apartment he unlocks the door and immediately discovers that she's not there. His mind mocks the hope he clung to; he should have known better. She's never been that stupid. It takes a few minutes to work up the courage to call Vladimir; once it's done, Shashenka will find out. He cannot avoid his fate now. *I am so damn dead.*

Fifteen minutes later, Vladimir and Anna walk through the door. Anna takes a seat beside Dmitri, trying to reassure him that they will find Elizabetta and get her back. Dmitri keeps shaking his head, his eyes closed. It's not that easy or simple. Even with Elizabetta's skills suppressed, there's never been another like her who has succeeded in escaping. *She could be anywhere by now.* His pulse quickens at the next thought. *What have we unleashed on the public?* She is unstable with her programming incomplete. The stronger her self-awareness becomes, the more likely the blocks hiding her true nature will fail. If that happens with no one there to explain and guide her, the risk rises exponentially for her to kill innocent people. She'll expose them all.

Vladimir says something about waiting with Dmitri until he talks with Shashenka. Their words fall into an abyss. Dmitri silently thanks them with his eyes and tries to smile, but he is drowning in a rising sea of panic he hasn't treaded for centuries. *Will Shashenka order her death this time? Will my life satisfy him? Will she survive without me? Who will protect her if I'm gone? If he doesn't kill me, how many years of torture are ahead? Is there any way out?* His hands are shaking so hard that it takes a few minutes before he's able to press the buttons and make the call.

Shashenka answers. Dmitri fights the urge to hang up. Teeth grinding, he flexes his jaw. "Master, I'm sorry to report ... Elizabetta has escaped."

An angry snarl is followed by Shashenka's deadly quiet voice. "Dmitri, this must be a bad connection. I could swear that you just unwisely told me that Elizabetta has escaped, and I know that's not possible."

"Yes ... I'm sorry, Master, that is what I said." Dmitri looks at Vladimir and Anna's worried, but supportive faces; what he sees doesn't reassure him. He knows they cannot stop the worst Shashenka can do to him.

The line is silent for a long minute before Shashenka explodes. "This is unacceptable. You've become a constant disappointment to me these last many centuries. I will not overlook this latest blunder. The team will remain to finish their mission and begin a search to recover Elizabetta. They will clean up your mess. You will be on the first plane to Prague and come directly to the estate when you arrive."

The moment Dmitri expected is here. His body begins trembling.

"I will deal with you then. You will pay for your incompetence."

Dmitri's hands shake violently as he ends the call. His fingers lace together, turning his knuckles white. Unable to meet Vladimir or Anna's gaze, he says resignedly, "I'm being recalled to Prague. The rest of you are to remain here and finish the mission. You're to start the search for Elizabetta as soon as possible."

Fear flashes through Anna's eyes as she wraps an arm around his shoulders. The Druzhinas know better than anyone the breadth of Shashenka's wrath and cruelty; they've seen it meted out against others, Dmitri included. The newest, disposable offenders receive a quick death. The higher-ranking, more valuable ones with the longest service suffer agonizing torture, and some are rewarded with a slow, gruesome death. Doubtless Anna understands that Dmitri will long for death before Shashenka finishes with him.

Vladimir sighs heavily. "I'll book your flight and take you to the airport. Try not to worry about everything here. We'll do our best to find Elizabetta. We will get her back."

"Thank you." Dmitri looks up at him and knows the Druzhinas will find her, but that it will likely be too late for him. His voice trembles. "I'm sorry for the mess this has turned into."

"Hush." Anna's faint smile fades. "We've been in worse

predicaments. I know your skills and doubt this is your fault. We'll get her back and set everything in order. Vlad is right—try not to worry."

Dmitri pats her hand and stands. Without another word, he goes to the bedroom to pack a bag. *There is no way out.* For a brief, foolish moment he considers running, but knows it's unrealistic. Shashenka will label him a traitor, task the Druzhina with finding him, and offer a reward to any bounty hunter willing to bring him in. Running is always futile. Even if his friends among the Druzhinas put minimal effort into tracking him, someone else greedy and skilled enough would do the job.

Tangled thoughts shred his mind, and numbness follows a burning ache as each thought is replaced by another. He is zipping his suitcase shut when Vladimir steps into the room.

"Direct flights are virtually nonexistent from here. Connecting flights will take two days." Vladimir pauses, eyes narrowing as Dmitri's shoulders slump. "I called Shashenka and explained the travel delay—he finds it unacceptable— and there are no estate jets in the area. He is chartering a private jet from Denver to pick you up here."

Dmitri nods, lifting the bag off the bed. "When will it arrive?"

Vladimir's tone is blunt. "Two hours."

Killing the time at Elizabetta's apartment would be unbearable. There are too many reminders of his time here with her, and he realizes they may have been his last moments with her. An indescribable pain settles in his chest as he prepares to leave.

After the two men arrive at the airport, they sit in silence in the airport café. There's little to say about the dire punishment awaiting Dmitri. Going unspoken, but known to all Druzhinas, is the one time Shashenka executed one of their rank. The incident occurred shortly after Shashenka rose to power and formed the Druzhina. Vladimir was there when it happened, but it was before Dmitri and Elizabetta's time—and it stands as a cruel testament to Shashenka's brutality.

The executed man, Ivan, was Shashenka's own brother, and the first Druzhina chosen to protect and enforce Shashenka's rule. Ivan realized Shashenka was turning into a monster and tried to murder him. Maria and the guards overpowered Ivan when he attacked his brother. Shashenka spent days personally carving away Ivan's flesh and dismembering his body—in full view of the other coven members—before killing him. The execution sent an ominous message, and centuries later it remains an active threat to any who might cross their ruler.

A similar fate may await him.

"Vlad, will you do me a favor?" Dmitri's somber tone shatters the heavy quiet between them. "When you find and return Elizabetta to Shashenka, protect her always from him and Alexander."

"We always protect one another ... that will not change."

"Although her defensive skills are intact—she can fight hand to hand—the block on her other capabilities will remain. All instincts to fight and survive are suppressed, and she will not know how to manifest her weapons. It ... she will be different now. The changes in her character and personality leave her more vulnerable."

Vladimir smiles slightly, perhaps understanding what Dmitri is trying to convey. "I promise that Anna and I will do our best to keep her safe." He looks down at Dmitri's hands and obviously sees the tremble in them. "I am sorry, brother. We should have helped you—I should have helped you. I'll always regret that we decided not to take a stand during the rebellion but remained silently in the shadows. I feel responsible for what you've endured since. We failed you."

Dmitri closes his eyes for a moment, thankful for Vladimir's candor. Anguish shows when his lids open, and his gaze becomes urgent. "Do not pity me, but grant me one act of kindness. Elizabetta surely hates me now, but please tell her—without explanation, of course—that I loved her and I am profoundly sorry for what I've done to her ... for failing her."

Vladimir grimaces. "If there is any way to do so, I will."

Rising from the table, Dmitri extends his hand. It is time; the plane is waiting on the tarmac. "Thank you for your friendship, Vladimir. I've always valued our bond of brotherhood."

Vladimir draws him into a tight hug. "I'm still hopeful Master will not kill you. Be brave, Dmitri." He pulls back and bows his head. "Until we meet again."

Numbly Dmitri climbs the stairs and enters the cabin of the wide-body jet—a long-range ten-seater. The pilot greets him at the door; there are no other passengers, and he's grateful for that much. He prefers to spend his last moments of freedom alone to reflect on what he's lost and prepare for what is ahead.

The flight will take nearly eleven hours to arrive in Prague. After the plane reaches cruising altitude, he unlatches the seat belt and lies down on the three-seat divan near the front of the cabin. He's exhausted but knows he won't sleep; agonizing thoughts will fill the time.

"Be brave," Vladimir encouraged him, but no amount of bravery survives Shashenka's wrath. It's impossible not to recall the thirty-five years of isolation and torture he endured after the failed rebellion. Now Shashenka promises a hundred years of torment, a time span almost seven decades longer than the last. Dmitri's pulse quickens. His mind doesn't want to accept that he can survive that long, but memories argue that he will; Shashenka will use Maria to make sure of it. He was nearly insane when he broke the last time. Now he wonders if it is possible for a broken mind to be so far gone that death never registers. *I don't know how much I can bear.*

Dmitri pushes the distressing thoughts of his likely demise aside. *What will happen to Elizabetta? Will the rest of her life be a lie? What if she discovers the truth?* He decides to focus on her for the rest of the flight. Thoughts of her helped him endure before, and while she no longer remembers their past, he does.

His memories drift to when Elizabetta entered his life. Dmitri discovered her in Venice only fifty years after he became a Druzhina. She was a governess for a wealthy family's children. He could not dismiss her striking beauty or her gentle nature that carried a hint of interminable strength;

she had an understated poise that screamed for his attention. Intrigue only fueled his curiosity, and he found himself stalking her for days. He fell in love with her before they ever spoke. Unable to deny his nature, he sought Shashenka's permission to bring her as his mate into the Belyakov coven. The request was denied until an unfortunate incident proved her worth.

Dmitri witnessed Elizabetta fight off a man who attacked her. She never gave the man a chance to rob, molest, or kill her; when she fled, leaving the man incapacitated and barely alive, Dmitri ended the man's life in a fit of rage. The natural survival and fighting instincts she displayed told him she'd be an asset—a key point that Shashenka couldn't refuse.

His master conditionally consented and made Dmitri solely responsible for her. Next, Shashenka extracted Dmitri's promise that if Elizabetta ever failed in her duties to the Belyakov coven, Dmitri personally would destroy her. Foolishly he agreed, fully believing she'd rise to be the best among them, and she did. The skills and abilities she exhibited were impeccable and without equal; she was perfect, unstoppable. When Dmitri, Elizabetta, and a few others rebelled eighty years later, Dmitri broke that promise; it was impossible for him to end her life. He should never have bargained with her life in the balance.

How does one kill the one they love most? How does one destroy a life that is the other half of their soul?

He knows that if the Druzhinas had backed them then, the rebellion might have succeeded, and it was a mistake to try without them. He still doesn't know why Maria and Vladimir pleaded for their lives to be spared; neither of them will explain their reasons for arguing against his and Elizabetta's execution. They did not plead for the lives of the others but stood by and watched while Shashenka swiftly executed their compatriots. Dmitri and Elizabetta were spared death, only to be subjected to this twisted and ongoing ordeal. If Vladimir and Maria had known how Shashenka planned to torment them for an eternity, he doubts they would have interfered.

The more than five hundred years that have since passed have offered him a measure of solace, at least: the pleasure of being near Elizabetta. Seeing her face gives him the strength to bear the loss of what they once shared. Still, nothing will ever replace the strength of their bond—the moments of loving each other, working as a team, and simply living their daily lives together. This last year has made a mockery of that.

Shashenka regularly has sent the Druzhinas to gauge and report the progress, and to ensure that Dmitri doesn't fail again. But although Dmitri has done his best, there's something about Elizabetta's mind that has made the reprogramming unusually challenging. What should have taken mere weeks turned into nearly a year of repeated attempts, continued delays, and new deadlines. Even Maria recognized it wasn't normal for someone to be so resistant to the techniques used. If not for her, Shashenka would have taken drastic action earlier.

What I wouldn't give to have Elizabetta back, all of her, for just one more day. Secretly he hopes that she will someday return to him as a mate, that her heart and mind are strong enough to lead her back to him, regardless of her lost memories. He won her over once before, and his desire to do so again reinforces his resolve to survive. Perhaps if he makes it through this and it is of her choosing, Shashenka will not prohibit it. *What are the—*

He startles when the pilot enters the cabin to tell him they will land soon. When they arrive not long afterward, a car is waiting for Dmitri on the tarmac, and Shashenka's personal guard, Peter, waits behind the wheel. Another guard, one he doesn't recognize, sits in the backseat. Dmitri places the suitcase next to him and rides in front. The men don't exchange greetings and drive in silence to the estate.

Clenching and unclenching his fists, Dmitri tries to stop his hands from shaking. He keeps his focus on the latch of the glove box and ignores the buildings and streets that blur by. When the car slows to stop at the estate gate, he finally looks up. The luxurious white four-story villa with its orange tile roof, sprawling lawns, pools, gardens, and guesthouse hasn't changed since he was last here. This estate is one of fourteen the Belyakov coven owns around the world. All are large, opulent mansions designed to house their numbers. Less inviting are the cells and torture rooms in the two or three subterranean levels built beneath each home.

The last time Shashenka imprisoned Dmitri was at the estate on the Volkhov River, in Novgorod, Russia; it is a medieval castle that Shashenka has owned since his rise to power. Quite fitting, Dmitri believes, given the horrors found within its walls. The dungeon is dank and dimly lit. Only the torture rooms have lamps; prisoners are deprived of light in their tiny stone cells. The memory sends a shudder through Dmitri as they enter the villa. *I can't go through this again.* The thought freezes him, and he stops walking.

Grabbing Dmitri by the elbow, Peter inclines his head toward the elevator across from the grand staircase, where three more guards are waiting. When the doors close, the elevator descends two floors. One guard shoves Dmitri hard in the back as the doors open. He stumbles forward.

The musty smell is mixed with odors of mold, rotting flesh, and blood. The drab gray walls show signs of moisture, and single light bulbs in ten-foot intervals on the ceiling light the passageway. Heavy, rusted cell and torture room doors are staggered diagonally on either side of the hall.

Suddenly overcome with fear, Dmitri abruptly stops and takes a step back. *No, I can't ... can't do it. The pain is too great.* Peter's hand tightens on his arm as another guard shoves him again from behind. It's irrational and futile, but he resists them and tries turning back to the elevator.

He makes a half turn, throwing a punch that connects with Peter's ribs, but the other guards move to halt his escape. After a brief struggle, they take him down to the floor before lifting him by his arms and legs and carrying him, writhing wildly, to the second cell at the end of the passageway. *No!* Peter unlocks the door and stands aside as the others forcibly throw Dmitri against the far wall of the small room. Scrambling to his feet, he runs for the door, but it slams shut in front of him.

The cell is nearly pitch black with exception of faint light illuminating the worn hinges and floor under the door. Methodically Dmitri's fingers trail along the cold surfaces, exploring the room for anything that will help him escape. He should know better. The ceilings are average room height, and the walls are bare except for marks etched by former prisoners. There is no furniture. It's a five-by-seven-foot stone box with no way out.

Dmitri stands for hours with his palms pressed against the cold steel door. When he finally moves, it's a few paces back. He sinks to his knees, staring at the sliver of light. *Elizabetta is my light ... she is my hope ... I will endure.*

CHAPTER 14: ELIZA

Friendship

The canopy of pine trees is thin overhead when the faint light of sunrise begins to shine through. Eliza is enjoying the run through the trees and bushes but stops and turns her face toward the sky. The warmth from the morning sun feels good, and she smiles. *I'm free.* Then a prickling sensation, like thousands of jabbing needles, turns into burning, an indescribable agony. Her eyes widen in horror. Her skin is blistering and turning black, with smoke actually wafting off her arms. She ducks into the shade of a large lodgepole pine; it brings a modicum of relief.

She tries staying in the shade of the tree, but streams of sunlight still burn her as the branches sway in the wind. *What the hell?* Frantic, she looks around and spots a thick grouping of elderberry bushes thirty yards away. Shrouded in the shade of the surrounding lodgepole trees, they offer another layer of protection from the sun.

Even the few seconds it takes to dive under the bushes are painful. Drawing herself into a tight ball, Eliza moves as the sun forces her to stay in the shade. Her mind races, trying to make sense of it, but she doesn't understand why this is happening. Although she's never been one to tan, she knows direct sunlight has never harmed her before. *Did the medication cause photosensitivity? Is it possible that I am sick?*

It's one more in a long line of puzzling enigmas that have appeared since she arrived at the hospital. Her low body temperature, undetectable heartbeat, lack of appetite, and inability to keep food down. Her surprising speed and stamina; she ran for miles without feeling winded or tired. Then she reflects on the way she moved at night, not slowing to pick her way through dense vegetation and dark forest that, although illuminated with moonlight, should have been difficult for her to see her way through. She even noticed details in the gloom as she ran. *Is that also a side effect of the drugs?*

She looks at her arms and sees that the blackened skin is returning to a normal, healthy state. She should feel relieved that her skin is healing, but it's freaking her out. *How is this even possible?* Echoes of Dr. Shelby's voice bounce all around her—something is severely wrong with her.

Her mind keeps racing in circles as the sun crosses the sky. When the evening shadows begin to grow, Eliza is still afraid to move. The full moon rises bright in the cloudless sky, nearly rivaling sunlight, and she tests exposing her skin. It has no effect. *Whew.* She crawls out from under the bushes and starts walking again, crossing a few more mountaintops before the moon sets and the sky pales to a predawn grayish blue.

The terrain is broadening into small valleys with hot

springs and mud pots. This area offers little shade, which frightens her. She doesn't know if she'll find enough cover to stay out of the sun. With daylight fast approaching, she finds a juniper bush near a few trees. It shields her better than the elderberry bushes of the previous day, and she closes her eyes in relief. She hasn't slept in more than twenty-four hours. Sheer exhaustion pulls her into a deep, dreamless sleep.

When she wakes hours later she feels refreshed and ready to run, but the sun is rising on the horizon. She slept an entire day and night away, losing any chance to put more miles behind her. She laughs aloud at the irony that a much-needed rest was likely at the expense of her stalker gaining ground on her. *I guess I should be happy that hasn't changed—I still need sleep.*

An hour before sunset she hears approaching footsteps. They aren't the soft treading steps of an animal's hooves or paws, but the heavier footfalls of a person. *Don't let it be Dmitri. Please don't let it be him.* She stops breathing as the footsteps draw nearer and stop in front of the juniper bush where she is hiding. Her heart thumps riotously in her chest, and she can't find enough saliva to swallow the lump forming in her throat.

A knee drops slowly to the ground, and Eliza freezes, locking every muscle, not even blinking. Then a hand lifts a branch and a man bends sideways to peer directly at her. She gasps and then inhales sharply—he's not Dmitri—but something about him unsettles her.

"Hmm, what do we have here?" The man is in his mid- to late twenties. His light-brown hair is unkempt, hanging over the top of his ears and curling slightly on the back of his neck. Bright hazel eyes sit wide over a straight nose, and the stubble on his face indicates he hasn't shaved for a day or two. She estimates him to be shorter than six feet, but he's brawny. He's wearing hiking boots, faded jeans, a tattered pale-brown shirt, and a pair of suspenders. He looks like a logger, but she's seen no signs of logging in the area.

When she doesn't respond, he asks, "What are you doing here?" His expression is a curious mix of amusement and uncertainty.

He's dangerous, run! The thought is irrational; he's made no threatening gestures. *Why does he scare me? At least he's not my stalker, and he doesn't look like he works at the hospital.* She can't stop staring at him.

The tension in his shoulders slightly relaxes. "Look, I'm not going to hurt you. I may even help you if you need it and if you promise not to attack me."

Eliza blinks in confusion. "Why would I attack you?"

"I know what you are. I can smell you."

Laughing nervously at his absurd reply, she blurts out with a hint of indignation, "Excuse me?"

"Oh come on, don't play dumb." He watches her, almost as if he is amused and wary all at once. "There's no need for games."

Oh boy, cuckoo. "I'm not playing dumb and I'm not stupid. I have no idea what you're talking about."

His eyebrows pitch up in disbelief. "You're kidding me,

right?"

When she continues staring, he says, "Look, I know we're supposed to be, like, lethal enemies and such, but you're the first of your kind I've ever come across. I vote for we don't kill each other, what say you?"

"Kill each other ... my kind? What the hell are you talking about?"

He looks incredulous and just stares at her.

"I honestly have no idea what you're talking about, beyond rambling like a crazy man."

His eyebrows arch again in surprise and doubt. "Oh, really?"

Okay, slightly nuts, exasperating, but cute and charming. Curiosity disarms the hyperarousal urging her to flee or fight. "Yes, really." She scowls at him, fed up with everyone not believing her.

He laughs, and a dimple appears with his smile. "Wow, you really don't know, do you?" Chuckling, he shakes his head.

"Don't know what?"

He whistles, a long, low sound. "What you are"—he gestures at her and then at himself—"and what I am."

And they thought I was crazy. "Other than you're a man and I'm a woman?"

Whooping with resounding laughter, he clutches his sides until he finally stops with wheezing breaths. Astonished by his reaction, Eliza stares at him in a mix of disbelief and fascination.

"Boy howdy, this is bizarre." A smile keeps curling his lip

as he seemingly struggles to regain composure. "What if I told you that I know why you're hiding under a juniper bush in the middle of the day? Would you believe me?"

"Maybe." Her brows draw together as she tries to figure this stranger out.

"You're a vampire."

Yeah right, and there are unicorns and flying elephants everywhere. "There are no such things as vampires."

He chortles. "Well, then I guess you won't believe me when I tell you that I'm a werewolf."

"Are you delusional?" If this is supposed to be a joke, Eliza doesn't find it funny.

Slapping his thigh in another fit of laughter, he chokes out, "Nope, but you may be."

The reminder of her recent hospital stay perturbs her. "I'm not crazy."

"Didn't say you were." His head cocks to the side. "I want to ask you something. Why are you hiding under this bush?"

"I was ..." She scrambles for an explanation that won't reveal her escape from the hospital and her stalker. "A recent illness left me sensitive to the sun. I ... burn quickly."

"And you're here, deep in the wilds of Yellowstone Park, because?"

"Yellowstone? I didn't know where I was. I've been walking a couple of nights trying to find a town."

He studies her face for a moment. "You're absolutely clueless. Amazing."

Before Eliza can respond, he offers to take her back to his place. She doesn't know what to make of it. "Why would you do that for me?"

"Because regardless which way you're wandering, you'll eventually come into a town, and people aren't going to want to help you. You've got to know that most humans instinctively shy away from our kinds."

The memories of her isolated life start to taunt her. She knows he is right in that. *No one has ever wanted me.* Uncomfortable, she tries changing the subject. "Why are you here?"

"Last night's full moon. I usually come to the park to avoid hurting people when I change."

He really is delusional. Her voice is hesitant. "Yeah right, okay."

"Seriously, I don't want to hurt anyone, and the park offers isolation and plenty of wild game. It keeps me from killing people."

Eliza recoils and shifts her body against the trunk of the juniper bush. *Run or not?*

Reacting to the terrified look now firmly set on her face, he says, "Let's start over." He releases the branch he's holding up, stands, and walks away a few steps. She watches his legs and feet turn and walk back. Once more he squats near the bush and lifts the branch. A broad, dimpled grin spreads across his face.

"Well, hello there, sweet lady. I'm Matthew Wolfe. My friends call me Matt. My favorite pastime is rescuing damsels in distress. May I be of service to you?"

His wit and charm touch her. He's the first young man ever to show any interest in talking with her, let alone smile at her like that, and it's difficult for her to ignore. Unable to stifle a laugh, Eliza says, "Perhaps."

"If you wish, we can travel in a few days to my castle." Eyes rolling, he corrects himself. "Okay, it's not really a castle—it's a small one-bedroom house with a queen bed and a decent couch."

He points to the west. "If you're interested, it's over the mountain in a little town called West Yellowstone."

When Matt extends his hand, Eliza shakes it and smiles in spite of herself. "Pleased to meet you, Matt ... Wolfe. I am Eliza Ross. Is that really your last name?"

Laughing, Matt sits on the ground. "Yes, believe it or not, but with an *e.* Ironic, huh? Anyways, my place is a full day's walk from here, but I can't leave for another couple of nights. If you want to go, we'll have to hang out here until the height of the full moon has passed."

Sounds sincere, if half-cracked ... werewolf, my butt. Kind of cute, though. Probably harmless. Regardless, she has nowhere else to go. Accepting his offer, Eliza promises to stay until he's ready to leave the park.

"I'll have to leave you here before the moon rises. I don't want to risk harming you when I change, but I promise I'll return in the morning."

It takes a few minutes to assure him that she won't run off. Apparently satisfied, Matt points to the south. "A watering hole is a couple miles from here. If you ... get hungry or thirsty, whatever it is you call it, you may be able to catch an animal near there tonight."

She rejects the implication, but nods politely. Night settles over the forest shortly after he leaves, and Eliza mulls over the facts of her life; unwanted, abandoned, stalked, and now among bizarre, unexplainable physical changes, she has a chance at friendship. A friendship with a crazy man. A man who claims they're mythical monsters. *I may be a bit desperate. Okay, I'm a whole lot desperate.*

Crawling out from under the bush, she wanders the area. Her thoughts are a tangled mess. Matt suggested she could find food nearby. She hasn't eaten since ... she doesn't know when, but she never really feels hungry. Since escaping her stalker—Dmitri, a name and face she'll never forget—she hasn't even sought a drop of water. After three nights in the wilderness, her body should be weakening, and it's not; it's getting stronger the longer she's away from the drugs they were giving her. They said her lungs don't take in or expel breaths, but it feels as if they do. How else can air move in and out of her mouth?

Eliza holds her breath and starts counting the seconds. At three hundred seconds—five minutes—she starts to panic. It's not a lack of oxygen, but the discomfort of not breathing she finds disconcerting. After fifteen minutes pass, she finally resumes breathing, taking in gulps of air.

Fifteen minutes. Dropping to the ground, she places a hand over her mouth. Humans cannot hold their breath that long and live. *Is Matt telling the truth? Am I dead, or undead, or ...?* She cannot finish the thought. Sitting with her knees drawn up, she starts to rock back and forth. Her hands tangle in her hair as if to pull it out by the roots.

This can't be real ... can't be. They don't exist. They are

*fairy-tale and horror movie monsters. I don't have fangs. I'm
not a monster. The idea of drinking blood is revolting.*

Her tongue flicks over her teeth—no, no fangs. But how
can she be so abnormal? What about the medical mysteries?
*Oh, no ... I am crazy. I'm losing my mind ... maybe it already
left and didn't even say good-bye.*

Her brain is numb. She can't dismiss Matt's conviction
that they are monsters. *If he's telling the truth, I'll never be
in sunlight again. It's just not possible. If it is ... I can't fathom endless nights of shadow.*

Either she's crazy, or vampires do exist. Overwhelmed by
the terrifying prospect, she starts hysterically shrieking. It
takes several minutes for her brain to catch a rational
thought and stop the delirium seizing her. The night sounds
of the forest slowly return as she sits silently quivering, hug-
ging her knees to her chest. She continues swaying until the
sun rises over the mountains; the first rays of daylight jar her
into reality.

The blisters on her skin are blackening, with smoke wafting from them, when she finally finds the juniper bush and
crawls under it. She's afraid to face Matt, yet she's hoping
desperately that he'll return. An hour after sunrise, he is still
not there. *He's not coming back. He's not coming ...* Her body
shakes with heavy, racking sobs.

The commotion she's making prevents her from hearing
the rush of footsteps coming nearer. She jerks back against
the trunk of the bush as a branch suddenly lifts.

"Eliza? Eliza, are you all right?" Matt's worried tone forces her to look at him.

A couple of minutes pass before she stops weeping. "No. If you're lying ... then, then ... I'm crazy. If you aren't ..." She can't finish the thought; it's too horrific, worse even than being mentally ill.

His lips form a silent "oh" of understanding, and he lies down and scoots under the juniper next to her. There's no room to turn onto his side, but he works an arm under Eliza's neck and his other arm brushes against the fist she's clenched to her chest. His fingers pry open her hand and then close around it.

She grasps it like a lifeline. In a whisper she says, "I can't believe it. I can't be ... a vampire. Not real."

"Eliza, can you feel how hot my hand is?"

Realizing he is warm, no, hot compared with the nurses and doctors she recently encountered, she nods.

"My normal body temp is 101. Yours changes with how hot or cold the air is. Right now I'd guesstimate the coolness of your skin to be about 75 degrees. Now inhale and tell me what you smell." Matt encourages her with a deep breath of his own.

Hesitantly she inhales until a pungent, earthy scent assaults her nostrils. "I ... I don't know how to describe it. It's like grass and bushes and trees and soil and something musky, something else that I can't quite place. It's very strong."

Matt chuckles. "That'd be me."

Eliza turns to face him. "What do I smell like?" The absurdity of asking a cute guy that question hits her, and she blushes.

"Compared to humans, your scent is fragrant and almost sickeningly sweet. It's like a mix of spices, flowers, and rotting fruit, not as rancid as death, but something uniquely its own. It's both a potent attractant and repellent to my kind." He grins at her.

A few moments pass in silence while Eliza considers his unabashed comment. *Is this why people don't want to be around me?* "Do I stink?"

"Naw, not really. It's just different from humans, and I notice it because it makes the hairs on the back of my neck bristle. It's sort of like a ... warning to my kind."

Why am I buying into his delusions? Should I go back to the hospital? They can fix crazy. But she can't go back there; she'd be institutionalized for the rest of her life. "I'm still not sure I believe vampires or werewolves exist, but if they do ..." She shudders at the thought. "If that is what you and I are ... what ... how did it happen to you?"

For a long moment Matt looks at her as if trying to decide what to say. "Do you want the long or short version?"

What if he's telling the truth? "We have time to kill."

He seems to reflect a moment, possibly organizing his thoughts, and then he begins. "It happened five years ago, when I went to Germany to see the area my ancestors came from. I left a pub on the edge of the village late one night, and a werewolf attacked me. The local doc there said it was an animal attack, duh. It wasn't until after I came home to Montana and the first full moon rolled around that I discovered exactly what type of animal."

Smiling sheepishly, he continues. "It freaked me out big-time. I had no idea what was happening to me. Instinct took me into the woods, where I stayed for several days until I stopped changing every night. I wanted to go looking for the one who attacked me—I wanted answers, wanted to kill him. I planned to go back to Germany and track him down, but didn't have enough cash to make the trip.

"During my third full moon, I came here to the park for the first time and ran across another like me. His name is Dave Jensen. We roamed together for a few days, and he began to teach me—told me everything I needed to know about the shadow realms. That included stories about your kind, too."

Matt's arm flexes under Eliza's neck as he squeezes her hand. "Your kind is supposed to be ruthless, untrustworthy, and will kill us for the hell of it. Our kind, well, we're angels by comparison, according to Dave." He winks at her. "I've heard a lot of stories about vampires. You're the first one I've met, and it makes me think the whole feud to the death thing is overblown."

I can't believe I'm even considering this. "Are there more werewolves? Are you part of a pack?"

Scowling, he's quiet for a few seconds before he answers. "Yes. There's this ragtag pack living on a ranch over near McAllister. Me and Dave sorta belong to their pack, but we're outliers." He shrugs. "Not a true lone wolf or lone werewolf, to be precise, but not a full-time member of a pack either. I see a few others like me sometimes, in the park."

Curiosity piqued, Eliza asks, "This is going to sound stupid, but do you only change when the moon is full?"

"Yes and no. We can control when we change just about any time we want to—day, night, moon, no moon, it doesn't flipping matter. The only time we can't resist changing is the week of the full moon. We change then whether we like it or not."

Matt stares through the branches above them. "It's kinda like tides. The moon pulls on us and forces the werewolf to surface. Our primal instincts are the strongest, sometimes the most uncontrollable, and dangerous then."

In books and movies, Eliza remembers, a good werewolf only kills bad guys, if at all, and the bad werewolf is always a murdering monster. She wonders how close to the truth myths and legends really are. Emboldened by Matt's forthcoming attitude she asks, "Have you ever hurt or killed anyone?"

The way Matt grimaces and looks away tells her that he has. While the awkward silence hangs between them, Eliza watches the conflicting emotions on his face and listens to his heartbeat slow to a lazy rhythm. *Let's play a grotesque game of tell me about your kills, I'll tell you mine. Way to go, Eliza!* She's heard the saying that the pen is mightier than the sword, but she thinks the mouth can inflict more damage than either of them. She's spent a lifetime being wounded by other people's comments, and now it seems her mouth may have cost her the first chance she's ever had at friendship.

Then Matt surprises her and lightheartedly turns the conversation back to her. "So ... tell me about you. What's your story?"

CHAPTER 15: DMITRI

Shashenka's Wrath

It's difficult for Dmitri to judge how much time elapses before the cell door finally opens again. Two guards enter, while another two wait in the hall. As he watches the first two guards approach, he realizes that he doesn't recognize either of them; they must be new to the Prague lair.

A standard prisoner-to-guard ratio is two to one, but for elite fighters like the Druzhinas, the guard is doubled. In an open and fair fight, when he's at his best he could take even these guards down. But the emotional toll of Elizabetta's escape hasn't left him at his best. Hauling him to his feet, the guards drag him through the corridor to a torture room two doors down.

Shackles embedded in the ceiling and floor of this room presage its purpose. Wrought-iron sconces on each wall are the only adornments, and the brightness, contrasted with the darkness of his cell, nearly blinds him. Once again he tries wresting free of the guards, but after a brief scuffle they lock his wrists and ankles into the shackles and leave the room.

Endless minutes and hours pass. His eyes adjust to the light long before Shashenka steps into the room. A malevolent glint is in his master's eyes, and fear paralyzes Dmitri. He's seen the look before; he knows and expects what Shashenka will do next. He battles his rising fear and tries to keep his expression neutral, but rapid, heavy pants betray him.

"You immeasurably disappoint me, Dmitri."

When he doesn't respond, Shashenka's tone becomes reproachful. "I had utmost confidence in you as a faithful Druzhina—if not for years of your exemplary service before the rebellion, and before this ... I'd be inclined to end you now."

Pausing, he looks hard into Dmitri's eyes. "Now you leave me no choice but to add to and prolong your misery."

Since the guards first tossed him into the cell, Dmitri has rehearsed what he wants to say, but now his voice quakes. "I am sorry, Master. I never meant to fail you again. In consideration for my long service with you, I beg of you, end my life."

Maniacal laughter echoes from the room and into the passageway. "I never thought I'd see the day when you begged for anything. Amusing as that is, I will not end your life. I will punish you immensely for losing Elizabetta, and you will pay a price for your incompetence once she's recovered."

Dread replaces his neutral mask with one of horror. Dmitri knows the brutality that Shashenka is capable of inflicting, and the unfathomable pain it brings. Unlike the last time, there will not be a decade of isolation for him to prepare for it; at most, he had only these last few days.

"I will personally torture you daily. Only at the point of death will you receive blood or Maria's spells to heal your wounds. When the others find Elizabetta and bring her to the estate at Big Sky, you will go finish her programming under Alexander's supervision."

A spark of hope flickers at the thought of seeing Elizabetta again. Perhaps being more merciful this time, Shashenka is giving him another chance and will bring a quicker end to this torture. *More time ... precious nights to be with her again and finish her programming so she'll be safe. I won't fail her. I will—*

Then Shashenka smothers that spark. "As part of your punishment for failing me again, I've decided to alter her programming. She will not return to me as a Druzhina."

A vindictive smile spreads across his face as his eyes rake Dmitri's body. "Instead you will program her to be a courtesan, a willing concubine to any who seek her favor at whichever estate I'm residing. She will submit to this, and you will break her if necessary to achieve her compliant submission."

A flood of repulsive images fill his mind: Elizabetta submitting to other men, being raped or tortured. His stomach twists at the thought of Shashenka or Alexander defiling her. Bile rises in his throat. "No! Please, Master, don't ... don't do this to her. It wasn't her fault she ran away—the mistakes are mine, not hers. Please don't do this to her, I beg of you."

Dmitri, barely thinking, continues to plead until Shashenka flies across the space between them and grabs him by the throat.

"How dare you! Who are you, Dmitri Markov, to champion

anyone? Who are you, that my ears should favor your pleas?"
He slams Dmitri's head against the wall. "You are no one."

The words hang in the air. "I am stripping you from the
Druzhina. You will serve the whims and needs of those in the
inner circle, including your precious Elizabetta. You will
watch her enjoy giving pleasure to me and others."

Dmitri writhes against the hold on his neck, and his eyes
melt into pools of pure hatred for the monster before him.

Shashenka chortles for a moment, and then his voice turns
sinister. "You will not have the luxury of hating me. I broke
you before and I will break you again, leaving you unrecog-
nizable even to yourself."

Without warning he pulls a knife from under his shirt and
slashes it across Dmitri's face. He tosses the knife aside as
Dmitri recoils from the blow, and unsheathes the saber hanging at his side. As soon as there is eye contact, he wields it
against Dmitri's arms, legs, and torso. "This is your first lesson."

The pain is excruciating. His body jerks at each blow. His
lungs fight to take air between each scream ripped from him.

Enraged, Shashenka growls as he plunges the saber
through Dmitri's stomach. "You will fulfill your end of our
bargain or I will torture you both for a century before executing her. Mark my words ... you will watch her die a
horrible death long before I ever consider granting you the
privilege of dying."

Seeming to tire of the saber, Shashenka tosses it aside and
unhooks a sadistic variation of a naval cat from behind his
back. Instead of the standard nine cords, a dozen strands of

thin, razor-sharp wire dangle from the baton. The flesh-shredding strikes jolt Dmitri's consciousness between horrifying remnants of past torture and sickening images of Elizabetta's future.

Moyata svyetlina. I have to save her.

Finally, seeming bored and satisfied, Shashenka drops the whip to the floor. Dmitri hangs limply against the restraints, his eyes barely open. Blood is pooling around him on the floor.

Shashenka pauses in the doorway and smiles back over his shoulder. "Remember this. You will obey me, and you will submit."

The pain and shock to Dmitri's system is overwhelming, preventing the words from fully registering in his mind as Shashenka leaves the room. He has no sense of the passage of time and is barely aware when the guards enter and unlock the shackles. They drag his brutalized body down the hall and pitch him onto the floor of the cell.

Unable to move, Dmitri lies in a crumpled heap. Blood seeps from his torn flesh and drips from his ragged clothes. He struggles to build resolve as his body repairs the damage inflicted. Shashenka will eventually break him. He must resist.

My light ... save her, protect her. Moyata svyetlina ... I must endure.

If he succeeds, it will prevent Elizabetta's fate for a few years; Shashenka will pour his energy into destroying Dmitri's mind first. The lingering hidden scars from the last imprisonment mock his will, reminding him that he failed then too.

Days blur together as Shashenka continues the daily torture. Dmitri's healing abilities are slowing, and his body is growing weak from blood loss. When the guards finally deliver a young woman for him to feed on—her scent calls like a healing attar he cannot resist—he barely has strength to draw her blood. After finishing her, he retreats to the corner to sit and stare at the corpse. Even in the darkness of the cell he can see that she bears a striking likeness to Elizabetta and undoubtedly was chosen for that reason. It's another cruel and unnecessary tactic meant to ravage his mind.

A soft voice lifts him from the black hole.

"Dmitri, please wake up."

He recognizes it—Maria—but his mind rejects her presence.

"Come on, Dmitri, you must wake up. I need to talk to you."

Her gentle ministrations—wiping a damp cloth across his forehead—argue for attention, leaving him unsure if this is a remnant of a memory. Fighting to open his eyes, he murmurs, "Maria, is that you?"

"Yes, I'm here." She dabs the cloth at the blood trickling over his jaw. "Shashenka sent me to ..." A strangled sound clears her throat. "He wants me to place you under a spell."

The revelation propels Dmitri's eyes open. He notices a towel draped across his naked, battered body, giving him a modicum of dignity. His voice is weak. "What spell?"

"One I'd rather not use." Maria looks over her shoulder,

rises, and peers through the open door and down the hall. Evidently seeing no one there, she kneels by his side again.

"We don't have long. This is one time I cannot, will not do as Shashenka demands."

What is she up to? "What is he asking?" Dmitri's eyes search hers.

"That I cast two spells—one to heighten your perception of pain, and the other to cause you to loathe Elizabetta."

Shocked and disgusted, he blows out a sharp huff. There are no limits to his master's cruel and hideous nature. Every time he thinks he's seen the extent of Shashenka's depravity, the vile creature creates whole new ways to ruin him. It's mind-boggling to imagine a spell that can inflict more pain than he's already suffered, or one that can possibly change what he feels in his mind and heart for Elizabetta.

Noticing a vial in her hand, he lifts his chin, growling, "What's that for?"

"Let's just say this is my way of complying while defying." A mischievous gleam seems to wash over her eyes. "I'm going to tell you how the loathing spell works, and you have to promise me that you will never balk or think twice about acting like it's in effect.

"I will have to place the pain spell on you. It will make even the gentlest touch feel painful." Jiggling the vial, she offers a tentative smile. "This prevents the increased pain from breaking you mentally, and it imparts a sense of invincibility regardless of what you endure. I will get you more later, should you need it."

What is she getting me into?

She shrugs. "It's the best I can offer you while lending pretense of complying with Shashenka's wishes."

Dmitri studies her face, deciding whether to trust her or not. Maria's powers as a witch are legendary. She's done Shashenka's bidding longer than anyone else, but she has never—since Dmitri's known her—gone against anything Master asks of her. In fact, her actions ended the failed rebellion; the spell she cast immobilized the rebels, and she didn't release it until they were locked in the dungeon's cells. *She's the reason Elizabetta's memories are lost and why I'm being forced to reprogram her. Why is she going against him now? What deceit is this?*

She seems to sense what he's thinking. "I don't have time to explain. The guards will return soon. You'll just have to trust me. Will you promise to follow my instructions to the letter?"

Given the alternative of having his feelings forcibly manipulated, Dmitri relents. "Yes, I will do what you ask."

"Then drink this while I cast the pain spell."

Their gazes lock as he swallows the contents of the vial. He listens to the faint hint of her Irish accent as she intones the Latin words of the spell. Seconds after she finishes it, he jerks away from her hand on his shoulder.

He readjusts the towel on his lap and growls, "You weren't joking about that spell. That was painful."

Maria offers a faint smile. "Listen to me, Dmitri. While under the loathing spell, at the mention of Elizabetta's name or when you're in her presence, you must feign expressions displaying anger, disgust, and hatred. Always treat her harshly and unkindly.

"You must show hostility and revulsion and make disparaging and insulting remarks, whether in the presence of others or not." Ignoring the appalled look on Dmitri's face, Maria sternly continues. "Any misstep will expose you. Shashenka's lackeys are everywhere. Never give anyone a reason to report your behavior as contrary to loathing, or I may be forced to do worse."

"I don't know if I can do this," he murmurs.

"If you want to protect Elizabetta and yourself, you will do it! Otherwise I will have no choice but to place the spell, and I detest the thought of robbing your feelings for her."

Dmitri purses his lips, absorbing the weight of the choice he's making. "I'll follow your instructions."

"Good. Maintain this artifice even when you think no one is watching or listening. I am truly sorry. I wish there were another way."

He can't bring himself to thank her. *It is bad enough that she no longer knows me—she will hate me now.*

"I must leave before anyone grows suspicious of the time I've spent here. No one will bother you tonight—I've convinced Shashenka that the pain spell needs time. You need privacy to practice your Elizabetta-loathing skills."

Realizing that Maria is waiting for him to react to her name, Dmitri feigns contempt. "Will this do?" It feels wrong and disgusts him.

"I know you can do this. I have faith in you."

He watches her walk out and close the door. Raking a hand through his matted hair brings a small sense of relief.

At least his own touch doesn't cause pain. Dmitri contemplates ways to show dislike for Elizabetta as his fingers pluck at the dried blood stuck to the strands of his hair. A plan forms slowly. Every particle of hatred he feels toward Shashenka is what he'll reflect at the mention or sight of her, and his love for her will be her shield. Unwilling to fail her again, he vows to perform flawlessly.

I will do anything to honor my oath to you.

CHAPTER 16: ELIZA

Monsters Exist

Over the next two nights, while waiting for the height of the full moon to pass, Eliza details her life to Matt. He stares up through the juniper branches, saying little as she talks about her childhood loneliness and the numerous foster homes she lived in. When she tells him about Dmitri, the hospital, and her escape, he doesn't say a word until she finishes.

"I think your escape was totally kick-ass, but that man, Dmitri, may not be who you think he is." Matt draws a deep breath. "I doubt he's a random stalker. He is probably the one who turned you."

She raises a hand to her neck. *Was I bitten by a vampire? Wouldn't I remember if some good-looking guy bit me?*

Seeming to notice her intrigue, he continues. "Vampires can control and manipulate people with just their voice, and some with their eyes. Gifted ones, they say, can wipe minds with a mere touch, but their tricks don't work on my kind, and I never heard of them using it on their own.

"The transformation must have blown your mind, and you freaked out and called the cops. They probably took you to the hospital before he could take you back to his coven."

Eliza's gut twists at the thought of going with her stalker to some vampire's lair. *Yeah, he looks like the Dracula castle type—not. Well, maybe a little.* "Do you think he'll come after me?" She's still skeptical, but she can't explain the many oddities she's discovered about herself. "I'm afraid he's going to find me."

That's a lie—I'm terrified.

Matt is silent for a few minutes. "When we get back to my place, I'll call Dave and ask if he thinks the pack will help. He's a cool dude and the pack is laid back, thanks to the way our alpha, Josh, leads them. If I tell him that you're just a new baby vampire I found lost, wandering in the woods, needing our help and protection, they might give it."

If they are delusional and believe this crap too, they are not going to like me. "What if it upsets them that I'm with you?"

He pats her hand reassuringly. "I'm an outlier. They don't have the same power and control over me, so I'm mostly free to do whatever I want. If there's a problem, it's theirs, not yours."

They spend the day making plans for her stay with him, and when they tire of that, they play anagrams and who'd-you-rather. *I've never laughed this much in my life. He's too funny.* It no longer matters whether Matt is crazy or delusional; she enjoys his company. Remarkably, he acts as if he genuinely likes her too. It feels wonderful finally finding someone willing to be around her—even if he's supposed to be her mortal enemy.

Eliza dreads the setting sun; it means Matt is leaving soon. "Do you really need to go away for the night?"

"Until I know you better and can trust myself, yes. I don't want to risk hurting you. I'd like to be your friend."

"Friends." She beams at the indescribable feelings swirling inside her. "I like the sound of that, thank you."

He flashes a brilliant, dimple-filled smile before jogging into the woods. Her eyes don't leave the spot where Matt disappeared from view until the last rays of sunlight yield to the mountain. Yes, she decides, she will miss her friend, and can't wait to see him again soon. Eliza leaves the protection of the bush and wanders through the park. *My life is bizarre. I ran away from a freakish stalker and now I'm moving in with a happy, crazy stranger.* She smiles to herself. It feels invigorating.

Still smiling, she returns to their meeting place before sunrise and is surprised to find Matt waiting for her already. She welcomes his familiar grin as she climbs under the juniper bush and lies next to him.

Knowing they will have a long hike when they leave after dark, they decide to sleep during the day this time. She snuggles into his side, drowning in the exhilaration of finding a first friend. Within moments, Matt is snoring. She chuckles—it is the first time she's ever heard anyone snore—but eventually the rhythm of his snores lulls her to sleep too. For the second time since her escape from Dmitri, her sleep is deep and restful.

At sunset they leave the shelter of the bush, and Matt leads her through unfamiliar territory, holding her hand as they head west through the mountains. Once true darkness blankets the countryside, he encourages her to run. The ground and scenery disappear behind them. The irony isn't lost on Eliza that for the first time in her life, instead of running away from someone and her isolated life, she is running toward an unknown future with a supposed mortal enemy—a friend.

They reach Matt's home as sunlight crests the horizon. He gives her a quick tour of the one-bedroom house. After Eliza showers she joins him on the couch in the living room, and his arm curls around her waist as she rests her head on his shoulder. A feeling of contentment is growing inside her, but it turns to tension at the underlying tone in Matt's voice when he announces that he wants to wait to call Dave.

Puzzled, she looks up at him. He explains it's best for them to spend some time together first—that it will enable him to blunt any fears or concerns the pack may have about Eliza. She smiles at his excuse. *I like him. Cute, funny, delusional. No way he's telling the truth. I am not a vampire any more than he's a werewolf. Greatest pickup line ever, and I fell for it!*

In the days that follow, a new routine develops between them. Earlier Matt told her he's self-employed in construction; he claims it enables him to disappear the week of each full moon and avoid questions. Her own strange physical quirks aside, Eliza still can't bring herself to believe he's telling the truth. Instead she focuses on settling into her new life.

At first while Matt is away, Eliza tests exposing herself to the sunlight. Within moments, her skin is burning and blistering. Resignedly accepting that the photosensitivity may never go away, she chooses to adjust to living nocturnally. The transition is easier than she expects it to be, and she adapts quickly to sleeping during daylight hours.

During the day, while he's working, Eliza sleeps in Matt's bed; at night she surfs the Internet, watches movies, or reads books until he wakes and goes to work again. Sometimes she wakes early and has dinner ready when he walks through the door in the evening. He eats alone—strangely, she still has no appetite, but neither of them dwells on the matter.

Weekends become the highlight of her week. On Friday and Saturday evenings, Matt often takes her to the local bar. She especially enjoys the nights with a live band, when they dance and do more than shoot pool while Matt drinks. Eliza revels in the new experiences. Being with someone who isn't repulsed by her is elating, and the dates and dancing exceed her dreams. Hope swells inside her as she embraces the opportunities before her—opportunities she once believed would never come into her life.

A few weeks later both have settled into a dating routine, and it almost surprises Eliza how comfortable they are together. While they've yet to share any intimacy beyond holding hands or cuddling, she's happy about the growing friendship with Matt. She smiles up at him as they enter the bar again. He squeezes her hand. They'll get to dance tonight; the bar has another live band.

As usual, Matt is consuming Black Velvet and Coke, his favorite drink. After downing nearly half the drink, he wipes the corners of his mouth with his thumb and forefinger and sets the glass on the table. He tips his head toward the dance floor—the band is playing a slow song.

Taking his hand, Eliza follows and doesn't resist when he pulls her close. Their bodies sway to the rhythm and her head rests against his shoulder. She opens her eyes and looks up when his fingers curl beneath her chin. The music and other dancing couples fade away as he lowers his head to kiss her. Matt's lips cover hers and soon his tongue is parting her lips. The sensation is familiar; it somehow feels right, yet wrong. But Eliza responds with fervor, her intensity sending Matt stumbling back. His eyes hold and search hers for a moment, and then he steps forward, reaching and pulling her close, ardently pressing his lips to hers.

After the second kiss, he breathlessly says, "Let's go home."

She understands the inference and follows him out to the pickup truck. Greedily she accepts his advances when he pins her against the driver's side door. Soon Matt's hands are exploring her body, and Eliza is tugging at his shirt to run her fingers over his bare back. She's reveling in the sensation of both his touch and the feel of him beneath her fingertips. His body heat is searing her in tantalizing ways; it's the first time she's felt truly alive.

Matt reaches behind her and pulls the door latch. Spinning Eliza around, hands firmly on her waist, he sets her on the seat. They continue kissing, pausing only when Matt climbs into the cab and inserts the key in the ignition. After another passionate kiss, he puts the truck in drive and takes them home.

Neither of them notices the woman and two men watching them.

Matt slams the door of the house shut with his foot while his arms encircle her waist. They're kissing and petting until reason runs away with sanity to another planet. He maneuvers Eliza down the hall to the bedroom, barely pausing at the edge of the bed as he pushes her down to the mattress and gently falls on top of her. Amid kisses, they are ripping and tearing at each other's clothing. Lying naked, Matt hooks an arm under Eliza's waist and smoothly shifts her to the center of the bed. Their lips and hands are sliding, gripping, kneading over stomachs, hips, legs, and chests as they explore each other.

Lost in the delirium, Eliza takes a few seconds to realize that his mouth and tongue are trailing over the most sensitive areas of her body. *Oh, wow.* But before she can get lost in the sensation, an abrupt and unbidden image of Dmitri flashes in her mind. *What am I doing? This is so wrong.* She freezes. Matt senses her sudden tension, looking confused; his eyes search for permission to proceed. Brusquely she shakes her head, wriggling away from him.

"Stop. I can't. I'm sorry, I can't do this." Horrified by what they were doing and unable to stop the words spilling from her mouth, she covers her face with both hands.

"What? What do you mean?" He releases her, panting, pushing against what his body is wanting, demanding.

"This." She gestures between their naked bodies. "I can't do this, I'm sorry." Grabbing her clothes, Eliza bolts from the bedroom, struggling into her jeans and torn top on the way to the living room.

Minutes later, Matt, wearing a pair of boxers, cautiously walks into the room and stops near the coffee table. His expression is puzzled. "Okay, what the hell was that? What just happened?"

She looks up and whispers, "I—I don't know." *Why does it feel like I just cheated?* Seeing the hurt in Matt's eyes, she apologizes again. "I don't know what happened. I only know that I can't—"

"Eliza." He takes a seat next to her on the couch. "If you're not ready, I can wait."

Tears begin falling as Eliza looks helplessly at him. She presses her face against his chest and doesn't resist as his arms wrap around her. A long while later, after she stops crying, he excuses himself and withdraws to the bedroom, leaving Eliza to sort out her conflicted feelings alone. *This is so messed up. Matt likes me and wants me. Why do I feel this way? Who is Dmitri, and why do I feel like I'm betraying him? Am I pushing Matt away because there's never been anyone in my life?*

None of it makes sense. *There's something definitely wrong with me.*

She falls into a fitful sleep, with confusing images of Dmitri plaguing her dreams. Instead of Matt she sees Dmitri, feels his touch, and his kisses sweep her away as they make love. When the sun sets she wakes, still feeling echoes of the dreams.

As the sensation fades, Eliza stands and quietly approaches the bedroom—it's empty. She slips inside and changes her clothes. Hearing a noise from the kitchen, she leaves the room to find Matt. There are too many unanswered questions, and she needs to know the truth. She pushes against the trepidation rising inside her; they can't avoid talking about what happened, but she is afraid of losing Matt's friendship. A sense of shame and fear makes it difficult for her to hold eye contact with him as she enters the kitchen, but she joins him at the table.

He speaks before she can. "I called Dave this morning."

I have to know the truth. Brushing his comment aside, she says, "Show me what you are."

"Why?" Matt barks.

"I need proof ... I need something."

Reaching across the table, Matt lifts her chin and forces her to look at him. He nods, stands up, and begins undressing—he explains it's necessary to prevent shredding his clothes. He lays his T-shirt, jeans, and shorts over the back of the chair, and steps away from the table. Then his body begins to tremble.

Stunned, Eliza looks on in horror as his body shifts and malforms itself. Claws grow from his fingers and toes. Dense light-brown hair erupts from his body, and his nose broadens and his full lips disappear into a snout. Her jaw goes slack and she recoils back in her chair. A very large wolf is standing before her. *Oh no ... no, can't be.*

Within seconds the wolf's body shimmers, and Matt's familiar human attributes take its place. His nakedness barely registers in Eliza's mind. At her frozen expression, he tugs his jeans on and sits again at the table, seemingly waiting for her to speak.

"Oh my God. This is real." She blows out a choking breath. "This is really real."

"I wasn't lying, Eliza."

"I—I didn't believe you." Shaking her head, unwilling to accept the truth, she murmurs, "I can't be ... I'm not ... n-not a vampire."

Matt strides to the fridge, opens it, and grabs a bowl of cut cucumbers and a package of beef hamburger. Squeezing the package of meat, he drains the watery blood into a glass and sets the bowl and glass in front of her. "Choose."

People eat. Why haven't I been hungry? Eliza looks at the cucumbers and the watery blood. It should disgust her. It does—until, hand shaking, she reaches forward, pushes aside the unappealing cucumbers, grabs the glass, and gulps the small amount of liquid in two swallows.

Mmm. The taste is tangy, not bitter, and sets off a burning hunger that twists her stomach and scorches her throat. She's trying to battle the overwhelming sensation when she feels a slight pressure inside her mouth, and fangs slide down in front of her eyeteeth. Her tongue stretches forward and curls around one before moving across her teeth to the other. Then a tingling sensation zings through her hands as fingernails reshape and grow into razor-sharp claws.

The sudden urge for more blood clouds her vision in a red haze. For a moment she looks at the vein pulsing in Matt's neck. *No good, that's nasty tasting.* Racing to the fridge, she grabs the package of hamburger and sinks her fangs into it. *Better, not great.* She's sucking it dry when she remembers Matt.

Comprehension of what she's doing slaps her in the face. Dropping the package to the floor, she dashes to the bedroom and flings herself onto the bed. *It's real, it's true. No, it can't be. I've lost my mind ... insane.* A claw scrapes against her upper lip as she cautiously fingers the fangs. *How did I not know that I had fangs or claws? What caused them to come out now?* She barely notices when Matt walks into the room.

"I wasn't making this shit up. I wasn't lying." Arms crossed over his chest, he leans against the doorframe.

Images of him transforming into a wolf and back to human form and the pressure of fangs in her mouth obliterate the life and world she thought she knew. She tries suppressing the tears threatening to spill over onto her cheeks. Doubtless letting them fall will not soothe the scorching ache now present in her throat. Tears won't stop her stomach from flipping between the undeniable hunger and extreme nausea threatening to consume her. She can no longer deny the truth, but a part of her clings to disbelief. Her horror and shock are slowly overtaken by one indisputable fact—Matt never lied to her, not once.

He's not crazy, and neither is she.

Finally she turns to him with a hand over her mouth. "Oh my. Matt, oh my G-god. Oh my God, we are monsters."

CHAPTER 17: DMITRI

Artifice

When Shashenka resumes the torture, Dmitri is ready to play his role. The pain spell elicits piercing howls with every touch of the knife, saber blade, or blow from the perverted naval cat. Shockingly, Maria was correct; even skin-to-skin contact is intolerable and worse than any pain he has ever known. Dmitri's breath catches as he pushes past the pain and works to strengthen his resolve.

But what Shashenka says next staggers him; it goes beyond what he expected to hear. Between each blow his tormentor boasts, "I heard very interesting reports from Kees and Katherine." He pauses. "The team has spotted your precious Elizabetta in the oddest of places. Seemingly she has fallen in with a pack of werewolves—to be precise, she's living with one. She seems quite fond of that werewolf boyfriend of hers. What do you think we should do about that?"

Trying to make sense of the words, Dmitri feebly lifts his head. His speech is thick. "That's not possible."

"Oh, it is quite possible. She has been seen on several occasions out dancing and having a good time." The naval cat again slices into Dmitri's back, eliciting painful screams as Shashenka speaks between each blow. "Do you have any idea how difficult this makes it to simply grab her?"

Another lash hits the back of Dmitri's thighs. Blood gushes past his knees. "Can you imagine how fouled she'll be after bedding a werewolf?"

No, no, not my Elizabetta. Dmitri mumbles, "That bitch would never do that. She kills their kind ... they kill us."

When he repeats it, Shashenka sets the naval cat aside for a saber. Running the blade through Dmitri's chest, he shouts, "She has. Both Alexander and Kees report that this werewolf rarely leaves her side. They've seen them out together, dancing, kissing, and having a grand time, and that's if they leave his house."

Dmitri feels his dead heart shatter, sending millions of pieces into an abyss. Cracks form in his resolve—this is a grave betrayal for one of their kind, and the Druzhinas would never hide it or lie about it. Accepting it as true means Elizabetta is lost to him forever. The thought is unbearable.

The words replay in his mind. *Dancing, kissing ... impossible.* He wants to reject it as a lie, but he heard the ring of truth even in Shashenka's tone. A lump forms in his throat and half strangles the scream rumbling up from the pain radiating through his chest. The image of Elizabetta in another man's arms—especially a werewolf's—is excruciating, and the thrusts and slices of the saber pale against it. Worse, he's responsible for driving her to such an extreme. Guilt, shame, pain, and heartbreak drown his mind as he barely holds on to consciousness.

The struggle between his internal torment and the outer torture begins to unravel his facade. Fighting desperately to keep his wits and maintain the charade, Dmitri almost slips up when Shashenka mentions Elizabetta's name and speculates what should be done with her.

Voice desperately spewing disgust, Dmitri replies, "I think, Master, that she needs a lesson about whoring with werewolves."

Head cocked, Shashenka pauses midswing. It gives Dmitri a moment for a few heavy breaths, and the chance to regain control of his spiraling emotions. Amusement crackles in Shashenka's tone. "Oh? Tell me, what should be done with her?"

Pulling on every ounce of hatred he has for Shashenka and looking the torturer in the eyes, Dmitri spits out, "She's trash and unworthy of your mercy, Master. I think she should kill the wolf that's defiled her."

"Ah." Shashenka grins maliciously. "That is one alternative, I suppose. Tell me, what do you think or feel about Elizabetta?"

Rage flashes in Dmitri's eyes. Thinking of the natural enemy they've hunted for centuries makes it easier for him to harden his glare. Biting back the words he wants to say, he snarls, "I think she's a whore betraying our kind. She disgusts me."

"Truthfully, you feel no fondness toward her at all?"

Nostrils flaring and his body quaking in pain, he says, "No. She's reprehensible."

"We shall see."

The naval cat strikes Dmitri's back. At the howl of pain, Shashenka laughs and sends another blow, ripping flesh from above his hips. Strike after strike exact more excruciating screams and make it difficult to hold on to the charade.

"Tell me what you'd do to Elizabetta if she were standing here right now."

Gasping, he says, "I'd run ... the saber through ... her heart."

Shashenka's tone turns mocking. "That's an intriguing choice. I thought you loved her. Tell me why you'd punish her now."

I never will, you evil son of a bitch! His body arching against three more blows, Dmitri struggles to answer coherently. "B-because sh-she-she's a v-vile wh-wh-whore, Mas-ter." Recalling the role he must play, he forces the lies past his lips. "I d-don't love that bitch, I l-loathe her slumming with werewolves. I h-hate h-her. I w-wan-want her d-dead."

It's enough to shock Shashenka into another pause. He leans forward and closely examines Dmitri's face. Pulling back, he says, "Humph. You might be telling the truth."

Through the rest of the torture session, Shashenka alternates between the knife and saber, repeatedly taunting and questioning Dmitri's feelings for Elizabetta. Dmitri's nostrils flare and his eyes flash in equal measures of rage, disgust, and revulsion that outwardly display the facade. It both veils the inner tumult of his mind and heart waging war to claim his mate, and rallies him to her side. The burden of withstanding the torture and maintaining the charade leaves him barely coherent as the weight of his body sags heavily against the shackles.

But when Shashenka leaves him alone in the room, a slight smile creases his lips as the master's footsteps fade—a small victory. *I will save her from this. I will protect her, always.* Thankful for the strength Maria's potion gives, Dmitri is still smirking when the guards arrive to take him to his cell.

The next several days pass the same way, with Shashenka torturing Dmitri and probing his integrity while he lies through bloodied teeth. Though the pain spell amplifies the pain, his assertions that he despises, rejects, and loathes Elizabetta remain consistent.

It's convincing enough that Shashenka switches the line of questioning. "What would you recommend I do with Elizabetta now?"

"I would make that bitch pay for her betrayal of you."

"Pray tell, how would you do that?" he asks as he runs the saber through Dmitri's heart.

It takes a moment to get past the pain and collect his thoughts. He's reluctant to suggest anything that he may be forced to harm Elizabetta with later, but he answers with as much venom as possible. "I will do whatever you wish, Master."

"Interesting." Shashenka hesitates, looking thoughtful. "If I tell you to beat her, will you?"

"Yes, to a bloody pulp, if you so desire." *She can survive that.*

"If I tell you to torture Elizabetta, will you?"

"Yes, Master." *I will not.*

Drawing a breath before asking the next question, Shashenka directs his gaze at Dmitri. "If I command you to rape her, will you do so?"

Swallowing the lump in his throat, Dmitri says coldly, "If you so command, Master." *I will kill you first.*

Shashenka still sounds distrustful. "And you would do so with pleasure?"

"Only if it pleases you, Master." Dmitri hangs his head in shame.

"Are you ready to return to work? Will you obey my every command?"

"Yes, Master." He struggles to block images of the atrocious acts Shashenka suggested—beating, raping, or torturing Elizabetta. Bile rises in his throat.

"Then I think it's time to prepare you for your next mission."

As Shashenka turns on his heels and leaves the room, Dmitri closes his eyes, feeling almost triumphant. The artifice is working in his favor.

When the guards arrive, they toss a robe at Dmitri and escort him to a bedroom on the fourth floor. He stands in the middle of the room, and as the door closes behind the guards, he collapses, exhausted, on the bed. Being released this soon stuns him; it's not what he expected. *What is Shashenka up to? Has he captured Elizabetta? Why is he doing this?*

A light rap on the door interrupts his thoughts. Pulling

the robe around him, he crosses the room and opens the door. A young woman with short blond hair smiles as she brushes past him; the painful contact forces him back a step.

"Yes? Who are you?" He's seen her before in the inner lair, but doesn't recall her name.

"I'm Sally Davis." She strides across the room. "Master sent me to help you clean up and dress. You're to join him in the ballroom."

Dmitri's eyes flash with anger. "You can tell Master that I'll be down shortly. I don't need your help."

Flopping into a chair near the hearth, Sally pouts. "I'm supposed to stay with you." The suggestive tone matches the flirtatious look she gives him. An icy tremor creeps through his bones as her hand fiddles with a button on her blouse. "I'm a token gift from Master. Until you leave, I'll be at your beck and call, and I'll stay in this room with you."

Clearly this is another ploy by Shashenka to test his loyalty. *We shall see.* Without replying, he walks into the bathroom and slams the door.

How soon will I be sent away? Where will Shashenka send me? It can't be soon enough or far enough from here. He doesn't know how many weeks have passed, or even what day it is.

Dmitri turns the shower on and steps into the spray, letting the soothing water run over his tender wounds for several long minutes. Water, hope, and dread equally drench him. He knows that until he leaves, he will be unable to avoid Sally.

Stepping out of the shower, he towels off and slowly

dresses, summoning the willpower to continue the charade. His reflection catches his glance, and he studies the loathsome expression deeply etched in the face staring back at him from the mirror—unveiled hatred for Shashenka, not Elizabetta. Somehow he needs to use this mask to convince the others of the lies he's perpetuating. A feat, he believes, that may be easier to pull off with Shashenka than it will be with his friends among the Druzhinas.

Sally is still reclining in the chair when he enters the bedroom. Her eyes roam over his body, and she smiles. "You clean up rather nicely."

Forcing himself to smile back, he thanks her. "Shall we go?"

She joins him at the door and places a hand in the crook of his elbow. Grimacing, Dmitri looks down and removes her hand. "Don't touch me. I can't bear anyone's touch."

Sounding confused, she says, "Oh ... right. You probably need a couple of days to heal and put the punishment behind you."

"No, the slightest touch by anyone causes me extreme pain."

Sally nods with an uncertain look still on her face. As they walk down the hall, she starts gossiping about those living in this lair. He recognizes a few names, but seven are new, and he wonders how large the Belyakov coven has grown in his absence. Sally continues rambling. Dmitri dismisses the inconsequential details of the lives here. *Is she ditzy or highly intelligent?* He's not sure which, and he's still suspicious she may be a spy. She reveals nothing of importance as they descend the staircase, walk through the villa, and enter the ornate ballroom on the ground floor.

Gold velvet drapes cover the tall windows, and plush highback furniture, in burnished shades of green, lines the edges of the room. Thin strips of gold separate the white marble floor tiles. Dmitri's eyes settle on Shashenka sitting with a small group of vampires in the corner near the windows. He recognizes two men and one woman, but is unfamiliar with the other two women.

The urge to leave is strong, but Dmitri complies when Shashenka waves him over. His lip starts to curl into a sneer; it takes some effort to force it into a smile and greet the men. "Master, Leonard, Charles."

Shashenka inclines his head toward the empty chair on his right. When Dmitri sits, the tyrant's voice is jovial. "It's so good of you to join us, Dmitri—"

As if I have a choice.

"I see you remember Leonard and Charles. These lovely ladies, Isabelle and Christina, are recent additions to our family, and you know Stephanie. Ladies, please welcome Dmitri home."

Rising from their seats, they approach him. He tenses. Two of them perch on the sides of his chair while Stephanie settles onto his lap. Unable to tolerate the painful contact, Dmitri abruptly stands, dumping the woman on the floor and nearly bumping into Sally. A mix of confusion, horror, and embarrassment flitters across Sally's face.

Roaring with laughter, Shashenka tells the women to return to their chairs. He leers at Stephanie. "I must have forgotten to tell you that our poor, dear brother is overly sensitive, so unfortunate."

After she's seated, he sighs and looks at Dmitri. "This party and feast are for you—our guests will arrive soon. I am giving you the honor of selecting the first among them."

Two vampires usher eighteen people, dressed in elegant evening attire, into the room. The party is a sham, and the guests, mere hapless humans, are the feast. Typically they are unaware that the invitation they accepted has sealed their fate. Still, it's rare when Shashenka forgoes choosing first.

I doubt it's an honor. What is he up to? "Thank you, Master."

Knowing what is expected, Dmitri rises from his chair and looks over the huddled group. The women share a likeness to Elizabetta, and although they are not her, it's difficult for him to consider feeding on the reminder. *This is a test.* Shashenka doubtless is watching his every move, leaving little choice—though his preference is culling a man from the lot. Unwilling to make such an error, Dmitri snatches the nearest woman, spins her around to face away from him, and pulls her against his chest. His face contorts with pain from the contact and his teeth grind together. With one arm wrapped around her waist, and clamping a hand across her mouth, he tilts her head to the side. A painful groan escapes him as he forces his jaws open and sinks his fangs into the warm flesh of her neck. *No mistakes.*

Her muted cry launches the feeding frenzy. Before the humans realize what is happening, the other vampires move inhumanly fast; brief chaos erupts as the men and women fall victim to their predators. Their shrieks of terror soon fall silent. Dmitri rapidly drains the life from the woman he's holding and lets her lifeless body gently slide from his grasp onto the floor.

Servants quietly remove the corpses, to cart them to the incinerator at the back of the estate. Music starts to play after the last one is taken from the room. Dmitri longs to retreat to his bedroom. Feeding on humans in this manner is barbaric in his mind. While blood is a necessary part of their nature, he doesn't feed needlessly and tries to show some compassion toward those whose lives he takes.

Wincing away from the hand suddenly clasping his shoulder, Dmitri bites back a growl. "Don't touch ..." His voice trails off.

Not surprisingly it is Shashenka, an insincere smile stretching across his lips. "Well done, Dmitri. Now stay, enjoy, go dance with Sally. You'll find her rather pleasing."

It's an order, not a suggestion, another way of torturing him; clearly it gives Shashenka perverted pleasure to watch him squirm in pain from being touched by another. Reluctantly Dmitri nods and walks over to Sally, and taking her hand and clenching his jaw against the pain, he leads her in a waltz. Every movement of her hands sends a stinging ache through him. The expression on her face suggests growing understanding, and she seems to be trying to reduce their contact. Dmitri appreciates the effort, but it's not enough; she's still touching him. As they turn, he sees Maria sitting in a chair—her green eyes furiously smoldering as they shift between him and Shashenka—perceptibly displeased to watch his torment.

It's a relief when Sally suggests they retire to his bed-room. With Shashenka watching them, he allows her to take his arm, and grimacing, he escorts her to the door. Sally swiftly removes her hand when they reach the hall.

"I'm sorry," she calls after him as he flees for the staircase. "I didn't mean to hurt you."

Fortunately she continues at a slow pace and doesn't rush after him. It allows him a minute alone in the room to collect his wits. Now he understands why Shashenka let him out of the cell; Maria's spell is its own prison and torture chamber. Until he's sent away, Shashenka will force him to engage in these twisted games. If the spell remains, he'll spend an eter-nity avoiding physical contact and never again know the pleasure of another's touch. *Is that a loss when it's not her touch? I will pay that price to keep her alive.*

He's sitting in the chair with his face in his hands when Sally enters the bedroom. He can feel her gaze, but doesn't look at her.

"Dmitri? Why does it hurt you to be touched?"

His chest rises and falls with a tremulous breath. "It's a spell meant to punish me."

"Oh." She kneels before him. "No one told me. I didn't know. I'm not cruel ... I'll try not to touch when we're alone."

Looking up, feeling grateful, he meets her eyes. "Thank you. I appreciate the kindness, Sally." She may be a spy, but at least she isn't cruel like their master.

CHAPTER 18: ELIZA

Meeting the Enemy

Before the next full moon, Matt contacts Dave to update him about Eliza and seek the pack's protection for her. The details apparently shock Dave; their conversation is heated and brief. Eliza waits nervously for Dave to call back after he relays the news to the pack leader, Joshua Cleary. If vampires and werewolves are the mortal enemies Matt claims them to be, she doesn't see any reason they'd want her around, let alone protect her from her own kind.

She is still struggling to accept everything she's learned. There are too many unanswered questions. The isolation of her life makes sense, but doesn't. Vampires are turned, not born, and she's been shunned since childhood. *At least people have a reason not to like me now.*

The lingering burn in her throat remains, and it continues to nag at her why she never noticed it before. The first few days after her fangs and claws appeared, they tended to stay present; it took a lot of coaching from Matt to learn how to retract them. Now it seems they only extend when she's feeding, and although she's tried to will them to come forth at other times, nothing happens. She's been ruining a lot of Matt's meals by sucking the meat dry before it's cooked. Oddly, instinct tells her his blood would taste awful; she's not even tempted by it.

The return call from Dave comes within the hour. Joshua—or rather, Josh, as he prefers to be called—is demanding a meeting to decide what to do with Eliza and has ordered Matt to bring her to the ranch that night. Nearly all pack members will be there, but ultimately the decision is Josh's to make; the safety of the pack is his primary objective.

After sunset Matt drives Eliza to the ranch near McAllister, eighty miles away. A few men and women are loitering on the porch when they arrive; they stare warily as Matt parks the pickup. *What if they attack me? How do I protect myself?* The hairs on her arms bristle when the combined scents of those on the porch reach her nose. Matt squeezes her hand reassuringly before getting out and walking around the front of the truck to open her door.

Matt guides her up the stairs, one arm around her waist. His tone is confident. "Hey, guys, this is Eliza. Eliza, meet Karen, Dave, Tony, Levi, and Sandra. Levi is Josh's beta."

Their inimical gazes freeze her in place. Swallowing twice, she says, "It's a pleasure to meet you."

"Yeah, we'll see about that." Levi nods toward the door. "Josh is waiting with the others inside."

Leading Eliza by the hand, Matt escorts her into the house. Several werewolves are gathered in the spacious living room, and seven pairs of hostile eyes narrow at the sight of her. *This may be a death sentence. I can't believe how stupid I am.* Matt pulls her forward until they're standing before a broad-shouldered man whose tanned complexion and black hair enhance his sharp blue eyes. Unstated power and strength ooze from the man, and Eliza realizes it sets him apart from all the other werewolves present—he is the alpha male.

Extending a hand, Matt greets him in a way that seems to confirm his outlier status but conveys deference toward the pack leader. "Hey, Josh."

Josh's nose wrinkles as he looks Eliza over. "Matt, I'm not thrilled about this ... Dave said she's possibly hunted by the one who made her?"

"Yeah, possibly." Matt pauses. "She honestly doesn't know much, other than that some vamp called Dmitri is stalking her. Like I told Dave, she's just a lost baby vamp."

Glaring at Eliza, Josh growls, "Baby or not, she's a threat to us. Aside from what she's capable of, we don't know if her creator is alone or in a sizeable coven. Why should we risk our lives for her?"

Not good. Defuse it or get out. Leave.

Matt responds before she can voice a willingness to leave. "She's been staying with me since the last full moon, and she hasn't attacked me." Matt grins. "She didn't even believe she was a vamp until a few days ago."

"Are you joking? How is it possible for her not to know?"

Eliza finally finds her voice. "I don't remember being turned or how it even happened. I didn't believe Matt was a werewolf either, until he proved it to me the other night. I

understand now what I am, but I don't want to be a monster.
I would never hurt anyone."

A red-haired woman steps forward. "I've never heard of
such a thing. It's impossible for her not to know. I think she's
lying."

Screw you!

"She's telling the truth." Matt's tone is protective, defensive.

"How do you know?" Josh's questions contain a hard edge.
"How can you be sure her master didn't send her to infiltrate
our pack and report our strength?"

Matt laughs. "I'm telling ya, she had no idea. You should
have seen her face when I phased to prove it to her. Eliza
completely freaked out."

The same redhead speaks. "Vamps are masters of deception. It's an act, a very clever one—one that is suckering you
in, Matt."

This is not going to work. Eliza grabs his arm. "Matt,
perhaps I should leave. It's clear that I'm not welcome here,
and I don't want to cause problems for any of you." *Actually,
I don't want to die.*

"I can't let you leave—you're too much of a risk," Josh
says. To Eliza's astonishment, he orders her to be taken to
the bunkhouse. There will be at least two wolves watching
her at all times, he says. He wants time to assess the threat
she poses before he decides to protect or free her. But it's his
underlying tone, an unspoken threat, that ignites her fear the
most—the pack will kill her and any other vampire that
comes looking for her. "If what Matt says is true, then she

has a chance to prove herself to us."

Eliza recoils. "What? You're going to hold me prisoner? You can't do that!"

Matt looks down at the floor, and she understands that Josh's decision is a direct command none of them will disobey.

He doesn't look up at her as he says, "I'm sorry, Eliza. You'll have to stay here."

Get out. Get out now! Panic puts her legs in motion, but before she can reach the front door, the wolves tackle her from behind. Hands clamp her arms and neck, restraining her. Matt walks over and takes her face in his hands.

"Eliza, please don't run. They only need time to make sure you're on the up-and-up." His hands move to her arms, trying to brush away the other hands restraining her. He glares at the men holding her and in a fierce tone says, "Trust me, I'd never hurt you or let anyone else hurt you."

That proclamation seems to stun everyone in the room—murmurs rise that it's unheard of for a werewolf to put the welfare of a vampire ahead of the pack. Several people are talking at once, but Josh silences them. "Quiet! Levi, Mark, show Eliza to the bunkhouse. Matt, I'd prefer you remain at the ranch until we sort this out."

Matt nods and follows the others out of the house. Mark and Levi hold Eliza by the arms as they march her toward the simple structure. It has a kitchen, living room, and two bathrooms, as well as two dorm rooms large enough to sleep twelve people each. Matt explains that it houses extra hired hands during the ranch's peak seasons of calving, lambing, and harvesting. The permanent pack members live in either of the two guesthouses set to each side and slightly behind the main ranch house—as pack leaders, Josh and his wife, Lois, are the sole occupants there.

Given their reluctant guest, the wolves decide that whoever is guarding Eliza will stay in the bunkhouse with her. Matt's questionable loyalties cause an argument when he announces that he'll remain in the bunkhouse too. Levi decides to allow it when Matt assures him that he will not help Eliza escape.

Odds of escaping without being killed or hurt aren't good. I have to trust him.

Taking Eliza's hand, Matt leads her to one of the dorm rooms. One wall has built-in shelves, drawers, and rods to hang clothes on. Six bunk beds line two sides of the room. Eliza sits on the lower bunk of the first bed, scowling. "How long are they going to keep me here?"

"I don't know ... it will depend on how long it takes them to decide you're not going to hurt them." Matt smiles. "They won't hurt you. They just need time to get to know you. They kinda suck at making first impressions, but they are good people. Be yourself, and they'll come around."

Eliza looks at the floor. "I'm sorry to cause all these problems for you."

Matt sits beside her. Gently grabbing her chin between his thumb and forefinger, he turns her face toward him. "Don't worry, everything will be okay."

She manages a timid smile and he jumps to his feet. "Now, do you want to share a bunk or do I need to call dibs on the lower rack?"

Her hand rubs at her neck as she does an exaggerated eye roll. "I sleep during the day."

"I don't think they will let you prowl around the ranch at night. It's probably best to be on our daytime schedule while we're here."

Valid point. Eliza gestures at the neighboring bunk beds. "I'll sleep on that bunk—you can have this one."

Silence settles awkwardly between them. She can tell by the look in Matt's eyes that he's also thinking of the night she bailed out on their lovemaking. They haven't slept together in the same room since. Now, given the threat surrounding her, it's a slight relief to know that he'll be so close.

"How much danger am I in?"

"With me by your side, very little." He shrugs. "If you were alone, I doubt they'd restrain themselves. They'd probably kill you."

Not what I wanted to hear. A shiver runs up Eliza's spine. "Are you sure you can protect me?"

Choking back a laugh, he shakes his head. "Truth is, you probably don't need me to protect you. You're a vampire, remember? If they try to harm you, your baby vamp self-protect instinct will rear its ugly head and you'll kick some serious wolf ass. I'm sure Josh knows that too, and I'm wagering he'll keep tight control on everybody."

It's a disturbing thought. *Am I capable of that kind of violence?* While she hopes he's right about her instincts, she can't imagine taking anyone's life, even one of a supposed mortal enemy.

They settle into their new quarters and adjust to her confinement. Early each morning Matt drives to work, leaving Eliza in the precarious care of his pack mates. She tries killing time by reading the numerous farm and ranch magazines spread on the coffee table, or by staying in the dorm room. And like a caged lion, she paces a lot; the similarity to her involuntary stay at the hospital isn't welcome. When Matt returns in the evening, they play cards or hang out with the others, or watch television until the sun goes down. The wolves take turns guarding her, with two always watching her. Ten men and women rotate in twelve-hour intervals, giving each pair forty-eight hours between shifts.

The week of the full moon is Matt's usual week off from work, and he prepares her for what to expect. Some of the pack members, he says, will stay in wolf form the entire week; others prefer shifting back to their human form during the day. With a crooked smile, he explains their propensity for entertaining dogfights. He equates it to sibling rivalry and friendly sparring and assures her that while it looks and sounds scary, they never seriously hurt one another.

The third night before the full moon, she's in the living room when some of the wolves begin to change. Squeezing Matt's hand, petrified, she watches him struggle against the shudders that tremble through his hand into hers as his wolf form begins to surface. He succeeds in denying the change four times and is trying to force it back again when Tony approaches her, snarling. Matt's hand is ripped away from her grasp as he bursts out of his clothes and fully phases into a wolf. Protectively he stands between them, and the menacing growl rumbling from his throat freezes Eliza on the couch.

I'm dead. They're going to kill me.

With a sharp, vicious snap of his jaws Tony just misses biting Matt's shoulder, and her instincts finally take over. Eliza leaps to her feet on the couch cushion and crouches in a defensive posture, hissing, fangs bared and claws extended. Levi reacts to her and moves next to Tony. Matt's muzzle twists into a terrifying snarl, and growls rumble from deep in his chest. His tail is rigid and straight behind him while his hind legs, set wide apart, remain firmly on the floor. His front paws adjust his stance and balance him as his teeth gnash at the two wolves. The message is clear: he will fight if they come any closer.

Somehow Eliza recognizes that the standoff is about to explode into violence. It goes against her defense instincts, but she must stop it from happening. *Trust Matt—don't get him killed. Do this for him.* Backing down is the toughest part, and for a few seconds she doesn't think she can. With deliberate effort, Eliza compels her claws and fangs to retract and cautiously lowers herself onto the couch.

It's enough to defuse the situation. Tony looks at Levi and both glance at Matt before backing away and leaving the bunkhouse. Matt turns and nuzzles her arm with his wolf snout. She understands that he wants her to leave the room. Retreating to the dorm, she shuts herself inside while he stands guard outside the door.

The next two nights go slightly better than the first. Although some have stayed in wolf form, those who reverted to human form change each night. Watching the werewolves phase with the rising moon still terrifies Eliza, so she stays in the bedroom. Matt's incessant pacing and the snapping jaws, gnashing teeth, and snarls coming from the other room keep her alert, on edge, and awake. No disturbances occur the second night, but the afternoon of the full moon brings an unexpected encounter.

Clearly still unhappy with their unwanted guest, Monica pays the bunkhouse a visit. She's heard about Eliza backing down from Tony and Levi. "Why don't you drop the act, vampire? We all know you're here to destroy our pack."

The two wolves guarding Eliza smirk. Matt starts to defend her, but Monica cuts him off. "Stay out of this, Matt. You're so twitterpated that you don't even realize she's playing you. Start thinking with your head instead of your dick and you'll see what I see."

You crude bitch. "We're not sleeping together," Eliza shouts. "I'm not using anyone. I'm not your enemy."

Anger flashes in Monica's eyes, her teeth sharpen into fangs, and she steps forward, shoving Eliza without warning. Immediately Eliza's fangs extend and she grabs the other woman by the neck, the tips of her claws puncture the werewolf's skin. Pushing Monica across the floor, she slams her into the wall. Her claws penetrate a little deeper into the woman's throat. With mere inches between their noses, Eliza hisses, "I am not your enemy, but I will protect myself. Don't ever touch me again or ... I. Will. Kill. You."

Monica's eyes widen in fear. The other wolves move closer, but don't intervene. Then at an inhuman speed, Eliza drags Monica to the door, opens it, and tosses the stunned werewolf out of the house.

Landing on her back twenty feet away, Monica scrambles to her feet. Before she takes another step, Eliza slams the door. Matt and the two guards burst into laughter.

Oh. Oh no. Realization of what she just did crashes over her. Mumbling apologies, she runs to the bedroom and slumps against the bunk frame. What she told Monica was not a hollow threat; she meant it. Somewhere deep inside she knows that she's capable, no, skilled at killing. *What kind of monster am I?*

CHAPTER 19: ELIZA

Odd Alliance

Tension between Eliza and the wolf pack remains high for six weeks, but there have been no further incidents—not even during the second full moon, which came and went two weeks before. She has not been let out of the bunkhouse since arriving here, and aside from Matt and her guards, she's seen nothing of Josh. Her frustration is turning to anger. She doesn't know how she's supposed to prove herself to him when he never spends time with her. When Levi announces—one afternoon while Matt is at work—that Josh wants her brought to the ranch house, her apprehension flips to terror. She's petrified—not of the sunlight on this gloomy, overcast, rainy day, but that they will murder her. One or two werewolves she may be able to defend against, but if more than that attack, she doubts she'll live through it.

Levi, Tony, and Mark escort her to the small office that Josh uses to run the ranch. Then the alpha dismisses the others and waves her to a seat in front of the desk. Eliza tries to veil her surprise in a mask of stoicism, but her nerves are jumping like a live wire. Josh's eyes follow her every move, further unnerving her, and she hesitates before sitting down.

"I know it's not been easy for you to be here, but we needed to test you." Josh's face appears open, friendly, but guarded. "We also needed to see if any of your kind followed you here."

He slides a folder across the desk and tells her to open the envelope inside. Eliza's hands tremble as the contents spill out: several low-light photographs of people she's never seen, although one man has features similar to Dmitri's.

Seeming to notice her puzzled expression, Josh says quietly, "They're watching the ranch. At least two of them show up prowling around here every night."

Watching the ranch? "I've never seen them before."

"None of them are this Dmitri you claim is stalking you?"

She looks at the photographs again and shakes her head. "I've never seen these people before."

"They're not people." Disgust saturates his tone. "They are vampires like you, Eliza."

Brows furrowing together, she inspects the pictures closer. There are two women and four men, and if she scrutinizes the subtle details, she can agree that they are, perhaps, vampires. There's an elegance and beauty to them, but also a strange familiarity—they're lethal. She almost asks how he knows for certain, but thinks better of it.

Josh passes her a half-folded note. "It appears they know you."

His comment sets her nerves on fire, and she has the sudden desire to flee. These vampires shouldn't know her. She almost stops breathing as she opens the note and begins to read:

> *Greetings Mr. Cleary:*
>
> *On behalf of Shashenka Belyakov, we respectfully request the honour of meeting with you and your lieutenants to discuss the return of one of our own. We understand Miss Eliza Ross is a current guest at your ranch and we seek an accord to secure her release. We desire a resolution that will spare bloodshed between us. Please give your reply to our courier within twenty-four hours.*
> *With regards,*
> *Mr. Vladimir Jagr*

She has to read it twice before her mouth catches up with her brain. *Dmitri's name isn't on here. Is he working for this bunch? What kind of screwed-up deal is this?* A tremor creeps into her voice. "I don't know these peop—vampires. I've never heard their names before."

"Oddly, I believe you. Still, they are expecting a reply." Josh smiles. "You've exceeded my expectations while you've been here. I know Matt was truthful about you, and that he cares a great deal for you." His eyes roam over her, weighing, measuring. "I'm going to give you a choice. They are your kind, Eliza. Do you want to go with them or stay here? Consider your answer carefully. If you go to them, we will be enemies, and as pack leader—"

"I have a choice?"

"Yes." He gives her a stern look. "If you go with them, I will forbid Matt further contact with you. If you stay here, you will be expected to fight by our side if they attack."

I can't lose him. The thought of never seeing Matt again settles like razor blades in her stomach. Something about these vampires scares her; instinct tells her to be on guard. "I'd rather stay here with Matt and your pack than go to them. If necessary, I will fight alongside you."

"Very well." Josh's cold stare matches his tone. "Don't double-cross me and make me regret this."

"I won't," she promises. "What will you say to them?"

"That you wish to remain here as a willing guest under our protection."

Instead of returning her to the bunkhouse, Josh shows her to a spare room in the ranch house; it's to be her and Matt's room as long as they need it. She doesn't want to offend them, so she says nothing about the sleeping arrangement— she and Matt will have to make do. Grateful to leave the confinement of the bunkhouse at least, she moves their clothes to the room—no guards in tow—before he arrives from work. The meeting with Josh replays in her mind as she sits on the edge of the bed. She can feel the weight of the responsibility and trust he placed on her.

The wolves gather for a meeting later that night. To Eliza's surprise, no one questions Josh's decision, and even more shocking is that none of them, including Monica, cast dirty looks her way. Matt explains afterward that the pack respects and trusts Josh's leadership. Moving them into his home, instead of one of the guesthouses, sent the message that she is directly under Josh's protection—she is not to be touched. Lower members of the pack rarely challenge the alpha male; doing so results in a fight to the death, with the victor always assuming leadership.

When they're alone in the bedroom, Matt beams. "Sweet. See, I told you you'd win them over." Playfully he flicks her nose. "Baby vamp."

At what cost? The pack's acceptance shifts her focus to the coming confrontation. "Do you think the vampires will accept Josh's decision?"

"Well, you must be important enough for them to try getting you back for this supposed leader of theirs. Still, how important is one baby vamp? I'd think they wouldn't put so much significance on one who got away."

"If they do? Will they attack us?" *How does Dmitri fit into this?*

"We'll find out soon enough." Matt draws Eliza into his arms. "You're worth fighting for."

Knowing he means that as a compliment, Eliza ignores the sick feeling growing in her stomach. A few months ago, nobody wanted her. Now she's someone werewolves and vampires will fight over. The notion makes her uneasy. *There's something I'm missing, not seeing. What is it?*

Matt accepts their sleeping arrangements better than she does, and he's already snoring next to her when Josh's wife, Lois, enters their bedroom. Breathlessly she explains that three vampires are downstairs, waiting to speak to Eliza.

Eliza's heart hammers against her chest, and Matt is on his feet before she can even blink. Scrambling out of bed, she pulls a robe on and fumbles with the belt. His hands push hers away and he deftly ties it into a slipknot. They exchange a quick glance before they follow Lois to the living room.

When they walk in, the uninvited guests turn to look at her and she skids to a stop. She didn't know which of the vampires had come, and the taller man is a near double to Dmitri—she has to look twice to make sure it isn't him. This man stands nearly the same height, and his dark-brown hair and eyes give him a similarly imposing appearance.

Josh's fangs are showing, and he growls, "State what you came to say to her, and leave."

The shorter, darker-complexioned man speaks first, directly addressing Eliza. "Hello, Elizabetta, I'm Stephan Vasilou, and these are Vladimir Jagr and Anna Kachida. Master Belyakov sends his regards and urges you to reconsider."

It angers her that this vampire, like Dmitri, insists on calling her Elizabetta. She folds her arms across her chest. "Josh gave him my answer. I'm staying here."

Anna takes a step toward Eliza and stops when the wolves tense. "Please hear us out. I'm sure everything is understandably confusing for you after what's happened to you these past few months. Our master wishes for you to come home and rejoin our family."

"I don't have any family," Eliza says flatly. "I don't know any of you." *Why does that feel like a lie?*

Vladimir's voice sounds calculating. "That will change if you come with us. As I've already explained to Mr. Cleary, Master is willing to go to war to get you back."

A cacophony of snarls and murmurs explode from the

pack members. Vladimir and Anna lower into a defensive crouch. Stephan remains measured and calm. "Mr. Cleary, will you kindly remind your pack that we are here cordially, and not here to fight?"

"Let them finish." Josh's eyes carry the order.

"Thank you, Mr. Cleary." Stephan smiles at her. "Elizabetta, I am personally appealing to you to reconsider. Our brother Dmitri is a good, honorable man—if you do not return, I fear he will greatly suffer your choice."

Ah, now I see. He's some low-level peon who screwed up a job. "Seriously? Are you kidding me? After what he did to me I don't give a damn what happens to him. He turned my life upside down and made it a living hell."

Anger flashes in Vladimir's eyes and he shifts forward, but Stephan places a restraining palm on his chest.

Smiling sadly, Anna says, "Sometimes, Elizabetta, circumstances and people are not what they seem. Right now you are ill informed, confused, and angered by what you think you know."

You got part of that right—I am angry, and I have no idea what you're talking about. Eliza holds back a retort in hopes that the woman will enlighten her.

Anna turns to Josh. "May I approach her? I will not harm her."

Josh nods and Anna moves closer to Eliza. She raises a hand to sweep Eliza's long dark hair back over her shoulder and then trails the back of her fingers down Eliza's cheek. "You are precious to me. If you remain here, some of your new friends will die. You may be hurt if you fight against us.

Our master is unrelenting and will not leave you among our enemies."

Something familiar tugs at the edges of Eliza's memories. Somehow she knows that Anna genuinely cares. *How? Why? Who is she?* Unable to keep the words from spilling from her mouth, she says, "May I have a few days to think about this?"

A hushed gasp comes from Lois, but Josh gives no outward reaction. Eliza hears a low growl rumble from Matt. An almost imperceptible shake of her head cuts him off.

Stephan and Anna look to Vladimir and his voice rings with sincerity. "We will give you exactly ninety-six hours. We do not wish a war with these werewolves. They, like you, are risking their lives for something they know nothing about."

"How will I let you know when the time's up?"

"If you choose to come home," Vladimir says, "you will come alone and meet us on the dam at Ennis Lake. If you fail to arrive, then we will know you decided to remain here."

Home?

Quiet to this point, and not willing to be silenced again, Matt interjects. "Why is she so damn important to all of you?" Eliza can feel the rage radiating from him.

Vladimir doesn't acknowledge the question or even look at Matt. "Choose wisely, Elizabetta."

The vampire places a gentle hand on her shoulder and stares at her in a way that seems to carry a hidden message, but she doesn't understand what he's trying to convey. Before she can respond, the vampires are gone and several of the pack members are rushing out of the house, chasing after them.

Josh's gaze is intense when he looks at her. "We need to unravel the mystery surrounding you. If you don't mind, I'd like to run a background check. We need to find out why they want you so badly."

"That's fine with me. I'd like to know that myself."

They agree to go over the search details in the morning. Matt and Eliza watch the others leave the room. When they're finally alone, Eliza sits on the couch and fidgets with a horseshoe candle holder, trying to focus the tumultuous thoughts that are blaring like a nine-alarm fire in her brain.

"Matt, that woman, Anna? When she was talking to me, I got a strong feeling that I should know her. I don't think she's lying about what their master will do."

"How can you possibly know that?" Matt sits beside her.

"I don't know—I just do." Traces of fear flicker in her eyes. "If I stay, some of you will die."

"There are only three of them and over a dozen of us. I think we can hold our own."

For their sake Eliza wishes it were true, yet something deep inside her is screaming that he is wrong. She keeps reaching for memories that may as well be in low-earth orbit; all she gets are wisps of smoke and shadows. She can't shake the feeling that she knows these vampires. Somehow she perceives that they're exceptionally deadly, but she has no idea why or how.

Matt's breath hitches in a snore, signaling that he's out until morning, but Eliza stays up and paces the living room. *I am missing something here.* Each thread she unravels brings her mind back to Dmitri. *What has he done to me?* Somehow he is to blame, and she knows it.

Just before sunrise, Eliza joins Josh and Lois in the kitchen. Matt is still asleep on the couch. While they sip cups of coffee, Eliza tells them about the thoughts and half memories she's struggling with.

"I can't stop this nagging feeling that we're outnumbered, and the three who were here are especially lethal. I don't want anything bad to happen to any of you."

"I'll send Levi and Tony to see whether any neighboring packs will support us in defending you. If you were human or even one of our own, I know we could count on them. We need to convince the other packs that you're different."

"Is that even possible?" A worried look creases Lois's forehead.

"A pack leader's word carries weight. They may think we're crazy, but they will consider the request for help. The fact that we may be about to start a war in their backyards will make them think twice, especially if the Belyakov coven's numbers are greater than our own."

It took almost two months to convince these guys. We don't have that kind of time.

"What if they refuse?" Lois counters Josh's position. "If Eliza is right about us being outnumbered, and the other packs don't help, we will be slaughtered."

I can't let these people die for me. "Maybe it's best that I go to the vampires when the time's up."

Josh slams his palm on the table. "Nonsense. Let's see what the other pack leaders say first. Give us time to do a background check on you and the vampires we have names for. Eliza is part of our pack now—she's part of our family, and we protect our own."

A lump forms in Eliza's throat. After a lifetime spent without family or friends, shunned by everyone, she feels Josh's words reverberate to her core. *Family? Can they really feel that way?* Humbled, Eliza says, "You have no idea how much that means to me. I don't know if I can ever repay you."

Matt stumbles into the kitchen, looks at them, and seeing the tears in Eliza's eyes, furrows his brows. "What's going on?"

"Nothing. We're just talking strategy." Josh pauses a second. "I want to fortify our fighting positions here at the ranch. I'm sending Levi and Tony to talk to other pack leaders and could use your skills. When Eliza doesn't show up at Ennis Lake, the vamps will bring the war to us."

CHAPTER 20: DMITRI

Battle Plans

Sally is true to her word, only touching Dmitri in front of others to keep up their charade. Their act convinces Shashenka the young woman is painfully pleasuring Dmitri. Grateful, Dmitri repays Sally's efforts with a cautious step toward friendship, and as it begins to grow, his trust in her increases.

When Dmitri tells her Elizabetta's story, he learns that he and Sally share a common hatred for their master. She is not the simple, willing concubine others foolishly think; similar to the other courtesans, she never had a choice and was forced into serving the inner lair. Sally's stories of the degradation and abuse the women suffer at the hands of Shashenka and his minions send shivers running down his spine. It's a grim reminder of what lies ahead for Elizabetta, and he's ashamed to admit there may be no way out for her.

One day she asks, "How can you bear what he's done to you? They say the bond between mates is powerful, undeniable, and it permanently connects and changes them."

"Sometimes it feels as if I can't endure it ..." He sighs, turning away from the window to look at her. "But if I'm to keep Elizabetta alive, I must."

He sees the unspoken question in Sally's eyes. "I always hope that she will fall in love with me again. It gives me the strength I need to keep trying to make this work. Unfortunately Master keeps adding challenges meant to destroy all chances of it happening."

"Do you think, if you win back her affection, there's any chance she'll try taking Shashenka down again?"

She'll never be capable of it after what we've done to her. He looks out the window at the moonless sky. "I doubt we will try again. After what Shashenka did long ago to Ivan, and since to Elizabetta and me, the others will not rally and turn against him. It's likely that no one will ever destroy him."

A knock at the door interrupts their discussion. Sally bounces across the room to open it. Maria is standing in the hall, a grave look on her face. Stepping into the room, she asks to speak privately with Dmitri.

When the young blonde closes the door behind her, Maria turns to him. "I wanted to warn you—Shashenka is returning you to the United States. Elizabetta is about to cause a war between us and the werewolves."

"What?" Dmitri nearly shouts.

"The wolves took her to some isolated ranch in the middle of Montana. Shashenka sought her return—they refused. The Druzhinas spoke with her, tried to change her mind." Maria starts to reach for his arm, but her hand stops midway and drops to her side. "She's still with the wolves."

Dmitri groans, not wanting to hear the rest.

"They gave her four days to decide. Shashenka has gathered the intelligence and is planning the logistics. If she fails to return willingly, he is sending force to destroy the werewolves."

Her programming hasn't failed, or she'd never have hesitated to come back. How self-aware is she at this point? Slumping against the wall, he rakes a hand through his hair. *She's going to get herself killed.* "How many is he sending?"

"In total, thirty. Besides the Druzhinas, he's pulling some of the Druzhinnikis from his lairs across Europe and Asia. Seven will go from here, apart from you."

"That's not a war, it's a massacre."

"Yes, it's more than twice the wolves' numbers, and it will be a successful campaign. Given the spells you're under, your master doesn't expect you to fight. He wants you there, waiting at the Big Sky estate when the others bring her in."

Dmitri's hopes surge at the thought of seeing Elizabetta again, but he doesn't relish the thought of a massacre. Then he notices the dark look on Maria's face. "What else are you not telling me?"

"I'm to go with you to ensure that we get Elizabetta under our control this time."

"Are you going to reset her?"

"No. I'll provide any necessary spells or potions to help you regain control."

He studies the witch. Shashenka rarely sends Maria on missions like this; it's a clear signal that they will succeed this time. The storm brewing in the witch's eyes tells him that she carries additional orders to punish anyone who fails in this task. She will not hesitate to carry those orders out.

"When do we leave?"

"They're making the flight arrangements now and need another day to pull everything together. Shashenka is hand-picking the fighters."

Scowling, Maria adds, "I want you to act fittingly shocked when you hear it from Master. You cannot risk revealing your true feelings. He doesn't plan to tell you until hours before the flight. He's still suspicious of you and your intentions and loyalty."

That revelation alone is a blatant betrayal of Shashenka. For the first time in centuries, Dmitri begins to wonder about her loyalty to his master. *Is it weaker than we thought?* Maria might be their greatest hope of ending Shashenka—or perhaps she is waiting to spring the trap.

When Shashenka comes to him six hours before the flight to the States, the feigned shock and disgust of Dmitri's response is successful and his bold request to include Sally in this trip to Big Sky reinforces the deception. Shashenka seems to assume Dmitri's increased interest in the concubine is due to his growing hatred for Elizabetta, an expected result of the loathing spell.

"Master, I humbly request removal of the pain spell. It greatly complicates my physical relations with Sally." Dmitri's tone is smooth, even.

Shashenka's evil smile suggests that he has no intent of

ever removing the spells Maria cast on him. "I will consider it if you successfully finish programming Elizabetta."

Of course not, always a catch. Veiling his hatred, Dmitri mutters, "I understand, Master."

"But I'll allow Sally to travel with you, painful distraction or not. I believe she's good for you."

Dmitri grins—a double victory in that it gives Sally a break from being one of Shashenka's playthings and provides Dmitri further cover in disguising his feelings toward Elizabetta. "Yes, she is."

"Do you have any questions about the steps you need to take with Elizabetta?"

"No, your instructions are clear. Regardless of my preferences, I am not to kill her. I will groom the bitch to take her place as a concubine in your inner lair."

"You will break her to submit if necessary. I trust you're capable of doing that, with Maria's help."

"Yes, Master." For good measure Dmitri adds, "I rather look forward to it. It will be my pleasure to break the filthy wolf lover's will."

Satisfied, Shashenka leaves Dmitri to pack, but not before he gives one final order: no one is to use Elizabetta's full name anymore, and while an occasional slip may be tolerated, a threat of punishment exists for willful disregard of this rule. At least Dmitri knows he'll have plenty of company in adjusting to it; those who have known her the longest will struggle with it the most.

He has barely closed the suitcases when Sally enters the room. She's giddy with the thought of being away from

Shashenka's daily control. Her enthusiasm as they drive to the airport is contagious, and for the first time in months, Dmitri's smile is genuine. *Soon, Elizabetta ... I will see you soon, love.*

Aside from Maria and Sally, seven others are on the estate jet for their flight. Most of them are newer Druzhinnikis—less than fifty years in the Belyakov coven—relative unknowns to Dmitri. With the nine Druzhinas already at or on their way to the Big Sky compound, the remaining thirteen fighters will arrive in two groups from Europe and Asia. They are ready to carry out their orders. Should Elizabetta fail to show up at Ennis Lake, they will launch an immediate assault on the werewolves' ranch.

When they arrive at the estate, Dmitri and Maria go with the Druzhinas to the library. The others, gathering in the great room, await their briefing from Vladimir. Katherine closes the door to give the Druzhinas' meeting privacy.

Justin, smiling, greets Dmitri warmly with a handshake. "Aye, you're looking better than I feared. It's good to see you again."

Dmitri withdraws his hand from the painful grip and smiles ruefully. "Looks can be deceiving." He changes the subject. "It must feel good to be back in your home country."

"I haven't had time to enjoy being back yet. Montana actually is the territory where my tribe is from, and I do want to take a few days when this is over to see my old stomping grounds and do a little fishing." Justin grins and casts an imaginary fishing pole.

Dmitri recalls the few times Justin has talked him into going along, and he smiles, remembering the exuberance the young Druzhina shows whenever he catches a fish, even though he releases everything he catches. Justin often invites him to go; the lack of an invitation now is a clear message that the other man doesn't expect him to enjoy free time in the days ahead.

When Dmitri turns toward Victoria and Sofia, Maria interrupts the greetings. "While I appreciate the reunion here, time is short and we need to go over the plans. Vlad, I understand you're leading this campaign."

Vladimir clears his throat. "Yes, of course. In the three months since Elizabe—Eliza has been with that wolf, we've surveilled the place thoroughly. We are deploying our assets on the assumption that she will remain at the ranch, but in the event that she doesn't, we will need at least two of us waiting to take control of her at the dam. I'd prefer you're one of them, Maria."

Thinking a moment, she says, "Sally can go with me."

"The Druzhinnikis will surround the ranch and wait for our signal—they are the main thrust of the initial attack. They will kill all wolves outside or in the guesthouses, leaving those inside the main ranch house to us. Their bunkhouse appears empty at this time, but they'll sweep it too."

Looking around the room, Vladimir continues. "The Druzhinas will take the ranch house. Stephan, Victoria, Justin, Alexander, and Sofia will enter on the ground floor, while Dmitri, Katherine, Kees, Anna, and I sweep the second."

Maria cuts in. "Master wants Dmitri to remain at the compound. He's under a spell which makes him a liability in a fight."

Dmitri knows that the Druzhinas were not informed of the spell or of his removal from their ranks; two facts that Shashenka wants to hide until after Elizabetta's capture. His voice is terse. "Master wasn't satisfied torturing me in a normal state—he had Maria cast a spell that causes extreme pain upon any touch or contact with another."

A chorus of gasps and hisses fills the room. Alexander laughs under his breath. "Astoundingly, you provoke Master's wrath like no one else, dear brother. It amazes me you are still alive."

I am going to kill you someday. Dmitri closes his eyes, biting off a retort.

"Hoka hey." Justin whistles long and low. "That's really messed up. It's just not right."

Victoria steps toward Maria. "You're here. Remove it so he can fight."

Maria shakes her head and seems to gauge the reaction of each Druzhina. "It's not advisable. Shashenka hand-selected those he sent here ..." She catches Alexander's attention, and after staring at him a moment, continues. "Some of them are under orders to watch Dmitri and immediately report any complications."

Vladimir strokes his chin, seeming to ponder her statement. "Dmitri, when you are touched, does the pain cripple you?"

"Nearly, but I doubt combat can feel worse than the pain I experienced under torture." He notices a range of sympathy and pity on some of their faces; he'd rather have their outrage and support to end Shashenka's reign of terror.

"Won't we need him there"—Kees rubs the back of his neck—"if he's supposed to regain control of Elizabetta?"

"Yes, he is." Maria's gaze shifts from Kees to Dmitri and Vladimir. "Though if we're abducting her, it won't matter whether he's there. I'll be working with Dmitri to ensure she falls under his control again after we get her back."

"I prefer him to be with us. We can provide a buffer— keep the wolves away, or interfere if he engages one in a fight." Vladimir glances between Maria and Dmitri. "If you don't mind us protecting you, will this solution work?"

Dmitri trusts the Druzhinas—with the exception of Alexander and his antics—they have fought and bled for one another for centuries. He's also not sure how far Maria will go in betraying Shashenka, and he knows others are watching, reporting him. Revealing his true feelings for Elizabetta is the greater concern. "I'm no longer a Druzhina—Master stripped me of that honor—but I will always fight with you if that is what you wish."

Without hesitation, Vladimir raises his voice above those murmuring disapproval of Shashenka's actions. "You will always be one of us. Our oath remains. You'll fight with us, and we will do our best to prevent the wolves from touching you."

Their meeting ends and Vladimir goes to detail the plans to the warriors waiting in the great room. The other Druzhinas follow him there. Maria leaves to talk to Sally, and Dmitri heads to the atrium. He needs time alone to think and prepare.

CHAPTER 21: ELIZA

Fateful Decisions

The ranch is buzzing with excitement. Crews have erected barriers and traps to thwart the vampires, should they bring reinforcements. The neighboring packs have refused to fight with Josh's mixed pack for the life of one vampire. Premonitions of what is coming take Eliza's mind hostage. She doesn't recall ever having visions before, and what they are showing is terrifying: werewolves lying dead in mangled heaps, and vampires—blood soaked, but with few wounds—surrounding her. *They can't die for me.*

The results of the background checks add layers of color to each vision, making them more portentous. They have learned that the Belyakov coven is the largest in the world, but it is composed of a network of smaller covens with sworn loyalties to Shashenka Belyakov, a one-thousand-year-old vampire who has built a controlling dominion within the shadow realms. He owns fourteen estates in eight countries, with at least ten full-time residents—commonly referred to as locals—at each. Most of them are mere servants and caretakers of the lavish estates. The entourage that travels with Shashenka, known as the inner lair, varies between a few to two dozen. It's rumored that Belyakov's lover is a powerful witch, nearly as old as he is, who routinely accompanies and protects him. Some speculate that she is the true strength behind Belyakov's power and control.

The balance of the shifting numbers is a specialized group known as the Druzhina. Their exceptionally lethal skills make them the most feared and respected among their kind and within the shadow realms. Apart from carrying out coven business—clean and dirty—they uphold vampiric law. They hunt down and kill rogue vampires, assassinate enemy vampires and werewolves, and enforce the general laws of the coven. A few legends claim they are adept at engaging and defeating their enemies, even when outnumbered two or three to one. The wolves' search confirmed that the three who visited the ranch are Druzhinas. So is Dmitri. That fact, along with learning his last name is Markov, stands out the most to Eliza. *Why does that name sound so familiar? How do I know that name?*

As ominous as that information is, the wolves' biggest surprise is discovering there are no records of Eliza's existence. Apart from false IDs and an apartment lease in her name they have found no birth certificate or foster care or education records. Resubmitting the search as Elizabetta Ross returns nothing either. The weight of these revelations and the recurring visions threaten to unhinge Eliza's mind. *Is my life a lie? Where did I come from? How can I be a living social pariah one day and not exist the next?* She doesn't even know if Eliza Ross is her real name.

The Belyakov vampires, especially the Druzhinas, may be a death sentence to Josh's pack. *I have a family. They are my family now.* Her stomach churns at the thought of losing her only friends, of possibly seeing Matt die. She questions her decision to stay with the wolves and tries voicing her concerns to Matt, Josh, and the others, but they remain steadfast, declaring they will protect her. Even Monica pledges to defend her.

Not giving up, Eliza tries persuading Matt when they're alone, and as usual, he turns to humor. "You know the saying about a dog's loyalty to man? Well, now that you're one of us, let's just say it's like that on steroids."

"God, that's not remotely funny. How can you joke at a time like this?"

"I'd tell you that life's too short, but for ones like you that's an oxymoron." His eyebrows wiggle and he takes her hands. "Eliza, some of us may get hurt, but we're a tough bunch and we're going to kick some serious vamp ass."

She frowns and he reaches up and ruffles her hair. "Besides, even with you on the sideline, those three vamps don't stand a chance against us."

What if you are wrong? We don't even know who or what I am to them. Eliza closes her eyes, trying to fight her suspicions that they are outmatched and that her friends are going to die. "Matt, I've—I'm sort of seeing things, like a waking dream or some weird visions. In them the pack is outnumbered ... the vampires are ruthless and without mercy, and they kill all of you." Terror grips her and adds a hint of sorrow to her next words. "I can't live with myself if they destroy you and the others."

His eyes narrow, and he's quiet for a long moment. Is he overconfident or downplaying her concerns? His tone suggests it may be both. "I think your imagination and the stress of finding out about them is getting to you. We're going to be fine."

No, you're not. You're going to be dead. "What if—"

He places a finger against her lips. "Jeez, Eliza, stop it—don't play these what-if games. I promise we'll keep you safe, and those vamps, bloodsuckers, Druzhinas, whatever you want to call them, will lose." Softening his tone, he gives an encouraging smile. "Now, enough of this. It's time to tuck you away for the battle."

Given what they've learned, Josh doesn't want Eliza in the fight; she's supposed to hide until it's over. She's not happy about being sidelined—she feels weak and useless—but no one will go against the alpha's command, and Matt's frustration with her resistance is taking a noticeable toll on him. Eliza reaches for his hand and tries easing his mood, saying halfheartedly, "Yeah, too bad I can't turn into a bat and hang from the rafters."

He grins. "I think I'd like to see that."

Hands clasped together, they head for the staircase, but look past the archway of the living room; the rest of the pack is assembling there. Her heart wrenches at seeing their determined faces. *They are all going to die because of me.* She hesitates when Josh motions for them to come over—she wants to run away.

But they follow Josh across the room, and when they stop near the couch, he turns and opens a curio cabinet, removing two weapons. "My grandfather and great-grandfather owned these," he tells Eliza. "They are old weapons but are in excellent condition. If they get past us and you need to protect yourself, I want you to use this katana."

Eliza takes the sword, slides it from its sheath, and tests the balance in her hands. Curiously, holding a weapon like this feels familiar. *Wouldn't I remember if I knew how to use a sword?* Sliding the katana back into the sheath, she looks up at Josh.

To her surprise, he's grinning. "And this"—he hands her a knife—"is an Arkansas toothpick. I'm hoping you won't need them, but I'd rather have them available to you if you do."

Eliza passes the sword to Matt so she can inspect the knife. Pulling the bulky twelve-inch blade from the sheath, she smiles. *It'd do wicked damage up close. Okay, that's disturbing. Maybe I do belong in an asylum.* "I hope they're not needed, but thank you."

Opening a large gun safe, Josh begins passing out pistols and ammunition to the pack. Eliza notices each member already has one or two knives hanging in sheaths from their belts. Josh reminds them to partner up and not get separated. He assumes the vampires will enter on the ground level.

The alpha sends the best fighters in pairs to guard the two exterior doors. Next he places another pair behind them near either end of the hallway leading to the staircase. Josh and Lois take position at the foot of the stairs, where everyone will fall back and go upstairs together if they lose ground. That leaves Matt and Eliza to go alone to the upper level. Matt will stay in the hallway below the attic door, guarding Eliza, and she is to hide in the attic until the attack is over. Josh doesn't want to give the vampires a chance to snatch her.

With everyone else in place, Matt unlatches the attic door and pulls the telescoping ladder down for Eliza to climb. She's not ready ... not ready to say good-bye. *I'm going to lose him—he's going to die!* She throws her arms around his waist. "Matt, whatever you do, don't let them kill you. Surrender if you have to."

Matt bends his head to kiss her. The urgency in the kiss is far different from the other passionate ones they've exchanged. Their lips knead and brush, pushing and pulling them into a private bubble where war with vampires doesn't exist. Then Eliza's thoughts become the pin that pricks it. Pulling back first, she lightly kisses Matt once more.

"Be careful," she pleads. *I can't lose you, don't die.*

A lopsided grin pulls up the corner of his mouth. "Always."

Then Matt spins her around toward the ladder. Swatting her on the butt, he says, "Time to be a bat—get up there, baby vamp."

Giggling, she shakes her head and climbs the ladder without looking back. She hears him close the attic door. The house is quiet, and the only sounds are the shuffling feet of the pack pacing the floors below her. Eliza knows that when the battle starts they will not keep their human forms. Her recent visions revealed them fighting and dying as were-wolves. The thought nauseates her, and she wonders if it's too late to change her mind.

She's still in the middle of that thought when the vampires launch their assault. The silence is shattered by a burst of gunshots and the sound of windows breaking and doors ripping off hinges, and it's coming from multiple areas at once; she realizes they've breached the house on both levels. *How many are here? We don't stand a chance ... we'll be slaughtered.*

Matt's wolf growl interrupts her thoughts and tells her he's already changed. Pulling the katana and Arkansas toothpick from their sheaths, she pushes the attic door open and drops to the floor below to join him. Adrenaline evaporates her fear, and her fangs and claws come out. She is ready to fight.

Matt is standing a few feet in front of her, and facing him—trapping Eliza and Matt at the end of the hallway—are two of the vampires who came to the ranch house. Vladimir and Anna were here mere days ago, but Eliza recoils and takes an involuntary step back at the sight of the third vampire—Dmitri. His eyes flicker between the wolf and her. For a fraction of a second she sees terror register on his face, but before she can fully comprehend it, his expression changes into the most frightening look of determination she's ever seen. *What the ... creepy ... deadly. Why do you want me so badly?*

Moving alongside Matt, Eliza holds the weapons ready. The vampires pause and exchange puzzled looks. Matt's body is in a tense crouch and his growls are menacingly low. His head turns slightly toward her as she steps into his peripheral vision.

Sounds of violent clashes from several areas on the floor below indicate the battle is raging between the wolves and vampires. Vicious snarling and gnashing teeth mix with hisses, thuds, yelps, and howls. A few final shots ring out before the rest of the wolves change form. The dull, fracturing noise of furniture splintering and walls cracking signals desperation. They are fighting for their lives.

The second floor is eerily quiet by comparison. Two other vampires, a man and a woman, appear from adjoining rooms off the hallway. They step forward to close ranks with the first three.

Vladimir's eyes remain riveted on Matt. "Katherine, Kees, we've got this. Go downstairs and help the others."

Without a word, the newcomers turn and dart down the staircase.

Dmitri ignores Matt, locking his eyes on her. "Elizabetta, you don't want to fight us."

"Trust me, I do." These vampires are killing her family. Rage coats her desire for revenge. *I've never wanted anything more in my life but to kill all of you.*

"Please, we don't want to hurt you." Truth echoes in every word, bolstered by the pleading look on Dmitri's face. "Tell your wolf friend to step aside, and come with us."

"Yeah, that's not going to happen." Eliza places her left foot in a leading position, angling her body, and raises her left arm across her chest, holding the katana tight over her right shoulder. Gripping the knife in her right hand, she holds it with the point inclined at her hip.

Suddenly Matt launches forward into the vampires, his shoulder knocking Vladimir to the floor, pinning him by the chest with a giant paw. Vladimir, claws extended, slices at his legs and chest. Anna and Dmitri are working as a team, attacking and slashing whenever Matt turns his head toward the other. He's boldly trying to ward them off, but he's losing the fight.

No! Matt, don't!

Matt shifts and half turns to put as much of his body between the intruding vampires and Eliza as possible. Undeterred, Eliza steps into the brawl, stabbing at the closest vampire—Dmitri. He recoils from the blow, howling in pain as Anna steps sideways to intercede. Blood seeps through his shirt near the shoulder. The movement allows Eliza to slip between Matt and the two other vampires.

Anna stands in front of Dmitri now, shielding him from further attack. Eliza's nostrils flare as she faces her. Before they can engage, Matt surges forward. His head hooks around her waist and he throws her back, away from the fight. Eliza's body crashes into the mirror hanging at the end of the hall. She lands feet first and rushes to rejoin the fray. Matt is in mortal danger because of her, and her only instinct is to save his life.

Vladimir is on his feet again, attacking Matt's flank and side. Dmitri lunges forward and wraps his arms around the big wolf's neck—painful groans match his grimaces as he chokes Matt. Anna's graceful moves look like a well-trained, macabre dancer's, but she is swiping, tearing, and stabbing the wolf's chest with her claws. The scene before Eliza seems familiar, but she doesn't recognize it from her visions. *Where have I seen this before?* She blinks and shakes her head, pushing the thought aside.

Only a few seconds have passed since Matt tossed Eliza to the end of the hall, and already the vampires are ripping his flesh apart. The deep gashes, dangling hide, and blood seeping from every wound propel Eliza forward into the melee.

Her body plows into Vladimir, sending him sprawling, and before he even lands, she grabs one of Anna's arms and jerks the limb forward and down, knocking Anna off balance. The vampire stumbles and scrambles back three steps to regain her footing. By now Eliza has reached Dmitri, and her teeth and fangs are sinking into Dmitri's forearm. An inhuman, shrieking hiss echoes in the hall as he wrenches his arm free and pulls back. The look on his face is horrified, wounded— as if he can't believe she'd attack and hurt him. It provides the momentary lapse she needs to push past Matt's big wolf body and crouch defensively in front of her now fallen friend. "Stop!"

The three vampires take a cautious step forward. Eliza hisses. "I said, stop. If you kill him, I will kill as many of you as I can before you kill me."

Anna says, "We don't want to kill you, Elizabetta ... we want to take you home. Your friend, however, will die."

Her soothing tone grates on Eliza. "No. If he dies, I swear you will have to kill me."

"You are far outnumbered." Vladimir points toward the

staircase, where several other vampires are now standing, watching. "Anna's correct ... we don't want to hurt you. You can end this right now if you come with us without a fight."

Eliza realizes the battle sounds from below have stopped—it is sickeningly, deathly quiet. "What about my friends?"

"All but this one are dead, and by the looks of him"— Vladimir nods at Matt's body—"he won't live much longer."

Her stomach drops through the floor. Her visions were right—they're all dead. *Not Matt, not him. I will save him.* She notices the cascade of emotions crossing Dmitri's face, and the way he, unlike the others, appears personally and emotionally invested in the outcome. He's struggling to keep his face neutral and detached. *Why? What is his angle?* Looking directly at him, Eliza says in a low, steady voice, "How about we make a deal?"

"What kind of a deal?" His tone is wary.

"I'll surrender, but we take my friend with us and get him medical help."

A ripple of laughter comes from the vampires lining the staircase before they start talking among themselves. Vladimir and Anna exchange an amused glance, as if sharing a private joke.

Dmitri, the only one not laughing or smiling, looks pained and uncomfortable. "We cannot take your *friend* with us."

"Then we're back to you kill him, you kill me, and some of you die." She brings the weapons back into fighting position.

In a familiar gesture, Dmitri raises a hand and rakes it through his hair twice, keeping the hand at the crown of his head for a lingering moment. The blood on his arm and shoulder, where she bit and stabbed him, is drying, but the wounds appear to be healing already. As he drops his hand, she sees the slight slump in his shoulders. They sag further when he looks from Matt to her. Pain is evident in his eyes, and his heavy sigh rings of resignation. "If we promise to heal this mutt, will you surrender and come with us without a fight?"

Several pairs of eyes flash astonishment in Dmitri's direction. Vladimir whispers in his ear, and Eliza hears him say, "I don't think it is a wise move."

Dmitri's body tenses and his fists clench before he says in disgust, "Every one of you knows her almost as well as I do. If she vows to fight to the death, she will do it."

A blond, curly-haired woman on the staircase says, "He has a point, Vlad."

Someone else shouts, "We need to end this now. The sun will be up soon, and unless you want to sit among a bunch of stinking, dead werewolves, waiting for sunset, I say we get in gear and get the hell out of here."

Dmitri hasn't taken his penetrating eyes off Eliza. "Is my proposal acceptable to you?"

Eliza's mind is whirling. *"Promise to heal this mutt." "Almost as well as I do." Just how well does this Dmitri know me? Who in the hell is he?* Regardless of the answers, Dmitri does seem to know her, and whatever he knows is enough for him to offer concessions the others clearly aren't happy about.

"Tell me first how and where you'll mend my friend."

Dmitri takes a cell phone from his pocket and punches a few buttons to make a call. It is on speakerphone, and everyone can hear it ringing.

A woman answers. "Do you have her? Is everything okay?"

"Maria, we need you to come immediately to the wolf ranch."

An Irish accent tinges the alarm in her voice. "Is someone hurt?"

It occurs to Eliza that only one of these vampires has an American accent, and he sounds Native American. The rest of their accents seem to be a wide range of European and Asian. It makes her wonder how such a disparate group ended up together.

"We, uh, have a situation here." Dmitri stares at Eliza. "We're fine. Most of the wolves are dead. The problem is that Elizabe—Eliza is guarding a dying mutt and won't surrender unless we heal him."

The woman bursts out laughing, and it takes a moment for her to stop. "I'm sorry. I shouldn't laugh. I'll be there soon. Sally and I waited at the lake, so we're not far away."

Dmitri hangs up and puts the phone back in his pocket. "Well, Eliza? What's your decision?"

Eliza is growing increasingly concerned about Matt's blood loss. His breaths are raspy and he hasn't moved or made a sound. He's dying, and she knows it. Inhaling slowly, she says, "I'll only surrender conditionally. First, you will save my friend's life. Second, we take him with us."

Dmitri looks like someone quick-froze him after dousing him with a bucket of ice water. "If you want us to spare his life, then trust me when I say that if we bring him along, he will die."

"Swear to me, then, that after you heal him, no vampire will hunt him down or bring harm to him."

The vampires are still haggling over her proposition when the woman Dmitri called arrives. Pushing past all the vampires, she moves immediately to examine the wolf lying behind Eliza.

The scent of her blood, detectable aside from Matt's, diverts Eliza's attention to her. Accusingly she says, "You're not a vampire."

The woman glances up. "No. I'm a witch. Now let me tend to your friend if you want him to live."

CHAPTER 22: DMITRI

Victory Concessions

The thorny standoff of the last half hour is at a stalemate, and the Druzhinas are debating whether to accept Elizabetta's conditional offer. Some of them are visibly upset. Dmitri himself understands he's risking Shashenka's wrath again, but he knows Elizabetta too well. Even with her altered mind, once she commits to act, she will follow through. The thought of injuring or killing her for the sake of one werewolf's death is too much for him.

He continues watching her, pleading silently with his eyes. Disgust, anger, and jealousy are waging an inner battle against devotion, loyalty, and love. He's never been this upset with Elizabetta in his life.

The way she keeps glancing at the wolf reveals genuine concern and caring, and the daggers she throws at him with her eyes make a thousand cuts that may never heal. It's a relief when Maria arrives, rushing to the wolf's side—perhaps she can end this madness. Dmitri takes a couple of cautious steps toward them, but Elizabetta's posture tenses, threatening death. It roots him to the floor.

Keeping his voice loud enough for Maria to hear, but not distract the others from their heated discussion, Dmitri asks, "Can you save him?"

"Some of his injuries are severe—he's lost a lot of blood, and being in his wolf form complicates matters." Maria rummages in her bag. "Let's move him into a bedroom and away from this horde. Then I'll need Elizabetta to convince him to change into his human form, or I may not be able to save him."

Dmitri looks at Elizabetta. "You'll need to let me approach, love, if you want me to help move him." His voice is low, soft, nonthreatening. He ignores the way Maria clears her throat.

Elizabetta barely nods, and Dmitri immediately crouches at the wolf's head and lifts his front legs. Maria opens the nearest door and motions for them to follow. Elizabetta grabs the wolf's hind legs, and within seconds they have carried him out of the hallway and lain the big wolf's body on the bed. Some Druzhinas follow them into the room, but Maria shoos out everyone save Dmitri and Elizabetta.

Closing the door, Dmitri surveys the room to avoid looking at Elizabetta; her apparent attachment to the wolf is almost too much for him to handle. Focused on the room, he determines it must be the master suite. A king-size bed with a knotty pine headboard is the centerpiece of the room; the bed looks smaller with the wolf's body sprawled across a sizeable portion of it. Neatly placed near a dressing area are matching blue pine cabinets and two dressers. A western-style leather loveseat with a cowhide coverlet sits beneath an alcove window. In front of the stone fireplace are two matching leather chairs with a small pine table between them.

Elizabetta's encouragements for the wolf to change— "Matt" is what she's calling him—grate on his frayed nerves. She's telling the mongrel that he'll be all right and that they are there to help him. The loving tone in her voice is ripping Dmitri's heart out. He wanders over and slumps into one of the chairs. Placing his elbows on his knees, he cradles his head in his hands, trying to shut out the torture she is unwittingly inflicting on him. *Will this never end?*

Maria is conjuring spells and using poultices to stop the bleeding. She tells Elizabetta that she's done what she can until the wolf returns to human form. "Keep trying."

Dmitri looks up when a whooshing sound comes from the cushion of the chair next to him. It's Maria. "Okay, tell me what's going on here."

Unsettled, he grumbles, "As you can see, she has quite an affinity for that mutt. We were about to finish the kill when she managed to get between him and us, and then she threatened to fight to the death unless we agreed to save his life and leave him unharmed. She has claimed him."

Maria stifles a laugh. Lowering her voice, she says, "It is so typical, classic Elizabetta."

It's typical, but right now it isn't funny. "The Druzhinas are debating whether to accept her conditional surrender or make another attempt to capture her, even if it means killing her in the process."

Shashenka would view her death as another failure on his

part; it would mean severe punishment for him.

"Let me go talk to them. Given my position with Shashenka, my word carries weight that none of yours will. I do not find her terms objectionable."

He winces as she pats his arm and says, "Everything will work out."

After watching her leave, he finds himself standing at the foot of the bed, studying Elizabetta. She is stroking her fingers across the wolf's forehead.

"Matt? Matt? Can you hear me? I need you to change back." Elizabetta's voice is a caressing whisper; it is the same tone she once used to murmur sentiments to Dmitri.

"Come on, Matt, change back. We can't help you until you do."

Finally the wolf's eyes start to flutter open. She bends down to kiss the thing between the eyes. It's disgusting for him to watch.

The wolf's eyes focus briefly on her face, and she smiles.

God, enough. For mercy's sake. This is killing me. She's ripping my heart out, can't she see that? "Maybe he's too far gone and you should just let him go." He can't hide his agitation or the tinge of hope in his tone.

"No, he's not." She glares up at Dmitri. Bending down, placing her cheek next to the wolf's head, she resumes encouraging the change until the wolf's body begins to shudder. Elizabetta cheers him on, every bolstering word another blow to Dmitri's spirit. "That's it, sweetie, you almost did it. Do it for me."

This time the shudders turn into a violent quaking, and

slowly the wolf features retract. Elizabetta snatches the blanket lying folded across the foot of the bed and prepares to cover him. Gently she lays it across his battered body.

The change complete, the mongrel says weakly, "Hey, baby vamp."

Smiling, Elizabetta takes his hand. "Hey there, thanks for coming back. We have someone to help you. You're hurt pretty bad, and we need to get you patched up."

"Mmm, okay." He glances at her and a moment later closes his eyes. "Is anyone else hurt? Is Josh and—"

Elizabetta dodges the question. "Let's just take care of you before we worry about anyone else. Okay?"

The wolf is nodding as Maria steps back into the room.

"Good, he's changed—now I can get to work. I want you two over there"—she points at the chairs—"or leave the room."

Without thinking, Dmitri reaches out and grabs Elizabetta's hand, and both recoil—he from the intense pain, she with a look of revulsion. Frowning at each other, they sit on the chairs as invisible walls rise up between them, strengthening their divide. Dmitri longs to tear them down; there are hundreds of things he wants, needs to say. Instead he calls over his shoulder to Maria, "Did the others say whether we're accepting Eliza's demands?"

"Yes, they'll abide by them," she hisses. "Now leave me alone."

His gaze locks on Elizabetta. "To be clear, your conditions were to save his life and mark him untouchable."

"Untouchable?" Elizabetta's brows scrunch together.

She has no idea how disgusting and risky this is. "Yes. Vampires mark their property—homes, cars, valuables, humans—in your case a damn werewolf—to prevent others of our kind from killing, harming, or stealing what we want to safeguard."

"So he ... what ... suddenly becomes like some damn cow to brand?"

"It's the only way to protect him. We mark humans in the hollow at the base of the neck above the collarbone—it's where his mark will go since he's half-human." Dmitri starts to reach to touch the area on her neck, but pulls back when she leans away. "All he needs to do is pull a shirt collar down far enough to reveal it if he's ever confronted by a vampire."

"And? What? They simply say, 'Sorry to bother you—have a nice day' and leave him alone?"

Dmitri smiles wryly. "Yes, unless they want to suffer the wrath of the Druzhina. We enforce the laws, and marked property is one of those laws." *Except I'm no longer a Druzhina.*

Disbelief is written on her face as she continues to glare at him.

He adds, "He will bear your mark. You're the one sparing him and claiming his life."

Elizabetta appears discomposed. "B-but I-I'm just a baby vampire. I don't have a brand."

He feels something hit the back of his head, and he turns to look at Maria. The witch's expression cautions him. The warning is understood, but he knows Elizabetta didn't pick up on the more significant fact—her mark precedes her knowledge of being a vampire. Now that the words are out there, he can't take them back. Still, he should be more careful around those who may report his behavior to Shashenka. His eyes narrow as he gives a subtle nod to Maria, and he says, "You have a mark."

"Oh really? And what else don't I know about my life? Do you care to fill me in on any of that mystery while we're at it?"

There will never be a time or place for that discussion, if you want to live. He ignores her question. "I will place your mark on him when Maria has finished healing him."

"Humph." Elizabetta rises, stalks across the room, and sits in a huff on the loveseat near the window.

Dmitri follows, but remains standing. "We weren't finished confirming your terms. We save the mutt's life, protect him from others, and you surrender. Correct?"

Her eyes blaze and her nostrils flare as she sneers. "Yes."

"You understand that by surrendering, you forfeit making any future escape attempts?"

"Yes."

Extending his hand, Dmitri braces for the handshake. "Then we, love, have a deal."

The quick contact and its accompanying pain are less than the worsening ache in his heart. Dmitri moves toward the bed and watches quietly as Maria finishes binding the wounds. She announces that she's given the wolf a sleeping potion that will keep him knocked out long enough to take him home. They humor Elizabetta by not interrupting her as she gives directions to the werewolf's home—a detail already well known to the Druzhinas from their weeks of surveillance.

Elizabetta asks for a moment to say good-bye, and Maria nods her approval. Sitting on the edge of the bed, Elizabetta takes the werewolf's hand. Her other hand strokes his light-brown hair. "Matt, when you wake up, please know that I didn't want to leave you. I am so sad and sorry about what happened to the pack. It's my fault they're dead, and I hope you'll forgive me someday. Take good care of you, for me. You mean so much to me ... I love you."

A wave of nausea almost brings Dmitri to his knees. Hearing her say those words to another man, especially one who is a werewolf, is devastating. It takes a moment for the tremble in his body to stop. He needs steady hands to prepare and place her mark on the mongrel.

"Maria, do you have a small bowl in your bag?"

She reaches inside and pulls out a stone mortar and pestle. Elizabetta looks at them with curiosity and, he suspects, a measure of distrust. As much as he'd prefer to destroy this creature, he could never hurt her that way. Dmitri gives her a slight smile of assurance; it's the best he can give her, considering what he's about to do.

Placing his fangs over the rim of the mortar, he expresses some venom and then spits into the bowl. Holding the mortar close to Matt's shoulder, Dmitri extends his claws to stir the venom and saliva. *If her memories weren't stolen, she'd never do this. She would have killed this mutt herself.*

Expertly slicing the werewolf's skin deep enough to leave the mark, he draws an extraordinarily straight vertical line.

Dipping the claw again—starting one-third of the way down from the top of the first line and stopping at the same height—he places mirrored lines that angle up on each side. Next Dmitri places a backward *E* with convex upper and concave lower lines. Opposite, along the vertical line, he carves a forward *R* with its free leg concave. Each letter sprouts from the center vertical line—sharing it as their spine.

Elizabetta's voice is almost a whisper. "What is that?"

A wistful smile is on his face when he looks up at her. For a moment he recalls the night she selected this rune, and why—she wanted something similar to his. Even that wasn't enough; she wanted more than an unseen bond between them, and had talked him into putting their marks on each other. The marks were placed at the lowest point of their backs, just above the tailbone, and remained there until Shashenka discovered them after the failed rebellion. The demented monster took great joy in filleting the symbols from their skin. When the wounds healed, the marks were gone, leaving only a faint scar of where they'd once been.

"It's your mark, love. To be precise, it is an Elder Futhark rune, the Algiz, with your initials to either side. The Algiz symbolizes protection or a shield."

"Oh." Elizabetta tips her head sideways, as if to view it at a different angle. "Why is it bubbling?"

"Our venom is poisonous and acidic, more so against a werewolf—our saliva slowly neutralizes it. Combining them allows the mark to penetrate deep enough, but stops it from eating away too much flesh."

"If it burns, then why did you have to cut him with your claw?"

Dmitri chuckles at the near repeat of a conversation they had long ago. "It breaks the skin, allowing us to neatly draw the design—much the same as a tattoo artist uses a needle to ink a body."

"Dmitri." Maria gains his attention, and her tone is sharp. "Your mask is slipping."

He stares at the witch, blinking several times. "Thank you."

Elizabetta looks confused but doesn't say a word. Tears pool in her eyes as Dmitri calls for Vladimir, Anna, Stephan, and Victoria to carry the werewolf out of the house. Protectively pulling the blanket aside to expose the wolf's mark, Elizabetta growls at the other vampires, "You will not hurt him."

The four Druzhinas nod in understanding. Lifting the werewolf from the bed, they take him downstairs and out to one of the ranch pickups. After placing him in the bed of the truck, Stephan and Victoria climb in, sitting on the wheel wells, while Vladimir and Anna get into the cab. Elizabetta, watching from the doorway, steps onto the porch and begins crying as they drive away. Unknowingly, she's giving Dmitri new material to draw on when he must pretend to loathe her—although at the moment, his glare is genuine.

The extra fighters have already left, and the remaining Druzhinas douse the house and the werewolves' bodies with gasoline. When everyone is clear of the house, Justin and Kees ignite the blaze from outside. A loud *whomp* precedes a fast *whoosh* and the gasoline-fed fire roars to life, but they have no time to watch it burn; they trust there is enough propellant to incinerate the bodies, and prepare to leave.

The stars have shifted across the sky, which means they need to run to reach the Big Sky estate before sunrise. The only nonvampire, Maria, will drive the estate car back to Big Sky. Despite Elizabetta's promise not to flee again, Dmitri asks Sally to hold her hand while they run; he doesn't want to take the risk. The young blonde tugs hard twice before Elizabetta pries her tear-filled eyes away from the burning ranch house.

Soon the eight vampires are racing through the countryside, playing beat the clock with the sun. They crest the last mountaintop when the sun's rays start breaking over the horizon. Keeping to the shadows when possible, they reach the mansion at the estate before the sun does any permanent harm.

Dmitri is thankful that Elizabetta didn't struggle, fight, or cause other disruptions during their flight, but he isn't looking forward to what comes next. Within a day, he must begin programming Elizabetta's life as a concubine for the Belyakov coven. The thought sickens him, and for a few minutes he contemplates running away and hiding her. It's impossible, of course; Shashenka's reach is too far, and he would hunt them down. He'd carry out his threat to torture and eventually execute Elizabetta while making Dmitri suffer endless centuries of torture before he'd grant him the relief of death. Dmitri still has one obligation—one promise remaining unbroken—to protect her always.

Soon Maria will cast a spell or use a potion to open Elizabetta's mind to Dmitri's control. He knows she will succeed where he's failed. Still, he wonders how far Maria will go in betraying Shashenka. Then he remembers her duplicity during the failed rebellion, and now with the supposed loathing spell, he speculates whether Maria is making up for past mistakes. *Is there a chance that I might yet live to see the end of Shashenka Belyakov? Do I dare hope?*

CHAPTER 23: ELIZA

Dr. Jekyll and Mr. Hyde

The sun is rising when they reach an estate nestled in the mountains. The house is a behemoth, a three-story log structure that Eliza estimates to be more than ten to twelve thousand square feet. Matching four-car garages, a guesthouse, and an unknown building flank the mansion on the manicured grounds. She slows to take in the spectacle of luxury, but the blond woman, Sally, keeps a firm grip on Eliza's hand and pulls her along. Much to Eliza's consternation, the vampire never slackened her hold the entire way from McAllister to the front door of the mansion.

When they enter the house, Dmitri demands that Eliza give up the sword and knife still in her possession, and he sends Sally away with them after she hands them over. The witch arrives just as Sally walks away. Dmitri acknowledges her by name, Maria, and then nods. Some sort of silent communication seems to pass between them. Taking Eliza's hand and loosely wrapping one arm around her waist, he propels her away from the foyer and down the hall. She watches an agonized look cross his face. *Is he grossed out or reacting to an injury from the fight?*

With the witch following, he leads Eliza to an elevator hidden in the back of the house, near the massive kitchen. They ride it down to a floor one level below, where he then escorts her down a long hall with many solid doors spaced at eight-foot intervals. Using a keycard, Dmitri opens the last door on the right.

It's only when the door swings open that Eliza realizes it's a cell. Panicking, she turns to run, but Dmitri seems to have expected this response; he wraps both arms around her, restraining her as his anguished cries and groans echo through the hall. Lifting her feet off the floor, he drags her, literally kicking and screaming, into the cell. The door slams shut and she hears the lock slide into place.

The windowless room is so dark that she can barely see its stark features. The cell is slightly larger than a mausoleum. The ceilings, walls, and floor are smooth concrete, with a circular six-inch drain in the middle of the floor, and no light fixtures. Eliza cannot hear any sounds from anywhere else in the house. There is no way out.

Why are they doing this to me? Sitting, staring at the door—blocking thoughts of Matt and the lives lost at Josh's ranch, which are shredding her heart—she focuses on the mystery of Dmitri Markov. Her mind replays the memories of him in her apartment, at the hospital, and at the warehouse and ranch. Nothing makes sense; there is something about him she can't figure out. His eyes say so much, and often contradict his actions or words. He kissed her at the warehouse and seemed genuinely taken aback by her reaction when she rejected him. *Why was he kissing me?* She tries not to think of the brief seconds when she enjoyed the feel of his lips pressed to hers.

Why did he negotiate? Why did he agree to spare Matt's life? The other vampires showed their surprise and disdain at her offer. The gentle way he placed the Algiz rune above Matt's collarbone—despite his obvious antipathy for were-wolves—displayed his compassion. *Is it possible to use his tender side against him?*

Several hours later the cell door opens. A half-dozen vampires flank Dmitri; they're holding a mattress, sheets, blanket, and pillow. Eliza rises, folding her arms across her chest as they enter and place the bedding in the cell. No one says a word, and the door closes after they step back into the hall.

Another couple of hours pass before the door swings open again. This time Dmitri is holding a box in his arms, and only two vampires are standing with him. Setting the box on the floor, he says coldly, "I don't know when you fed last." Then he leaves, locking the door behind him.

At first Eliza tries to ignore the box. Curiosity piqued, she crawls over to it and lifts a flap to peer inside. The contents are from a blood bank: eight pint-sized bags of blood. *Oh thank you, Dmitri. I'm so thirsty I could drain a bear.* The entire time she was at Matt's and the Cleary ranch she never fed more than sucking dry whatever package of meat was being cooked for that night's dinner. She's become used to the dull, burning ache in the back of her throat.

Lifting a bag, she extends her fangs, puncturing it to

drink. The flavor shocks her—it is scrumptious. Her eyes close as she delights in the sweet, tangy mix of iron, salt, and spices. *Way better than animal blood.* Famished, Eliza goes into a feeding frenzy that doesn't stop until she realizes there is no more blood. Still, she is satiated for the first time. The fire in her throat is gone. She squeezes the few remaining drops onto the box lid, and using her fingernail, scrawls, "Thank you." Tossing the empty bags into the box, she folds the top closed and leaves it sitting in front of the door.

With nothing to do but think or sleep, Eliza lies on the mattress and stares up at the dark. Dmitri's stalking, the hospital stay, and her time with Matt lead her to one inescapable conjecture: Dmitri is the key. *He's the only connection to everything. What will it take for him to unlock the mystery of my life? I will find out, one way or the other.*

Many hours pass and no one comes back to the cell. Eliza shifts between sleeping, pacing, and scheming. She's asleep and in the middle of a nightmare about the battle at Josh's ranch when she wakes to someone's fingers lightly brushing her cheek. Startled, she knocks the hand away and leaps to her feet.

In response, there's a sharp gasp and hiss. Next, Dmitri's voice is trying to soothe her. "Shh, shh, it's okay."

Warily Eliza looks at him and then toward the three others standing outside the door. The witch is among them. "Why are you doing this to me?" she snarls.

He grimaces. "You won't have to be here much longer. This will all be over soon." Dmitri motions to the two men, who step to either side of the door. "Walk with me." The command seems contrary to the polite dip of his head toward the hall and the almost-pleading look in his eyes.

She decides to test him. "If I don't?"

"Then you will leave me no choice but to move you to the other room by force."

His expression turns threatening, so she nods and steps out of the cell. The two men take positions at her sides; Dmitri follows close behind. Then the witch, Maria, leads them down the hall to a room a few doors away.

Maria opens the door and Eliza stops midstride and gasps. It's roughly the same size as her cell, but on the wall opposite the door are arm and leg shackles. Two chairs are pushed against another wall, and a single bright light bulb illuminates the room. The vampires on either side of Eliza grab her arms as she struggles against them, and they turn and press her back against the wall with the shackles. Dmitri refuses to make eye contact with her as he slowly, deliberately secures the shackles around her wrists.

She screeches at them, "Why are you doing this to me? What kind of monsters are you?"

Dmitri turns to the two men. "Thank you, Justin, Kees. You may go rejoin the others."

When they leave, he says to Maria, "She's all yours."

Eliza bellows, "No. You tell me why you're doing this. I surrendered. I'm not fighting you or trying to escape."

"It's necessary." His tone is harsh.

"Bullshit. You said nothing about torture or imprisonment." She glares at the vampire. "If I had known, I would have fought you to the death."

Dmitri gives a faint smile to Maria. "Please, do what you must."

Swinging a wild kick toward him, which narrowly misses, Eliza screams, "I hate you. I hate—"

Maria cuts her off. "Dmitri, be a dear and leave the room until we're ready for you."

Appearing stunned by Eliza's outburst, he takes a moment before collecting himself and leaving the room.

Maria, smiling, turns toward her. "Elizabetta, please calm down. We really aren't going to hurt you."

Seriously, Elizabetta? Probably not my real name any more than Eliza is. "Then why"—she tugs on the wrist shackles—"is this necessary?"

"Because ..." Maria pauses. "You may not react well to what I'm about to tell you."

Eliza is silent.

"None of this is what it appears to be. We are ... preparing you to come home."

What a farce. "God." Eliza, exasperated, breathes out again. "Who are you people?"

Maria shakes her head, and her green eyes flash with urgency when she looks up. "There is something I wish to say before doing what I must, and I need you to listen carefully."

Eliza's chest is rising and falling with heavy breaths. When she doesn't speak, Maria continues. "What I'm about to do will not alter your memories but will leave you questioning them—all of them. That is my gift to you, and I expect one favor in return. Very soon Dmitri will give you many reasons to hate him. Even when he is most vile, never judge or treat him harshly."

Before Eliza can make sense of the statement, Maria is muttering something in a foreign language. Then Eliza's eyes roll back, and she blacks out.

Coming to, she finds herself slumped in a chair across from Dmitri. The red-haired witch is gone.

Dmitri smiles apologetically. "Hello love, how are you feeling?"

Blinking rapidly to focus and gather her wits, Eliza shifts to sit upright. *How did I get here? I was in a cell. What is happening to me?* She looks around the room. "I—I think I'm fine."

His smile falters. "Good. Now I need you to hear me."

Her eyelids droop and she replies without compunction, "I hear you."

"What is your name?"

"Eliza Ross."

"Who am I?"

"Dmitri Markov."

Her reply appears to rattle him. "How do you know my last name?"

"I ... um, I—I don't know." Eliza lifts a hand to her forehead. Tangling fingers in her hair, she looks around again. "But that is your name"—she looks directly at him—"is it not?"

He doesn't push the issue. "What are you?"

"I'm a vampire."

"Who is your master?"

"Shashenka Belyakov." She knows it is the truth, but the notion pricks her distrust.

He sighs, sounding relieved. "What is your position in the Belyakov coven?"

"I ..." *I'm a ... something.* It makes her brain ache trying to recall it. "I don't know."

Looking at her with frustration, he says harshly, "You are a courtesan in our master's lair."

"A courtesan?" She knows what the word means, but it doesn't make sense to her.

"Yes." Dmitri swallows hard, draws a deep breath, and looks away. "You serve our master and any who seek your favor in his lair."

"My favor?" Eliza blurts out. "What, like for sex?" *No way, no how. Not happening.*

He grimaces and tries meeting her gaze, but then averts his eyes to the floor. "Yes, if that's what they seek."

The idea is repulsive to her. "Um ... no ... no, I don't think so."

"Elizabetta, when you hear my voice, you must obey. You are a courtesan in the Belyakov coven. You freely and willingly give your favor to any who seek it."

Nice try, dream on, never going to happen. "Go to hell! I'm not a whore!"

Dmitri stands and begins pacing the room with what seems like agitation. She watches shame turn to determination and back to shame; both seem to battle across his face. When he returns to the chair, he takes her hands and winces from the contact. "Can you still hear me, Elizabetta?"

"Yes," she says automatically.

"Will you do as I say?"

"Yes." She feels like an automaton with no free will.

He pauses and says softly, "You live a good life among us, in beautiful homes, with fine clothes and many friends, and never wanting for blood. You do not want to leave; you wish to stay with us. Would you like to see your friends?"

Matt's my friend. He was hurt. "Is Matt here? Are you going to take me to see him? Is he okay?"

"No, your other friends." Dmitri sounds frustrated. "Maria, Sofia, Anna, Victoria, Katherine, Sally, Vladimir, Stephan, Kees, and Justin. Do you want to see them?"

The names sound familiar, but aside from the recent introductions to Sally, Maria, and Anna, she can't recall having a friendship with any of them. "I don't know them."

"Yes, you do. You were ... they are your friends."

"Oh."

"Your friends miss you. Would you like to see them?"

The idea is appealing to her; she feels hungry for friendship. "Yes, I would like to see my friends." Her head dips down and forward as she peers at his face; he's looking at the floor. "Are you my friend?"

Dmitri ignores her question. "Good. I will arrange for you to see them tonight. You will be happy here."

"Yes," Eliza answers without hesitation.

"Would you like to go to your room now?"

"I don't want to go back to the cell."

"Your bedroom is upstairs—you don't stay in a cell."

She blinks, confused, and her fingertips wipe and pull at the corner of her eyes. Her mind is trying to race for answers but trips and falls. "Then yes, I would like to go to my room."

Dmitri snaps his fingers and her brain becomes fuzzy. For a moment, disoriented again, she looks around the room. *Why am I here? How did I get here? Brain damage or bad memory? Huh, probably both.*

"Come, love, we're done for the day." He extends a hand.

Eliza takes it and he winces again. *What is up with that?* "What are we doing here?"

Leading her from the room, he says, "Nothing. You got lost looking for your bedroom."

The answer sounds like a lie. *Room? I thought I was in a cell. Did I imagine that? I'm really losing it. Still, a bedroom sounds like an upgrade—I'll take it.*

When the elevator arrives, they step into it, but Dmitri pushes the hold button. He suddenly wraps his arms around her in a fierce embrace. A painful-sounding moan rises in his throat before he whispers near her ear, "I'm so sorry, love." Just as abruptly, he lets her go.

Whoa! What just happened? Eliza stares at him as the elevator begins to ascend, but he refuses to look at her. They get off on the main floor, and Dmitri leads her to the grand staircase and up two flights of stairs. Halfway down the hall, he shows her a bedroom, explaining that this is her room. Her clothes, he says, are in the closet and wardrobe. He tells her to shower, mentions a selection of her favorite soaps, and leaves the room.

No matter how hard Eliza tries to make sense of the

strange encounter, she cannot. Equally disturbing is her acceptance of being here, when she clearly remembers that they forced her to surrender. The need to stay is so strong that she knows she'd refuse to leave even if they threw the door wide open and told her to go. *What is going on? What did he do to me?*

Remembering that he said something about seeing friends, she opens the wardrobe and recognizes most of the clothes, but there are some she's never seen before. Eliza starts to wonder how her clothes got here, but she knows the answer—Dmitri. She selects a pair of jeans and a purple sleeveless blouse from a hanger. Then she tosses them on the bed with the undergarments and heads for the bathroom.

Turning on the shower, Eliza chooses soap, shampoo, and conditioner from a small cabinet next to the shower stall and steps into the spray, letting the hot water pour over her body. She hasn't bathed since the morning the vampires attacked the werewolves, and it takes a while before she feels relaxed and clean. Having all of her favorite bath and hair products here—doubtless, thanks to Dmitri again—helps ease her tension. She's toweling off when someone raps on her bedroom door.

"Come in." She peeks around the bathroom door.

It is Dmitri, and he hesitates when he sees her head wrapped in a towel. For a few seconds he seems to dither between leaving and staying. He closes his eyes for a moment and then steps inside, shutting the door behind him. "I'm sorry to intrude. I'm here to escort you downstairs."

Eliza steps back from the bathroom door, leaving it

cracked open. "It's fine. It's my fault—I took a long shower. I'll be out in a minute."

Frowning, she looks around the bathroom and then remembers that the outfit she selected is lying on the bed. *Great, shinola, I get to flash my stalker.* She holds a towel securely around her body as she darts into the bedroom to snatch the clothes and run back to the bathroom. From the corner of her eye, she sees the surprised look on Dmitri's face. *Yeah, he got an eyeful. Just peachy.* Ignoring him, she dresses quickly and runs her hands through her wet hair. If Dmitri and her friends weren't waiting, Eliza would blow it dry. Not wanting to delay, she deftly weaves the damp strands into a single braid and smiles at Dmitri when she reenters the bedroom. "I'm ready. Sorry I took so long."

He again offers his arm, and flinches as she takes it. *Really, what is up with that?* She ponders his weird reaction while he leads her through the hall and down the staircase. There's an inexplicable comfort being this close to him, and she can't resist taking sideways glances at him while trying to figure it out. For once she is looking at more than his face.

Her eyes trail over his long, lean body, taking in his easy and assured stride. Dmitri radiates power and strength. Although it's difficult for her to see much beyond a side profile, she moves her head to take in as much of him as she can. *Great hands, fine ass, and oh, those legs. Even his forearms are sexy. Damn, he's hot.* A blush tints her cheeks and she can feel the heat spread. *Shit, seriously, I didn't just check out my stalker.* Yet she knows she did, and quickly she looks away, hoping he didn't notice.

Wherever he's taking her, she knows they'll soon be surrounded by others, and a part of her wishes they could spend
a few hours alone; she'd like to get to know him and ask him
some questions. But on the ground floor, he ushers her to a
billiards room sandwiched between the great room and the
theater. At the doorway Dmitri withdraws his arm from hers,
putting a foot of space between them. She briefly wonders
why, but that thought as well as her earlier ones fall away;
her eyes are riveted on the scene before her.

The room is huge, with four mahogany pool tables well
spaced in the middle of the floor. A rich dark-green felt covers the tables, and a single brass light bar with three pale-
green shades hangs suspended above each one. The marble
floor is a shade of green nearly identical to the pool tables'
light shades. Matching dual sconces with white frosted glass
globes rimmed in polished brass adorn the walls. A few
couches and several wingback chairs with small mahogany
tables between them line the walls. The heavy fabric of the
furniture has thin curving, nondescript lines in shades of
brown, deep red, and green set against a dark tan background. *Beautiful.*

She counts nine vampires and the witch in the room, smiling, laughing, talking, and shooting pool. These vampires
and this house are in a class far beyond her own. Unsure
what to do, she takes a side step toward Dmitri. He scowls as
he places a hand on the small of her back, and she doesn't
understand why.

Dmitri's tone is saturated in sarcasm as he raises his voice
above the laughter and murmured conversations. "Everyone,

I'm pleased to announce that Eliza"—to her surprise, he uses the correct name—"is back home with us. Please welcome her." He roughly shoves her into the room.

Several vampires leave their pool tables to greet her, and Dmitri introduces her as each one comes forward. Then they are urging her toward the pool tables, talking animatedly and smiling. *I don't understand. I know them. Was I wrong about not having friends?* They ask her to join them and find a partner for a straight game of pool.

With several eager faces looking back at her, she doesn't know whom to choose. She laughs nervously. "Who needs a partner?"

Several voices ring out. "Dmitri."

Her heart flutters at the thought, but then she sees him turn. His eyes close for a few seconds, and when he speaks, his tone is spiteful. "No thanks, I'm still trying to get rid of the fleas."

Eliza flushes at the abrupt shift in his demeanor. Before she can ask what's wrong, a young woman with a pale-olive complexion, long brown hair, and big brown eyes speaks up and introduces herself as Sofia. "She can be mine."

A chill creeps along Eliza's spine. Somehow she does know these vampires, and it's more than what she learned from Josh's files about the Druzhinas. Afraid to show her confusion, she smiles at Sofia.

"But you're my partner and we're the winning team," the one called Justin says.

"Get another. I'm going to play with Elizabetta." Sofia wraps an arm around Eliza's waist and leads her over to a rack to select a cue stick.

Memories of the time spent at the bar playing pool with Matt seep to the surface, but they are too raw for Eliza to deal with, and she shoves them aside. Turning her attention back to Dmitri, she watches as he partners with Sally for a game. A weird pang of jealousy stabs her. Her emotions tangle into a larger mess when Dmitri seems to go out of his way to avoid her. She notices that he and Sally have played against everyone in the room except for her and Sofia. Anger flashes in his eyes and he gives Eliza a cold look when Sally accepts Sofia's challenge. His actions trigger uncomfortable reminders of the way many others have rejected her.

Eliza won't allow Dmitri's obviously cranky attitude to ruin her night, and with deliberate effort she remains friendly and polite toward him. During their game, Dmitri barely looks at Eliza, and when he does, he's glowering. He keeps the pool table between them and moves away if she tries standing on the same side. When she speaks to him, he either ignores her or responds with biting comments. It rattles her so much that she can't focus on the game, so her team loses. *Was that his plan all along?* It has Eliza's mind reeling. The way Dmitri apologized and hugged her fiercely in the elevator contradicts this open hostility, leaving her with one thought: getting to know this guy is like hanging out with Dr. Jekyll and Mr. Hyde.

CHAPTER 24: DMITRI

Cad King

After enduring a game of pool against Elizabetta and Sofia, Dmitri deliberately tosses the next game against Kees and Victoria. Sally doesn't play well enough to win on her own, and she doesn't object when he decides to retire to their room.

Since arriving at Big Sky, they've kept up the pretense of being together. Behind the closed, locked door of the bedroom, they don't even sleep in the same bed. While Sally changes into a nightgown in the bathroom, he grabs the comforter off the bed, folds it in half, and lies on the floor. He closes his eyes when he hears the bathroom door open. Sally's sleepwear is usually skimpy and revealing—Shashenka imposes a dress code on the concubines of his lair—and Dmitri tries to give her a modicum of relief from roving eyes.

She turns off the light after crawling into bed. "Are you okay?"

"I'm fine."

"I know tonight was hard on you. I think everyone noticed

the foul mood you're in." She pauses. "If you want to talk, I'll listen."

"I don't want to talk about it." Dmitri blows out a breath. "I'm sorry—it's not fair to you."

"I'm okay. I can help you get through this, if you'll let me."

Rolling onto his side, he faces away from the bed. "Sleep well."

The false loathing is difficult enough to manage in front of others, but the way he directed it at Elizabetta fills him with shame. *She doesn't deserve this.* But how can he stop? As his mind pulls one way, his heart tugs the other, and he can feel a chasm open and tear his soul. Swells of pain and numbness cycle through him as he sits on the sidelines and watches his mind wage war with his heart. Hours pass before he finally falls asleep.

When he wakes, Sally is showered already and is sitting with an e-reader in the armchair. She doesn't look up while he places the comforter on the bed, collects his clothes, and goes to shower. When he comes out of the bathroom, he tells her that he has business to attend to and will meet her later in the evening. She nods without saying a word.

He needs to speak with Maria before he takes Elizabetta for another brainwashing session. There is no other way for him to think of what they are doing to her; it's despicable and wrong. His part of it has been ongoing for over a year now, and frustration and failure plague his efforts. The many times the others slip up and call her Elizabetta instead of Eliza aren't helping him either. Now with her back under his control, the pressure on him to complete the mission has increased, but he cannot ignore the warning signs for failure any more than he can embrace the potential for success.

Dmitri finds Maria in the great room, but she's hesitant to discuss the matter until he promises to be brief. She follows him to the seldom-used kitchen. It's unlikely anyone will be there; it serves little to no purpose in a Belyakov household.

Maria leans against an island counter and waits for Dmitri to speak. He's unable to hide the disgust in his voice. "Yesterday during Eliza's session, she balked at the command to be one of Shashenka's playthings."

"Well, I hope you didn't put it to her like that."

"No, of course not. The point is that she resisted that part of her programming. Your spell worked fine. She wasn't out of my control when she refused."

Maria's eyes narrow and the muscles in her neck tighten. Her tone is dismissive. "I'm not sure what I can do to help you."

His eyes widen and a muscle twitches in his jaw. She's supposed to be here to help him, but seems fickle and unpredictable. Exasperated, Dmitri says, "Can't you cast another spell or give her some kind of potion that will make her promiscuous?"

"Spells and potions that influence behavior aren't permanent. They serve to drop inhibitions, but only work when a person is predisposed toward having that trait. If she's naturally resistant to the suggestion, it will create a bigger problem for you to deal with."

"Damn it." He knows such loose behavior is contrary to

Elizabetta's nature. The suspicion that Elizabetta's reprogramming was always doomed to fail begins to grow. He tugs
his hand through his hair and turns to leave.

"Wait." She takes a step toward him as he turns back.
"About last night," she says. "Overall, your performance toward Eliza was convincing."

Too convincing. I saw her hurt, the confusion. He can tell
by the way Maria's looking at him that there's more. "And?"

"You can hate someone and not be unpleasant to everyone
else."

Agitated, he snaps, "I'll work on that."

Leaving her in the kitchen, he goes to the library and
finds Elizabetta standing in front of a tall bookcase, holding
an open book. She looks up, slides the book back on the shelf,
and eyes him warily as he comes into the room and marches
straight for her.

"I need to talk with you. Come with me."

Elizabetta folds her arms across her chest. "I'd rather
not."

Pushing frustration aside, he softens his tone. "I'm sorry
about last night. Please come with me."

"We can talk here." She starts moving toward a chair.

"No, we need to go where we won't be disturbed."

Her body language appears stiff and guarded, but she
steps forward and takes his outstretched hand. Clenching his
jaw against the pain, Dmitri leads her out of the library and
to the elevator. The tumult raging inside him seems to esca-
late his intense physical discomfort, and he drops her hand
when the doors close. They remain silent until they reach the

first subterranean floor. Dmitri doesn't look at her. "Follow me."

"Why? Are you putting me back in a cell?"

"No. We're going to the same room as yesterday."

He sees defiance in her eyes before her chin lifts and her shoulders square. Elizabetta is clearly averse to it, but walks toward him, mumbling, "I don't understand why we have to talk down here in this—this dungeon."

"The rooms are soundproof." He knows she grasps that their sensitive hearing allows their kind to hear sounds beyond normal human ranges.

"Will you tell me why I only remember finding myself in that room just before we left it yesterday?"

He ignores the pause in her step and says smoothly, "I don't know what you're talking about."

They enter the room and he closes the door, motioning for her to take a seat. For a moment he isn't certain whether she'll cooperate; he dreads the thought of placing her in shackles to start this session.

She watches him, but complies. "Okay, I'm here. Now tell me what you want to talk to me about."

He wants to tell her the truth and reveal everything she's forbidden to know. Perhaps someday he'll be able to defy Shashenka and do precisely that. Unfortunately, until she readjusts to life within the coven and becomes comfortable with her new identity, it's not possible. She'd never successfully feign being someone she's not.

"Sometimes, Eliza, things aren't always what they seem in the Belyakov coven." Before she can respond, Dmitri's tone turns harsh. "Hear me."

She immediately falls under his control. Her responses to the baseline questions come quick and true to the false history of her life. However, when they reach the point in the session where he suggests her role as a concubine, she balks once again. Simultaneously frustrated and relieved, he tries repeatedly over the next hour to get her to accept the command, but fails. *Master may have taken her memories and half her heart, but the other half keeps fighting. Ah, it dooms me to failure and gives me hope. Which half will win?*

"Eliza." He pulls her to her feet and into his arms, welcoming the searing pain of her touch. "May I kiss you?"

Tilting her head up, she leans in and initiates the contact. He ignores the intense sting of her mouth as it moves against his, and he lovingly kisses her back. *My half ... my half will win.*

Reluctant to stop, he pulls away from her and opens the door to return her to the ground floor. Before they step off the elevator, Dmitri snaps his fingers in front of her face and walks away.

Leaving her dazed, Dmitri exits the back of the house through the enclosed breezeway connecting it to the gym. The courts and gym are rarely used, and he finds both racquetball courts empty. *I am ruining her. She never wanted this, yet I condemn her to it. I never deserved her. I deserve the hell it puts me through. She trusted me, and this is what I have brought her to, this is the fate I leave her with because I can't do what she asked.* He chases and slams the little blue ball around the court until his self-loathing is spent.

Afterward, he joins the others in the great room. The Druzhinnikis have left and only the Druzhinas remain. Dmitri learns that seven of them, and Maria, will depart the following night. Shashenka is sending them to different locations to contend with various matters that won't require more than one or two to handle each problem.

He, Elizabetta, Sally, Justin, and Alexander will remain, but Justin plans to travel to the Flathead Valley the day after, to go fishing. He'll go directly to Prague from there a few days later. Dmitri's not looking forward to their departures. The minimal interaction with the ten full-time residents— locals, as they're often called—allows too much opportunity for Alexander to harass him, and not enough excuses to avoid time with Elizabetta and Sally.

Before sunrise, he finds time to talk with each one of the leaving Druzhinas, and thanks them for aiding in Elizabetta's return. There will be less contact with the Druzhinas now that he's been stripped of his position. Their sporadic and brief visits to the Belyakov estates will give little time for the friendships they have forged. His mood is darker by the time Sally accompanies him to their room. He refuses to even look at her as they get ready for bed.

Later that night, after sunset, Dmitri has no desire to be around others. He just wants to be alone with his thoughts and release the tension that festered during the day. Over the next few hours he pounds another set of racquetballs to death; it helps some. When he returns to the house, Elizabetta, Sally, and Alexander's voices are wafting from the entertainment room. They're trying to decide on a movie to watch.

He's about to go to the library alone when he hears Alexander ask Sally if there's a lover's quarrel going on between them. The chance of Alexander reporting a problem is too risky; Dmitri turns around and joins them.

Elizabetta quickly looks at and then away from him when he enters the room. Forcing a smile that doesn't reach his eyes, he sits next to Sally on the divan and braces against the torment of contact as he cups her chin in his hand and kisses her. Politely he inquires about her evening, and she prattles on a few moments, quieting only when Alexander puts a movie in the DVD player. Discreetly Dmitri shifts to put a slice of space between them.

Alexander is focused on the movie, allowing Dmitri's eyes to linger on Elizabetta. His eyes keep darting to her face, distracting him from paying attention to anything else. She glances his way and refuses to meet his gaze. It doesn't escape his notice that she is also keeping her distance from Alexander—a small relief.

Conflicting thoughts and questions run through his head. He's growing concerned about her resistance to the role Shashenka expects her to fill. He is also finding it difficult to play his part. In a battle of willpower, he wonders, who will break first?

When the movie ends, Elizabetta asks to speak with him. He rebuffs her curtly, grabs Sally by the hand, and leaves the room, breaking the contact when they're out of sight. They go to the indoor pool for a swim. Sally tries to engage him in conversation, but he doesn't feel like talking. She then tries to get him to play, even splashes water at him, but he ignores her. After an hour of this, she leaves to play video games in the arcade room. Dmitri swims another hundred laps before he joins her there.

He finds Alexander and Elizabetta with her; they are gathered around a pinball machine, their playful banter filled with teasing and laughter. Alexander is playing while the women stand to each side. Walking up behind Sally, Dmitri steels himself for the unwelcome contact and slides his arms around her waist, kissing her neck. Smiling, he suggestively encourages her to come to their room. He knows the look that flashes through Elizabetta's eyes before she abruptly looks away—jealousy tinged with hurt. Hating himself, Dmitri keeps an arm painfully around Sally's waist as they leave the room.

He knows his behavior is erratic; he needs to stop taking his frustration out on Sally. Once in the bedroom, they discuss it further, and he promises to rein in his rude behavior. Jointly they develop a schedule that will further their charade of being together. They will avoid Elizabetta and Alexander whenever possible and offer excuses to be alone, which will provide him the cover he needs to avoid suspicion.

The next several nights fall into a routine. Each evening starts with another failed session with Elizabetta. She simply rebuffs his every attempt to plant the courtesan role into her mind. After calling Maria to report the problem a second time, Dmitri begins to wonder how long this can go on without Alexander—and Shashenka—finding out.

Another week passes without progress, and tension is growing between Dmitri and Elizabetta. She no longer follows him willingly to the basement; he has to put her in a trance wherever he finds her after sunset and deliver her back to that spot before breaking it. He knows it appears to her as if he arrives, seeking to talk with her, changes his mind, and leaves. He's seen her bewildered and angry expression; he is certain she is confused by his actions.

Finally he reports the ongoing problem a third time to Maria. "She hasn't relented one inch. She remains as resistant as on that first day."

"Shashenka's getting eager to see her returned. You're going to have to report the problem." Maria sounds sympathetic.

"I feared you might say that." Inwardly he cringes. He must take the risk of revealing his feelings. "Maria, I don't know how much longer I can do this."

"You know the consequences if you fail."

"What we're doing to her is killing me. She tries so hard to be friendly to me, and I'm an absolute cad toward her." He has watched the confusion, hurt, and distance growing in her each day. "It's tearing me apart. I miss her so much."

Nearly a full minute passes before Maria replies. "I am truly sorry, Dmitri. You have no idea how sorry I am, but you have to find a way to endure this. If you don't succeed ... I won't be able to live with it."

The phone goes dead, leaving Dmitri stunned by her comment. *What did she mean by that?* She confounds him regardless of his efforts to figure her out. Anger rises within him as he mulls over the enigma that is Maria, but then he bursts out laughing. Doubtless Elizabetta thinks the same of him, and the irony is humorous to him.

Unable to unravel the mystery surrounding the witch, he seeks out Alexander; there is no way to put off the inevitable. Once more he finds the man in Elizabetta's company. The growing interest Alexander is showing her isn't helping Dmitri's mood.

Interrupting their banter, he looks at Alexander. "May I have a word with you privately?"

Alexander nods, excuses himself, and follows Dmitri to the library. "What do you want? I have plans to watch a movie with Eliza in the theater tonight. The locals are setting up the film reel now."

Keep your hands off her! Dmitri fights to keep the jealousy off his face. "Since Eliza returned, I'm having a problem with her programming."

"What kind of a problem?"

"She's refusing to accept her assigned role."

A huge grin spreads across Alexander's face, and he mutters, "Hmm ... nice to know it's my charm and not your brainwashing."

Anger flashes in Dmitri's eyes. It takes extra effort to keep his palms pressed to his legs instead of curling them into fists and ending Alexander's life.

The vampire's expression is smug. "I'll report this to Master and let you know what he decides."

CHAPTER 25: ELIZA

Puzzle Pieces

Since she arrived at the Big Sky estate, the vampires have forbidden Eliza to use a phone. She desperately wants to call Matt to let him know what happened to her. She wonders how he's coping with grief over the loss of the pack—a luxury she denies herself. There is no time for mourning among the vampires of the Belyakov coven.

Finding an unguarded moment, she tries sneaking a call out, but one of the younger permanent residents—Jacob—catches her before Matt answers the phone. He knocks the phone out of her hand before she can utter a sound. The back cover pops off and the battery tumbles out of the phone.

Jacob roughly escorts Eliza to the study, yelling for one of the others to find Alexander, and holds her there until Alexander arrives. The older vampire's eyes narrow, trapping her gaze as Jacob explains. After calling Shashenka, he tells Jacob to watch her. He leaves the room, but is back five minutes later and dismisses the young vampire with instructions to find Dmitri.

An uncomfortable silence falls between them before Alexander says flatly, "I've cut the phone lines, at Master's request."

"Why would you do that?" Eliza shrieks as her body quakes with rage. "I just wanted to make sure Matt's all right."

"You need to forget about that damn dog and let him get on with his life."

"Matt is not a dog—he's my friend. You guys slaughtered his pack, my family. If you had a kind bone in your body, you'd let me check on him. I left him behind and I don't even know if he's still alive."

Dmitri, frowning, enters the room, and Alexander turns to him. "She tried calling the mutt."

He nods. The stern expression on his face is formidable. Jaw flexing, Dmitri opens his mouth as if to say something, but Eliza is suddenly in a daze and he's walking away, leaving her confused. She's starting to realize this is a pattern whenever she's alone with him, and it's infuriating. Looking around the room, Eliza can't even recall why she's in the study in the first place. *What is going on? Why do I keep blacking out?*

Strangely, she has a sudden urge to go for a swim, but doesn't know why. Comprehension sneaks up on her; after each bizarre encounter with Dmitri, she feels compelled to do an activity that hadn't been on her mind. She needs to know why he acts so bizarrely and what he is doing to her. Sally is the best candidate for information, and Eliza invites her along to the pool.

Several minutes later, they are frolicking in the water and chitchatting about unimportant matters. Eliza finally summons the courage to ask the questions that are now nibbling at the edges of her mind. "Do you mind if I ask you a few questions about Dmitri?"

Sally laughs, submerges for a few seconds, and surfaces. "Why would I mind?"

"Well, because he's your mate, and I didn't want to cause problems between you."

They tread water, staring at each other for a moment. Sally's voice is tight, clipped. "I'm not Dmitri's mate."

"I'm sorry. I thought because you live together—"

"I'm only with him as Master wishes."

A pucker forms between her brows. "What are you saying?"

"I serve our master, as you do." Sally chews her lip. "I'm a concubine—I serve at Master's pleasure."

"Oh. Oh!" Eliza flushes. *That's what he's into, whores? Awful.* "I'm sorry, I didn't realize." She tries to collect her wits as Sally remains silent. "I can't figure him out. He wants to be around me and doesn't, he's polite one minute and rude the next, and he approaches and leaves without saying a word." *Obviously prefers someone like you, but won't give me a chance. That's mean, I shouldn't judge her.* "Somehow I offend him all the time, and I don't know what I'm doing wrong."

The uncomfortable look Sally gives her is disconcerting— she is convinced the other woman knows something. "Sally? Can you tell me what I'm doing wrong? I want to like him, be a friend, but his mood swings are driving me crazy."

"It's not you." Sally swims closer, scanning the pool room. She whispers, "Don't ever repeat what I'm about to say, to anyone. Dmitri serves our master—sometimes he must do distasteful, despicable tasks that no one else has to do. He likes you more than he's supposed to, or allowed to ever show."

In bewilderment, Eliza says, "I don't understand."

"I've already said too much." Swimming away, Sally climbs out of the pool and doesn't look back as she heads into the shower room.

Eliza floats for a few minutes, trying to make sense of the bizarre conversation. Nothing about it—or Dmitri, for that matter—fits. She leaps out of the pool and runs to the shower room. "Sally, wait."

Slowly turning around, her normal spunk subdued, Sally says in a sad tone, "Don't judge him. It's not his fault." Then she opens the door and leaves.

Dmitri is a puzzle with pieces missing, and I will find them. Eliza showers and dresses hurriedly; she plans to start looking now. The next one on her list to ask is Alexander. She finds him in the entertainment room, and they exchange pleasantries and make plans for later that night. Then the opportunity arrives for Eliza to find another missing piece of the puzzle. Given what Sally said in the pool, Eliza frames her questions carefully.

"It's my understanding that Dmitri serves the master. What does he do?"

Alexander tenses and waves her to a chair. "Why do you

want to know?"

"Well, you are a Druzhina, and you're here to make sure I don't run away again. The rest of the Druzhinas left. Sally's an"—Eliza chooses a euphemistic label—"escort. The locals are merely servants for the estates, and I'm curious what job Dmitri does."

"Our dear brother Dmitri is a fool. He's the first Druzhina ever stripped of the honor of serving, by displeasing our master too many times. Now he's a simple personal servant to whomever Master assigns him." Alexander actually sounds boastful.

"I see." Eliza, recalling the several times she has seen Dmitri and Alexander meeting or speaking privately, is deliberate in her assumption. "He's attached to you right now?"

Roaring with laughter, he chokes out, "Oh heavens, no, sweet Eliza. He's attached to you."

She expected the assumption to provoke a response, but his answer stuns her. "T-to me?"

"Yes, he's to oversee your training, so you may return to Master's inner lair."

"Return? I've never been there."

"I suppose it may seem so to you, but you have met our master before, and he is ... shall we say, quite enchanted by you. That enchantment led him to select you for service in the exclusive brothel of the inner lair."

Intuitively Eliza knows he's lying about how their master feels toward her. Then his words hit her, and she blenches at the thought. She gasps. "No!" Learning she is a vampire was horrifying enough, but to discover this is beyond appalling.

They want me to be a whore. No flippin' way. Still reeling, she barely hears Alexander abruptly excuse himself. *Dmitri. He's done this to me. He prefers that sort ...*

Anger over everything that's happened to her begins to build. *That bottom-dwelling, scum-sucking pig. Now I know I'm crazy. So insane to think he's sexy and worth getting to know.*

Within twenty minutes she's in a consuming rage and needs an outlet for it; only one comes to mind. *Dmitri.* Jumping to her feet, Eliza bolts from the entertainment room and runs from room to room, searching for him. She finds Alexander in the study on his cell phone; she slams the door shut. Next she finds Sally alone in the bedroom she and Dmitri share.

"Where is he?" Eliza roars.

Clearly startled, Sally says, "I—I don't know."

The doorknob crumples under her grip and comes off the door when she slams it shut. She drops the mangled handle to the floor and keeps searching. Dmitri doesn't seem to be anywhere in the house, including the cells in the basement. She doubts he has left the estate, and that only leaves the outbuildings. Determined to confront him, she speeds through the breezeway to the gym. Jerking the door open to a racquetball court, she finally sees him, and tastes rage like a flavor on her tongue. *I am going to kill you.*

Dmitri barely turns and registers surprise before Eliza rushes forward and grabs him by the throat. His strangled cry dies there. In a streaking blur, she slides him across the floor and smashes his body into the wall. The fiber resin court wall cracks with a loud, splintering rip. Then she pulls him away from the wall and slams him into it twice more. A dent appears behind him in a mosaic of spider fissures across the surface. A wild and agonized expression covers his face. Eliza's chest is heaving with heavy breaths. Her eyes flicker with fury; she's too angry to speak. A strangled groan escapes Dmitri's throat and his eyes turn pleading. When she releases him, he immediately pitches forward, coughing and gagging.

She doesn't give him time to recover. "You did this to me." Her tone grows louder. "You did this to me, you son of a bitch!"

Looking up at her, he asks warily, "Did what?"

"Ruined my life," she wails. "I know what you're here to do."

"Oh, that." Dmitri slumps to the floor, legs extended, and his back and head fall against the wall. He raises a hand and gently rubs his neck.

"Yeah, that." She gives him a murderous look. "You have no right. I will not submit to this, and I will fight you every inch of the way."

Hanging his head, Dmitri speaks softly. "I don't want to do this to you. It's not my choice."

"We always have a choice, and what you're choosing to do to me is reprehensible."

"No, I don't. You don't understand." He pats the floor next to him. "Sit down, love. Please."

I hate how his voice gets to me. Reluctantly she sits on the floor next to him. "You had better start talking before I change my mind and beat you to death."

"I will tell you what I can, but understand there are details I cannot reveal. Whatever I tell you, you must swear never to repeat. Okay?"

"I don't buy it."

Dmitri turns his head to look at her. "As I said, love, there are facts you do not know or understand. Anything I withhold from you protects our lives."

A vague memory surfaces: Maria telling her that none of this is what it appears to be.

"Everything I do to you is what Master commands. He chose you to serve the inner lair, and it's my ... duty to prepare you for it—it is my punishment for displeasing him. If you refuse and I fail, he will torture or kill us."

That disconcerting ring of truth she's heard before is evident in his voice. *Is it possible he's not responsible, that he's only acting on our master's orders?* She doesn't want to be killed, and a part of her doesn't want Dmitri dead either. "If it's that dire, why don't we just run?"

"Shashenka Belyakov's reach extends too far—there is no place in the world we can hide. The Druzhina can find anyone, anywhere, and remember this ... he will send them, and others, to find us. I was one of them—a Druzhina. Most of them are our friends, but loyalty to Master supersedes friendship and even blood oaths, and it'd be a death sentence to any of them if they refused an order or looked the other way to let us stay on the run."

"Well, maybe we can outrun them, since you know their tactics."

Dmitri shakes his head. "They haven't failed in their tasks for more than eight hundred years. Trust me, love, we can't run, and if we want to live, the best we can do is obey the master's wishes."

He won't budge. Eliza changes course and tries for answers to the many other questions she has. Perhaps they'll provide missing pieces and explain why she's a vampire—why he is involved with every bad thing that has happened to her. "Did you turn me?"

His smile looks bittersweet. "Yes."

"When?"

"I can't tell you."

"You said you don't want to do this to me. Why?"

"I can't answer that either."

"Can't or won't?"

"Can't."

Eliza ponders how to proceed. Recalling the background searches Josh did leads to the next question. "Something tells me you also won't tell me my real name or where I'm from, will you?"

He eyes her cautiously. "Why do you question your name?"

"I, um, let's just say that I have my reasons to suspect it's not my name. Now do you care to enlighten me?"

"No."

She slams her palms down so hard that she cracks the court floor. "God ... shit, this is making me insane." Infuriated, she leaps to her feet, snarls, and begins pacing.

Dmitri laughs, his tone sardonic. "Me too, love, me too."

"Is this why you're always acting like a deranged lunatic around me?" *Like I'm one to talk. Sheesh, pot meet kettle.*

"You have no idea, love, but yes."

"Why do you call me love?"

He shrugs and gives a pained smile. "Old habit, perhaps."

Eliza considers the comment before walking over to sit by him again. "You said you're supposed to prepare me. What does that mean?"

She watches his hands clench into fists on his lap. When he unclenches them, stretching his long fingers wide apart, he answers, "Learn to dress, and how to tease, flirt, submit willingly, and please without reservation or complaint any companion seeking your favor."

The detached, almost emotionless way he speaks sounds more like someone parroting another or reading from a script. "What if I can't?"

"Shashenka will find ways to force you."

"When are you supposed to start teaching me all of that?"

A regretful tone makes his reply almost inaudible. "Several weeks ago."

Oh. She assumes this is why he often approaches her and leaves without saying a word. *Perhaps he isn't morally bankrupt and finds it as repugnant as I do.* His earlier comment about torture or death echoes in her mind. Eliza says simply, "We can't avoid it much longer, can we?"

"No."

The muscles tense in her jaw and neck. She swallows hard, once, twice. "Perhaps it's best we start on it tomorrow."

Dmitri looks astounded. "You'd do that?"

Rising to her feet, Eliza nods once and starts for the door. She opens it and then turns to look at him. "Dmitri?"

"Yes, love?"

The realization of what she's just agreed to hits her like a lit stick of dynamite. *There's got to be another way out. I can't do this.* "I am not a whore and I will still fight you on this. Every inch, at every turn, I will fight you."

She leaves the door open and storms through the gym and into the house. A dark mood has engulfed her, and she doesn't want to see or talk to anyone. Eliza goes to her bedroom and draws a hot bath. Her mind has so much to digest that the water turns cold before she processes everything she's learned. Letting some water out, she adds hot water to the tub again. It's daylight before she finally drains the tub and gets out.

Lying across the bed, she can't get thoughts of Dmitri out of her mind. Although he doesn't reveal much with words, his body language shouts loudly enough. She notices he hides it well from most, but she catches the minute slips in his facial expressions. Sally and Maria are right; he cares more for her than he should, and he and the position they're in aren't what they seem. *What are they all hiding? What is really going on?* When she and Dmitri are alone he shows a tenderness and compassion that don't suit the role of one willingly forcing her into sexual slavery.

Often she's seen him flinching, wincing, and grimacing in pain whenever someone touches him, yet there are no obvious wounds. *Can vampires feel pain after an injury heals?* He's deathly terrified of their master, and Eliza suspects the despicable creature has tortured him. Doubtless that's why physical contact with others causes him discomfort; it infuriates her that his gentle soul should know such pain. *Jeez, I'm no better. I grabbed his throat and threw him into a wall.* In retrospect, she feels ghastly about it.

Admittedly, his striking good looks attract her. When she saw him on the racquetball court, even in her rage, she couldn't ignore his physique. The shorts and tank top he was wearing, and his long legs and arms ... *He is so damn hot.* His six-foot-three-inch height forms a lean body that's muscular, but not bulky. His deep-brown hair is nearly black, and it matches the smoldering eyes that penetrate her more than she cares to acknowledge. Every time she looks at his lips, she fights the urge to kiss him. *Even with the scars I saw, he's the walking definition of tall, dark, and handsome.*

Eliza rolls onto her side, snuggling the extra pillow in her arms against her chest. She wonders what it would be like to feel Dmitri's body lying next to hers. It's easy to imagine his arms, one tucked under her neck and another wrapped around her waist. She pictures their legs entwining, their bodies fitting, molding together, with nothing awkward or out of balance between them. He would lightly kiss her neck and shoulders, nuzzling his face in her hair and falling asleep.

At one point Eliza drifts off to sleep, and the fantasy gives way to a dream about Dmitri. She feels a tender kiss on the back of her neck, his arm tightens around her waist, and the full length of his body presses against her. Dmitri rolls her onto her back and moves his body over hers as his mouth takes her lips in a hungry kiss. Next they're making love, and everything about it seems so right, so perfect that nothing else in the world matters to her anymore.

CHAPTER 26: DMITRI

Shattered

What a remarkable woman. I've never seen another as strong as her. For a long time after Elizabetta leaves, Dmitri sits staring at the open door. His gaze shifts to the two indentations where her hands cracked the floor, and he wonders if she even noticed the raw power she exerted. Her parting comment echoes in his ears; it bemuses him and oddly gives him hope.

When she suggested they start on her training tomorrow, his heart soared and plummeted in the same dead beat. He felt relief that she accepted the role being thrust on her, sparing both of them additional torment. But he has always believed in her strength, and it is devastating to see her break so easily. Not to mention what it will do to him to watch other men defile his mate.

It's daylight when he finally makes his way to the bedroom. He notices the doorknob is gone, but doesn't care why. Sally is already asleep on the bed. Dmitri places the comforter on the floor and is about to lie down when he hears a knock. He rips off his shirt, tosses the comforter across the bed again, and dives under it before saying, "Come in."

Sally stirs and looks as surprised as Dmitri feels at seeing Alexander standing in the doorway. The look on Alexander's face is menacing. "What happened to your doorknob?"

Before Dmitri can respond, Sally quickly offers what sounds like a lie. "Oh, I accidently did that ... was in too much of a rush and I pulled it right off when I closed the door."

Alexander nods, but doesn't look convinced. "Get dressed and join me in the study. Master has new orders for you, dear brother." He doesn't wait for a reply.

Sally whispers, "What is that all about?"

"Whatever it is can't be good. Go back to sleep. I'll return later."

Putting on a clean shirt and a pair of jeans, Dmitri struggles to calm the sudden tremble in his hands. A sense of foreboding spreads through him and slows his stride on the way to the study. He pauses at the door before pushing it open and entering the room. Alexander is watching his every move. Trying to appear relaxed, Dmitri sits in a chair and inquires, "Master has new orders for me?"

"Yes. It seems your reports on Eliza's progress are less than forthcoming, and she is—rather, was—ignorant that Master expects her as a concubine for the inner lair."

Dmitri clears his dry throat. "Yes, it's a problem I've been trying to resolve before alarming anyone. I told you, the bitch is resisting."

Anger flashes in Alexander's eyes. "What you didn't tell

me is that she didn't seem to know that important detail. I discovered that part of your problem in a conversation I had with her last night. I had no choice but to report it immediately. Once more, you disappoint our master."

"But—"

"Master considered your problem for a few hours and called a short time ago with a solution."

Dmitri's stomach begins to churn. "A solution?"

"Yes." Alexander sneers. "Since you were incapable of informing Eliza of her role, and I had the unfortunate circumstance to reveal it to her, our master assumes that if it's not her, then you are the one delaying. Are you sure it is only her resistance? Which is it?"

Dmitri looks down. "It's her resistance. I've been erasing her memory of those discussions until she reacts favorably toward it."

"Then that removes option one."

"Option one?"

"Master gave me two orders, one to fit either possibility, and since you insist it is the latter, the first no longer applies."

The lascivious look in Alexander's eyes unleashes the dread Dmitri has been holding in check. "What are my orders?"

"You will break her under my direct supervision."

"Break her how?" *Don't say it, don't.*

"You know how."

The intent is clear: forcible submission, rape, a dual punishment meant to cause suffering to each of them. Dmitri tries to stall. "I'm not certain I can do that. The ... unseen shackles Master left on me hamper my ability to perform."

"There are other ways to rape a woman, Dmitri. I'm sure you're intelligent enough to figure it out. Master expected your refusal, and says if you do not do this, then I will have to—and you will watch."

Over my dead body. Dmitri thought his hatred for Shashenka was unparalleled, but this ... *Mine!* The thought of Alexander raping his Elizabetta just put the other man on the same rung of the ladder as their master. Briefly forgetting to display loathing toward her, Dmitri says, "If you—" Then catching himself, he replies coldly, "That won't be necessary. I will do the deed myself."

"Good. We'll go to her room right now and get it started."

Fleetingly Dmitri prays that Elizabetta recalls their conversation on the racquetball court, when he told her that everything is at their master's orders. Otherwise she will never forgive him for what he's about to do to her.

I have to get her away from here.

No, keep her safe, protected. Detestable as it is, he cannot avoid this, but neither will he ever forgive himself.

As they approach her room, Alexander grabs Dmitri's elbow. He says earnestly under his breath, "Brother, we have not always gotten along, but I have always been fond of you. We have served and fought together for centuries, and in respect for you, I will not enter the room to watch. Remaining in the hall, listening, should be sufficient for me to give a status report to Master tonight."

Dmitri's mind whirls as the words sink in. *What is his an-*

gle? Think. There has to be a way. Stiffly he nods and walks to Elizabetta's door. It is locked. He breaks the handle and, removing the outside half of the broken handle, uses a claw to trigger the bolt, sliding it free of the doorjamb. He pushes the door open, steps inside, and closes it behind him.

Elizabetta is sleeping in the middle of the bed. Her long brown hair splays across the pillow, and she's holding a second pillow to her chest. Memories rush to the surface; how many times during their years together did he stand and watch her sleep for hours? *Wasted hours when it could have been me she held.* Often when she sensed his absence from the bed, she'd grab his pillow and hold it against her that same way. Oddly, it gives him resolve now to move forward.

Leaping on the bed, Dmitri lands astride her body and quickly clamps a hand over her mouth, ignoring the pain of contact. The moment her eyes fly open, he leans forward and whispers, "Don't scream, and listen fast. I'm under orders to break you—to rape you—now. Alexander is on the other side of the door, waiting to hear proof of that vile act."

He draws back to look in her eyes. "I will not do it. When I lift my hand away, you will start screaming. We will have to make noises sounding like a struggle, a fight. We will say vulgar comments to each other—threats, curses, demands."

Ignoring the panic and terror crossing her face, he says, "We'll need to trash the room. Then you will start crying, and we'll make it sound like you're submitting to the rape. Starting tonight, you will show everyone how much you despise and fear me. Understand?"

Wide-eyed, Elizabetta nods. Dmitri removes his hand and

springs lightly to the floor. She lets out a bloodcurdling scream as he's pulling the blankets and top sheet loose.

"Stop it! Stop. Get off me!" Elizabetta screams again. "Don't do this to me. Stop."

Dmitri hears both terror and courage in her plea as he jostles the nightstand, knocking the lamp to the floor. Its ceramic base breaks as it lands. "Shut up, bitch!" Shocked and embarrassed by the rancor in his tone, he freezes.

"I'll kill you!" Suddenly she flies off the bed, tackling him to the floor. He cries in pain as she lands on her knees, straddling his hips. Keening, she tells him, "I told you to get off me."

Elizabetta rips his shirt. Bending down, she whispers near his ear, "Slap me so he can hear it."

"I can't do that."

Elizabetta's claws come out and she rakes Dmitri across the face. Under her breath she hisses, "I said, hit me."

No. No. In the almost six hundred years since they met, he's never once raised a hand to her. There is a familiar determination in her eyes, and he knows she's right; she needs to look abused when this is over. Feeling another stinging swipe of her claws across his chest, he swings his left arm. The slap sends her tumbling across the floor and into the wall. Guilt immediately turns him rigid as stone.

Elizabetta runs at him, picks him off the floor, and throws him on the bed, moving it sideways a few feet. Their body contact rips another guttural cry from his throat as she leaps on him. He recognizes the anger and compassion that blaze in her eyes, but he startles at the menace in her voice. "I'm going to kill you."

Snapping out of the shock, remembering he still has a role to play, he bellows, "You filthy whore, you will do as I say."

Elizabetta shifts off Dmitri and starts bouncing on the mattress on her knees, making it sound like they're jostling for control.

"Don't. Stop! No! Don't! Please, don't do this to me."

"Shut up! This is for your own good," he growls.

"I hate you." Elizabetta mouths, "Sorry," then says aloud, "I hate you."

Dmitri laughs and sneers. "Well, welcome to club hell."

Getting off the bed, he moves around to the footboard and starts pushing and pulling the bed, banging the headboard against the wall. With Dmitri shaking the bed, Elizabetta tears at her pajamas and the bottom sheet. What she does next immeasurably astounds him. In two swift moves, she rips the shredded pajama top and bottoms from her body, throws them to the floor, and using her claws, rakes her legs and torso. Then she collapses, lying on her back, and starts wailing. The move catches him by surprise, and for a moment he is impressed by her performance. But something about the way she's crying is ... off... not right.

She's not acting. Mortified, Dmitri stops shaking the bed. *Oh no ... no, what have I done?* Elizabetta's closed eyes seem unable or unwilling to stop the torrent of tears now flowing from them. Watching her beautiful naked body heaving with racking sobs—it is heart wrenching. Although the rape is pure artifice, he knows something deep inside her just irreparably shattered. It's sickening. He can feel her agony shred his soul. Shame and humiliation unlike anything he's ever known begin to eviscerate what is left of him. He wants to take everything back, undo what just happened.

Gasping and choking, Elizabetta rolls over, curling her body into a tight ball.

Oh my God, what have I done? Forgive me, love, please forgive me. Dmitri grabs the rumpled top sheet off the floor and gently covers her body. He strokes her long hair and places a feather of a kiss on her temple. "I'm so sorry, love. You will never know how profoundly sorry I am."

His hatred for Shashenka reaches a height Dmitri never thought existed; it is now a flavor on the back of his tongue. Somehow, someday, he will kill that evil, despicable, vile vampire. The master will pay for what he's done to Elizabetta.

Hair disheveled, tattered shirt open and untucked, Dmitri unbuttons the top two buttons of his jeans and stumbles toward the door. He jerks it open and steps into the hall, rebuttoning his jeans. Not looking Alexander in the eye, he says dejectedly, "It's done."

Alexander peers around Dmitri and into the room, looking at Elizabetta's huddled figure on the bed. Then he looks at Dmitri with guilt and pity in his eyes. "Perhaps you should stay with her. Get her calmed down and cleaned up." Mumbling, he walks away, saying, "I'll let Master know you did the deed."

Dmitri watches Alexander descend the top of the staircase; then he turns and reenters the bedroom. Waves of remorse crash into him as he shuts the door. Unable to look at

Elizabetta, at what he's accomplished, he sits on the edge of the bed with his back to her. She's still crying. Cradling his head in his hands, he wonders if anything will ever be good or right between them again. He has broken her. In a cruel twist, one of the things he vowed never to do, he has done.

Turning slowly, keeping his eyes averted from her face, he places a hand on her hip. She doesn't move. The weight of her pain is too much for him. Dmitri repositions himself on the bed, wrapping his body around hers. For the first time, he welcomes the agonizing sensation of full physical contact, and shockingly, finds it's not enough—he deserves worse. He buries his face in her hair at the back of her neck, and his tears begin to spill across his nose and cheeks, soaking her dark tresses. He tightens his arms around her, silently begging forgiveness, and tries to hold her and himself together.

Then Elizabetta's voice trembles, barely audible. "Dmitri, please leave."

"I can't ... I can't leave you like this."

"I don't want you near me." Her voice, slightly stronger, whispers, "I don't want you to touch me again—ever."

There it is, the last shard falling into an abyss where Dmitri will never be able to recover it. They were once one, and then broken in two, but now they have shattered together—leaving both of them utterly destroyed. He pulls away, and without looking at her, leaves the room.

Numb with grief, he finds his way to the bedroom he shares with Sally; she doesn't stir when he closes the door. Going straight to the bathroom, Dmitri strips his clothes off and crawls into the empty tub. *I've delivered her one step away from final death. All my promises ... forgive me, moyata svyetlina.* He extends his claws and slices the veins running from his elbows to his wrists and watches the blood gush to the surface and run down the sides of his arms. Then he leans his head back, closes his eyes, and longs for a death that will not come.

When the wounds close too soon—the curse of a vampire's immortality—Dmitri reopens them. It's a curse with a flaw; while his body will repair itself, it cannot create and replenish his blood out of thin air. It takes feeding on a human to restore this amount of blood loss. He will never take another human life; there is no redemption for him.

Reopening the veins a third time, he stares at the crimson liquid covering his arms and legs, trickling toward the drain. The blood loss is making him weak; he fights to stay conscious. He needs to finish what he started, and if he passes out, he will fail. Slowly his head tips back and rests against the wall. As life seeps out of him, his eyes grow heavy. Darkness overtakes him.

From deep within the blackness, he hears voices and feels hands grabbing, tugging, and lifting him from the tub. Unable to open his eyes, he feebly tries to resist. Then he realizes there are two pairs of arms holding him, one under his shoulders and the other behind his knees. His body is numb—barely registers pain—floating, his head tilted back, lolling with each movement. Then he is being settled on a bed, and excited voices clamber in chaos.

"Dmitri, what have you done?" Sally is shrieking. "Alexander, do something. He's dying."

"Jacob, get Lee and take the utility van with the tinted windows into town. Quickly find two humans and bring them back here. He's going to need them to recover from this."

"You want them brought to the room?" Jacob sounds confused.

"Yes." Alexander's tone is brusque. "Also, tell Anita to stay with Eliza until I say otherwise. Have her tend to her needs. Sally, go to the utility room and get a bucket."

"A bucket?"

"Yes, get a damn bucket," Alexander shouts. "You'll need to clean him up. You can fill it in the tub. Now go get it."

Barely conscious, Dmitri notices the shift in the bed as Sally climbs off. There's still a pair of hands on him, bringing a dull ache to his numb body, but he lacks the strength to remove them. Then the darkness envelops him again and the commotion around him goes silent.

Next, a male voice penetrates the obscurity. "Drink. Damn it, Dmitri, drink."

Something thick and wet is trickling over Dmitri's lips into his mouth; its sweet, tangy, metallic taste reaches his tongue. *Blood.* He tries opening his eyes, but the lids are too heavy. The pressure of fangs pushing against the inside of his upper lip involuntarily opens his mouth. A wrist is rotating to line up with his fangs, and instinct closes his jaws—even though he's willing himself not to do it—locking the wrist in place as his fangs puncture the vein.

Dmitri's eyes fly open as his strength returns. The pain grows with each swallow. The petrified look on the face of the man being held next to him by Alexander and Jacob comes into focus. Sitting up, pushing the man's arm away, he bellows, "No. Let me die."

The man sways from the blood loss, but he can recover—he's not been drained to the point of death. Alexander shoves the man at Jacob and tells him to take the victim to the corner of the room, where Lee is restraining a woman. A flash of sympathy crosses Alexander's face before he nods and tosses a length of rope to Sally. "I will not allow that, dear brother."

CHAPTER 27: ELIZA

Last Spark

When Eliza woke to find Dmitri hovering over her body, it took her a second to realize he was real. He tore her from a dream that felt more like reliving a memory. The brief confusion cleared as she listened, horrified, to his rushed explanation and plan. But in executing it she saw his conflict, a wound so deep it was crippling and damaging him to the core. The staged rape, beyond his capability to do convincingly, forced Eliza to seize control.

She orchestrated the fight between them and brought it to its conclusion. Near the end, when Dmitri collapsed, his body wrapped around hers—ignoring his own physical pain—epiphany struck like a thunderbolt: he has been protecting her at considerable risk to himself.

Now Eliza understands that his burden is too much for any soul to bear, and it is killing him; he is too fragile to endure if she fights against him too. Inexplicably she feels the need to protect him, as if failing to do so will doom her in some unknown way. *I will never allow anyone to hurt Dmitri*

again. I must save him ... preserve his last spark of life.
Achieving that lies in shielding him from what will come, and
putting herself between Dmitri and who, or what, is destroying him. It means sacrificing herself, becoming the Phoenix
reborn. Lying on the bed, staring up at the ceiling, Eliza
knows she's made the right decision. *Who is destroying our
lives?* The answer comes slowly, but it feels so saturated in
truth, she accepts it.

I will kill Shashenka Belyakov.

Eliza rises from the bed, collects fresh clothes from the
closet and armoire, and prepares for a long, hot shower. The
first step of her plan is to distance herself from Dmitri to
protect him. Then she will submit to the role of courtesan,
and she will subvert Shashenka's inner lair. Fixing the image
of Dmitri, broken and unraveling, in her mind, Eliza finishes
showering, dresses, and winds her long hair into a bun at the
nape of her neck. After what happened—at least what others
will think happened—no one will expect her to leave the bedroom for a while. Settling into the wingback chair, she
watches the daylight seeping around the edges of the curtain.
Until she reaches the inner lair, it's impossible to strategize
the third step of the plan. Instead she begins preparing herself for what she must do.

A light knock at her door disrupts her thoughts. One of
the locals, a young brunette named Anita, is here; she's to
stay with Eliza until Alexander sends word. Nodding, Eliza
turns and resumes her vigil in the chair.

The local follows her into the room and busies herself
with righting the room from its disarray. She swiftly removes

the reminders—the broken lamp, shredded pajamas, and bloodstained bedding—of the supposed rape. When she finishes putting clean linens and bedcovers on the bed, she fidgets, unsure what to do with herself.

Motioning the young woman to the other chair, Eliza asks, "How did you come to be here?"

"Alexander sent me."

Eliza rolls her eyes and lets out a sigh. "No, I meant, how did you come to serve Belyakov here?"

The young woman gulps. "I grew up in Missoula. I went to an outdoor concert one night, and next thing I knew, I was this." She shrugs. "They brought me here to serve our master and those he sends to stay on this estate. I mostly spend my time cleaning and keeping the main house in order."

"And you're happy with that?"

Anita nods. "Yes. At least I get to stay in my home state, and most the time we're left alone. They treat us well. We get to feed when we need to, as long as we do our jobs and have everything in order when Master arrives."

She explains that their master doesn't come often, only once or twice a year. "The rest of the time we're free to do almost whatever we want. Pretty lucky from what we've heard—there are some estates Master stays at longer or visits more often." Anita smiles mischievously. "We have a pretty good time when there aren't any extras around."

Concluding the Big Sky compound is too remote to learn anything of value about Shashenka Belyakov, Eliza focuses again on the window. She watches the light around the edges of the curtain begin to fade. Twilight, the harbinger of an endless series of long nights of shadow, and on this one, Eliza fully embraces being a vampire and the darkness it has brought to her life. *There is no going back. The only way out is forward.* She will destroy any who stand in her way to freedom. She will stop cowering, being afraid.

I will be strong ... deadly.

Uninterested in further conversation with Anita, she grabs a book off the end table and flips it open. She's still pretending to read it when Sally bursts through the door, a panicked look on her face.

"I need you to come with me. It's Dmitri. He's trying to kill himself."

Instantly Eliza is out of the chair and following Sally down the hall. Within moments they enter the bedroom where, tied to the bed, Dmitri is shouting at Alexander. She notices the fading red lines on his forearms, the sallow and ashen tint to his skin. But his eyes trouble her the most; they hold the haunted look of a man who has lost the will to live and has the determination to end it. Then her attention is drawn to a corner of the room, where Jacob and Lee are re-straining a young man and woman. Eliza rapidly takes in their trancelike state and their muted, stiff posture; they are under vampiric control. She's beginning to understand the dynamics of the problem.

Bellowing, Dmitri glares at Alexander. "I told you, let me die. I have lost my dignity, and if you truly are my brother, you will grant me this one request."

Alexander ignores the outburst and greets Eliza. "Thank you for coming, dear. We need some help convincing him to stop this nonsense."

In a low voice she asks, "What happened?"

"He tried bleeding himself dry in the bathtub. Fortunately for him, Sally found him passed out before he could finish it." Disgust drips from every word. Alexander gestures to the two humans. "We brought these to restore his strength, but as soon as his wits returned he started fighting us. He's not had enough to repair the damage he's done to himself."

"Let me talk to him." Profound understanding and sadness settle over her. Dmitri is trying to extinguish the last spark she's vowed to save. *I will not allow it. You are going to live.* Her eyes fill with compassion as she sits on the edge of the bed. "Why are you doing this?"

He looks away.

She turns to Alexander. "Bring him here"—she points at the human first and then Dmitri—"and untie him from the bed." *You're not going to die on me now.* Bending near Dmitri's ear, she whispers a plea, "Don't fight me."

With blinding speed, Eliza grabs the young human by his hair and shirt and pushes him down until his throat is over Dmitri's mouth. Firmly she snarls, "Drink."

His hands shoot up and grab the terrified man by the head and shoulders. Dmitri grimaces and groans painfully as he stares at her. Questions flash in and out of his eyes. Adjusting the man's neck, he exposes the jugular vein. His eyes focus on Eliza as his fangs come down and plunge into the man's throat. When the body falls limp and lifeless, he shoves it away. The corpse lands with a thud on the floor.

Ignoring it, Eliza brushes past Sally, takes the young

woman from Lee, and marches her to within two feet of the
bed. With one arm around the powerless human's chest, Eliza uses her free hand to pull the woman's hair aside and position her for Dmitri to feed. "Get off that bed and finish this."

He's already rising from the bed, and she catches a
glimpse of his bare butt. Embarrassed, she watches as he
wraps the sheet around his waist. In spite of herself, her gaze
travels down his bare chest, over his V line, and pauses at the
sheet before drifting further down. *I'd like to see him without that sheet.* Her breath quickens as he closes the distance
between them. When he grasps the woman by the waist and
winces, it helps to douse Eliza's inappropriate thoughts. It's a
small relief to her that Dmitri doesn't touch her as he drains
the life out of the human. His eyes are another matter; the
scrutiny is as if he's trying to decipher the mysterious change
in her behavior. She intends to keep that secret.

When he steps back, Eliza drops the body to the floor between them. Turning to Alexander, she rocks her head toward the door. "It's done ... may I go back to my room now?"

The older vampire looks puzzled and his tone turns suspicious. "Why would you so willingly save his life after what he
did to you earlier?"

I have to save him. We will be free. Looking back at
Dmitri, she smoothly slides a lie past her lips. "Because I'll
need him alive if Master ever grants me the privilege of killing him myself."

Oddly, she sees relief flicker in his eyes. "I'll have Anita
return to your room and keep you company."

"I'd rather be alone, if that's all right."

Alexander allows it, and she leaves the room. A bitter smile spreads across her face as she walks down the hall. The earlier incident in her room may have lit the spark, but what just happened in Dmitri's room brought the fire to life; she can feel the bloodlust in her core. There is only one whose death will sate it—Shashenka Belyakov.

In the privacy of her room, she analyzes scenarios for moving against the monster who rules them. For her plan to be successful, those closest to him—the witch, the Druzhinas, and any others protecting him—must be swayed or killed. She'll need to use her role as a concubine to gain access to the right people.

Shashenka ... I am coming, and the Grim Reaper is coming with me.

By the end of the next day, Eliza is ready to proceed. Seeking Alexander, she finds him looking out at the mountains from the great room. His attempts to befriend her are obnoxiously overt, and she has no doubt he wants more than friendship. It turns her off and leaves her feeling cold, but it is something she can use to her advantage.

He smiles as she enters. "Are you feeling better, dear?"

"Yes. I understand what I must do now, the role our master expects of me." Dramatically she shudders. "I've resigned myself—it's inevitable—and I wanted to let you know that I don't want, or need, any further lessons from Dmitri." *I need to keep him away from me.*

"Ah, I see." He gives her a sympathetic smile. "He will still need to finish your training."

She snarls, "I don't want him to finish my training. I don't want him anywhere near me, ever again." Softening her tone, she proposes an alternative, one that will provide the buffer between her and Dmitri. "I know Sally serves Master in this regard. I'd prefer her to do it."

Alexander seems to consider it, to evaluate Eliza's demeanor. "I'll see if Master will allow it." He hesitates, then asks her to wait until he returns.

It is becoming obvious that no one makes a move or decision without Shashenka's approval. *Just how much control does he really have around here?* She is beginning to wonder whether the master is solely responsible for everything that's happened to her.

While waiting for Alexander to return, she wanders over to a reproduction of a Charlie Russell painting and studies it. She's seen a picture of it before, but never knew its title: *Loops and Swift Horses are Surer than Lead.* It depicts two cowboys roping a grizzly bear on a sage-covered hillside in the wilds of Montana. Eliza feels like the grizzly in the painting, cornered, trapped, and snared. It's representative of the coming fight: they may have captured her, but they have failed to subdue this angry female grizzly. She will fight back and she will kill Shashenka Belyakov and anyone who stands in her way.

She moves toward the window and looks at the mountains; these hills have no sagebrush. The painting's inspiration must come from an area further east of this southcentral part of the state. Her home state, supposedly, or at least she once believed it was, but now she isn't sure. They've taken everything from her. *My human life ... identity ... name. They've stolen my past and my future.*

She's still staring at the scenery when Alexander returns twenty minutes later. "It's a breathtaking view, isn't it?"

"Yes." She wonders what it looks like in daylight. Although she knows that her vision acuity is far advanced compared to a human's, it is not perfect; darkness still bathes everything in the color of night.

Alexander clears his throat. "I spoke with Master about your proposition. It pleases him that you're willing to serve him. He's arranging a flight for us to join him in Prague. He'll decide on your training after we arrive."

Fear starts to creep into her bones, but she quickly gains control. "When will we leave?"

"Within the next night or two."

"I should start packing, then—may I use the suitcases in my closet?"

"Yes, they are yours."

I've never owned a set of luggage. When she returns to her room and pulls a garment bag from the closet, she notices it looks used. Flipping the owner's tag over, she finds her name, written in her own handwriting. *What the ...? Will the mysteries never end?* Not knowing if or when she'll return here, she packs all the clothes and items she can find. She can't focus; she keeps speculating what life in the inner lair is like for ones like her and Sally.

What am I walking into? How can I find out before we arrive in Prague? Closing the carry-on bag with her toiletry items in it, she goes to find Sally.

A few minutes later, she locates her and Dmitri in the entertainment room watching a movie. *You can ... I have to do this.* Knowing she needs to drive the wedge deeper, she meets his questioning look with a fierce scowl before smiling at the woman next to him. "I don't want to interrupt your movie, but when it's over I need to talk with you, Sally. Alone, please."

Sally speaks cautiously, and with a hint of anger. "Sure."

"Thanks. I'll wait for you in the library." Without looking at Dmitri again, Eliza leaves the room. She's glad he didn't try talking to her, but the concern she saw in his eyes bothers her.

In the library, she murders minutes scanning the books that line its tall shelves. Their conditions range from new to old and tattered, and the collection contains works from both classical and modern, contemporary authors. A newer novel about a mutinous escape catches her eye. It may prove a fitting read given the daunting challenge ahead of her. Eliza decides to take it with her to Prague and sits down to start reading it until Sally arrives.

When Sally enters the room there's obvious tension in her posture. "What do you want to talk about?"

The harsh tone catches Eliza off guard. "I ... um—are you mad at me?"

"I am not liking you much at the moment. Dmitri told me what happened a couple days ago. It's not his fault he had to do that to you."

Eliza opens her mouth, but Sally doesn't give her a chance to speak. "You're lucky it was him and not someone else who can stand physical contact. It undoubtedly shortened the whole ordeal for you."

"I—" is the only word she utters before Sally cuts her off again.

"I've seen other girls punished or broken that way, and I can tell you, the men who normally do it will take hours and sometimes days before they stop. From what I heard, Dmitri finished with you in about an hour."

Remarkably, she barely comes up for air as her tirade continues. "I told you not to judge him, and now you want to kill him. I'd say that's judging him in the harshest way. Dmitri is my friend, and what you did pisses me off. I won't let you kill him, so you better get past that idea, pronto."

It's a small victory, learning others believe the ruse. Eliza is unwilling to tip her hand; her tone is dismissive. "I don't want to talk about it. The reason I want to talk to you is because I need to know what it's like, doing what you ... we have to do, and I have no idea what to expect."

Sally's chest is still puffed out, but her anger appears to cool slightly. "What do you want to know?"

"Everything from our living conditions to"—she shudders—"how it works. I mean, are we used every night and day, or do we get any time off in between?"

"We have private quarters on the same floor as the master. They're very lovely rooms, much like these here." She seems to relax and finally sits down. "Master uses us as it pleases him. When he's interested in or is busy with one of the other girls, he'll assign us to someone or leave us free to select somebody else. We get ten consecutive days off for every four weeks we work."

Four weeks on? She hopes this will leave her enough time to cultivate her plan. "So we're what, expected to perform twenty-four hours a day?"

"Depends." The other woman shrugs. "Like right now, you could say I'm on twenty-four seven. I'm with or available to Dmitri around the clock, but I still find time for me. It helps that he likes time alone too."

Given the weird way he acts with physical contact, and the amount of time he spends without Sally, Eliza assumes their sexual encounters are few and brief. Biting against jealousy—irrationally, she doesn't want Dmitri touching other women that way—she remembers to ask what she dreads most to know. "What's it like ... being with so many men all the time?"

"You get used to it after a while, and you may even find you have favorites among those who return often."

It's midmorning when their conversation ends. Eliza has compartmentalized key details that will either help her cope with this new life, or aid in her plans; with what she's learned, she'll go to Prague with more courage and determination than trepidation. Her biggest question, though, is still left unanswered: how much power and control Shashenka exerts over those in the coven.

CHAPTER 28: DMITRI
Calm Before the Storm

The mixed signals Elizabetta sent during the debacle in his room following his thwarted suicide attempt present a challenge for Dmitri to figure out and understand. Even with her altered mind, certain qualities of her behavior, character, and personality remain as they were before. Her sense of justice, the fine line between her compassion and mercilessness, and her all-or-nothing attitude—there are no half measures for her. None of that has changed. The puzzling part is trying to reconcile her plea to her threat; both rang true, but they lack congruity. He wasn't detecting any malice or deception from her, but regardless of how he looks at it, they don't fit together.

The simplest and likeliest conclusion is for him to trust that she will kill him. *I will not reject such a fate.* After all he's done to her, he owes her at least that much.

His only regret is that she likely will not do it in time to spare him the horror, humiliation, and heartache that are coming. They—Alexander, Sally, Elizabetta and he—are returning to Prague the following night. Dmitri will have to maintain a consistent level of false loathing toward Elizabetta, and the thought sickens him. But he has no idea what exactly Shashenka is planning for him there, and he can't risk the backlash for failure. All he's known among years of torture is serving as a Druzhina. After centuries of traveling, it will be difficult to adjust to a semi-stationary life. Whatever Shashenka tasks him with, he hopes it allows him to avoid watching Elizabetta's new life unfold.

When sunset arrives, Dmitri heads to the racquetball court for an hour of distraction from his own thoughts. Afterward he'll meet Sally in the pool room for their nightly swim. The time at Big Sky has lent them the opportunity to start an unlikely friendship. He thinks she has enjoyed the time off from the constant groping of men. Although she's prone to chatter, it's been a welcome distraction to have someone to talk with. She's beginning to prove her trustworthiness, too—he let slip a few inconsequential details that he expected her to report to Alexander, and she hasn't. The ultimate test—when he confessed that there is no loathing spell—Sally not only passed, but even began to covertly help him maintain the artifice.

She's already in the water when Dmitri steps to the pool deck, and they smile in greeting as he walks out on the diving board. Gracefully Dmitri launches into the air. His body arcs and his fingers touch his toes, before he straightens and dives into the pool. There's barely a splash as he disappears beneath the water. When he surfaces, he moves to an outside lane to swim laps. It's ironic that he makes the effort, because vampires don't need exercise—he does it because he finds it relaxing. Something in the way the water rushes over his body soothes him.

He's midstroke when he painfully bumps into Sally. She swims back and splashes water in his face. "Play."

"What?"

"I said, play. Don't you ever do anything for fun?"

"This is fun."

Sally rolls her eyes. "No, this ... is you escaping. Now play." With palms forward, she shoves a wall of water at him.

Grinning in spite of himself, Dmitri lunges forward and dunks her, forgetting his limitations. The pain is a quick reminder. "This is why I don't play," he growls when she surfaces.

"No one said you had to touch me." She giggles, turns onto her back, and starts wildly kicking her legs, sending a torrent of splashes his way.

Grabbing the ledge of the pool, he launches his body up to the pool deck and stands there waiting as she swims over.

"Why did you get out? Are you leaving?"

"Never." Then he catapults into a cannonball to douse her, erupting in a hearty laugh when he sees Sally sputtering and gagging. The moment she recovers, Dmitri sends another deluge of water her way.

Sally surrenders when their splashing war gets the better of her. "Okay, time out. I wanted to ask you something."

"What?"

She looks around before speaking. "After everything that's happened, have you considered moving on from Eliza?"

Dmitri doesn't hesitate. "No, I could never do that. It's impossible."

"I didn't mean find another mate. I meant move on, enjoy life, and at least enjoy the company of a few lady friends."

Revolting thought. I expected she knew better by now. His eyes smolder in disgust. "Even without the pain curse, I will never be with another woman, Sally."

She sighs and shakes her head. "I'm on a roll lately for either being too blunt or muddling my words. I'm not seeking a relationship with you. I'm talking about going places, doing things, having fun, not necessarily involving sex, and probably far better without that."

Dmitri rakes his fingers through his wet hair. He has enjoyed her company over the last few weeks, and now that he is no longer a Druzhina he has been isolated from his friends. "On a platonic level, it's something I might consider."

"Good." Sally smiles warmly. "I've thoroughly enjoyed our time together and think we have a good start on a friendship. Not that sex couldn't be fun between us, but it's nice being around a man who isn't demanding that from me. It'd be wonderful having someone, a friend aside from the estate women, to spend my time off with."

An awkward silence envelops them as they tread water. Dmitri hopes Sally won't change her mind later; he likes their friendship uncomplicated. She is a good woman and deserves a mate; yet she seems to be alone. Tentatively he questions that, and is stunned by her reaction—she doesn't want a mate.

"Why not?"

Her tone is sharp, bitter. "I'm a whore, Dmitri. Our world is small. Most men who move in our circle know what I am, and if they're looking, it's not for someone like me. I can't exactly move to a new city, forget my past, and start a new life."

Appalling. I am a cad. I never gave a thought to how Master ruins these women. "I'm sorry. Forgive me ... I didn't think of ... mean it like that."

"Thank you." The tension in Sally's face eases. "A few of the girls have mates—but it's a rare breed that tolerates other men intimately touching their woman. That's the real issue for you, isn't it, Dmitri?"

The ambiguity of her question leaves him unsure how to answer. "What do you mean?"

"You're wondering about Eliza, if she falls in love with you again. But the question you need to ask yourself is this— can you tolerate sharing her that way?"

Dmitri sighs. "It's a question I've been asking myself a lot lately."

"For what it's worth, it's not one I think you need to worry about having an answer for anytime soon. Her feelings for you seem to be moving toward hate rather than love." Sally's gaze is sympathetic and she whispers, "I'm sorry."

She doesn't wait for his response, but climbs out of the pool, heading for the showers. Dmitri floats for a while longer and ponders her last statement. If Elizabetta doesn't kill him, centuries of hatred await him. Maybe the best he can hope for is that she will kill him soon. *It is far easier now for her to end my life, than I hers.*

Not wanting to be alone with his thoughts any longer, Dmitri leaves the pool to spend time with Sally in their room. This might be their last night to enjoy their growing friendship. As the hours pass, it strikes Dmitri that it's not dissimilar to the last day of a vacation; they've seen and done everything there is to see or do, and now they want to enjoy killing the remaining free time with mindless activity before resuming their normal lives. Neither mentions their discussion in the pool room. Sally is right; only he can answer the question of what he can accept.

Both are uncertain what will happen when they return to Prague. There's been no word from their master as to whether he'll allow Sally to continue as a distraction for Dmitri, or if she'll resume her role as a courtesan, or be assigned to another man. Now that Elizabetta's reprogramming is complete—he released her from his control, returning her to self-awareness during their last session—there's no further work for Dmitri, nor any hint for what the master will have him do next.

Dmitri and Sally avoid discussing the what-ifs of an unknown future, but as usual, the topic turns to Elizabetta. It seems that if he isn't bringing her up, she is. Dmitri's concern for Elizabetta is growing. He's already heard that she's sought Sally's help in finishing her training. Control of the concubines is often left to the inner lair guards to manage, and Shashenka's preference toward them suggests that Dmitri may not be expected to finish it.

"Sally, promise me you'll watch over Eliza when she reaches the inner lair."

She seems to hesitate. "All the girls look after each other."

"That's not what I'm asking." He sighs. "I don't want to see her hurt by Shashenka or anyone else. She can be quite stubborn when she gets a notion set in her mind. If you see her acting foolishly or doing something that will bring her harm, please try to stop her."

She rolls onto her side. "If that's what you're after, then I already have an item on my list."

"What's that?"

"Change her mind about killing you."

Dmitri's tone is brusque. "Don't. After everything I'm responsible for, that I've done or allowed to happen to her, my life is the least I can repay her with."

"I think you're wrong." Sally sounds scornful. "Perhaps I need to protect both of you from yourselves."

"Good luck with that, then. We failed miserably at it ourselves the last time around."

"Do you mean the rebellion?"

"Yes."

He sees the curiosity in her expression. A couple of minutes pass before he says, "Tragic errors were made—it ended badly. We trusted the wrong people, failed to bring the right people to our cause. We used too few for the plan we had, and the death knell was the mole—Master superbly played us. When we realized we were set up, it was too late."

Sally appears genuinely inquisitive. "If you had to do it all over again, would you?"

"Not under those circumstances—like our eyesight, hindsight is always crystal clear."

"If the circumstances were different and those key things fell together with the right people, and Master stayed ignorant, would you try it again?"

And if Elizabetta's mind wasn't altered, absolutely, we'd succeed this time. With a sliver of a chance that Sally's friendship is phony, Dmitri dodges the question. "Why does it matter now?"

"I've always hoped someone would. Those of us forced to live in the inner lair see the worst this coven offers. It's not a happy existence."

When Dmitri remains silent, Sally continues, sounding wistful. "You had potential supporters that you never considered or used. We see and hear just about everything that goes on with the master. They knew things, we know things, and no one even talked to those who were there when it happened."

The guards maybe, but the concubines? "Are you serious?"

"Yes, I'm serious." Sally rises, propping herself on an elbow to look down at Dmitri on the floor. "You have no idea what we're forced to endure. Those who complain or resist go missing rather quickly. Many of us don't want to be there and several, like me, just want to be free."

Scowling, he asks, "Then why didn't any of them warn us about the mole?"

"Those working the inner lair know a lot, more than most, but it doesn't mean we know all. From what I heard, the mole was one detail Master kept very quiet, and no one knew about him until it went down."

Interesting.

"Now that you know you would have our support, tell me, would you do it again?"

Why is she pushing this? Have I made another mistake in trusting her? "I think it doesn't matter now, not after how Shashenka killed the rebels—and the way he's punishing Eliza and me, no one is going to consider it again for centuries." *I could never do it without Elizabetta, and she'll never be that type of threat again.*

A wry laugh breaks low in Dmitri's throat. "Well, I certainly have nothing left to lose, but I think I'll sit the next rebellion out."

CHAPTER 29: ELIZA

Trouble in Paradise

Just before midnight Alexander announces that their travel plans have changed. They are to leave in thirty minutes. Shashenka is routing them to the small vacation estate in Arecibo, Puerto Rico, where he and a small entourage will meet them. They'll stay there for a week before going on to an extended stay at the castle at Novgorod, Russia. It creates a commotion as the locals carry luggage to the van and the travelers prepare to leave. Dmitri seems to be avoiding Eliza; she doesn't see him until they gather on the front steps to wait for Jacob to bring the van around. Alexander rides in the front, putting Dmitri in the backseat with both women.

Fortunately Sally sits between them. It's difficult for Eliza to act distant toward Dmitri when they're forced into close quarters. She notices that he seems particularly subdued and tense; Sally is either oblivious or ignoring it. She hasn't been to Arecibo, but has spent a lot of time in Novgorod, and she rambles on about taking Eliza to see her favorite places when they arrive in Russia.

Once everyone has settled into the jet's passenger cabin, the women begin bombarding Dmitri and Alexander with questions. Alexander deflects them to Dmitri, given his familiarity with the island.

"It's been months since I've gone on holiday! What type of fun activities can we do there?" Sally is nearly bouncing in her seat.

Dmitri sounds uninterested. "Hang out in the house. Go to the beach. Visit the lighthouse. Hike to the caves, or the observatory."

Eliza's face brightens with excitement. "The big radio telescope observatory in the mountains? I wrote a report about it for my astronomy class." Smiling, she adds, "It has always fascinated me. I'd love to see it."

"I'm sure Master has your itinerary planned, and doubtless it will include seeing a lot of skin, a bed, a ceiling, and four walls."

Whoa. What is his problem? Still, it makes it easier for her to pound the wedge deeper between them. "Well, at least it won't be your bed."

He glares. "If I'm lucky, it won't be. Bedding a mutt-loving whore with fleas doesn't appeal to me."

"I rather look forward to seeing little of you in the week ahead. You disgust me."

Sally, apparently fed up with their bickering, interjects, "Dmitri, what are your top two favorite places to see there?"

"The observatory"—he sneers at Eliza—"and the lighthouse."

"Great. I'll cross those off my list of things to do," Eliza mutters.

"Trust me, being around you is no picnic."

Well, keeping you alive isn't either. Eliza bellows, "I can't even stand to be in the same room with you."

"Yeah, well, being in the same house with you is worse, much, much worse."

To her astonishment, it actually sounds like he means it, and she stops herself from clutching at the ache radiating from her chest. *Why am I protecting him? He's a jerk.*

"That's enough!" Alexander rebukes them. "Both of you had better check this shit by the time we land. Master may find it amusing at first, but he won't tolerate it in the long run."

It effectively subdues the conversation for the rest of the flight. Eliza takes in what each of them are doing. While she sulks, Dmitri looks as if he's ready to kill someone. Alexander has his nose stuck in a book, and Sally, obviously afraid of setting them off with any more questions, fidgets in her seat. Inwardly Eliza feels torn; Dmitri engaged in the dispute better than she expected, and while it helps her achieve her goals, his rejection stings deeply and leaves a lingering ache. She can't tell if his feelings are genuine or if their pending reunion with Shashenka has him on edge.

It's nighttime when they land at the airport, and a car with dark-tinted windows follows the jet into a hangar. After loading their luggage in the car, the driver takes them to the estate. It's beautiful, and oddly similar to the way Eliza imagines an island dream mansion would be. To be more accurate, it feels almost as if she's been to this island before, though she knows she has not. She doesn't know if she should feel amused or disconcerted by all the strange familiarities since she came to the Belyakov coven. There are the little and many déjà vu moments—a recognition of others when they've only just met. Then the oddities—others calling her Elizabetta, or acting like they've known her for years, and the well-used luggage set with her name on it but that she doesn't remember seeing before. And Dmitri somehow knows all of her favorite scents and had the bathroom stocked accordingly. Why do all these things keep happening?

Breaking away from her thoughts, Eliza takes in the house's appearance. It is a modern, geometric three-story structure, with rounded walls and sharp lines and angles, and the exterior's modern design flows to the interior living space. Raised and sunken rooms create the ground floor. Stark white and clear glass walls create an airy, open space while still giving each room a modicum of privacy. Highly polished white marble floors and staircases complete the look.

The decor is modern too, and bursts with a sweeping range of colors everywhere, but tastefully done and not garish. The solid and glass furniture share geometric themes in their design or patterned fabric. Immediately Eliza feels comfortable and welcome, almost like coming home.

Then alarmingly, she notices there are no curtains—anywhere. Wondering where everyone hides during the day, she is about to ask when she sees the glint of a silver strip in the ceiling. It lines the outside glass walls, and seems to be a metal shuttering system designed to block the sunlight.

Three men are sitting in the raised living room, watching their arrival. The man in the purple chair is blond with pale-blue eyes, and of average build and height. There's nothing distinct to his features. In a yellow chair, a man with shocking red hair is staring at them. He appears taller and brawnier than the first man, and his green eyes offset his chiseled features. The third man, sitting in the middle of the couch, is smaller than the other two. His slight, diminutive frame, light sandy-brown hair, and hazel eyes are nonthreatening. His smile is even impish.

Eliza assumes the man with red hair must be Shashenka; he's the most intimidating and fierce looking among the three. As they climb the few stairs to the living room, the smallest man stands. His mischievous grin broadens. "Ah ... dear, lovely Eliza, how good it is to see you here at last." Stepping forward, he takes her hand and kisses it. When he stands to full height, he's eye level with her.

Oh, crap. Eliza immediately realizes her error. "Pleased t-to meet you, M-master."

"Oh-so proper and polite, what a delight you are," he croons as he points her toward the couch. "Sit there, Eliza, we'll catch up in a moment. First I must greet my other guests."

Turning to Sally, his voice still dripping with phony courtesy, he grins. "Sally. Dear, dear Sally, it's wonderful having you home. I've rather missed your company."

"Good to be home, Master." Sally smiles and doesn't flinch

when he embraces her.

When Shashenka gives Sally a kiss, Eliza is unable to turn away. Her mouth hangs agape and she shudders. She has barely recovered from the revulsion when he glances at her after releasing Sally.

"Join Eliza on the divan—and leave the cushion in the middle for me, my dear."

His smile appears more genuine when he greets Alexander and Dmitri. "Gentlemen, I trust your stay in Big Sky was enjoyable."

"As always, Master," Alexander replies, inclining his head. "We achieved our goals."

"Yes, yes, we'll discuss business later. Just enjoy your week here, Alexander. You'll be back on assignment next week."

The smile drops from Shashenka's face as Dmitri's body goes rigid. "Honestly, Dmitri, I thought by now you'd be getting over being mad at me."

"Begging your pardon, Master, I mean no disrespect."

Everything about Dmitri is screaming disrespect, hate, and fear, and Shashenka, contrary to his words, seems to be relishing the way he makes him squirm. The difference in their stature makes Eliza almost laugh at the absurdity. Dmitri exudes power and strength. Shashenka, over a half-foot shorter, is so slight by comparison, he looks weak. Then Shashenka reaches out, takes him roughly by the arm—Dmitri winces—and leads him to the chair near the blond man. Humor is gone; her anger is building. *Get your filthy mitts off him!*

She has to do something to stop this torment. "This ... this place is beautiful, gorgeous. It's very welcoming and comfortable."

It works to draw Shashenka's attention away from Dmitri. "I knew you'd find it to your liking, sweet Eliza."

Shashenka's strides are catlike as he comes toward the couch. He perches on the cushion, his body angled toward Eliza. Now she understands why he placed Dmitri in the chair closest to the left of the couch; it allows him to watch Dmitri's reactions while he engages her in conversation. *He's not acting this way toward the others, why Dmitri? It doesn't make sense that my escape should cause this level of animosity.*

"Yes, I do like it." She realizes she almost forgot to respond.

He pouts, patting her leg. "I thought that after all that unpleasantness in Montana and at Big Sky, you might like a few days to enjoy yourself."

No one else is trying to join the conversation or even talk among themselves. Shashenka's ego and vanity clearly demand the full attention of those around him. She holds no doubt now; he is the cause of everything that has been happening to her.

Shashenka shoots Dmitri a spiteful look. "I'll have Dmitri take you to see the Arecibo Observatory tomorrow. Its dish is spectacular in the moonlight."

Dmitri stiffens, and Eliza sees the first opportunity to step between them. "Master, if you don't mind, I'd rather not ruin this vacation by accompanying him anywhere. I find him less than enjoyable to be around."

Shashenka laughs. "So direct." Then his eyes narrow. "Such directness can be refreshing, but easily unbecoming if used too often. Don't you think so, sweet Eliza?"

She catches the veiled threat. *Two can play that game. How adept are you at catching barbs in return?* "Yes, even boorish when overdone."

The pout returns. "True, so true. Perhaps I will not bore you with Dmitri's unfit company while we're here. He is churlishly moody and irritable, after all."

Shashenka, zero; me, one. Pleased, Eliza smiles, realizing Shashenka is intelligent, but not immune to being outwitted.

Suddenly a mechanical noise rumbles through the house, and the metal shades descend from the ceiling. *Sunrise.* Eliza wonders if they're automatically triggered by a certain level of natural light. Then she sees the witch, Maria, descending the staircase and speculates that she must have activated them. *I didn't realize the witch came too.*

She isn't sure how to feel about Maria. Eliza recalls the warning she gave about appearances, but now that they are in Shashenka's presence, the shift in Maria's demeanor is subtle, yet drastic. Watching her now is like looking at her for the first time; her bearing is nowhere near the same as it was at Big Sky. It leaves Eliza even more clueless as to how integral Maria is to Shashenka's power, other than protecting him or doing his bidding.

After Maria warmly greets everyone, including Eliza, Shashenka directs orders to all of them. "It is getting late in the morning. Alexander, Leonard, and Charles, you may go to your rooms on the second floor. Dmitri, you're to stay in the room at the west end of the hall on the third floor."

As the men stand, he continues. "Maria, will you show Sally to the room next to yours? I'll escort Eliza to her room in a few minutes—we have a few matters to settle.

"Afterward I'll fetch you," he says to Sally. "I've missed the pleasure of your company."

A chorus of "Yes, Master" comes from the group as each of them comply with his commands.

As everyone leaves the room, Dmitri pauses at the foot of the stairs to look at Eliza. She sees a surge of emotion on his face, but it's subtle, and he's clearly trying to hide it.

Shashenka's jaw flexes. "I didn't invite you to stay, Dmitri, but if it interests you so much, then I can surely invite you to watch when I take Eliza to my bed later."

Did he really just say that? Not going to happen, you crass, pompous piece of shit.

Dmitri's hands begin to shake. "That won't be necessary, Master. I've seen quite enough of this whore. I was merely curious if she will please you or need another lesson in learning her place."

"Oh, I'm certain she will please me quite well."

Poor Dmitri turns and races up the staircase. Shashenka's grating laugh now sounds malevolent; although the master feigns charm and warmth, Eliza is just beginning to learn how deceptive and detestable he is. *What else has Dmitri suffered?* She will take Shashenka down, but his ruthless cunning will be a daunting challenge. Advancing her plans will take the utmost caution and diligence.

"Now, dear, let's discuss your proposal."

"Excuse me?"

"Alexander relayed your desire to have Sally prepare you for the inner lair."

Seeing that I don't have a choice. "Oh, that. Yes." Pushing against revulsion, she playfully pouts. "I want to serve and please you, Master. Dmitri is so hostile, rude, pigheaded, and arrogant that even the sound of his voice grates on my nerves. I'd rather not be around him at all."

Amusement flickers over his face. "I didn't realize he'd been so dreadful toward you, but as much as I'd like to give you what you ask, I cannot remove Dmitri fully from your presence."

Her hope simultaneously shines and dims. "But you will not force him to finish my training?"

"No, of course not." The puckish grin returns to Shashenka's face. "I'd already decided that before you arrived."

"Thank you, Master." Eliza bows her head, mimicking what she has seen the others do.

"I will allow you the privacy of your room tonight." He pauses as if gauging her reaction. "Tomorrow Sally will prepare you for the rest of your stay here and begin some of your training. When we return to Novgorod, she will complete your training within two nights and have you ready to serve by the third. Is that acceptable to you?"

Try the complete opposite of acceptable. Given Shashenka's ego, though, she understands he sees this decision as a great kindness, a gift. "It pleases me, Master. Thank you."

Watching him rise to his feet, Eliza decides his short stature and nasty temperament aren't impish at all—something cute, adorable, or even lovable in her mind—no, he's a goblin, a repulsive goblin king. *And I have no choice but to let that slimeball touch me.* He extends an arm for her, and when she stands and takes it, he leads her toward the staircase.

"I'll show you to your room and say goodnight."

He keeps an arm around her waist as they climb the stairs to the third floor. At the top she sees five doors, three on one side and two on the other; Shashenka guides her to the middle room on the wall with three doors. He leaves the door open while they enter, and quickly explains what she'll find in her bath and bedroom. Then he grabs her by the waist and pulls her in for a kiss. It is repugnant—too soft, wet, and sloppy—and leaves Eliza fighting the urge to pull away and throw up.

Not enough mouthwash in the world to take that taste out of my mouth. Instead she forces her arms to wrap around him and presses her body into his. Shashenka gasps in excitement and his hands leave her waist, groping her body. Then he regains control of himself and pulls away.

Breathlessly he says, "Your eagerness quite suits me, sweet Eliza." He shrugs. "I did, however, promise you tonight alone. It appears we both have some preparing to do for tomorrow morning, or your passion will be my undoing."

You have no idea, you son of a bitch. Fluttering her eyelashes, she teases him some more. "It's wonderful to know I can please you. I look forward to tomorrow morning, Master."

Shashenka looks stunned, as if a woman being the physical aggressor is something new. Maybe she can use that to her advantage.

"Goodnight, Master."

"Goodnight, sweet Eliza."

CHAPTER 30: DMITRI

Nine Levels of Hell

Rerouting the group to Arecibo was another dig at Dmitri. The master knows he and Elizabetta often spent time off from their Druzhina duties there, although Elizabetta has no memory of it now. When Dmitri said the observatory and lighthouse were his two favorite places, he meant they were theirs. Their last visit together was long before the observatory or lighthouse were built, but those locations were among their favorite places on the island. The mountain the radio telescope sits on is one of the best in the world for watching the night sky and stargazing. The shoreline, near where the lighthouse stands, was a place they often enjoyed taking walks or making love.

Will I ever know the feel of her again? Will she ever rediscover our bond?

He expects a long, unpleasant week ahead, and so far it is following that trajectory. First, the roughness of the road and Jacob's driving forced him to endure accidental contact with Sally when they left Big Sky. The emotional hurt was worse; the hundred questions from both women and his spat with Elizabetta on the plane left him feeling unsettled. Seeing Shashenka touch and flirt with Elizabetta just to spite him was so enraging that it was all he could do to act with loathing toward her and not his master. Finally, his master's suggestion that Dmitri watch his mate subject herself to another proves it will be one of the worst weeks of his existence. It's just another way Shashenka torments him—insulting the higher principles and morals Dmitri has always kept.

Which is easier, cutting my eyes, heart, or tongue out? She's never going to forgive me.

Within a few minutes of retiring to his room, he hears Elizabetta and Shashenka's muffled voices through the wall; though the bedrooms are mostly soundproof, a vampire's exceptional hearing still picks up some sound. That explains why he isn't in the usual room on the second floor. *Ah yes, another lovely week in paradise hell.*

If there were controls for the window shutters in each room, Dmitri would raise his and let the sun end his miserable life. Unfortunately there are no manual controls, and the shutters magnetically seal tightly against the edges of the window. Even his inhuman strength can't force them apart enough that he can wedge his body between them—he knows, he tried.

When it finally becomes quiet, Dmitri gets off the bed and approaches the wall between their bedrooms. There is little noise; he assumes Elizabetta is exploring her room, and then he hears the water running in her private shower. He keeps listening, merging memories with imagination of her every move, until she goes to bed.

Sleep eludes him, and he spends the day staring at the ceiling, tormenting thoughts filling each moment. He's not looking forward to tonight; he doesn't want to bear witness to the destruction of his mate. To him, that is the end result for successfully completing Elizabetta's reprogramming.

When the evening begins, the small house staff has eight humans seated at the dining table—Shashenka typically holds one of these debauched affairs weekly. The humans, however, are unknowingly consuming their last dinner. It's a typical ploy: send out phony invitations and offers for deals too good to be true, and bring the fools to him. Worse is that frequent feeding is a choice, not a need, for vampires. A single, full feeding sustains their kind for four to six months, but Shashenka enjoys wielding his power and insists on these weekly snacks. It's gluttony, senseless murder.

Once the visiting members of the Belyakov coven gather in the music room, Shashenka leads them to the dining room, and the vampires move behind the low-back chairs of each person. These orchestrated events are routine, and by Elizabetta's actions, Dmitri assumes someone told her what to expect before she came downstairs. He doesn't want to look at her, but she has taken a position directly opposite him.

The nasal, almost whiny tone of Shashenka's voice is sickening. His warm, eager smile doubtless has the humans believing a happy and wonderful evening lies ahead, when in actuality the monster is salivating over his dinner.

Then Shashenka asks the humans to close their eyes to receive a surprise gift. When they comply, he nods once, and

each vampire steps forward and restrains a human while biting into their neck. The shrieks and open eyes of horror last
only a couple minutes. In silence the vampires exit the room,
leaving the drained bodies slumped in the chairs; the locals
will dispose of the corpses.

In the living room, Shashenka dispenses with business
first. He assigns Sally to spend the next few hours preparing
Elizabetta for the day ahead. Leonard, Charles, and Alexander are free to do whatever they choose the rest of the week.
He orders Maria to return in two to three hours, claiming he
needs time for some local business. Dmitri, he says, is to remain here.

After the others leave, Shashenka has Dmitri follow him
to the study. "Close the door. I wish to speak with you privately."

"Yes, Master." He shuts the door, steals a moment to prepare, and turns to face the monster he despises.

"Sit down ... really, Dmitri. This will take a few minutes."
Shashenka smiles as if they are friends.

They have never been friends, and if Dmitri had known
what being a Druzhina for the vilest of all creatures had
meant, he would never have given Vladimir acceptance to
change him.

"Alexander tells me you did very well in Big Sky as far as
securing the return of Eliza to us. It seems there was a problem, however, with you finishing your task. I want to hear in
your words what happened."

Dmitri rattles off the facts, remembering to sound loathing. "The spell Maria cast helped me regain control of Eliza

so I could finish her programming. While I successfully claimed control, the bitch resisted and rejected the commands to be a courtesan."

Scowling, Shashenka asks for clarification. Dmitri takes a breath and continues. "Eliza would argue and refuse. We couldn't progress on that single point. Everything else went fine."

"And you had full control each time this happened?"

"Yes, Master."

"I'll have to discuss this problem with Maria later. It's not an issue I want to see happen again." A lascivious smirk spreads across Shashenka's face. "At least it appears breaking Eliza was successful. Tell me about it."

The subject is grotesquely uncomfortable for Dmitri, and it takes a minute for him to form a sufficiently loathing version to tell. "I entered her room. She fought back. She struggled, screamed, and cursed until I gained control, pinned the whore to the bed, and forced her to my will. It only took one round to break the bitch." *No, what I did was worse than that.* "She curled up and bawled for hours."

"Yes, Alexander reported it was fast, and relayed what he saw when you finished." Raising an eyebrow, Shashenka adds, "I must compliment you ... well done. It's almost too bad that we won't be adding more concubines in the near future—you'd be perfect for getting them in line."

When Dmitri doesn't respond to the nauseating statement, he says, "Between that and programming her to feel worthless and unloved, you did a fine job snapping her will in half. In fact, it seems she's wholly resigned to being an inner lair concubine now, and there's not a shred of fight in her. Her eagerness to please me so quickly last night was refreshing."

The thought sickens him, but given his hatred for Shashenka, it is easy to keep his tone disgusted. "Yes, Master, I believe she is. I'm sure she'll be a fine whore, a good addition for you."

"I do fear that you've left out at least one detail. Why is that?"

The evil monster looks genuinely curious. Confused, Dmitri searches for, but can't find anything missing from his story. "I'm sorry, Master—I do not understand. That is all that happened."

"Are you sure?" He chuckles, looking amused. "What about your physical pain? You mention nothing of it, yet Alexander tells me you tried to bleed yourself dry afterward because of it. Then ironically, Eliza saved your worthless hide ..." He's laughing hard and it takes a minute for him to finish. "Only because she's hoping for a chance to kill you."

The physical pain is nothing in comparison to what I've done to her. Dmitri looks down in shame and confusion. Remarkably, Alexander distorted the truth and didn't reveal the real reason behind the attempted suicide. Surely he knew that Dmitri hadn't wanted to live with what he'd done to Elizabetta? "The unbearable pain is something I have to cope with every time someone touches me."

He briefly looks at Shashenka and shifts his focus down to the desk between them. "It greatly interfered with the pleasure of Sally's company, and in breaking that bitch, Eliza, with the way she struggled against me. Her anger is why I complied with her demands and drank those humans. Her death threat enrages me. That whore will have one hellacious fight on her hands if she tries." Dmitri's lies are smooth, polished, and his sneer makes them more convincing.

"Go on."

"I understand that it will not please you, Master, to keep complaining about the pain. I'm resigned to live with it." That part is at least true.

Looking smug, even pleased, Shashenka gives a dismissive wave. "Yes, well, about that, I've made a few decisions in those regards. First, I have ordered Maria to remove the pain spell. While I found it amusing for a while, it is boring me to hear other people constantly complain about it. I've also instructed Maria to remove the loathing spell." He watches for Dmitri's reaction.

Dmitri feigns ignorance. "Loathing spell, Master?"

"Yes." Shashenka's expression is a mask of hatred. "I will never tire of punishing you, and I need Eliza on my side to do that. Maria placed a loathing spell on you to help things along, and it appears to have worked beautifully. While you falsely accepted a growing hatred for Eliza, it planted the seeds for her to hate you. I will have years of pleasure watching her reject you."

Biting back a retort, Dmitri decides to play it up with disbelief. "No ... no. I hate that whore. She disgusts me. I don't know why I ever loved her in the first place. I find everything about her vile and repulsive."

"Oh yes, I'm certain you think you do. See? The spell

worked perfectly, and once it's removed you will fully feel her repudiation of you, while your true feelings suffer her wrath." He tosses his head back in another full-throated laugh. When he finally stops, his tone turns businesslike. "Others have reported the bickering and quarreling going on between you, and that will become tiresome to watch every day if you both believe the lies."

Dmitri hangs his head at the truth of that last statement; everything about Elizabetta is a lie now. The worst of it is that she will never know.

Looking up, he sees that Shashenka's eyes are hard and cold and a spiteful smile is on his face. "It's my opinion that Eliza's dislike of you has taken strong enough root that you will not weed it out of her, regardless of how you feel or act toward her."

A lump Dmitri can't swallow is threatening to choke him. He struggles to keep his expression neutral.

"Lastly, I am assigning you as personal servant for Maria and the courtesans of the inner lair." Shashenka is clearly enjoying himself. "You will see after their needs. Escort them when they shop, protect them in public, report problems, and resolve disputes between them. You will, however, not be allowed to touch any of them. Their affections are off-limits to you."

Shock and contempt leave Dmitri speechless and fighting the urge to kill the man where he sits. Shashenka prompts the praise he's looking for. "Does this please you?"

No, no, it doesn't ... only your death will please me. "Yes, Master, thank you. Thank you." Knowing the monster seeks assurance, Dmitri adds, "I will not disappoint you again."

"Good. After Maria removes the spells, go enjoy the island tonight. I'll expect you to remain at the girls' disposal the rest of the week." He watches as Dmitri rises from the chair. "Oh, I almost forgot about your time off. I'll give you what the courtesans receive, ten days for every four weeks of service. That is all—you may go, Dmitri."

He leaves the study, feeling drained. Although there is some good news, getting rid of the cursed pain, the bad news is a new invisible shackle. He honestly doesn't know how to cope with seeing Elizabetta every night. The opportunity he's waited centuries for is finally here, but after the damage he's done to her, it may be too late. That, combined with her new role, one he doesn't want to watch, is enough to destroy them both.

If there are nine levels of hell, surely this is one of them.

Maria is sitting in the living room and smiles when she sees him. Clearly Shashenka has already informed the witch about the removal of the spells. Dmitri is still trying to figure her out; she's back to acting as she always has around Shashenka, as if nothing has changed. Rising from the chair, she lays a book on the coffee table and asks Dmitri to follow her. She leads him past the pool and doesn't speak until they reach the gazebo in the garden. After Dmitri sits on the bench opposite her, Maria finally says, "It will only take a moment to release the spell."

Her Irish accent colors the Latin incantation, making it

sound mystical. When she quiets, Dmitri feels no different than he did a moment ago. Then Maria grabs his hands, pulls him to his feet, and fiercely hugs him. "I'm so sorry you had to endure that horrendous spell. It's a relief finally to remove it. I don't think I could have withstood watching you suffer it daily at the inner lair."

At the relief of feeling nothing but the pressure of physical contact, Dmitri is nearly at a loss to process the normal sensations running through his body. When he does, he pulls Maria into a tight hug. He had resigned himself to living with the curse for the rest of his existence, embraced it even as a penance for what he's doing to Elizabetta. *Perhaps one day it will be Elizabetta's touch I welcome again.* "God, thank you, Maria. You have no idea how wonderful this feels."

She starts laughing. "It doesn't take much to please you these days."

For the first time since he can't remember when, he laughs heartily. When their laughter dies down, he asks if she knows what's expected of him when he serves the inner lair. Sitting on a bench together, they discuss the duties, the atmosphere, and the rotating schedule the courtesans have for time off. She also gives him tips on Shashenka's habits, so Dmitri can avoid him as much as possible. When the conversation ends, it leaves him feeling slightly better about surviving and working the inner lair.

Afterward Dmitri spends most of the night alone near the observatory in his and Elizabetta's favorite spot. He misses her presence, but then he thinks of the time they'll be spending together in the months and years ahead, and cringes. Maria clarified that the four-week work cycle is actually a twenty-eight-day work period; the women's ten days off are staggered to ensure there are courtesans available at all times. Dmitri plans to time it so his ten days come after Elizabetta's do. He knows it will create a repeating twenty-day period where he won't have to endure watching her daily, leaving only an average of fifteen days each month where their work days overlap. The solution brings apprehension and relief, but somehow he must find a way to live with it.

When day arrives, he receives the first reminder of how daunting this duty will be, especially as long as Shashenka seeks ways to torment him with it. He's drifting off to sleep after sunrise when a thrumming electrical noise pulses and starts broadcasting a passel of sounds—murmurs, groans, moans, the wet slap of ...

Then he distinctly hears Elizabetta's voice. Frantic, he tries to fill his lungs with air, but it gives no reprieve from the constriction in his chest. *No! He's defiling my mate ...* His mind lurches between the desire to storm her room and rescue her, and the knowledge that he must not—he's powerless to stop it. Dmitri flies off the bed, hunting the source of the sound, and finds a baby monitor tucked next to a back leg of the dresser.

Does his cruelty know no bounds? It's enclosed in a small wire cage, a padlock on its latch, with a note on top: "Dmitri—Do Not Touch." The cage is just large enough and the mesh so tightly woven that there is no way to slide the power switch or adjust the volume control knob without breaking the lock. If he does that, Shashenka will know he violated the order not to touch it.

Dmitri traces the power cord, hoping to unplug it, and discovers Shashenka expected him to try to silence the monitor. The monster drilled a hole through the wall; the plug end of the cord goes into the next room and is siliconed in place. It must be plugged into an outlet in Elizabetta's room. *That dirty, rotten bastard.* The volume is just loud enough to ensure that Dmitri hears everything, but low enough that Elizabetta won't hear the echo of it in her room through the mostly soundproof bedroom walls.

Leaving the room is probably impossible; the locals, no doubt, are under orders to report if he's out of his bedroom all day. The short legs on the dresser prevent him from stuffing thick pillows around it. *There has to be something ... some way ... I can't think.* The sounds coming from the unit are already driving him into a rage. He can hear their conversation, laughter, the groans of the bed frame, and every sucking or slurping noise they make. He flies into the bathroom, grabs a couple of towels, and wraps them around the baby monitor. It stifles but doesn't block the sounds coming from her room. He pulls the pillows over his head, squeezing them against his ears as the muffled moans and grunts start again.

Stop, make it stop. This is killing me, make it stop! Dmitri thought the five hundred years separated from Elizabetta were torture, but this is much, much worse. When the noises from Elizabetta's room finally cease, it's slightly more than an hour before sunset. It has been the longest day he's ever known, and given the almost seven hundred years he's existed, this is something extraordinarily rare. His heart is shattering in ways he never dreamed possible.

The moment the sun sets and the shutters retract, he speeds out of the house to the pool room, changes into a pair of swimming trunks, and dives into the pool. It's the best he can do, since duty binds him to be on call for the women. He'd rather run into the hills of Arecibo and not come back until predawn.

The next three days are a repeat of the day before; trapped in his room, Dmitri desperately tries not to listen to what's happening in Elizabetta's room. Then inexplicably, the fifth and sixth days are quiet, and he feels grateful for it. For the first time in centuries, he's looking forward to going to Novgorod, if for no other reason than to get away from here. Shashenka will not be able to pull the same stunt at the castle. The courtesans' rooms are separate from the other living quarters, so at least he'll have that distance from her.

On the day of their departure, Dmitri rises in the late afternoon to help the women finish their last-minute packing. It's a relief that Elizabetta apparently finished hers before going to bed that morning; he doesn't have to help her.

Shashenka's private jet and pilot will meet them at the airport an hour after twilight. When the limousine arrives to take them to the airport, Dmitri sits as far from Elizabetta and Shashenka as he can manage. Sally sits nearest him and prattles on about the wonderful time she's had in Arecibo. He tries to be polite, but he is ill tempered. The long car ride and the flight to Novgorod border on unbearable.

CHAPTER 31: ELIZA

History and Future

The week in Arecibo is a grueling marathon course in the art of deception. Sally prepares Eliza well for what Shashenka expects, likes, and allows. It also helps that Eliza's isolated life led to her reading scores of books, some in the romance genre; it makes her role easier to adapt to while fighting back the bile that rises during Shashenka's frequent kisses and touches. Still, there are moments when Eliza feels unsure of succeeding at or even surviving their first encounter.

Fortunately Sally also explained his sexual fetishes—most romance novels never mention such bizarre proclivities—leaving her less shocked, but no less sickened when they finally occur. Eliza shudders at the thought of Shashenka's repulsive touch; losing her virginity to such a vile creature is degrading. *I'm never going to feel clean again.* Her dreams and fantasies have always pictured someone caring, kind, compassionate, and loving, someone with tenderness ... *Someone who looks like Dmitri.* She'd even take Matt—

regardless of how wrong it felt between them—over the ... the disgusting goblin king.

She spends her limited free hours each evening with Sally and Maria, and has been pleasantly surprised to find she likes the witch. When the two women mention Dmitri, both speak well and protectively of him, unwittingly raising Eliza's respect for them. Still, Maria confuses her, especially the witch's connection with the pain spell. Why would she openly acknowledge doing that to him? Everyone acts like it's common knowledge, but what purpose did it serve? If Dmitri's suffering upset the witch so much, then why did she place such a cruel spell on him? It's a riddle Eliza intends to solve.

On the fifth morning, before Shashenka arrives in her room, Eliza is unwinding the twisted braid her hair is in when she carelessly drops the hair stick on the dresser. It falls off, hits the floor, and rolls underneath. She's kneeling to find it when a small white box near the dresser leg catches her eye. It takes a moment before she realizes it is the listening half of a baby monitor system. *What is this doing here? Vampires don't need these things.*

Eliza searches for the control end of the unit and can't find it. Then she realizes a cord goes through the wall into Dmitri's room, and she assumes the missing monitor is in there. She notices it is plugged in behind the decorative floor vase that's partly covering it from view. *Dmitri wouldn't do this. He's not sick, twisted, or perverted.*

But Shashenka is. Clearly the master is tormenting Dmitri with the intimate sounds coming from her bedroom each day.

Humiliated and outraged, Eliza rips the cord out of the socket. *You filthy, disgusting, maggot-infested slimeball. What's next, set up a camera and live-stream it?* She can only imagine what Dmitri heard and must think. *God, I'll never be able to look him in the eyes again.* This stunt raises her hatred and contempt for Shashenka to a new level, and it exposes what she's facing as a concubine in the Belyakov coven. It's an effort for her not to confront the nasty little goblin king when he arrives minutes later.

When Shashenka finally falls asleep, Eliza's thoughts return to Dmitri. She's seen little of him, and the few times they have interacted, his suddenly cordial attitude toward her has been disturbing. She has no idea what brought about the change, but doubts the removal of the pain spell is behind it. Then she considers the baby monitor—would it cause Dmitri to feel embarrassed enough for her that he would treat her better? For whatever reason, the rude, cantankerous disposition is gone, and in its place is an unsettling caring familiarity. He uses the word *"love"* in almost every sentence when he addresses her. Thinking back, she realizes that he's done so since their encounter at the warehouse. He doesn't use endearments for Sally or Maria. Why her and not them?

Unfortunately for him, Eliza has been continuing her sarcasm, insults, and threats. Each time she hurls one at him, she sees the weight of it on his face and feels monstrous. There's no way to tell Dmitri why she's doing it, and part of her wishes that he had continued acting atrociously toward her; it would make the situation easier, although no less painful.

If it weren't the only way to protect him from Shashenka, she'd be begging for his forgiveness. But the more she comes to know the others, the more she feels certain she is doing the right thing. It's imperative to shield him from the one thing—her—that Shashenka most delights in using against him. Instinctually, she knows protecting him is central in securing the inner circle against the goblin king.

If her uprising against Shashenka is successful, she will apologize to Dmitri and seek his forgiveness afterward. Until then, she must strive to act as intolerably as possible toward him. *Will freedom pay the debt I'll owe him after being so cruel?*

The stay in Arecibo has also given Eliza the opportunity to start learning about Shashenka and the way he runs the coven. Both Sally and Maria are providing a copious amount of information about Novgorod, far more than she expected this early in her plans. According to what they've told her, the Belyakov coven lives in one of the few remaining ancient castles. Astoundingly, it is open to public tours, with the public's movement through the castle tightly controlled. Anyone who sneaks past the barriers or takes a wrong turn disappears forever. The public sees what Shashenka wants them to see, and given what is lurking in the depths behind the castle walls, he doesn't show much.

Eliza finds the history of the castle and city engrossing. Novgorod is one of the oldest places in Russia, its history rich and colorful. It served as a merchant trade route early on; in fact, as a human, Shashenka worked the trade routes until he crossed paths with a Viking vampire and was turned. After learning all he needed from his master, he slew the older vampire and took possession of the castle in the twelfth century. It was then that their coven's history began. Shashenka's rule, continual brutality against his own, has made him more feared than respected.

The human rulers were not free from his wrath, either. Eliza's perception of recorded history shifts and leaves her aghast after she hears about one particular incident. It also gives her another glimpse into the goblin king's mind.

According to Maria, Shashenka succeeded in murdering the great historic prince, Alexander Nevsky. Through a series of bribes, threats, and a half-dozen murders, Shashenka aided the prince's rise to power; the man never knew about the trail of blood and corruption behind his success. Shashenka became enraged a decade later when Prince Alexander unwittingly went against his interests and allied with the Golden Horde. Shashenka dispatched the Druzhina to intercept the prince returning from a meeting with the Golden Horde in Sarai. They subdued and wiped the memories of the prince's guards, and presented him an offer: accept being turned, serving Shashenka and retaining his own rule for a few more decades, or perish. One of the Druzhinas—they never revealed whom, according to Maria—injected their venom into the prince and gave him three days to decide.

Vampire venom is poisonous to a human body, and unless neutralized by vampire blood—permanently setting the changed DNA and allowing the transformation to vampire to complete—within seventy-two hours, the person experiences a slow, miserable, painful death. Prince Alexander was a pious man and a moral leader; he refused to drink the blood when the Druzhinas returned for his answer. They left him to suffer a terrible death, and history recorded only his legendary contributions and his untimely end.

Keep talking, girls. Unknowingly, Sally and Maria are giving Eliza the details she needs to understand Shashenka and end his rule. They are also revealing kernels of useful insight on certain members of the Druzhina, whom she'd rather co-opt than kill when the time comes.

Trying to uncover more information about the Druzhinas, Eliza presses for their current numbers. "So, there are eleven Druzhinas then?" From the names Maria listed, two seem to be missing.

"Yes, but Dmitri lost his position with them when you escaped to your wolf friend." Maria smiles apologetically.

She tenses and blinks at the reminder of Matt, and immediately shuts down the unwanted and horrible thoughts and tries to refocus on the Druzhinas. *With Dmitri included, that's ten ...* "Who's the eleventh?"

Without seeming to think, Maria contradicts her earlier statement. "No, there are only ten, the ones I told you about."

Number eleven, the mystery guest. Will I learn who it is after we arrive in Russia? Not wanting to draw suspicion, Eliza changes the subject. "Novgorod sounds like an enchanting city. I think that I'd like to see some of the historical places when I finally get time off."

Concealing her true intent, the insurrection and escape

she is planning, Eliza listens patiently as Sally describes local cathedrals, castles, and churches and her favorite late-night shopping and dance clubs.

"I can show you if our nights off overlap." Excitement bubbles in every word Sally says.

"I'd like that, thanks, Sally." Eliza smiles. "Would you like to go, Maria?"

Maria declines, offering another valuable tidbit of information. "I never know what duties Shashenka will expect from me when I'm there. I don't work the same as you. I serve your master, but I am not subject to him in the same manner as those in his coven. My alliance with him requires me to meet certain obligations; beyond that, my time is my own."

Then the next Dmitri hurdle Eliza faces arrives: the flight to Novgorod. Fortunately it's less chaotic than when they left Big Sky. Seated in the jet's cabin, everyone quietly waits for the aircraft to take off. Sally, sitting near Dmitri, reaches for his hand and smiles. Eliza watches as he squeezes it, smiles back, lets go, and returns his hand to his lap. Another pang of irrational jealousy shoots through her, and she looks out the window, trying to push the thought away.

"Master, I want to take Eliza to see the Kremlin tomorrow. May Dmitri escort us?" Sally is batting her eyelashes; Eliza rolls her eyes.

Shashenka scolds her. "That's wolf territory, Sally."

"Yes, I know, and that's why Dmitri needs to go with us." She pouts. "Please, Master."

Relenting, Shashenka taunts Dmitri. "You'd best go with

them. Return Eliza's weapons to her, and Sally, make sure you go armed as well. I don't want to lose either of you lovely ladies to a wolf."

Eliza flushes at the unexpected reminder of Josh's pack and Matt. For a moment her heart constricts with the memories and the loss. She misses the chance to complain about Dmitri going along.

"Yes, Master." Dmitri gives Sally a cold look.

Smiling triumphantly, Sally says, "It'll be fun. Besides, it's the only chance for Eliza to see something before we resume working. Speaking of, do you know which days you'll take as your first time off, Dmitri?"

"I haven't decided. I thought I'd wait to see what rotations the women are in before I settle into a routine." His tone is stoic.

Shashenka says coolly, "That won't be necessary, Dmitri. I expect you to take the same days as Eliza for your rotations."

Eliza grinds her teeth. *Crap, so not helping me.* It's obvious from Dmitri's reaction that he's not pleased either. At least that is good news to her; it means her offensive attitude is pushing him away, even if he's had a change of heart about her.

"Dmitri!" Shashenka snaps his fingers to gain his attention.

Eliza almost gasps at the intensity smoldering in Dmitri's eyes when he turns toward their master.

Shashenka doesn't seem to notice; his tone is jovial. "You'll have new permanent quarters. I'll have the pilot radio a message ahead to Peter, and it will be ready for you when we arrive."

Eliza hopes that it is far from hers. Dmitri only nods, and no one says a word. The awkward silence that keeps settling among them is making the trip to Novgorod unbearably long. Making another effort to disrupt it, Eliza looks at Maria. Perhaps she can get the witch talking again; it doesn't matter if it's chitchat or has substance, Eliza needs to focus on something other than Dmitri's black mood. "Your historical knowledge of Novgorod is great, but I was wondering if you would mind taking me sometime on a tour of your favorite places of the past. I'd love to hear the history as you know it."

"Let us get settled and see what our schedules look like first. We'll be here at least the next three months, and there'll be plenty of time to take in the sights."

Eliza has no idea where they will go after Novgorod; there's no pattern to Shashenka's rotation of estates, at least none she's aware of yet. From what she understands, he is unpredictable and may transfer them on a whim to one of the other estates. The most time the inner lair spends in one location is roughly 90 to 120 days. At places like Big Sky and Arecibo, the stays are often one or two weeks—mere vacations or holidays, as Shashenka and many of the others refer to them. His three favored places to stay with the inner lair are the castle in Novgorod, the estate in Prague, and the villa in Venice. The remaining estates fill the time, often between transfers to or from Shashenka's top three.

The unpredictable relocations will make it difficult, but not impossible for her to go forward with her plans. Still, she'll need to be ready to adapt rapidly, or she'll be at risk of failure. Trying to remain optimistic, Eliza is at least looking forward to seeing all of them, if for no other reason than to travel and visit new countries. She hopes that each location will provide something useful for her plan to overthrow Shashenka.

Sally is again prattling on, and her favorite target for discussion is Dmitri. "Which estate is your favorite?"

"For holiday or work?" he asks, sounding uninterested.

"Both." She gushes enthusiastically about the perks—free use of the estate jets and no lodging costs—that come with taking a holiday at an estate not currently occupied by the inner lair.

Eliza's trying not to pay attention, but cannot keep herself from grabbing for each word parting his lips. *I'd like to part those lips.* Sometimes she can't believe her own thoughts, but worse, she knows it's true. Keeping her eyes on the nighttime horizon through the plane's window, she listens and pretends not to hear.

"Going on holiday at Arecibo was one of my favorites in the past," he says, and it increases her curiosity about him. "Venice and Cusco are my next favorites. They are—were— important to someone I love."

She catches the stumble in his response and notices Shashenka's glare, followed by Sally darting glances between Dmitri and her. It happens frequently when Dmitri is talking, as if he's revealed something that Eliza should, but doesn't know. It only deepens the mystery surrounding her life since his strange appearance in it. She is certain that Dmitri knows more than he's willing to admit, and when she destroys Shashenka, she intends to find out. Combining that with what she's seen in Arecibo, she is equally convinced that Shashenka is the driving force behind these strange occurrences.

Evidently bored with Sally's chatter, Shashenka takes Eliza to the private suite at the back of the jet. She spends the rest of the flight submitting to his sexual perversions, and they are late in exiting the plane after it lands. Everyone else is already waiting in the limousine. It's not nearly as bad as spying on her with a baby monitor, but it is bad enough. *It's humiliating that everyone knows what I do behind closed doors.*

They begin their drive through Novgorod to the castle. Arriving after dark allows Eliza to catch glimpses of the nightlife in the city as the car cruises past it. Whatever she expected, it wasn't this. There are many people out enjoying the pubs, casinos, and cinemas or theaters, and there appear to be bands playing to large parties that spill into the streets. To Eliza's relief the city's distractions, along with the quiet ride to the estate, allow her to keep her face toward a window and not look at Dmitri.

The crowds thin, and she notices they are driving alongside a river. Then the outline of the castle rises out of the dark. Maria told her that it is located on the southern end of the city, and well north of Lake Ilmen, near the Volkhov River, but Eliza is unprepared for how the city falls away from it almost as if it is shunned and isolated. The rest of the castle finally looms into view, with several cupolas of various heights standing sentinel against the night sky. Eliza cranes her neck back while taking in the height of the castle walls as the car passes through the gatehouse. The castle is stunningly impressive, in architecture and history, and still she shudders to think of the horrors contained within its walls. *Welcome to Dracula's castle, where I have no future and life dead ends.* Then the familiar prickling sensation of a memory that's out of reach teases her mind. *Why does it feel like I've been here before?*

The car stops at a side entrance. Shashenka offers Eliza his arm to lead her inside. The corridors are dank, gloomy, and lit with lights in sconces designed to look like torches; it is a step back in time, but for the modern amenities. After passing through a series of halls, they enter a large interior chamber—the great hall, Eliza learns—with many passageways leading from it. Her elusive memories seem to echo and beg for attention. *Is this some serious déjà vu, or have I been here before? This place gives me the creeps.*

Shashenka stops to greet other vampires, all locals serving him. When they pay deference and welcome their master and his entourage home, she notices a hint of fear in their eyes. Eliza tries to decide whether they will help or hinder her when the time comes. Will fear hold them back or rally them to action?

He dismisses Leonard, Charles, and Sally; they quickly hurry away through the passageways. After barking a few orders to others, he turns to lead Eliza and Dmitri to their quarters, down the same hallway where Sally disappeared.

Stopping in front of a heavy wooden door hung on iron hinges, Shashenka shoves it open and strides into the middle of the room. "This"—he waves—"is your room, Eliza. You'll find it's been upgraded to modern standards, and shares a bathroom with the connecting room. Dmitri, follow us."

In the moment he allows, Eliza takes in her new surroundings. The room is large enough to contain a queen-size bed, wardrobe, dresser, and a dressing table with a mirror. A tall, narrow window, cut through the thick outer wall, provides the only view—an inner courtyard accessible from somewhere within the towering castle walls. Dmitri steps into the room as a local places Eliza's suitcases at the foot of the bed—her bed. Ignoring him, she starts to follow Shashenka into the next room.

Leading them into the bathroom, Shashenka barely pauses long enough for them to look around the small room. There's a toilet, a sink vanity with a mirror, and a tub-shower unit with a narrow floor-to-ceiling cupboard between it and the toilet, but no window; the only light is a row of lamps on a brass plate above the mirror.

Pushing open the adjoining bedroom door, Shashenka steps into a room almost identical to Eliza's. With a flourish he announces, "This, Dmitri, is your room."

Oh hell, no!

Seeing the horrified looks on their faces, Shashenka cackles with laughter. "Now, now, surely you two can put aside your petty differences and share a bathroom." He adds in a snide tone, "Don't worry, dear, Dmitri's room has its own door to the hallway."

Dmitri, clearly well conditioned after years of serving Shashenka, answers immediately, "Yes, Master."

It takes a moment for Eliza to recover from the shock and stammer her own response. "Y-yes, M-master."

Shashenka uses the pouty face he's fond of when chastising and mocking someone. "Let's not have squabbles over whether Eliza leaves her bra and panties on the floor, or her stockings hanging from the shower rod. The same goes for Dmitri not rinsing toothpaste off the sink or leaving the lid up on the toilet."

Eliza's holding a hand over her mouth to hide her gaping, and Dmitri is staring daggers at the floor and breathing hard. She knows that Shashenka set this up to torment Dmitri further; it has very little to do with her. *Why is he doing this? What purpose does it serve?*

Looking at them both, Shashenka laughs. "Good. I'll let you two settle in then." He's walking toward Dmitri's bedroom door when he stops and turns to look at Eliza, a lecherous smile spreading across his face. "I'll expect your company again soon."

When Shashenka leaves the room, they stand rooted to the floor for a horrified minute. Dmitri's eyes lock on hers— they are pleading, searching, apologetic, and hopeful.

Don't look at me like that. Don't fall for it now. Move! Recovering before he does, Eliza storms out of Dmitri's room and into the bathroom. She slams his door behind her, and after passing through hers, slams it too. She collapses on her bed, knowing this is the beginning of a humiliating and degrading life in the Belyakov coven. It will be a test of her endurance to see if she remains sane until she takes Shashenka down, or if she'll go utterly stark, raving mad before she accomplishes it.

Either way, this is her future.

CHAPTER 32: DMITRI

Purgatory

I have passed through the nine gates of hell and have arrived in purgatory. Dmitri stands staring at the bathroom door that Elizabetta just slammed. The limited contact with her in Arecibo was enough for him to conclude that he is no longer her favorite person. Now, with this arrangement—Shashenka ensuring he experiences her growing hatred daily—it's only going to get worse.

After unpacking all his clothing, he tentatively opens the bathroom door—it is empty. He sprints across and locks Elizabetta's door. Knowing her habits and preferences, he takes the bottom drawer for his brush, comb, and colognes, placing them in two neat rows on the left side of the drawer, front to back. His toothbrush and toothpaste go in the holder next to the sink.

He has no shaving kit, one advantage to being a vampire with body and hair frozen in time. He was fortunate to be clean shaven when Vladimir turned him; others with facial hair—stubble, beards, moustaches—must live with it. Cutting their hair or shaving is pointless, as their original appearance regenerates minutes later. His only regret is not getting that haircut he put off the day before he was turned. Centuries later the shaggy mess, falling into his face, still bothers him.

Dmitri checks out the linens and extra towels in the narrow cupboard, then unlocks Elizabetta's door and retreats to his room. He has no urge to wander the halls of this old castle; he's seen too much of its darkest side. Instead he spends a few minutes gazing out at the courtyard, where a few locals are enjoying the night air. Unhooking the drapery tieback, he drops the curtain across the window. The room feels as desolate as his heart. Elizabetta could fill them both, but she stormed out. He longs for the time when it was easier to draw her in—when he could sing to her, or play a song on his violin. Years ago he lost that fine instrument too. *I should buy another violin ... it's been so long since I've played. I wish I knew what happened to it or who took it.*

Stacking the pillows against the headboard, Dmitri reclines and begins to read a book, glad for a way to kill the time. It's only a couple of hours until sunrise but he doubts he'll be able to sleep, knowing a dozen paces and two walls separate him from Elizabetta.

He loses his place when he hears Elizabetta enter the bathroom. He has noticed the lock on his side never engages. Born in an era when people used chamber pots and didn't have locks on most of their doors, if they had interior doors at all, Elizabetta still habitually forgets to lock bathroom doors. *Even after all this time.* He needs to be careful about forgetting the barrier between them and entering while she's in there.

The sound of Elizabetta opening the bathroom drawers redirects his attention. He listens as she places her items in the drawers, and smiles when he hears the bottom drawer slide open; she always starts top to bottom. He knows it must please her to find it tidy, with enough room to store her remaining items.

Perhaps living in a room next to Elizabetta won't be so bad after all. The thought bursts almost as quickly as it forms—he's reclining on a bed that is not hers. *I'll be sleeping alone forever, unless I can turn back her hatred toward me.*

It's late afternoon before Dmitri finally falls asleep, and an unwelcome knock on his door wakes him at twilight. Groggy, he gets up to find Sally is standing there, bouncing on her feet, eager to take Elizabetta on the tour of the Novgorod Kremlin. He promises to meet them in the solar in twenty minutes.

He has mixed feelings about the outing, wanting to be with Elizabetta but not wanting her scorn. *Perhaps this small adventure will be fun. This is my first real chance to make a good impression. I need Elizabetta.*

After a quick shower, he dresses in a pair of black trousers, a button-down shirt, and a leather jacket. He almost forgets to grab Elizabetta's weapons before he leaves the room. She insisted on keeping the sword and knife they found her with, but they're too large to be practical and on display in public. Crossing to her room through the bathroom, he leaves both on her bed; he has a better plan, and a more suitable weapon. Dmitri smiles to himself, recalling the fierce fighter she was before they altered her mind.

He returns to his room and opens a hidden compartment on a travel case. Inside is a ten-inch horse-head dagger with a handle crafted from dark marble jade that is streaked with green and inlaid with gold; the wooden scabbard is wrapped in black leather, with elegant gold-plated throat and drag. Dmitri slides it out and smiles at the delicate embellishment of Elizabetta's mark on the blade. Ovals of matching jade, set on both sides of the sheath, are similarly carved. Dmitri had it custom-made for her before they began her reprogramming. He intended it as a gift to welcome her return to the Druzhina. *She may as well have it now, since that will never happen.*

Sliding the dagger into his waistband, he goes to join the women in the solar. Sally's endless chattering about the city leaves off mid-sentence. Her eyebrows pitch up and she's smiling, saying something he doesn't hear because he's watching Elizabetta's eyes sweep over him and widen. He can't suppress a smile; everyone dresses finer here, forgoing the jeans, T-shirts, and flannel shirts of Montana. *She may hate me, but she can't hide that the attraction is still there.* He takes a moment to appreciate the way the women are dressed, too. Each is wearing slacks, a long-sleeved silk blouse, casual leather shoes, and a lightweight jacket.

"Peter said we should take the red Lada Granta." Sally tosses Dmitri the keys, and he leads them to the garage behind the castle and asks Elizabetta to take the front passenger seat.

Before starting the car, he takes the dagger from his waistband and hands it to her. "You should have a smaller weapon, love." He's waited years for this moment and is surprised by the nervous burst of energy coursing through him—and the worry, concern. While she won't understand the significance, he does, and if she rejects him now, he's not sure that he can stand it.

Scowling, Elizabetta turns it in her hands, inspecting it. He watches and holds his breath as she draws the dagger slowly out of its sheath, but she gasps when she sees the fine embellishment parting and delicately encasing her mark on the blade. A muscle in her cheek twitches as she pushes the blade back into the sheath. "Where did you get this?"

"I had it custom-made for you in India."

"Why?"

To remind you. Dmitri's laugh dies in his throat. "It was to be your welcome-home gift from me, before we decided we were going to hate each other."

Dmitri sees that she's struggling to maintain her composure, and he's not certain if that's a good sign. She starts to hand it back; her hand is trembling, and tears well in her eyes. "I can't accept this. It's too much."

She can't reject it—me. I won't let her. "It's etched with your mark, love. It belongs to you."

"But ... but I can't repay you."

"It's a gift, Eliza, nothing more. Keep it. I insist." To lighten the sudden tension, he says with a smile, "Besides, it suits you better than that bulky Arkansas toothpick you were packing."

Elizabetta drops the dagger in her lap, covers her mouth with her hand, and hurriedly turns her head to look out the passenger window. Dmitri sees a tear rolling down her cheek. He assumes his reminder of the other knife brings back memories of when she last used it, and of her werewolf friend, Matt. As if this wasn't going wrong enough on its own, he's driving nails into their coffin as fast as she hands them to him. *Probably gave her another reason to hate me more. Wait until she learns I have her dagger's twin. She'll kill me ... and probably use it to do so.*

"I'm sorry," he murmurs as he starts the car.

Sally, stone quiet, is staring at him in the rearview mirror, and she looks as if she's about to cry too. His eyes silently ask what the matter is, but she shakes her head and looks out the window. Dmitri glances at Elizabetta; she's wiping tears away. Putting the car in gear, he starts to drive toward the castle gates, shaking his head.

After a couple of miles he breaks the awkward stillness. "Sally, did you remember to bring a weapon?"

She chirps, "Have two, just in case."

"Good—we're all armed and off to see the Kremlin."

It doesn't lighten the mood. Elizabetta is still staring out the passenger window. Dmitri sighs. It's not how he wanted to begin the uncomfortable stay in Novgorod. He had hoped the gift would be better received, that it might lessen the hatred she's building toward him.

As they drive through the city, Sally starts pointing out nightclubs and other places she likes to frequent. It's a welcome distraction, but Elizabetta's responses are monosyl-labic. She's lightly stroking the dagger with her fingertips. Dmitri doesn't know if it's because she likes it or because she's plotting his demise.

When they approach the end of the developed area sur-rounding the fifteenth-century Kremlin, Dmitri parks the car near an old brick building with a tall, round chimney. "We need to walk from here. They're closed to tours this time of night, so we have to sneak in."

"Oh." Elizabetta's tone is quiet.

"We'll cut through the patch of woods next to us, cross the road at the bottom, and run up the motte. We'll use the trees closest to the nearest guard tower for cover when we reach the wall. We can climb in from there."

"Okay." Elizabetta puts the sheathed horse-head dagger into her waistband at the small of her back.

Sounding enthusiastic, Sally playfully whines, "Come on, Eliza, this will be fun."

"Yeah."

Her responses lack inflection and are starting to worry Dmitri, but he tries to shrug it off as they walk toward the trees. Taking a path into the small patch of woods, they barely are beyond the outer edge when he sees movement in the shadows. The hair at the back of his neck begins to prickle. He takes a few cautious steps forward and realizes the shadows are following, pushing. Something tells him they don't belong to humans.

Dmitri stops and waits for Sally and Elizabetta to come alongside him, and whispers a warning to the women. He knows they can smell the werewolves too. Their noses wrinkle as their eyes scan the shadows around them.

A lanky man steps from behind a tree, speaking in Russian. "Well, well, well. Look who's come to join the party."

The area around the Kremlin is known pack territory; Dmitri was hoping to avoid them, yet is not surprised to see them. His hand slides up his back to the handle of his dagger. He notices the women do the same.

"Are you sure that's her?" a voice calls out from behind the trees.

"If not, she's a dead ringer." The lanky man tilts his head and grins at Elizabetta.

Strange. Dmitri wonders if this pack is descended from a werewolf Elizabetta killed as a Druzhina. Sometimes they place bounties and pass the wanted list to the next generations. Longest he's ever heard of a bounty lasting is three hundred years, as the current generation tends to be more forgiving about what happened to some long-dead ancestor they never met. What's baffling here is that Elizabetta hasn't served as a Druzhina for more than five hundred years.

"I say we hold them until Grigori can bring the foreigner to ID her." A young female approaches the male.

Foreigner? Dmitri eyes them warily, noting their tense posture and ready stance. Sally and Elizabetta are glancing at Dmitri and scanning the movement in the trees around them. They're outnumbered on pack turf; it's likely one, if not all, of them will be injured or killed if they try to run.

"You heard the lady—make the call, Shasha." The lanky man directs the others to tighten the perimeter. "We don't want her going nowhere until Grigori gets here."

Dmitri glances toward Elizabetta. She's clearly confused as to what is going on. His eyes narrow and he speaks to the lanky wolf in English. "You. You're the leader of this pack?"

Seeming to ignore the change in language, the werewolf continues in Russian. "Grigori leads this pack. I'm just part of the security detail."

"What's your name?" Dmitri notices more movement in the shadows around them. His hand tightens on the handle of the dagger and he inches it slowly out of the sheath. If they have to fight, it might be best to do it before the wolves have them tightly circled.

"Pavel. What's yours, bloodsucker?"

"Dmitri. What's this all about?"

Swaggering forward, Pavel points at Elizabetta. This time he replies in English. "There's a bounty on that one."

"Why?" Dmitri knows Elizabetta is taking everything in, and he dreads hearing the answer.

Pavel growls, "None of your business."

"She's mine—I'm making it my business."

"I think you should shut up and wait for Grigori. He'll be here soon."

Sally slowly draws both of her daggers. "I don't like this, Dmitri."

Elizabetta finds her voice. "It may be none of his business, but if the bounty is on me, I have every right to know."

Laughter erupts around them. "How are you finding Novgorod, Eliza?" Pavel smirks.

"How do you know my name?"

Eliza? Shit, this has something to do with that wolf pack we annihilated in Montana. The curious expression on her face tells him that she hasn't made the connection—not yet.

Pavel rolls his eyes. "Told you, there's a bounty on you."

"For what?" Elizabetta demands.

"For crimes against our kind."

Damn, another mistake turning to bite me in the ass.

"Be silent, Pavel." A tall, muscular man strolls out of the shadows.

By the reactions around them, Dmitri assumes the man is Grigori. "You're their leader?"

"Yes." He stares coldly at the three vampires. "I'm going to step close enough to shine a light on her. I need to verify it's her."

Dmitri crouches and brandishes the dagger, hissing, "You're not going to touch her."

Grigori takes a piece of paper out of his pocket, unfolds it, and holds it up. A photograph of Elizabetta covers half the page. Below the image, in bold print, is a monetary sum— over 1.7 million rubles. Under it is her name, height, and weight. It also includes a list of the Belyakov covens world-wide.

A flashlight turns on, and Grigori shines it in Elizabetta's face. She pulls back, turning her head to the side.

Dmitri's mind races through ways to escape, but without a way to communicate his intentions to Elizabetta and Sally, he knows it's impossible. Instead he cautions the werewolves. "I doubt your pack wants to incur the wrath of Shashenka Belyakov. You might want to think twice about that bounty."

Grigori ignores him. Looking over his shoulder into the woods, he shouts at someone still hiding in the shadows. "It's her."

Murmured voices rise around them. Dmitri counts at least fourteen wolves and has no idea how many more are still in the shadows. Regardless, they're outnumbered by over four to one. Two to one they could take, provided Sally has any fighting skills and Elizabetta's skills haven't completely been suppressed, but this ... this would be suicide.

"I'm still waiting for someone to tell me what this is about," Elizabetta shouts.

Grigori smiles and laughs ruefully. "You marked one of our kind—an unusual event in our world. Something like that gets noticed and talked about."

Confirmation. Elizabetta's damn mongrel from Montana. Dmitri should have known it was a mistake leaving him alive. "What of it? It only means there's at least one of your kind that ours will not touch."

Ignoring Dmitri again, Grigori turns to the male, Shasha, who made the call earlier. "Is he about here?"

"Who?" Elizabetta is clearly starting to panic. "What are you going to do with me and my friends?"

"We couldn't care less about your friends—they can leave if they want." Grigori shines the flashlight on Elizabetta's face again, and smiles wickedly. "As to you, well, we'll all find that out soon enough."

Dmitri takes a step sideways, shielding Elizabetta's body from those in front of them. "If you want her, you'll have to go through me."

Then another voice shouts, "Eliza? Eliza, is it really you?"

A distinctly American voice, one he's heard before. His stomach drops. If she escapes with that American mongrel, they could be searching for months. He starts reaching behind to grab her by the wrist.

"Matt?" Elizabetta shrieks, jerking her arm away from Dmitri before he closes the grip. "Oh my God, you're here? You are really here. How—what are you doing here?"

Matt steps out of the shadows and Elizabetta runs to him, her dagger still firmly grasped in hand. Jumping up, she wraps her arms around his neck, and his arms envelop her waist.

"Damn, it is sure good to see you, baby vamp. I was beginning to think I'd never find you." Matt swings Elizabetta in a circle.

Sally tugs on Dmitri's sleeve, a puzzled expression on her face. She whispers, "Do you have any idea what's going on here?"

"Yeah, my nightmare doing what it always does. Getting worse."

Clearing his throat, Grigori lifts his chin toward Elizabetta. "We want the bounty paid before you take her."

Matt puts Elizabetta down, draws a slip of paper from his pocket, and makes a call. "Wire the funds, it's her." Looking at Grigori, he says, "You should have it within the next few hours."

"Matt, what are you doing here?" Elizabetta sounds incredulous, breathless, ecstatic. She's actually laughing. "I can't believe you're really here. God, you look great! I was so worried about you. I can't believe you came all the way to Russia for me."

The werewolf laughs heartily, picking her up again. Dmitri struggles to lock every muscle in place to keep from attacking the mongrel for touching Elizabetta. "The answer is, I'm here for you, and yes, I came all this way for you. I told you I rescue damsels in distress, and you, baby vamp, are at the top of my list." Still holding her feet off the ground, he kisses her, and groans and howls go up around them.

Horrified by the possibility she will go with Matt, Dmitri raises his voice. "Eliza, no! Think about this. Do you have any idea what Shashenka will do to him or this pack?"

She pushes against Matt and he sets her feet fully on the ground. Looking at Dmitri and not taking her eyes off him, she bites her lower lip. "Matt, I need to talk with you. Is there somewhere quiet we can go?"

Matt grins at the pack leader. "Grigori, mind if we wait at my hotel room until you have that confirmation?"

"Only if I and two of my pack go with you. I'm not letting her out of my sight until we're paid."

"They're going with us too." Elizabetta points toward Dmitri and Sally. "You have my word, they will not harm anyone."

Matt frowns and Grigori starts to object.

Dmitri drags a hand through his hair. *This is getting ten shades uglier by the minute. What is she up to? Doesn't she understand how dangerous and reckless this is?* Still, while he doesn't want to be cooped up in a hotel room with four wolves, at least it offers a solution for getting him and Sally out of the middle of this pack of werewolves—and it keeps Elizabetta within his grasp. It may present an opportunity for him to get her away from Matt.

"Baby vamp's word is good enough for me." Looking at Sally and Dmitri, he waves them forward. "Come along! Looks like it's a party in my room tonight."

Baby vamp? You juvenile imbecile. There was a time she would have killed that mutt without thinking twice.

"I didn't say they could go," Grigori snarls.

Matt barks, "I just gave you 1.7 million reasons to do what I want." Curling an arm around Elizabetta's waist, he looks at Dmitri and Sally again. "Let's go."

CHAPTER 33: ELIZA

Scores to Settle

Eliza can hardly believe it, barely accept she's not dreaming. Since leaving McAllister, she has often blocked thoughts of Matt; being inside the Belyakov coven left her no other choice. She didn't believe that she'd ever see him again. There's never been a way or an opportunity for her to contact him, and now that he's here, there's much she needs to know and tell him.

With Matt's arm around her waist, they leave the small woods to go to his hotel. Dmitri and Sally get in Matt's car, while Grigori and two of his pack mates follow in another. She's doing her best to ignore the confused and hostile glares coming from the others.

Chuckling, Matt is saying, "This will blow your skirt up, but believe it or not, I'm staying in a snazzy suite on the top floor. We can leave the other vamps and wolves in the living room while you and I go to the bedroom and talk privately."

Dmitri is sitting diagonally from Eliza, and she catches his reaction to Matt's statement. His fangs are showing, his dark eyes are smoldering, and he's acting as if he wants to attack Matt from behind. Ignoring him, she squeezes Matt's hand. "You have no idea how many times I've wished for a few hours alone with you since this all happened."

"Speaking of ... why is it that when I woke up back in West Yellowstone, in my own bed, I may add, I found this on me?" Tugging the collar of his shirt down, he points at her mark.

Eliza looks down at her hands. "Everyone else ... the pack was dead, and you were badly hurt. The vamps wanted to kill you too, wanted me to surrender. I wouldn't, couldn't if they came back to kill you once you were out of my sight."

He's looking at her as if waiting for more of an explanation.

"Dmitri told me how a vampire can mark something ..." She takes a deep breath to finish. "Something they own and want to keep other vampires from stealing or harming. He branded it on you before they took you back to your house."

"But it has your initials, baby vamp."

"Yes, all vampires have their own mark. Dmitri said that one is mine, and since I was the one claiming you, he used it. It's a protection rune; it shields you from other vamps."

"That explains some of the batshit-crazy reactions I've had from vampires I've crossed paths with these last few months looking for you. Talk about feeling the love—I don't think I made anyone's gift list."

Dismissing his sarcasm, Eliza remembers that Matt, while not broke, had little financially. "How can you afford all of this, Matt? I mean the reward, that's like what—fifty thousand dollars? Where did you ever get the money?"

Grimacing, Matt says, "Josh was thorough in planning for our last stand. I went back to McAllister after I woke up, and everything, everyone was gone, the house burned to the ground. I searched the ranch, but I knew they were all dead, probably burned to ashes in that smoldering shell of a house. I realized too late how badly the vamps wanted you."

The images of the ranch house burning flicker through her mind. Until now, Eliza has managed to block the horrible scene from her mind. When they took Matt to the pickup, they walked past several mangled bodies, and she was horrified to see how it mirrored her visions. Now, as she imagines Matt standing by the charred remains of the house, her stomach churns. She watches him blink back his own memories, leaving her unable to find the words she needs to say.

"Evidently, before Josh died he planned for the worst outcome. Their life insurance was paid to me as a sole beneficiary. He and Lois didn't have children, and his estate was held in a time-limited trust for the first pack member located after their deaths. If no one else comes forward within three years, everything goes to that lone pack member. I was the only one they found ... the only one left."

Matt snorts one short laugh; his tone is bitter. "Josh was actually quite wealthy. He had millions. I never had a clue he was worth that kind of money—he was always so down to earth and didn't act the way I thought millionaires did. I've been working as Josh's replacement CEO for his businesses. Eventually it will all come to me."

He takes a deep breath. "And I was determined to find

you, baby vamp. I would have spent every last dime to get you back." His grin widens, deepening the dimples in his cheeks.

Brief memories begin to surface of the moments she shared with Josh and the pack. One particular memory lodges in her mind: the moment Josh said she was one of them, part of their pack. It was the only time in her life when she can recall true hope ... the hope of finally having a family. When she lost them, she had to bury the pain so deep inside that it will never surface. *I'll never have a family. This hurts too much. Don't think of them.*

Then she recalls when Josh handed her the katana and Arkansas toothpick. Hope shone in his eyes, hope that they would succeed in protecting her. *I owe them so much. How do I ever repay them? Is there anything that equals the price they paid?* Not knowing what to say to that, pushing against the pain, Eliza murmurs sheepishly, "I still have the sword and knife he gave me that night."

Matt reaches for her hand, and silence settles over their shared grief.

They arrive at the hotel and go to Matt's room. Before leading Eliza to the bedroom, Matt gives a warning to the mortal enemies they are leaving in the living room of the suite. "Here's how this works. They"—he points at the vampires—"protect her. I protect her. She protects me. If you attack the vamps, I'm on their side. If you vamps start anything, I'll let the wolves fight you."

Tugging on her arm, he smiles. "Come on, baby vamp, we have a lot of catching up to do."

After he closes the door behind them, Matt's tone becomes rushed, urgent. "Okay, tell me what's going on. You're not acting like you want to be rescued from them."

Eliza sits on the bed and stares at the closed bedroom door. "Is there any way to make it harder for the others to hear us?"

Both species have exceptional hearing, although the wolves less so in human form. Matt shakes his head and grins. Taking a MP4 device from a dresser top, he puts a playlist on loop, plugs it into a portable dock, and turns the volume up as a buffer. Pressing a finger to his lips, he leads her to the bathroom and turns the water on in the shower.

Leaning against the counter, he gestures toward the toilet. "The throne is all yours, baby vamp. Now tell me why you don't want to leave them?"

"I do and I don't. I have a score to settle first." She wonders whether Matt will help her destroy Shashenka. "Before I can do anything, I need to know how you found me."

"I was insane with worry, had no idea where they took you."

Eliza knows their time is limited, and redirects his focus. "The greater concern is who we're up against here. The reports Josh got on the Belyakov coven only skimmed the surface—"

His smile melts into a scowl as he cuts her off. "I've learned a lot about the Belyakov coven ... including the three most frequent places that bastard leading it likes to stay. Dmitri is evidently well connected to him, and I figured that if you were important enough for them to wipe out an entire wolf pack on the other side of the world, they'd keep you wherever the leader is."

He's wrong about Dmitri, but the other information is helpful.

"Before coming here, I checked the places he keeps in Venice and Prague. I left a flyer with your description with each wolf pack in the areas near those Belyakov estates. I was about to go back to the States to check on my construction business—then you suddenly showed up tonight."

"I'm glad you came. I need you to help me."

"Wa-huh. I'm telling ya, little lady, that is why I'm here."

Matt is impersonating John Wayne, and laughing, Eliza jumps up and slips her arms around him. Pressing her cheek to his chest, she hugs Matt tightly. "I still can't believe you're here, but I really do need you." Pulling back, she looks up at him. "This is going to sound wacko, but I need to be back at the Belyakov castle before dawn. We only have a few hours, and there are a million details you need to hear."

Sitting back down on the closed lid of the toilet, Eliza details what happened in Big Sky and the terrible week in Arecibo. The longer she talks, the more her eyes harden in determination. "I'm going to take that nasty goblin king down. I still don't know how or when, but it is going to happen. Being in Novgorod is the first chance I've had to begin my surveillance and build alliances."

Matt's voice drips disgust. "Yeah, that's not nutso, that is insanity—or sheer stupidity. God, Eliza, they've made you a whore in their master's keep. Can't you do this from a distance?"

Angrily she snaps, "I know what they're doing to me, and it drives me to ruin them. If I leave, they will hunt me down, and I've learned enough already to know there is no place on the face of the earth where they won't find me. I'm not going to risk you being killed, or have others killed like what happened to Josh's pack."

Matt is leaning against the counter, his arms folded across his chest. Ignoring the disapproving look on his face, she continues. "It has to happen this way—there is no other way to do it. I'll never be free unless I kill that little son of a bitch."

"It makes me want to storm into that castle right now and rip his throat out." He spits in the sink. "I can't stand the thought of him or any of those other vamps touching you like that."

You have no idea how dirty it makes me feel. "Trust me, I'm not wild about it myself, but it's something I have to endure."

Breathing out slowly, he asks, "Okay, baby vamp. What do you want me to do?"

Eliza explains about her time off from the role she's playing. "I don't think I'll be able to meet you as long as I'm expected to be near the inner lair. But I'll find some way to communicate with you, and as I gain more of their trust, I'll be able to take advantage of my days off and see you. We'll have to be extremely careful in case they're watching me."

"What about that leech, Dmitri? He was the one stalking you, ruining your life, and I find you out on the town with him and that blonde." Matt tilts his head toward the living room.

Where do I even start? Since settling into her room at the estate, she has been unable to keep her thoughts from dwelling on Dmitri sleeping on the other side of their shared bathroom. It took hours of searching, struggling to find any good in the arrangement, before she finally convinced herself that having him so close would actually work to her benefit. Her plan was simple: use the close quarters to further the discord between them, and take advantage of him being near enough to protect him. She will know if someone harms him.

Then Dmitri presented her with the dagger, a dagger so exquisitely stunning it threatened to undo her. A gift, he said, making it sound simple, but it's not, and that makes it even more difficult to explain to Matt. No mere acquaintance gives a gift like that, not when love, adoration, and devotion clearly have designed every detail. *What is he hiding from me?* She tried to refuse it, knowing that her keeping it erodes distance between them, but he refused to take it back. At the same time, she knows that Dmitri has no idea how this gift touched her, filled her with desire that he might see her as something other than a whore someday.

He can't love me, not yet—it's too dangerous. Unsure where the thought comes from, Eliza goes rigid as her mind whirls around the notion. *Are my fantasies about him getting out of control? Do I want him to love me?* Then she remembers that Matt is standing across from her, and it shocks her that her thoughts would drift this way.

Matt's eyebrows arch upward, indicating that he's still waiting for an answer.

Seeing Matt's frown, she says defensively, "Dmitri isn't a monster. I don't think he's what we thought he was."

"So—what, he's like a good guy now?"

"No. Yes ... I don't know, but ... yes, maybe."

The dubious expression on Matt's face spurs her on. "Some have hinted that he's protected me, or is still protecting me, and I have no idea why. All I know is that the goblin king delights in tormenting him daily, putting him through hell, and he is using me to do it."

She can't explain it, but her gut instinct is telling her this is important, that she may need Dmitri to finish this, to get out. "I'm doing my best to put distance between us so I can shield him from Shashenka's brutality. Regardless, I owe him at least that much."

"Hmm." Matt grunts and flexes his jaw as he seems to consider her comments. "What's the story with the blonde?"

"Sally is like me. I'm not sure where her loyalties are, but I suspect she's not happy being a"—Eliza makes air quotes—"courtesan of the inner lair, any more than I am. She may be an asset for what I need to do."

"And you trust her, why?"

"Trust." Eliza huffs. "Aside from you I don't trust anyone, but at some point I am going to need to trust others, or this nightmare will never end."

Matt doesn't hide his concern, and it hardens his gaze. "So your bad-guy stalker is now a good guy, and his little blond sidekick is just a poor misunderstood vamp? Really, Eliza, is that the best you can come up with? This doesn't even make sense. Look what he's done to you!"

How can I make him understand when I don't get it my-self? "Sally is not misunderstood. She is another of Sha-shenka's victims. There seems to be a whole coven full of them, under the goblin king's control. Everyone cowers and no one confronts him, not even vamps twice his size. He's evil personified. Sally's life was stolen from her, much the same as mine was, and like me, she has no choice."

"You have a choice! You can leave with me."

"No, I can't." Eliza stands and crosses to where Matt is still leaning against the counter. "This has to be done right. I won't have anyone else lose their life because of me, especial-ly you."

Matt winces and then pulls Eliza into a hug. "I'm sorry. It's just so damn frustrating to finally find you and hear that you want to stay here with them."

"Then help me. Help me take down Shashenka so we can walk away without this hanging over our heads."

"I'll do anything for you, baby vamp."

Together they strategize the early stage of her plan and how best to achieve the ultimate goal—Shashenka's death and her freedom. Emboldened by the chance of working to-gether, they grow optimistic, end the gloomy discussion, and return to Matt's bedroom.

Reclined on the bed, Eliza cuddles against Matt, her head on his chest. She relishes the familiar warmth of his body and finally begins to relax. But when he kisses her and they begin making out, images of Dmitri's disapproving eyes flash through her mind. She stops and pulls away, again feeling like she's cheating. *What is wrong with me? Why does he keep coming between us?*

She grimaces, fishing for an excuse, and then says with a sympathetic smile, "You're my best friend and I love you to the moon and back, but I can't complicate my life with a relationship until this is settled."

He tugs her back into his arms and they lie on the bed, holding each other. "This is enough for now, baby vamp. I'm just glad to have you back."

An hour before sunrise they leave the bedroom, where they find Dmitri and Sally sitting alone in the living room. Dmitri explains that Grigori and his goons left as soon as the payment confirmation arrived. The expressions on their faces—Sally looks ill and Dmitri, irate—tell Eliza that they're going to bombard her with questions on the way back to the castle.

How can I turn this to my advantage? What am I going to tell them? Somehow she must keep pushing Dmitri away while keeping him close, and yet convince Sally this night was no threat to any of them. Then she realizes this meeting presents an incredible opportunity to start driving the wedge deeper.

Leaning into Matt, she pushes against the doubts. She knows precisely what step she'll take next. She looks up and gives Matt her most heartwarming smile. "I can't thank you enough for tonight, Matt. It is the best night I've had in a long time."

Bending his head down, he places a series of kisses on her face before pressing one to her lips. "I just wish you were going home with me."

He voiced the same sentiment earlier when he told her that he doesn't want to lose himself in the darker world of feuds with werewolves and wars with vampires. Eliza wishes there were another way, but there isn't one. "I know, but we're doing the right thing. Just you take care of you, for me."

"Always." Matt winks at her. "If you get in trouble or change your mind, make sure you give me a call. Those bloodsuckers won't stop me from getting you out of there."

Dmitri is suddenly on his feet and hissing. Sally moves in front of him and places her hands on his chest to hold him back. He continues pushing forward until Eliza moves alongside them, grabs Dmitri's arm, and tugs him toward the door.

Glaring at Matt, Dmitri snarls, "You'll stay away from her."

"Don't get your panties in a bunch." Matt returns an equally menacing stare. "She's leaving with you."

"You're not listening, mutt. You will stay away from her."

Eliza opens the door and pulls Dmitri into the hall with Sally's help. Matt follows them to the door and leans against the doorjamb. "Not too late to change your mind, baby vamp."

"It's getting late. We need to go." Sally nervously fidgets with the hood on her jacket. They are risking exposure—daylight is coming.

Rolling her eyes at Matt, Eliza turns and gives Dmitri a fierce look that tells him to stay put. She walks over to Matt and cups his face in her hands, forcing him to look at her. "I'm sure about this. Take care, Matt." Rising on her tiptoes, she places a trail of kisses on his lips and over his jaw, stopping near his ear. Then she leaves Matt standing in the doorway of his hotel suite and storms past Dmitri and Sally to the elevator.

CHAPTER 34: DMITRI

Ashes

There is complete silence among the three of them on the walk from the hotel back to their car near the Kremlin. Unlocking the doors, Dmitri is about to get in when Elizabetta suddenly spins Sally around and pushes her against the rear car door. Her forearm is across Sally's upper chest and the horse-head dagger is in her other hand, at the startled blonde's throat. "If you ever breathe a word of what happened tonight to anyone, I will kill you."

Dmitri is too stunned to move. Elizabetta lifts Sally away from the car and slams her against the door again, leaning in until their noses almost touch. In a low, menacing whisper she says, "Do you understand me?"

Sally's eyes dart between Elizabetta and Dmitri. "Y-yes. I-I won't tell anyone. I p-promise."

Unbelievable. She may look and sound like Elizabetta, but I don't even know her anymore. Dmitri can't contain his anger. For hours he and Sally sat in that hotel room wondering how the night would end, and it was worse after the werewolves left.

They could hear the water running behind the music playing, along with the soft, murmured voices from the bedroom. Neither he nor Sally picked up on more than a few scattered words of their conversation. *What were they talking about for so long?* Jealousy grew as seconds surrendered to minutes and hours gobbled both. When Elizabetta finally emerged from Matt's bedroom, Dmitri was convinced that they'd spent their little reunion having sex. Unlike with the men at the inner lair, she has a choice with this one, and it hurts him worse than Shashenka's torture.

How dare she do this to me! When they're finally in the car and driving away, Dmitri bellows, "What the hell was that?"

Sally chimes in. "Yeah. Why threaten me and not Dmitri?"

Elizabetta scowls at Sally. "You need to be kept quiet." Softening her gaze slightly, looking at Dmitri, she says, "Don't cross me. You know Shashenka will punish us, and you will get the worst end of it if that happens. I'll make sure of it."

Dismissing it—he knows well what their master would do—he growls, "Not that. I'm talking about what the hell happened in that bedroom between you and that damn dog all night."

"I needed to say good-bye. I sent Matt away."

She's lying; there are too many years between them for her to try hiding a lie from him. "You expect me to believe that you took a long shower with that damn mutt, made love to him for several hours, and then just said *Dovizhdane, arrivederci,* have a nice life?"

Elizabetta clenches her fists, and her retort is filled with vehemence. "What I did or did not do with Matt is none of your damn business, Dmitri. I promised you when I surrendered in McAllister that I'd never run again. I am keeping my word."

"I don't know how you're going to hide this from Master." Sally sounds scared. "There's too many connections. He always knows what the wolves are doing or have done."

"She's right, Eliza, Shashenka will find out," Dmitri snarls. "What do you expect us to tell him?"

There's a long pause. "Exactly what I said, and if he asks for details I'll give them to him."

Dmitri's rage turns to worry. "Do you know what he does to get the truth, love? He tortures to get it. He cuts, stabs, slices, and whips to get it, and he does it for weeks, months, and years without end. The more you fight back, resist, and beg, the more that little son of a bitch enjoys it."

He hears Elizabetta gasp and watches her bite down on her lip again. Realizing he just revealed too much of his persecuted past, he lowers his voice. "Trust me, love, you don't want to experience it." *Never pity me. I am not worthy of it.* For the ways he has failed her, and his participation in destroying the woman she once was, the last thing she should ever feel toward him is pity.

"That's if he doesn't kill you. Dmitri's right." Placing a hand on Elizabetta's shoulder, Sally croaks out, "Master has killed and tortured many of us in horrible ways. I don't want to see that happen to you."

A wry smile spreads across Elizabetta's face. "I'll be fine, and I can handle dealing with that gob—our master."

Dmitri doesn't know what dangerous game Elizabetta is playing, but he's terrified that it's going to get her killed. His thoughts scatter as Sally presses for details that Elizabetta won't give. He wonders if Elizabetta understands the seriousness of her betrayal in meeting that mongrel. The anger she's directing at them, while displaying wanton ignorance about their master, astonishes Dmitri. He's not seen this level of reckless behavior in her since before ... *No, impossible.*

When they reach the castle, Elizabetta storms straight to Shashenka. In front of all present, she gives a condensed version of their encounter with the werewolves; that they collected her for a bounty paid by some man who was looking for someone else. She assures him it was nothing more than a simple case of mistaken identity. When Shashenka begins questioning her, the lies she tells remain consistent.

It wrenches Dmitri's gut as she declares her loyalty and devotion to their master. *She can't mean that, can she?* If there's anything in her story Shashenka doubts, she seems to find a way to calm his suspicion. Apparently satisfied that the situation was dealt with, Shashenka dismisses them and asks Elizabetta to freshen up and join him in his quarters.

Unable to sleep, fearful the monster is torturing Elizabetta or worse, Dmitri paces until he hears her return to the adjoining bedroom. He listens as she takes a shower, and it tears at his battered heart as her sobs rise above the spraying sound of the water. *What has that monster done to her?* His hand rests on the doorknob as he fights the urge to open the unlocked door to comfort her. When the water finally shuts off, he hears her go into the adjoining bedroom and he assumes she went to sleep—it is finally quiet.

Worried, he listens for any sound from her throughout the day. *How much can she endure before it's too much?* She's up before twilight, and Dmitri waits until he hears her bedroom door open and close. He steps into the hall to follow her, wanting, needing, to know she is all right. It's been one of the worst days of his life, and it suddenly becomes worse when she looks back over her shoulder and glares at him.

Dmitri expected her to look worn, defeated, but instead her body language is defiant, self-assured. He doesn't understand; he assumed ... *But why was she crying, then? What am I missing here?* Watching Elizabetta and Shashenka throughout the night, Dmitri feels relieved the master shows no signs of displeasure. In fact, Shashenka interacts with Elizabetta as if she pleases him. The night passes without incident, leaving Dmitri more confused.

The temperature in his living hell climbs another few degrees as the nights pass. While Elizabetta's friendship with Sally thaws, she treats him more coldly than she did before. Without reservation or complaint, she genially accepts intimate advances from Shashenka and whatever men the master sends to her. The muffled sounds coming from her room as she entertains her paramours burns a hole straight through him.

Each evening he swears not to look at her, and fails—he can't keep his eyes off her. The pain inside is growing by the hour, and Dmitri longs for the ability to hate the willing and playful concubine Elizabetta has become. *Mate bond, the worst curse leveled against a vampire's damnable soul.* No matter what he tries, he can't stop loving her, and isn't even capable of disliking her. It's driving him insane. A small part of him wishes that Shashenka had reset both of their minds.

When their first set of nights off arrives, he's determined to spend his time trailing Elizabetta. Something is not right; the way she seems to embrace the life they thrust on her is out of place and even nonsensical. Unexpectedly, Shashenka helps in that regard, seeking him out the night before.

"Eliza's going to London for holiday. I have the Druzhinas busy with other assignments and can spare none of them for this task. You must go. But," Shashenka says, a note of caution in his voice, "don't lose her and disappoint me this time. I've already arranged a flat for you next to the manor. The locals will contact you whenever she comes and goes, and by what entrance, so you can follow."

"Yes, Master. Thank you, Master."

"I want you to arrive ahead of her—you fly out tonight in two hours. I don't need you held up in traffic and losing her right away."

"Yes, Master. I'll go pack my bag."

"She'll arrive by private jet at midnight tomorrow. Be ready." Shashenka turns away, then turns back. "Dmitri, don't disappoint me this time. Call the moment there's a problem."

Dmitri bows his head. "I will not fail you, Master."

While rushing to pack a bag and meet the jet on time, Dmitri prepares for the trip in other ways. His Druzhina skills are rusty, but not forgotten. He has had centuries of successfully stalking and surveilling targets, and provided he can keep reminding himself that Elizabetta is a target, she will not elude him. Fortunately Elizabetta's memories are suppressed. *I will discover the game you're playing, what lies you hide.* He cannot believe her programming was so successful that it would alter the truth written upon her soul— so complete that she would forsake him. To admit that would mean accepting she is forever lost to him.

A shudder courses through him as he steps off the plane in London, and he draws his jacket closed. The damp weather in England makes it one of his least favorite cities to visit. After settling into the flat, Dmitri orients himself to the estate's driveway exits and takes the car back to the airport to watch for her arrival. The black Vauxhall Corsa he's driving will help him blend into traffic if Elizabetta drives anywhere. If she takes public transit, it will complicate his tracking of her movements but not render it impossible.

She arrives just after midnight; a Belyakov driver is waiting for her on the private jet tarmac. As the car leaves the airport, Dmitri slips into traffic behind it and follows it all the way to the manor. He's surprised—he half expected her to ditch the driver somewhere along their route and make a run for freedom. Still, he'll need to remain vigilant. If she disappears again, Shashenka will not stop at punishing Dmitri. That evil monster will torture Elizabetta, and Dmitri cannot bear the thought of seeing her brutalized that way.

Dmitri parks at the flat so he can easily go either direction when she leaves next. An hour later his phone rings; it's a local with an update. She's going out. *That didn't take long.*

Elizabetta is supposedly going sightseeing—by herself. He snorts. When she pulls out of the west gate, Dmitri puts the car in gear and starts following the dark-blue sedan. For a half hour, Elizabetta drives in seemingly aimless circles around the streets of London. *Is she lost, or looking for something?*

Then he realizes she is driving to spot a tail and shake it if she needs to. Dmitri isn't sure if she's made out his car. He turns the signal on to suggest he's taking another street, and slows down. When a couple of cars take the space between them, he turns off the signal light and keeps tailing her. Within moments Elizabetta drives straight to a luxury hotel in the heart of Mayfair. *I knew it. She's meeting someone, but who?*

Taking a side entrance to the lobby, Dmitri seeks cover behind a pillar. Elizabetta seems to be waiting for someone; she keeps looking up and around the lobby. Then a familiar face comes into view.

Matt.

So this is what her lies were hiding after the Kremlin incident. He should have known. Anger boils as he sees them embrace and go to an elevator. When the door closes, he watches the number above the doors; it stops on the fifth floor. Without losing sight of the entrances on the front and side, Dmitri walks outside and crosses the street to examine the fifth floor from the ground. It contains luxury suites with balconies. He had hoped that Matt was exaggerating about the money he'd inherited, but after seeing the suite he had in Novgorod and now this place, Dmitri begins to wonder if they have underestimated the mongrel's influence and power.

Returning indoors to wait, he finds a chair in a quiet corner with a partially concealed view of the elevator. It does little good, but Dmitri keeps checking the accuracy of his watch by comparing it to the lobby clock. Both are working, yet time is dragging slower as each hour passes. It isn't until just before dawn that Elizabetta and Matt return to the lobby. He kisses her before she leaves. Dmitri's fingers grip the chair to keep from launching an attack, and it takes great effort to not confront the wolf as Elizabetta leaves the hotel. Instead he slips out of the lobby and follows her. She seems less wary returning to the manor, making only a few last-minute zigzags in the route and eventually driving back through the west gate. With the sun about to rise, Dmitri supposes she's in for the day, and goes to the rented flat.

The next eight nights are the same. Elizabetta leaves the manor and takes a cautious route to the luxury hotel, either staying in the room with Matt the entire night, or heading out to the pubs and sightseeing with him. Dmitri isn't sure if she is escaping or plotting something, but his hatred for the wolf is blocking his ability to sort it out. *I cannot have lost her heart to a werewolf, never.* He decides to wait in her room at the manor to confront her when she returns at the end of their last night in London.

There's a smile on her face as she pushes the door open; it irks him. It fades with an audible gasp when she sees Dmitri sitting in a chair near the bed.

"Do you want to tell me what's going on, love?" The toll of watching her sneak around with Matt the last nine nights makes his hands shake uncontrollably. He can barely contain his hurt and anger.

"What are you doing here?" Elizabetta hisses. "Why are you in my room?"

"Your room, love?" His eyebrows pitch up. "This hasn't been much of a room during your stay here, has it?"

Dmitri recognizes Elizabetta's stiff posture; she used to adopt this falsely relaxed stance just before attacking her foe. He tenses, ready to respond if necessary. His eyes follow her as she drapes her jacket on the foot of the bed.

"Are you spying on me?"

"I asked you, and I will ask again, what's going on here?"

"That's none of your business. I can do what I want on my time off."

His tone becomes harsh, bitter, and he leaps to his feet. "Not when it includes sleeping around with some mangy mutt."

Anger flashes in Elizabetta's eyes. "So you are spying on me. Why? Did that despicable goblin king send you to do his dirty work?"

"Goblin king ..." He has to stifle a laugh in spite of himself. He has never thought of Shashenka that way, but it fits. Then Dmitri remembers why he's confronting her. He snaps,

"Answer my questions. You need to start talking, right now. I need to know why you're sleeping with that damn mongrel and if you're plotting an escape."

Elizabetta flies across the room and shoves Dmitri in the chest, knocking him back two steps. "What I do on my own time is my business. I am not running away—I'm returning to the castle on a flight tonight."

Her answer shocks and puzzles him. His brows pull together. *She's telling the truth.* "Then tell me, love, why are you sleeping with that stinking mutt?"

Her voice rises slightly and has a raw edge to it. "Who I sleep with is none of your damn business, Dmitri Markov. You don't own me. But if you must know, Matt is here to spend time with me. He's catching a flight back to the States right now ... he's going back to Montana."

More honesty, something he didn't expect. Confused and hurt, he mutters, "Why him? Why does it have to be *him?*"

"Matt"—Elizabetta sits on the bed, shoulders slumping, and looks down at the floor—"is the only real friend I have. If I'm going to survive my tour of that monster's version of hell, I need his friendship to keep me sane."

The answer freezes his core. *More truth. How can that be?* Not once has he considered how isolated she feels, how frightened and alone she is in this world. Of course she's running to the only one she feels happy and safe around. It is a devastating thought. *I've completely lost her. Another piece of my world burned to ashes.* Looking down, he mumbles, "I'm sorry, love."

Before she can say anything more, he flees the manor. The

first rays of sunlight catch him as he parks the car and dashes into the flat. For a moment he considers going back outside and letting the sun have him, but the one thought stopping him is that he did this to her. It's his fault she feels she
has nothing in this world; it is exactly what he left her, at
Shashenka's command.

Dmitri slumps onto the divan and rakes his hands through
his hair. *My world is gone ... it's burned to the ground ... I
have lost her. I'm sifting ashes and picking amid bones for a
scrap that doesn't exist.* He's done this to her, he's done it to
himself, and resignedly, he'll pay the boatman for an eternity.
Somehow he must make it up to her, even if she never speaks
to him again.

There's no need to wait until she flies out; she is telling
the truth about returning. He catches an earlier evening
flight back to Novgorod and gives Shashenka his report
when he arrives. The lies he weaves portray a solitary holiday: Elizabetta stayed alone at the manor, each night spending her time wandering the streets of London and visiting
pubs. As they programmed her, she prefers to be alone. She
saw no one and barely spoke to others. Dmitri's hoping he
still knows her well enough to assume that she'll tell
Shashenka a similar story, regardless of their confrontation.

Claiming to be weary from the surveillance, which isn't a
lie, he asks to spend the rest of the night in his room. Five
hours later he's still sitting on the bed, staring at the bathroom door, when he hears Elizabetta enter the adjoining
room. She is late. He suspects the little goblin king, as Elizabetta called him, demanded her time.

Dmitri stands and mindlessly undresses, uncharacteristically dropping his clothes to the floor instead of carefully folding and laying them across the chair. He lies down and listens as Elizabetta unpacks and takes a shower. Exhausted and numb, he falls asleep to the sound of the water running.

CHAPTER 35: ELIZA

Adjustments

Arriving at the castle from London, Eliza cringes when Sally tells her to report immediately to Shashenka's quarters. *Truth and consequence, great ... here we go.* Knowing that she won't want to leave her room once she reaches it, Eliza goes straight to his room—with luggage in tow. When he shows surprise over the bags, she claims that it's because she's so excited to see him.

He waves a hand, directing her to leave them near the door. "It's good to see you home, sweet Eliza. I've missed your company."

Inwardly she squirms as he hugs and kisses her, but she forces a smile when they pull apart. "I missed yours too."

"Come, sit down and tell me what grand adventure you had in the Big Smoke." Shashenka sits on the divan, draping an arm along the back cushions.

Deliberately putting a bounce in her step, Eliza slides onto the cushion and leans in, resting her head on his shoulder. His arm curls around her. "London," she begins, "is an intriguing place. I discovered a few pubs to enjoy, but I mostly saw the traditional and not-so-typical tourist attractions."

Drawing lazy circles on his shirt, Eliza starts to unbutton it while she spins her tale. "I enjoyed seeing places like the Tower and the Thames." She chuckles. "I couldn't resist taking the Jack the Ripper tour—they hold it at night. It was oddly humorous to me, being a monster on a tour about a monster."

Shashenka laughs. "Dear me, sweet Eliza, you are anything but a monster."

She kisses him for effect. He takes her chin in his small, slender fingers. "Did you discover a favorite place there?"

"Surprisingly, I did." This part is true. One place she and Matt went became a siren call to another life, another era—one she may have enjoyed had she lived then. The eighteenth-century furnishing and decor of the house felt authentic and were more than visually appealing. Eliza closes her eyes and recalls the voices of people heard, but not seen, the lingering scents of a half-eaten meal, and the burning wax of the candles. "I influenced the manager of the Dennis Severs' House to bump a scheduled paying customer's Exclusive Silent Night visit. Extraordinary ... it is beautifully done, a unique way to step back in time."

The expression on Shashenka's face encourages her to continue. Her eyes narrow as she remembers the nagging ache the place left within her. She tells him how the ambiance of the house disconnects from the modern world and allows the perception of going back in time. She doesn't mention the strange feeling—as if that time period somehow bypassed her own life. It was too easy for her to imagine such a simple life filled with basic necessities and surrounded by family. "I like it so much that I plan to go again."

"I've never seen it. Maybe we shall see it together when my lair returns for a visit."

I'd rather see you dead. Smiling, taking care to keep the truth hidden, she says, "I'd like that. Knowing you lived through that time, it'd be riveting to hear your take on it."

"Were you able to make friends among the locals at the manor?"

She avoided them, and he already knows it. "To be honest, I was selfish. They probably think I'm some rude American. Going there, having this time off ... it is the first I've had to myself since ... before Big Sky. I didn't even try to get to know any of them."

Eliza takes a deep breath. She knows he's waiting for an explanation, but there is so little from her past or present to draw from that she can use, and she goes with what she knows best—isolation. "I hated the time I spent alone growing up, but didn't realize how much I'd crave it once it was gone. I'm not complaining or anything, it's just that these beautiful homes of yours never give one a moment of peace. There's rarely a place I can find solitude and be alone."

He pulls her into a hug. "You are so right. After ten centuries of constantly having others around, I have forgotten what it's like to be alone. You make it sound like I'm missing something. I may have to take a solo holiday to find out."

The ruse works, and Shashenka seems to lose interest in Eliza's stories of London. He spends the next two hours using her as he often does. Finally satiated, he dismisses her.

Shashenka zero, me two.

Her relief is palpable when her bedroom door closes behind her. Eliza glances toward the bathroom. After her earlier encounter with Dmitri, it took only a few minutes of self-loathing before her mind went into overdrive. By the time she reached Novgorod, she was nearly sick with worry that her cover for the London visit was blown. Then in utter astonishment, she discovered that Dmitri had kept his mouth shut.

Why didn't Dmitri rat her out? If he had, she doubts her homecoming would have been so welcoming. It's another item to add to her growing list of things she needs to make up to him someday. Then she laughs to herself. *He's horrible at helping me, but he's not making it easy to fake hating him, either.*

Hastily she unpacks the suitcases and goes to shower; no amount of water or soap is enough to make her feel clean after Shashenka has touched her. Gritting her teeth, she rakes a bath brush over her body nearly to the point of abrading her skin. Her thoughts engage in battle as she continues scrubbing.

In some ways, she feels, Dmitri is no different from Shashenka—maybe even more cruel and twisted because of the tender way he acts toward her. She wouldn't be here if not for him. *It's his fault. I should have killed him in Bozeman ... or Big Sky. I don't get this perverted game.* He stalked her—still is stalking her. His overbearing presence smothers her one moment and chills her the next; his moods pitch wildly one way and then the other. *Why is he doing this to me?* But she can't ignore what she's seen with her own eyes—his tenderness, and the longing he conveys in looks or touches. *Who am I kidding? I don't hate him ... a part of me wants him.* "Ugh. This is so messed up," she mutters aloud.

Sliding down the shower wall to sit on the floor, Eliza wraps her arms around her sides and holds her breath, trying to stop the tears that are starting to spill over. Maybe some of the psychological tests were right about her having a split personality. She can't reconcile the two extremes. Half of her mind is achingly being pulled toward Dmitri, while the other half is growing increasingly resentful of what he's done to her life. *I can't have it both ways. It's tearing me in two.*

Rocking back and forth, closing her eyes, she regains control of her emotions and scrubs her body once more before leaving the shower and reclining on her bed. Her life is a disaster. Matt wants a relationship with her, but it just feels wrong. Dmitri is an enigma she can't figure out. Then there's the coming destruction of Shashenka, but she doesn't know when she'll be able to put that in motion. *How is this supposed to all work out?* Deeply lost in the tangle of unsolved dilemmas, she startles when a light knock at the door gives way to three sharp raps. Cautiously she gets off the bed and opens the door to find Maria in the hall. The look on the witch's face makes Eliza uncomfortable. *Why is she here?*

They sit on the bed to talk. "I'm thrilled to see you return. I was afraid you wouldn't." Maria pauses, giving her a hard look. "Why did you come back, Eliza?"

She blinks at the unexpected question. Maria's on her kill

or turn list, and she doesn't know enough about her yet to trust or approach her. Maria seems less fearful of Shashenka than many of the others, and Eliza has seen enough to understand that while the witch does his bidding, she keeps her distance from him whenever she can.

Deciding to be as honest as possible, she says, "I have nowhere to go. I've already figured that much out."

A faint smile creases the witch's mouth. "You always were smart. May I be just as blunt as you?"

What an odd comment. "Yes."

Maria lowers her tone, almost to a whisper. "I told you once that many things are not as they seem in this coven. Dmitri is one of those things. I don't know what happened while you both had your time off, but I know him very well. He returned here, obviously in pain. Would you like to tell me why?"

This is no time for me to mess up. Play it up. "I have no idea. He always seems miserable and unhappy. Is this all you came to talk to me about, Maria? If so, I'd rather not—it's enough that I have to put up with him here, not to mention share my bathroom with him. My time off doesn't include Dmitri."

"Then we shall not talk about him." Her expression adds an asterisk: except when Maria thinks he needs protecting.

The witch may be useful to me yet. After Maria leaves, Eliza lies in her bed and lets her mind wander over her earlier encounter with Dmitri and the recent meeting with Matt. She still feels rattled by the way Dmitri quietly closed the door behind him as he left her room in London. She doesn't know which is worse, the way he yelled at her, or the abrupt way the fire in him extinguished and his eyes filled with pain. Either way, she understands that she needs greater distance from him. It's too risky having him stalk her every time she's away. *What difference does it make if I am with Matt? Why is he being so obnoxious and acting like this is personal to him? What kind of game is he playing?*

In truth, Dmitri has little to worry about right now. His inexplicable pull on her is almost an insurmountable road-block between her and Matt—something she constantly stumbled over during her holiday with her friend. When Matt expressed interest in a committed relationship, it trig-gered an eerily similar feeling to the one she experienced during their near sexual encounter in West Yellowstone. How could she explain what she didn't understand herself? Instead she used the excuse of still settling into her role in the Belyakov coven and lamely explained their need to re-main focused on turning the inner circle against Shashenka. Next she brought up her lingering doubts about who she is, and the nagging suspicion that several in the inner lair are keeping the truth from her. When Matt tried to poke holes in her argument, she claimed it was impossible to complete their plans if her attention became distracted by a intimate relationship. Her redirection worked and allowed them to awkwardly resolve some of the tension between them. Matt finally agreed not to complicate matters by moving beyond friendship right now.

Convinced she saw hurt flicker in his eyes when he con-ceded, she couldn't help telling him that friendship is a good place to start. Eliza can't lie to herself, though. She groans and rolls onto her side. *As long as Dmitri is standing between us, there is no starting point. Do I even want him to stand aside? Why does it feel like I don't have a choice?*

She doesn't want to give false hope to Matt any more than she wants to give false encouragement to Dmitri. Her actions toward Matt are unlikely to cause permanent harm—their bond of friendship is strong. She can't say the same about Dmitri, though. She's seen it in his eyes, or the way his body tenses and trembles. Somehow she must minimize the damage or hurt she is inflicting on him and keep him distant but safe, nearby but protected. *Is there a happy medium? A fine line, a balance?* The pendulum keeps swinging between the two halves of her mind, leaving her feeling hideous; she must continue acting cruel toward Dmitri, and she hates that. *Why do I care if I hurt him?* She ponders that thought before answering herself. *Because I'm not like him. I'm not a cold-hearted monster like Shashenka either.*

That thought reminds her of what she learned during her time in London. The nine nights she spent with Matt were productive. He brought more information about the network of control Shashenka exerts over his coven—the goblin king has made himself a virtual monarch. While the Druzhinas are few and elite, their duties are kept to enforcing law, conducting political assassinations, and hunting and killing rogue shadow realm species. More frightening, Matt told Eliza, are the Druzhinniki. Unlike their elite counterparts, this group numbers several hundred and its members are spread around the world to do whatever legitimate or illegal work

Shashenka has for them. He pulls his bodyguards from their ranks. Their duties include manipulating and controlling the smaller covens loyal to Belyakov, and they enforce his business interests—and they have no compunction about using violence.

The thought of Shashenka having his own twisted version of a mafia was terrifying. Eliza almost gave up her plan to overthrow him. But after several hours spent debating the Druzhinniki, both agreed that someone must put a stop to the goblin king's reign of terror. Matt joked that it is freedom or bust. He may be right; if they fail, it will be a spectacular defeat.

Eliza's next step is to decide whom she wants to subvert or mark for killing alongside the goblin king. Matt has promised to research Shashenka's personal guards, the Druzhinas, the courtesans, and the witch. The information will help her narrow the target and approach those critical to her plan.

News travels fast in a coven, and she has learned that some of the Druzhinas will be rotating through over the next couple of weeks. *Without them, we're doomed.* No one ever knows in advance which of them will arrive first, but generally at least half will trickle through in staggered arrivals and departures over several days. While she may not be able to co-opt them before Matt's next report, Eliza decides to work on cementing their developing friendships.

It's time to make friends. I wonder how long I'll need to wait before telling them I need their help to take Shashenka down? God, this could take decades. Twisting thoughts cede ground to sleep and keep her tossing and turning most of the day.

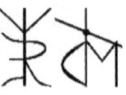

The sickening routine of the inner lair helps to blur time. *Yeah, nothing like normal for a house of horrors.* It is all made worse by Shashenka's needless feasting on humans once a week. He expects those in the inner lair to partake in the practice, and Eliza loathes the disgusting habit. To her it's little more than senseless murder. Feeding on blood to survive is one thing, but doing this is beyond anything she's ever known. It is the one night of the week she wants to remain in her room and not come out, but is unable to avoid. She'd love to be normal and only feed a few times a year. *Normal? Is my humanity gone?*

As everyone gathers in the great hall for the so-called feast, Eliza notices that Victoria and Stephan are there—the first of the Druzhinas to arrive. *Besides killing, what are their skills? I really need to get to know them.* Working her way through the crowd toward them, she nods in hello. They barely get pleasantries exchanged when the guards escort the doomed humans into the room. Clenching her jaw, Eliza avoids looking in the face of the person she grabs. As her fangs sink into the young man's neck, she tries not to speculate on his age or the life he might have had if his fate were different. She bends to one knee, gently lowers the body to the floor, and then reaches to close the eyelids over his now sightless eyes. *I'm sorry.*

Victoria is chuckling as she rises to her feet. The woman leans to whisper in Stephan's ear, but Eliza still hears what she says. "Her and Dmitri ... it's nice to see that some things never change."

Stephan seems to notice the question building on Eliza's face, and deflects it. "Life in the inner lair is treating you well?"

A phony smile spreads across her face. "As well as a monkey in a gilded cage."

Before either can comment, Dmitri joins them and places a hand on the small of her back. She tries arching away from his touch, but he lets go when he extends his greetings to the pair. "Victoria, Stephan. It's good to see both of you again. Undoubtedly you have earned some time off."

Eliza watches as he shakes Stephan's hand and hugs Victoria. When he steps back, she feels his shoulder brush against hers, and she subtly takes a step sideways. Victoria's eyes dart between them as Stephan says, "Time away from our Druzhina duties is always a welcome respite, especially when said duties trend quiet and mundane."

Dmitri's eyes slide toward Eliza, and she looks away as if she is searching the room. He says, "Quiet times ... often the calm before the storm."

Somewhat abruptly, Victoria says, "Do you think Master will ever reinstate you? It's not the same with those we're missing."

All three briefly look at Eliza, and between their conversation, looks, and Dmitri's near presence, she is beginning to feel rather uncomfortable. *What are they not saying ... hiding? What do they know that I don't?* Sadness tinges Dmitri's response. "No. It's clear my time among you is finished."

The air suddenly heavier around them, Eliza decides to engage Victoria. "Why don't we leave the men to talk shop? I need girl time, and it looks to be a slow night for me, what with everyone else fat and happy after another lovely feast."

The couple exchange glances and Stephan dips his head in agreement. Victoria smiles as she moves alongside Eliza, locking their arms together. "I'd enjoy taking a stroll in the garden."

The women leave the great hall and exit the castle through the nearest door. Neither speaks until Victoria stops and motions for Eliza to join her on a bench. "How are you doing here? Is everyone treating you kindly in the inner lair?"

"I'm adjusting. I'm sure everyone treats me as well as can be expected."

Eliza notices the muscles in Victoria's face and neck tighten. "It's not easy for you here, is it?"

Seriously, should it be? "It's not a life I want." Seeing warmth and sadness in her eyes, Eliza adds, "I'm sure it's nothing like being a Druzhina. Tell me what's it like doing what you do."

"There is a freedom to it that I enjoy. We get to travel a lot and meet many different people, but it has its downside too." When she remains quiet, Victoria says, "We enforce the law, and that sometimes means carrying out harsh punishments and justice."

Eliza's hoping for more than a general job description; she needs to know Victoria's skills. "What's the worst thing you've had to do as a Druzhina?"

"I'd rather not talk about it."

The two women fall into an awkward silence. Finally Victoria draws a deep breath. "How are you getting along with Dmitri?"

Why is everyone so bent on us getting along? "On a good night we put up with each other, but if you don't mind, I'd rather not talk about him."

"You don't like him much, do you?"

Biting back a retort, Eliza responds with as much honesty as possible. "I resent what he's done to my life. I know he tries making up for it, but I wish he was still serving the Druzhina and had less time at the inner lair." She pauses. "Do you know why he was fired from being a Druzhina?" *So much for not talking about him. Sabotage yourself, much?*

"It's something I'm not at liberty to share details about." Victoria shifts uncomfortably, signaling she is holding back something of importance.

Trying a different tactic, Eliza prods further. "Do Druzhinas get replaced often?"

"No. In fact, we've only ever lost three Druzhinas since they were formed."

"Oh?"

Her lips draw into a tight line. "All three lost their positions because they went against Master's wishes."

Clearly, the woman is dancing around revealing anything of value, and Eliza recognizes it for what it is. "Dmitri was reassigned to the inner lair, but what happened to the other two?"

"It's not a matter we should be discussing." Victoria

stands and starts to walk down the path.

The subject is closed, but she has to find something Victoria will talk about that will give her the information she needs. People often complain about their jobs and bosses—maybe vampires do too. During her brief time here, Eliza has seen Shashenka's quick temper and cruel brutality on display. Often when he's not physically hurting someone, he is emotionally tormenting those around him. Strangely, it tempers her fear and increases her courage and determination to end him. "Are you happy in your job? It seems many are unhappy here, but no one ever confronts Master about our work conditions."

Turning swiftly, Victoria grabs Eliza by the shoulders and hisses, her tone grave, "One word of advice—keep these thoughts to yourself. It's not safe to speak of such things."

Stunned, she watches Victoria hurry off toward the castle. *Well, that didn't go the way I hoped. Was she warning me or threatening me?* The Druzhinas have more freedom than anyone else in the coven does. She wonders if they are using fear of Shashenka to keep everyone in line, or if they fear him too.

CHAPTER 36: DMITRI

Barely Holding On

The day after Stephan and Victoria leave, Justin and Sofia arrive, providing Dmitri some distraction from the tedium of working the inner lair. He tries not to think of it as living vicariously through the Druzhinas, but he's only fooling himself. Dmitri misses working with them. On their second night at the castle, Justin and Sofia go with him while he escorts Sally, Elizabetta, and another courtesan to a tavern where they're meeting some of Shashenka's shady business associates.

Normally when they go out, Dmitri stays in the shadows, where he can watch the women and protect them if necessary. Tonight Justin and Sofia join him at a corner table not far from where the courtesans sit with their dates.

"So, Master has you babysitting these days." Justin's tease is laced with sarcasm.

Dmitri's jaw tenses as he bites back a retort. "One could say that."

Winking, Justin says, "At least it gets you out of the castle for a change of scenery. There are some good-looking women here." Dmitri watches as Justin scans the crowd and makes eye contact with a tall woman whose black hair flows past her waist.

Sofia scowls at Justin. "I'll keep Dmitri company. Go mingle."

"I'll take you up on that." A broad smile is on his face as he leaves the table.

Sliding into a chair next to Dmitri, Sofia asks in a low tone, "How's Eliza doing?"

He looks across to where Elizabetta is sitting on a man's lap, fawning over him and laughing. "As you can see, she is doing exactly what Master intended."

"No, I mean how is *she* doing."

Taking a deep breath through his nose, he exhales slowly. "I don't recognize her anymore. She's not who she was, but it appears she's accepting and adjusting to this life quite well."

Sofia gazes at the other table and watches as Elizabetta and the man head to the dance floor. "So it seems." She turns back toward Dmitri. "How are you doing?"

"Fine."

"You can't fool me. Anyone who knows you can see otherwise."

He ignores the comment and keeps his eyes on Elizabetta. The way she's suggestively pressed against the man she's dancing with is boiling the rage inside him. *Sofia sees through me, but can't see that?* "Would you care to dance?"

Looking at his outstretched hand, Sofia nods and takes it. Dmitri leads her to the dance floor and immediately pulls her close. When Elizabetta notices them, he whispers in Sofia's ear, "Watch her reaction—it will tell you what you want to know." He cups Sofia's face and looks at her. "Forgive me, but play along, please."

Then he presses a kiss to Sofia's lips.

She immediately tenses and pulls back, hissing, "What are you doing?"

"Watch her. You'll understand." He kisses her again as his hand slides down over her hip, keeping her turned to observe Elizabetta's reaction.

Sofia's eyes widen and he knows without looking behind him that she's reacting to Elizabetta. A moment later they turn and his eyes lock with Elizabetta's. Her back is against her dance partner's chest, and she is swaying provocatively against him. But the look she's giving Dmitri is cold.

When the song ends, they return to the table. Elizabetta is glaring at them, and Dmitri's scowl matches her intensity. He leans toward Sofia. "What did you see?"

"I'm not really sure. Anger mostly, I suppose. Maybe some jealousy, confusion—but something is off, not right."

"It's called hatred." Dmitri looks down at his hands. "Eliza acts abhorrently toward me now. Master got what he wanted."

Sofia takes another long look at Elizabetta. "It's that bad?"

"Yes. She avoids me when she can and will not speak with me unless she has to, and when she does it is often rude and disrespectful. I've lost her." His hands rest against his legs, palms up, and he briefly stares at them before curling them into fists.

Before Sofia can reply, Justin rejoins them at the table with the woman he was dancing with moments ago. "Dmitri, Sofia, this is Katya. Katya, my friends Dmitri and Sofia."

"Pleased to meet you," Dmitri offers dryly. Sometimes he's not sure why Justin bothers. This woman, like many others, will likely be forgotten by the end of the night.

Katya exchanges pleasantries with them, but mostly flirts with Justin at the table and on the dance floor as the night goes on. The distraction keeps the conversation from returning to Elizabetta or Dmitri's life in the inner lair, and he's grateful for that. Living it is hard enough, but talking about it only drives his failures to a deeper level inside him.

When they return to the castle after the tavern closes, Sofia goes to visit with Elizabetta while Justin stays with Dmitri in the great hall. Only a few others are in the room; most have already retired for the day. Dmitri asks about the other Druzhinas, and Justin updates him on their current assignments. Mostly their activity is routine, with nothing spectacular to report: a violation of marked property, a business associate caught skimming profits, a dispute with a rival coven in New Zealand, and the capture and execution of a werewolf in Peru who assaulted one of the locals at the estate in Cusco.

Dmitri learns there will be a slight gap before the others cycle through for time off and their next task. "How long before you're sent out again?"

"A night, two at most. I'm supposed to speak with Master later tonight about my next assignment." Justin shrugs.

"We're not getting as much time off since you were sidelined, and it's wearing thin for some of us. Vladimir intends on discussing it with Shashenka when he arrives. He's going to ask for your reinstatement first, but will push for adding a new Druzhina if Master resists."

A spark of hope ignites, but Dmitri smothers it. He knows it is hopeless. "Doubtless the odds favor a new member. Master will not allow my return."

"I hope you're wrong. You have the support of all the Druzhinas—that should mean something."

"It will mean nothing."

After the night ends, Dmitri is alone in his room when he hears Sofia and Elizabetta talking in the adjoining room. His thoughts drift to the time when they were all Druzhinas. Life wasn't perfect, but it was better than this. Elizabetta was his, and she was remarkable in skill and grace. He can't reconcile Eliza with Elizabetta—they are two different people. It is a victory for Shashenka, and even that win fails to quell his master's anger toward him. Still, it is enough to trigger thoughts of the failed rebellion. A subject, he recognizes, that is increasingly crossing his mind.

He doesn't know if it's desire for another chance to end Shashenka or the longing for Elizabetta that he seeks in such memories. Perhaps it is both. He's still sorting through it later that morning as he drifts off to sleep, and it sets up another day where Elizabetta is with him in a dream. It's the only place where she belongs to him now; the only time where she is kind to him and loves him.

Too soon, twilight arrives, chasing the dreams away, and

Dmitri readies for another long night of work. He watches for Elizabetta, needing to see something in her that tells him the dreams are not lies. As usual, she ignores him. He can't let it go. Trying to keep the hurt off his face, he offers a smile. "Good evening, love, how are you?"

No response as she looks away. He tries again. "May I assist you with anything tonight?"

Her glare matches the acid in her tone. "You don't get it, do you? Try catching a clue for once. I don't want or need anything from you, so why don't you do something novel for a change and leave me the hell alone!"

Dmitri's throat tightens, and her cutting words leave his chest heaving for air as she walks away. Closing his eyes, taking a moment for a few steadying breaths, he waits for the ache in his heart to stop. It doesn't. Then he hears Shashenka's low laugh as a hand clasps his shoulder.

"I told you, her hatred for you grows nightly, and you'll never stop it." A malevolent grin spreads across his master's face. "Indeed, it gives me immeasurable pleasure—among other things. Would you like to know what those other things are?"

There is only one acceptable answer, and Dmitri knows it. He tries but fails to look the evil vampire in the eye. "Yes, Master."

Shashenka pats Dmitri's shoulder as if they are old friends. "Our lovely Eliza is truly a remarkable lover. I should compliment you on teaching her so well over the years you had with her. She pleases me like no other."

Bile rises in his throat. Dmitri stops breathing, and pain

and hate battle for control of his expression and body. An image of permanently removing the arm grasping his shoulder comes to mind. He knows a response is expected, but the words never reach his tongue.

Shashenka's grip squeezes tighter. "There is one thing that pleases me even more than her skill in bed. Would you like to know what *that* is?"

No! "Yes, Master."

"My greatest enjoyment is in knowing that you will never again feel her sweetness, whether in a tender word or a loving touch. You'll never taste those luscious lips or feel the roll of her hips while deep inside her. You'll never lay your head upon her breasts or take pleasure in them. Yes, it all suits me quite well, watching you suffer and knowing you'll do so for an eternity as you pay the price for your treachery."

The words shred his mind and hurt as much as a blow from the naval cat. *I need to get out of here. It's too much.*

"I have to admit, it's rather more satisfying than expected. When you tried killing me, I wanted you to suffer a slow, torturous death, but this ..." He shakes his head, smiling, and his eyes turn cold. "This exceeds the pleasure I would have taken in executing you, and it will last far longer. Oh yes. As they say, this is the gift that keeps on giving."

It takes every ounce of discipline he has to lock his body in place. Hatred and pain are strangling the words in his throat. His jaw is tight, teeth nearly clenched, as he says, "Is that all, Master? I have work to do."

Patting him on the back, Shashenka starts to walk away. "Yes, by all means, return to your duties. I'm sure the other courtesans appreciate your help."

Dmitri keeps his distance from Elizabetta for the rest of the night and tries to ignore her while she playfully teases Charles, laughs with Peter, and eventually leaves with Shashenka. Not once does she look his way, and he cannot decide if that makes the night worse or better. He's still pondering it when he climbs in bed that morning.

Then his thoughts return to the last conversation they had when they were still mates; every movement and word between them is inexorably etched in his memory along with the pain, hope, and love those moments held. It was the night before Maria erased her mind and placed Elizabetta in the catatonic state.

They were locked in the cells beneath this castle, awaiting their punishment for treason. Vladimir was granted unsupervised time to visit them, and he used it to give them a few last minutes together. Dmitri recalls the shock of seeing the cell door open and watching Elizabetta and Vladimir step into the room. A haunting ache echoes through him as he remembers the way she rushed into his arms.

"I've been given an hour to visit with you both. If you haven't changed your mind, then Master will carry out the alternate punishment tomorrow night." Vladimir's tone was somber.

Dmitri remembers how Elizabetta pressed firmly against his chest, and the kiss they exchanged. At the time and even now, he cannot fathom taking her life, but the pain of living near her is almost as insufferable as living without her. He still hears himself saying, "I cannot execute my mate if it means existing after she's gone. If I must live, so must she."

Elizabetta tried once more to get him to reconsider. "Death is a better fate. I cannot bear the thought of living and never knowing you again. Please, *amore*, let me go. I'd rather die."

He tucked a loose strand of hair behind her ear, never breaking eye contact. "Do not ask that of me. I cannot kill you. I need you to live, *amore*."

Vladimir leaned against the wall. "Death may be a more favorable outcome for her, and kinder for you, brother. If it were Anna, I would find it easier to live with her death than to watch her go on never knowing she's my mate. You know the bond is too strong, and leaving it intact for you and not Elizabetta only invites centuries of torment that may be intolerable."

Vladimir didn't mean to be unkind, yet his words cut deep. Dmitri still wouldn't change what he said in return. "Could you kill Anna if Master commanded it? Could you end her life with your hands? I do not think so. It is too much to ask of any mate." Dmitri shook his head and looked pleadingly at Elizabetta. "Keeping you alive is a risk I am willing to take. I believe in our bond, and trust that you will come back to me. Master has not forbidden that. You will love me again."

"We know how evil he is. Shashenka will manipulate and control every aspect—he will make it impossible for me to find my way back to you."

"*Amore, ti amo e non smetterò mai di amarti.*" He gently brushed a kiss on her lips. "I swear that I will never leave your side. I will endure this for us, and I will protect you. When your mind believes you are someone new, I will court you and I will win your affections again. You will love me as you do now. I promise to never fail you."

Elizabetta will never know how prophetic her words were, or how he's learned the lesson of foolish pride since.

"If I should fail you, *amore* ..." Elizabetta cupped his face in her hands. "What you will endure is unfathomable. I do not wish to see you under such circumstances, even if I do not know you. It will be too much for my heart to bear."

"You are my heart, my soul. I will not lose you." He kissed her forehead. "Your heart will never forget where it belongs."

She sighed heavily, and tears welled in her eyes as she pleaded for his forgiveness should she not remember. "I will ask for you to kill me if the burden becomes too great. If you can endure, then I charge you never to give up. Fight for me. Return my heart where it belongs."

"There is nothing to forgive, *amore*. I will not end your life—I will fight for you, always."

Those were promises he made, the oath given that final night together. It was the last thing he said to her. Shashenka sent for them the next night. They were kept separated, not allowed to touch or share a final word, when the guards brought them to the great hall. Their hearts broke together as the last of the Elizabetta they knew was taken away by the witch's spell. He can still feel the burning ache in his chest and the helplessness that coursed through him as he watched her lie on the table. Tears streamed down her face while Maria muttered the words that sealed their fate. Even now, he can hear the last words Elizabetta kept repeating until her voice fell silent. *Ti amo e non smetterò mai di amarti. I will never cease loving you.* It was as if she meant to imprint them on her soul and never forget.

Now Dmitri wonders if Vladimir was right, that this is too much to overcome. *I am failing her. I cannot break my oath. I cannot live with this pain. I must not fail her again!*

He is determined to be persistent and continue his efforts to reverse Elizabetta's hatred of him. Dmitri keeps up his nightly pattern of talking to her, asking after her needs, and she rebuffs him at each turn. The more he tries, the more distant she becomes, but he won't give up; it is time for a new approach. After seeing to the other courtesans' needs, he seeks Elizabetta's whereabouts and begins following her from a discreet distance. Finally an opportunity to prove she needs him presents itself.

Elizabetta is escorting one of Shashenka's many human business partners for a night of entertainment. The man doesn't know what they are and is oblivious of the dangers lurking around their kind. Like many other men, he assumes her cool skin is a product of the chilly castle or the cold winter air of Russia. When they leave the theater, Dmitri watches from the shadows as the man drapes his coat around Elizabetta's shoulders. She looks up, giving the man a warm smile. They are nearly back to the car when a group of thugs surrounds them, demanding money and jewelry.

Dmitri briskly walks forward as Elizabetta pulls the horse-head dagger from under the borrowed coat. The sight of it thrills him. Not only is she armed, but with his gift. The businessman's fear is evident. He's ignoring Elizabetta's attempt to protect them, and his shaking hand is already reaching for the wallet he intends to hand over. Brandishing the dagger, she faces the thieves. "Evgeniy, leave your wallet where it is. They are not taking anything from us."

"We're outnumbered, dear, and our possessions can be replaced, but our lives cannot." His voice sounds tight with panic as he holds the wallet out.

Elizabetta ignores the man. "Which one of you is stupid enough to take me on?"

"Just give us the goods, lady. We don't want to hurt you." A gangly youth with greasy hair takes another step forward, showing a pistol in his belt.

"I suggest you move on." Dmitri stops just outside the group surrounding Elizabetta and Evgeniy. "Their valuables are not worth your life."

The youth draws the pistol and points it at Elizabetta. Dmitri's pulse quickens.

"I don't need your help," Elizabetta hisses at Dmitri, and she flies into motion. Before the thugs can blink, she is behind the greasy-haired kid and the dagger is at his throat. "You're going to hand that gun over to my date, and the rest of you are going to put your weapons on the ground. Then you are going to walk away."

When the boy hesitates, she yells, "Do it now, or I'm going to cut you. You will die." She presses the blade into his neck, and a drop of blood slides down the front of his throat.

The youth's hand is shaking as he points the pistol toward

the ground and holds it out for Evgeniy to take. The other
four exchange nervous looks before laying their knives and
guns on the ground. Elizabetta waits for them to back away
several paces before she releases the one she's holding. She
roughly shoves him forward, and he takes a few stumbling
steps before breaking into a run.

That's my Elizabetta! So ferocious, so strong. Dmitri feels
a small sense of pride; her fierceness and ability to fight are
traits she's always had, even when she was human.

When the hooligans are out of sight, Elizabetta ignores
Dmitri at first, instead instructing Evgeniy to collect the discarded weapons.

"How did you ..." Evgeniy begins as he bends over to pick
up a knife. "How did you move so fast?"

Looking at Dmitri, she says, "Well, since you're here, why
don't you take care of that." She places the weapons in a pile
on the ground.

Nodding in understanding, Dmitri clasps a hand on the
man's neck. "You did not see anything other than Eliza
greeting me as you left the theater and returned to your car."
He steps toward Elizabetta. "Hello, Eliza, how is your evening?"

Her eyes smolder in a mix of gratitude and animosity. "It's
fine. Now if you'll excuse us, we have to go."

Dmitri watches as Evgeniy curls an arm around her waist
and they begin to walk away. In a low tone she hisses as they
pass by him, "I told you, I don't need you. Leave me alone."

Shaking his head, he retrieves the small pile of weapons
and continues following them. She's right, he wasn't needed

to protect her, and it's disappointing. She's never really needed him in that regard, but where it used to be a point of pride, it is now another blow to his mind. Then he wonders if Shashenka is aware that Elizabetta still hasn't learned how to use her skills to alter human memory. Should he mention it or not? *Ah, but she at least needed me for that much.*

Dmitri follows them inside the hotel where the man is staying, and when they step onto the elevator, he takes a seat in the lobby. *Keep fighting, never give up.* He doesn't expect Elizabetta to return for the next few hours, but he is happy to wait.

An hour before dawn, Elizabetta enters the lobby and storms straight toward him. "Why are you still here? I thought I told you to leave me alone."

"You know I can't do that, love." He offers an apologetic smile and turns to follow her outside.

They're within walking distance of the castle when she cuts through an alley on the way back. It's there she turns on him, dagger in hand. "I'm going to make this really clear one last time. If you don't stay away from me, I will hurt you."

He blinks as the words strike him. *You're already hurting me in ways you'll never know.* "It's my duty to see after you."

"Unless that goblin king sends you, no, it isn't. Stop talking to me, and stop following me! Don't you get it? I don't want to be around you, period."

Desperation drives him to brashness; he reaches for her hands, but she quickly steps back. "Elizabetta ... please, *amore*, remember I hold your heart."

"Excuse me, what? Are you flipping kidding me?" She

takes a menacing step toward him. "Listen, buckwheat, you're certifiable. My *heart*"—the word reeks contempt— "belongs to no one, least of all you. I want nothing to do with you. Stay away from me. I'm not going to tell you again."

The weight of the words staggers him back a step. He gulps and swallows hard. "I'm sorry, love."

Elizabetta lets out a frustrated growl and runs away. For a second he considers chasing after her, but doesn't. *How am I supposed to do this? Forcing myself on her is driving her further away.*

Then he recalls when she asked him to kill her if it became too much to endure. A fleeting minute passes while he considers it. *No, I cannot kill her. Perhaps it is time to back off a little. Keep watch from a distance and don't let her see me following. Don't speak to her unless it's demanded of me.*

Somehow ... someday ... he will win her back.

CHAPTER 37: ELIZA

Unchecked Fury

Nights begin passing as they should, at least as expected of Eliza. Daytime, when she's free to sleep alone and is not sharing her bed with another, is becoming the loneliest time for her. Dmitri barely talks to her anymore—it makes her longing for him worse. She knows feelings toward him are inappropriate and hopeless given their circumstances. *I wish he never put that thought in my head. Hold my heart ... yeah right.* She sighs; at least she's mostly kept busy at night and can't dwell on it.

As the weeks go by the stagnant pattern of pursuing her goal to take down Shashenka begins to wear thin. Eliza constantly reminds herself to remain patient—she knows this may take years. But still, she is looking forward to the next rendezvous with Matt. She is eager for new details that she can use in manipulating others, especially the Druzhinas. Working without information leaves her going by first impressions. Disconcertingly, those she's becoming familiar with act as if they already know and genuinely have liked her

447

for years. It leaves her pondering her mysterious past.

Somehow, Dmitri is the key that will unravel all of her riddles. *May as well be a lost key for all the good he's doing.* Even though it's because of her that they're not talking, she's growing increasingly and irrationally angry with him over it. Worse, he's still stalking her—and everyone knows it. The annoyance Eliza feels over it is testing her self-restraint, and she decides to channel it for better use. If given the opportunity, she will use it to drive the final blow, firmly setting the wedge between them so it remains until she's ready to pull it out. Maybe then he will stay away until she can finish taking down Shashenka. *I'm going to have a lot to apologize for when it's done.* She laughs aloud, wondering if by then he will hate her again.

A chance to take that step comes sooner than expected when a dozen vampires gather in the great hall late one evening.

"Eliza, may I have a moment of your time?"

She knows who it is before she turns around. "No, Dmitri, you cannot."

"Please, love—"

Eliza cuts him off. "Fine. Fine." She closes her eyes, nods twice, and explodes into her planned tirade. "Let me tell you something, Dmitri. You are making me wacko. I see you lurking about, watching me, always watching, following me. It's creepy. You're like some crazed, maniacal vampire stalker. What is wrong with you?"

Then something snaps inside her, and planned speech cedes ground to hurt, anger, shame, and disappointment. It swells into a torrent she can't restrain. Lying and honest words race off her tongue like a bunch of lemmings over a cliff. "I hear you in your room, hanging on everything going on in mine. I half expect you to waltz in and watch what I'm doing. Hell, you even pick up after me if I so much as leave a brush on the counter or a towel on the bathroom floor. You're not my maid. If I drop a towel, I expect it to be there when I return."

Dmitri stands there flinching while she lashes out at him. Eliza doesn't give him a chance to jump in. She knows it's unfair and that most of what she's saying is a lie, but she can't stop.

"Let me tell you something else. Your stalking of me in Montana ruined my life. Then when you forced me to go to Big Sky, I tried ... God knows, I tried ... being friendly to you, to get to know you, and you treated me like dirt. I felt sorry for you because you seemed so lonely, and others spoke so highly and seemingly think you're worth knowing. I don't. In fact, I've decided they are wrong.

"You're pathetic, and that's why no woman wants you. You're a pathetic, weak man with no life, and I hate every-thing about you. I wish I had never laid eyes on you, and if I never saw you again, that would be too soon. Do you hear me, Dmitri Markov? I regret the day I ever laid eyes on you. I hate you. Do you get that? I hate you!"

A single set of hands slowly clapping returns Eliza to her senses. It's then she realizes that all eyes in the room are on her. Dmitri still hasn't moved an inch; tears are welling in his eyes. He keeps swallowing hard, jaw tense, and he is clearly struggling but failing to keep his bottom lip from quivering. *Oh crap, what did I just do?*

Mortified, Eliza flees the great hall. She doesn't stop running until she's at the top of one of the guard towers. Others rarely come here; it's one place she can be alone without anyone bothering her. Standing in front of a window, Eliza holds a hand over her mouth as disgust and shame rage inside her. Pandemonium explodes in her mind, berating her the same way she just did to Dmitri. *Oh God, he didn't deserve that. I'm heartless ... a malicious, cruel monster.* She is as locked in her own dressing down as he was in hers moments earlier, and she doesn't hear the footsteps enter the room behind her.

An ominously low voice mutters something, and without conscious will, Eliza finds herself spinning to face the door. Standing ten feet away is Maria, her eyes murderously enraged. Eliza can't move or speak; her body and mouth are frozen. "If you ever humiliate Dmitri that way again, no agreement I have with Shashenka will protect you or keep me from killing or cursing you for the rest of your life."

Eliza still cannot move or speak. The witch's eyes are narrowed in fury. "He is an honorable and strong man who has endured far more than you will ever know. He has done more to protect you than anyone else has. He was humiliated, shamed, stripped of his dignity, and tortured because of you. He has given up far more than you ever have, just to keep you alive. Your ignorance is no excuse for treating him with such ingratitude and hatred.

"How dare you! How dare you, Elizabetta Rossellini. If you value your life, you'll never do that to him again."

Maria mutters something and is gone before Eliza realizes she's free to move again. Slumping to the ground, she begins to cry as the witch's words strike her repeatedly. *She's right, I'm ignorant—I don't know the truth. He is honorable. Protected me ... given up ... saved me?* She deserved every word, and more.

Then gradually she settles on the one detail buried among the others; it should have screamed at her from the start. *Elizabetta Rossellini—a name, a complete full name. Elizabetta ... Rossellini. Elizabetta.* When she first came to the Belyakov coven, and even before, when Dmitri was stalking her and when she was in McAllister, that's the name the vampires kept calling her. It took weeks of correcting them before they finally stopped; even now, some still slip and call her Elizabetta before they catch themselves. Elizabetta Rossellini—Eliza Ross; it is so astoundingly simple and obvious, it leaves her thunderstruck.

Elizabetta Rossellini. Could it be— She knows it, she feels it, and even her bones are singing the truth of it. It will be the first name at the top of her list when she sees Matt in a week.

It's time to learn who I really am.

CHAPTER 38: DMITRI

Final Straw

Shashenka's triumphant laugh echoes mockingly down the hall after him as Dmitri flees to his room. There, the tears he's been choking back start to flow. Everything she said is true, but hearing it directly from her punches more holes in his heart than he's ever managed on his own. He stalks her ... hangs on ... looks after her. He has ruined her life, but in more ways than she'll ever know. Dazed, he wanders into the bathroom and he looks around, unsure why he came in here. Picking up the brush Elizabetta left on the counter, he starts opening a drawer to put it away. Then he remembers this angers her. He puts it back on the counter as she left it.

He stumbles back to his room. *I can't take this, go on like this any longer. Nothing good is left.* There is no way to undo the terrible acts he's committed against her. He has no way to atone, amend; there is nothing left for him. Nothing left of him. *She was right ... all those years ago, she knew her own heart and mine. She knew we'd fail.*

That woman is not his Elizabetta. Yet he cannot kill her, even now he cannot. *It has to end. I have to set her free. I cannot exist.*

Dmitri removes his shirt and then pulls the mate to Elizabetta's dagger from his drawer. Backing into the corner of the room, he lays the blade against his arm and begins to cut, deeply slicing the veins. He sees the blood, but his body and mind are too numb to feel the pain. Sinking to the floor, he switches the dagger to his other hand and slices the second arm. Still he feels nothing.

He watches as the blood flow starts to slow and the wounds begin to close several minutes later. All strength and will have left him; he is incapable of releasing himself from this destroyed life. *Eliza is right—I'm weak and pathetic. I can't go on ... I can't. I've lost everything.* The only action he's capable of now is bawling like a broken child. Curling onto his side, Dmitri lets anguish take him, and he greets it like an old friend in a warm embrace. He gladly follows it and allows it to bury him in the deepest, darkest pits of grief. Soon there is no sound or sight, only fading images of an unnaturally long–existing nightmare. He'll spend an eternity here; he has no will to leave.

CHAPTER 39: ELIZA

Aftermath

Eliza returns to her room at sunrise. Luckily Shashenka is nowhere in sight when she enters the great hall on the way back from the tower. The prideful and approving look he gave her as he clapped will haunt her forever. In that moment, she knew she was just like him—unadulterated evil. A few people are still lingering, but Eliza can't look at any of them. Sally calls out and then chases after her as she slips into the hall leading to her room. She has to ask the other woman twice to leave her alone and go away before she finally does.

In her room, exhausted, she prepares to go to bed. Cautiously she opens the bathroom door to make sure it's empty—it is—and steps to the sink vanity to turn the water on.

She's hanging the hand towel when she hears a sound from Dmitri's room. Stopping to listen, she realizes he's crying. Only it's not the soft sounds of gentle weeping, it's the heavy, racking sobs of someone in the throes of tremendous grief.

I did this to him. Eliza has never felt more atrocious in her whole life, and it's tearing and gnawing at her in ways she never expected or has experienced before.

Compelled to do something—short of revealing every-thing—Eliza slowly turns the knob on his door. What she sees drives spikes through her feet and pins them to the stone floor. *Oh my God, not again.* Curled on his side, shirt-less, Dmitri is lying on the floor near the corner of his room, his body quaking and shuddering with each sob. A bloody dagger is lying in the limp grasp of an outstretched hand. The other arm, tightly wound over his head from front to back, entangles his fingers in the hairs at the nape of his neck. Blood covers his arms—elbow to wrist—and is matting his dark hair. Her dead heart lurches at the sight of the blood pooled around his head and smeared on the floor.

He hasn't noticed she's in the room. "Humiliated, shamed, stripped of his dignity, and tortured ..." That's what Maria said. Dmitri alluded to that torture the night Matt found her near the Kremlin. Her eyes sweep over the numerous scars on his chest and back—her stomach clenches at the sight, picturing the horrors he's suffered. Now she has done worse. Fighting tears, trying to choke them back, Eliza steps toward Dmitri and kneels next to him, unsure if she should touch him.

"I'm sorry. God, I'm so sorry, Dmitri. Please, please ... please, I shouldn't have done that to you. I am sorry."

He doesn't respond; it's as if he can't hear her, doesn't know she is there. His eyes are open, unblinking and unseeing. The heavy sobbing sends spasms through his body. Eliza gently places a hand on his hip. He still doesn't respond. Wherever Dmitri is in his mind, it's far from his body, far from here, and she doesn't know how to find him, to bring him back. Not knowing what else to do, Eliza grabs a pillow and blanket from his bed. She tenderly lays the blanket over his body and tucks it around him, lifting his head and placing the pillow underneath.

If I ask Maria to help, she'll tell Master. I've done this to him. I have to fix it. How do I fix someone I broke? She places a tender kiss at his temple, mumbling, "Sorry, so sorry, forgive me," and then she sits with him, holding his hand and silently shedding her own tears.

Unable to withstand his pain, Eliza snatches the dagger and runs for her room. Then she looks, really looks at the dagger covered in blood. *What was he doing with my dagger?* Studying it, she walks into the bathroom and washes Dmitri's blood away. She dries the blade and returns to her room. Then she realizes it's not her dagger, but one so eerily similar that it's nearly a twin.

In the middle of the blade is a different Elder Futhark rune, this one with a backward *D* and forward *M*—Dmitri Markov. Eliza read about these runes after arriving here, to understand her own mark. This rune, the Naudiz, looks like a *t* or cross with its horizontal arm skewed—the left side raised, not touching the *D*, and the right side lowered, touching the last peak of the *M*. Where they intersect the vertical line, a slight dot binds them. The sources she read said this rune represents need or hardship. It is fitting for Dmitri.

Still, it has not escaped her notice that this dagger, his dagger, is a twin to hers. *Why?* Something this finely crafted—custom-made with these materials—isn't something one buys on a whim. They doubtless were very expensive, and seem to have been intentionally planned before they were created. *Why would he pour that much love and attention into a matched set of daggers expressly meant for him and me?* It's another mystery to solve.

The sobs from his room are quieting. Eliza undresses and gets into bed, lying awake, unable to sleep—listening for Dmitri, thinking. When sleep finally comes, she becomes lost in more memory-like dreams. Her life makes sense inside the dreams, and somehow she knows they bring her closer to the truth.

CHAPTER 40: DMITRI

Going, Going, Gone

Light and sound return. Disappointingly, all his senses awaken, but he's not the same; he'll never be the same again. He realizes someone has put a pillow under his head and tucked a blanket around him on the floor. It stupefies him why someone would bother. He is not worth anyone's compassion or pity.

Quietly he gathers clean clothes and takes a shower, not wanting to disturb Elizabetta should she be in her room. *No, not Elizabetta ... Eliza.* He doesn't listen for her; he can't do that anymore. Instead he dresses, leaves his room, and finds his way to the dungeon. He goes to a cell and stares into the gloom. This is where Elizabetta was still his mate, where they spent part of their last night together. *This is where she ceased existing, and she knew it, expected it. This is where we ended.* A venomous thought occurs to him. *That woman ... that thing upstairs is an imposter.* After several hours, he wanders over to the cell where Shashenka tortured him for decades. He physically left these rooms, but he understands now that his mind never fully did.

When he returns to the ground floor, he realizes the night is half over. Others are murmuring, looking, staring, watching, and Dmitri lowers his head, avoiding eye contact with everyone while torpidly going about his duties. Some try speaking to him, but his words evaporate before they reach his mouth. The constant tremble in his body distracts his mind and disconnects his tongue. If asked for help, he complies with the request, doing only what needs to be done. He doesn't know if he'll ever speak again. *Don't care, don't want to ... nothing left to say.*

Kees and Katherine arrive a few nights later. They try repeatedly to talk with him, but his silent, unresponsive staring seems to unnerve them. Katherine takes his hand and leads him to a table. He remains standing, staring down at the floor. "Dmitri, what's wrong?"

Seconds fall into oblivion. "Go find Maria. I'll stay with him," Kees urges her. They exchange a worried look before she leaves. While she's gone, Kees asks, "Did something happen? Is Elizabetta okay?"

Elizabetta ... my Elizabetta. The pain sears every cell in his body. *She's gone.* He can't breathe. He collapses to his knees, with arms wrapped around his sides, and leans forward. His forehead presses against the cold stone floor. *I failed you. Forgive me, amore.* Squeezing his eyes shut, waiting for the color behind the lids to turn black, he seeks the darkness.

Kees tries to pull him up, but Dmitri won't budge. His friend rubs a hand across his back and shoulders. "Tell me, brother, what has happened?'"

Then another hand is on his neck, and voices grow louder around him. "He wasn't like this when I saw him earlier. I don't know what's wrong with him." Maria's hands frantically move across his body. She's looking for a wound that she'll never find.

"I don't understand. What's going on?" Katherine's tone is waffling between concern and anger. "Did he say anything while I was away?"

"He collapsed a minute after you left. I tried getting him to his feet, but he's locked in position and refuses to move."

"Oh, this is priceless." Dmitri cringes as he hears his master's voice. Shashenka prods Dmitri with a foot. "Stupid fool."

Katherine asks again, "Master, what happened? What caused this?"

The witch is muttering and continues searching him for injuries. Dmitri is desperate to pull the darkness over him. *She's gone, no more. I lost her. I failed ... failed her.*

"*Ciach ort!* We need to move him." Anger radiates in Maria's words. "Kees, Katherine, Peter, let's get him off the floor and back to his room."

He does not resist as the others carry him away. He is busy figuring out the puzzle of darkness. He's felt it before, the way it starts settling over his body, but is unsure how to grab and hold on to it. *Is it a fabric, a cloak? Is it an oil, water?* The hands holding him go away; he is on a bed. *I need the darkness ... the void where nothing exists, where I'll cease to exist. It's where my heart and spirit will die.*

Maria pries his eyes open, and the thin veil of darkness he's pulled in falls away. He blinks rapidly for several minutes and then stops and stares without seeing. "You need to stay with us. Don't you do this, Dmitri."

"Is he injured?" The bed shifts as Kees sits on the edge of the mattress. Dmitri stares blankly and doesn't react.

"Not physically." Maria mutters, swears again, and then slaps Dmitri's face when he closes his eyes. "I said, stay with us!"

A sinister laugh rumbles through the room. "He's going out of his mind. Eliza was correct—he's pathetic and weak."

The room suddenly falls silent. Dmitri wills his mind to follow suit as he reaches once more for the darkness.

"Stop wasting your time, Maria." Shashenka says. "I have other tasks for you to do. Let's go."

"Stay with him," Maria whispers to someone.

The room is quiet once more. Then Katherine is stroking his head, murmuring, "Everyone else is gone now—it's just Kees and I. Talk to us, tell us what happened."

Dmitri's fingers touch the darkness; it's smooth, like polished marble or the softest silk.

Kees places a hand on Dmitri's shoulder. "I think Master is right. It's his mind."

"What do you think happened?"

"I'm not sure, but whatever it was wasn't good."

Their voices eventually fall away. There is no concept of time. Then Sally is there sitting on the bed, rambling on, as she often does. "I heard about this when I got up tonight. I know Eliza did this to you somehow, and I'm so upset with her right now ..." She sighs. "I believe mates should be together, but you deserve better than this. It's not right. Don't let her get away with this. If she does, it means Master wins. You've fought so hard and too long to give up now."

She grabs his chin and forces him to look at her. "Fight! Damn it, Dmitri, you fight this. You can't let Shashenka win. We need you. Eliza's too far gone. You may be our only hope."

A black shroud finally drowns her out, and for some time there is nothing. When it lifts, Dmitri is standing near the narrow window in his room, and Vladimir is speaking. "Someone needs to figure out how to fix this. We both know Master won't be patient forever with him in this state."

"Maria should be back here any minute. I don't know what to do for him." Anna's soft voice sounds sad.

Looking out the window, Dmitri can't shake the feeling that he's meant to be doing something—but what, he doesn't know. *I'm not supposed to be here.* He turns and walks out of the room. Halfway down the hall to the great room, Vladimir grabs his arm, turns him, and pushes him against the wall. It confuses him, and the nagging thought that he's supposed to do something returns.

"What's he doing out here?" Maria calls out as her footsteps draw nearer.

"I don't know. He just walked out." Vladimir is searching his eyes. "Can you hear us? Do you understand us?"

Anna snaps her fingers in front of his face. "Say something, anything."

"Let's get him back to his room. I'm going to try a potion

that may wake his mind."

Realizing he's going the wrong way—he should be doing something, not going to his room—Dmitri jerks out of Vladimir's grasp and starts walking away. They don't try stopping him, but follow; he can feel their eyes watching his every move. When he reaches the great hall he looks around the room, searching for something ... someone. *Who am I looking for? What am I doing here?*

Maria, Vladimir, and Anna form a semicircle in front of him. Several minutes pass as they try eliciting a response. His eyes look at everything but them. When Maria tries giving him the potion, he refuses to open his mouth. Vladimir pries his jaws open, but Dmitri twists his head as Maria begins to pour the vial, and more ends up on his shirt than in his mouth. He refuses to swallow; the liquid dribbles over his chin.

"Is there anything else you can try?" Anna asks, wiping the front of his shirt.

"I don't even know if this will work, and if he's going to fight us, we're not likely to get it down him. I've already tried several healing spells." Maria lowers her voice. "Given that Eliza directly caused this, she may be the only one who can bring him back."

"What did she do?" A hint of anger tinges Vladimir's voice.

"She blew up and had a hissy fit right here in front of Shashenka and everyone else." The witch shakes her head. "I suspect there have been similar encounters between the two, because there was nothing said that should have done this in one blow. He's stronger than that, we all know it. We've seen him go through hell for centuries. One outburst shouldn't have unraveled his mind."

Anna leads Dmitri to a chair. "This is because of their punishment?"

Maria looks around the room before answering. "Yes."

"So our master is ultimately to blame," Vladimir says with a note of finality. "I sometimes wonder if it would have been a kindness to allow their execution."

"Don't you ever say that! We did what's right."

"Are you sure, Maria? This is on us now. We pleaded for their lives. Do you see what it's done to them? I swore a blood oath to keep them from harm. Look at Dmitri. Look at what Elizabetta's done, at what she's become. We failed to protect them and gave them a fate I fear is far worse than death."

A dark look comes over Vladimir's face, and it catches Dmitri's eye. He cocks his head to the side, wondering if it is the darkness he's looking for, or something else. Little makes sense to him, other than the urge to find the void.

"We've got to keep trying to get him back somehow. We all know Master will tire of this sooner rather than later." Anna kneels in front of Dmitri. "Hang in there, come back to us. Don't quit. Elizabetta needs you."

His mind screams echoes of her name. *Amore ... gone. I failed her.* Still, he must find something. He's searching ... looking down, looking up, looking through them, and eventually they go away. He realizes it must be daytime; time for bed. He lies on the bed fully clothed, but it doesn't feel right. Someone should be here with him. Then he remembers, Elizabetta. His heart wrenches, and tears begin to fall.

A new pattern develops as the nights pass. Most have given up talking to him and now leave him alone. The solitude suits him. When he's not in his room, he wanders aimlessly around the castle, but he's not thinking or searching. He is just existing, with nowhere to go and no one to go to. Simply it is the way he is now, the way he moves through each night. This is all he has left, beyond avoiding *Eliza* in every way possible. He doesn't hope for her anymore; grief massacred that in its black pit. When she leaves for her days off, he remains at the castle, hiding in an unlocked cell—where he and Elizabetta said good-bye—during the night. He finds it as disturbing as it is comforting, and returns there each evening.

There, the last memory of *his* Elizabetta replays in his mind: every word spoken, every touch shared, and their final kiss when Vladimir said it was time. Dmitri relives each second, holding on to each moment. Then he skips ahead to the last sharp words Eliza—the imposter—threw at him. In that moment he knew that she had cut his Elizabetta from her soul forever. The pain is too great; he's determined to find a way into the darkness, permanently residing there until his bones turn to dust.

Soon the days and nights turn upside down. He spends each day wandering the castle and stays every night in their cell; it's the only way he can hold on to her … let her go. It brings the darkness he seeks, and eventually it will keep him there forever.

CHAPTER 41: ELIZA

I am a Monster

The next evening and for several nights afterward, Eliza sees nothing of Dmitri. She knows he's around; she can hear him crying in his room each day when they're supposed to be sleeping. Shashenka made her feel more humiliated by reveling in what she did to Dmitri. The night after her outburst she apologized to Maria and Sally, the only two who, in her estimation, matter to her besides Dmitri. She wants to make amends to him, but he's giving her no opportunity to do so, and others are constantly in and out of his room. Maria warned her to stay away and leave him alone. Avoiding him leaves her feeling more guilty.

Since that disastrous night, her memory dreams have been coming daily, and stronger with each one. In those dreams she is always with Dmitri, and they're laughing, talking, and doing things she doesn't understand. They're working together like a precision team, hunting down and killing rogue vampires. In other dreams they're making love, and increasingly it feels right, like that's the way it's supposed to be. Eliza has examined her thoughts, feelings, and emotions dozens of times. It feels like she's been weighed, measured, and found wanting.

She's grateful when her next ten-day holiday arrives and she can leave the whole mess behind her and join Matt in London. Seeing Matt and spending time with him feels like her one mooring for sanity in the messed-up world she lives in. It's refreshing to hear his laugh and see his smile. It's the only time she can be herself, unlike in the farce of her life in the inner lair. She's constantly on guard there—someone is always listening or following her every move.

Eliza pays extra attention for any sign of Dmitri or anyone else trailing her, but sees no one. If Dmitri came to London this time, he either is not stalking her or is staying well hidden. Still, she keeps up the charade of being solo on this trip, returning to the London manor each morning and leaving it each night. This time she makes an effort to be friendly to the locals. They will be integral to her plans in the future.

When she reaches the hotel, Matt greets her with a lopsided grin and a hug. Eliza savors the moment and suggests they go do something fun. Matt flicks her nose. "Business before pleasure, baby vamp."

"Tyrant," she teases as he hands her portfolios of information on the witch, the guards, some of the courtesans, and each member of the Druzhina. He tells her that they are also making progress in uncovering the scope of Belyakov's financial empire. A good sum of Shashenka's money comes from businesses he owns solely or in a partnership with unsuspecting humans. He leaves CEOs to run the businesses and only attends critical board meetings. Not surprisingly, he gains some of his money by illegal means: drugs, sex slave trade, and stolen antiquities.

Matt has hired the best mergers and acquisitions experts to assist him in making inroads into Shashenka's businesses. When the time is right, they'll help leverage a few hostile takeovers ahead of moving on Belyakov. In the meantime, Eliza needs to act on the intelligence Matt has gathered on the inner circle members. She will study their files during this holiday and put the knowledge to use when she returns to the castle.

Next, she tells him about the name Maria revealed: Elizabetta Rossellini. When she explains how important it is, Matt makes a couple of calls and launches the search immediately. They don't know when preliminary word will come; it may take some time, and time seems to be their biggest enemy and hurdle. Both are eager to finish this, but there is no way to bring Shashenka down faster or sooner. They are resigned to staying the course.

The coven will likely be in Novgorod another month, and Shashenka hasn't yet revealed where the inner lair is going next. Eliza is nervous that Matt may have to start searching for her again when they move. He reassures her that there are wolf packs now in his employ, keeping constant watch over activity at all the Belyakov estates. He'll know within hours which place they go to next.

Two nights later, with the serious discussions behind them, Matt and Eliza decide to enjoy their remaining time sightseeing and having fun. They've both been under tremendous stress, and planning to end the reign of a thousand-year-old vampire has been more involved than either expected. Eliza smiles as she watches Matt down another drink. He's earned it, deserves it—she doesn't know where she'd be without him.

After a few hours in a local pub, dancing and laughing, they return to his plush suite at the hotel. He's a little tipsy from the suds, and she keeps him from falling over as he stumbles through the lobby. She could pack him back to his room, but bystanders would find it odd that someone her size can lift someone of his.

Goofball ... he needs to sleep it off. Eliza helps strip him down to his boxers. He's laughing and trying to find a way to help her out of her clothes too. She rebuffs him by playfully swatting his hands away.

Falling onto the bed and pulling Eliza on top of him, Matt slurs his words. "Baby vamp, I know we agreed, but tell me again why we have to wait until this is all over before you decide if we're going to be together?"

She raises her upper body to look at him. "You know why. Right now you're my best friend, my closest friend. If we cross that line, it can ruin everything between us."

The lopsided grin on his face fades as he becomes serious. A breathless rush of words tumbles over his lips. "Do you know how much I want you? Do you know how hard it is letting you go back to those bloodsuckers after one of these visits?"

"Matt, sweetie"—she nuzzles his nose with hers—"I'm a bloodsucker."

He laughs. "You don't count. You're my baby vamp. I found you and I'm keeping you." Then he pulls her close and kisses her.

What if I'm not yours to keep? She politely finishes the kiss and pulls away. The kiss reaffirms that nothing has changed for her. Even as bad as things are between her and Dmitri, his pull on her is stronger than ever. Making out with Matt only gives him false hope and complicates their friendship.

"Ah, come on, Eliza, don't be like that." Matt's eyes lock on hers. "I want you. I want you so badly. I need you. Please."

"You're drunk." She pokes his ribs. "You need to sleep it off. I'm going to step out and go do a few things before I go back to the manor. I'll see you tonight."

Defeated, Matt tosses his arms wide on the bed and groans. As she's walking toward the door, he says, "Hey, baby vamp."

Eliza turns and looks at him. "Yes, Matt?"

"I love you."

Smiling, she blows him a kiss. "I love you too. Now get some sleep."

Eliza drives around London until the first color shift in the sky signals the coming sun and forces her to return to the manor. If Matt doesn't stop pushing, she's going to have to tell him everything about Dmitri. *Yeah, and what exactly can I say? Oh, by the way, I went total psycho-chick, but hey, everything's cool. I left him a blubbering mess, and oh yeah, I think I'm in love with him. But don't worry about me—I've got it all under control. I refuse to be a victim anymore and*

I've completely taken charge of my life, even if I totally don't know who the hell I am. What do you mean you spell winner l-o-s-e-r?

Something is not right. There are too many déjà vu moments and missing pieces to the puzzle of her life—even without her looking, they find her. It's like Maria's revelation of what Eliza intuitively knows is her real name; but Eliza has no proof, and there's a slim chance she could be wrong. When she started this crusade against the goblin king, she wanted to put the search for her past off until after he was destroyed. The incident with Dmitri has left her feeling that it's necessary to piece together who she is first—it may be the only way to achieve her goals. If she doesn't, she may fail in keeping him safe. After Shashenka's glee over the way she hurt Dmitri, she is more convinced than ever that Dmitri is pivotal to everything surrounding her. *Someone should have protected him from me.*

When she sees Matt on the last night of her holiday, she decides to talk to him before they go out. Apart from her growing feelings for Dmitri, Matt needs to know something about her personal struggle. "How much do you remember of last night?"

He groans. "All of it. I was pathetically stupid, wasn't I?"

"Yeah, you were." She grins. "I still love you, though, and you're still my best friend."

"That's good. I was afraid you'd get mad, and I'd find out that I royally messed everything up between us." Matt sighs and shrugs apologetically.

"Well ..." Eliza leads him to the couch. "I want to talk to

you about it before we go do anything tonight."

"Am I ... in trouble?" He gives her an overly dramatic wounded expression.

"Keep that up and you will be." She punches him in the arm. "No, what I need to tell you is something I don't quite understand myself. I'm hoping some of your research about the Belyakov coven may help me sort it out."

"You're spooking me, baby vamp." He takes her hand, looking concerned. "Are you all right?"

Not really. "I'm fine." She breaks eye contact for a moment. "In any of your research, have you seen or heard much on vampire mates?"

She listens as Matt tells her what he knows. Then, drawing a deep breath, Eliza finally shares the doubts and questions that hold no answers for her. "I mean, I don't get it. Why would a vampire, a man, do so much, risk so much, and endure so much for a woman? Does that make sense to you?"

Matt looks worried. "What little I've read or heard matches what you're describing. These sound like the actions of an avenging mate."

"But we're not mates, and that's the biggest part that stumps me. Why is he doing all of this? Why did he spend so lavishly on a matched pair of custom-made daggers? Why is he subjecting himself to such brutal torture from that vile goblin king?"

"Like I said, maybe it's an avenging thing." He shrugs.

Shaking her head in exasperation, Eliza says, "There's nothing to avenge. We haven't known each other long enough, and I'm not his mate. From what you've said, it's a two-way street, not a one-sided affair."

"So what's all that got to do with me acting like a fool last night?"

Several seconds jump off the clock. *I've got to say it ... break it gently.* Taking his hands in hers, Eliza gives him a sympathetic look. "Do you remember that night back in West Yellowstone, when we almost had sex and I couldn't do it?"

"Yeah, I try not to think about that too much. It was a seriously weird night for us, baby vamp."

"Things haven't changed for me since that night, and in some ways it's worse. I'm sorry, but it's true. Whenever we get too intimate, images of Dmitri flash through my mind. It's absurd, but I feel like I'm cheating on him. Like he's standing between us, and I don't get it. That shouldn't be happening."

She gives him an apologetic smile. "It's not right ... me, you, together like that, with Dmitri in my head, it's not right. It's not fair to you, Matt, and I love you too much to—"

Anger and hurt creep into his voice. "What? Are you telling me that you prefer a man, no, a bloodsucker you've thoroughly chewed up and spat out, over me?"

Yes, maybe. No, I need both of you. Groaning, Eliza says, "No, that's not what I'm saying. I'm saying that I need to solve the mystery of why Dmitri is acting the way he is—why he's affecting me the way he is—before I can in any way, honestly, come to you as something other than a friend."

She flushes with embarrassment. "I'm acting monstrously evil toward him, and I'm so ashamed ... I never wanted to be a monster, and around Dmitri ... with him I am one. I don't like me this way, and if you knew just how atrocious I've become, you wouldn't like me either. It's not fair to him and it's not fair to you. Do you understand?"

"Yeah, I think I do." Matt grabs her into a hug. "Go figure it out and make amends where you need to. No matter what, baby vamp, I'll always be your friend."

I hope so, because I don't know what I've done to deserve you or what I'd do without you.

They part without unresolved problems between them. There's a glimmer of the old Matt, the man who became her friend under a juniper bush, when they say good-bye. It lifts her spirits as she once more returns to the Belyakov castle.

Unfortunately the search for Elizabetta Rossellini is still incomplete, and she's returning to Novgorod without so much as a scrap of information that may shed light on her past. Regardless, there is one thing she must do when she reaches the castle. She begins looking for Dmitri as soon as she arrives. While she will not yet reveal her plans, it is finally time to pull the proverbial dagger from his heart. *Better hope it's not too late.* She doesn't want to fight with him or hurt him anymore, but she has to keep him safe. Her apology will be meaningless if she says the wrong words. *I have to make each one count. I need him to trust me. I can't shake the feeling he's my missing key ... I need him or I will fail.*

CHAPTER 42: DMITRI

Ignite

Word comes that Eliza has returned from London, but Dmitri remains far away from her. Even when others tell him that she's looking for him, he hides from the imposter—she is not his Elizabetta, never will be her. *I can't face her. I won't look at her ever again.* Then Sally is blocking his path in the hall, arms outstretched, thwarting his efforts to move past her.

"Dmitri, Eliza wants to speak to you, and she says it's important. She's waiting in her room for you."

He nods and ducks under her arm, going in the opposite direction. Sally rushes past him and repeats the message. Again he nods and keeps moving further away from the corridor leading to their bedrooms. *I need to get to our cell.* Apparently undeterred, Sally grabs him from behind and forces him to turn to face her. She looks as if she might cry, and he doesn't understand what's wrong. Without a word she grabs his hand and forearm and begins pulling him the other way. He doesn't have the strength to resist. He trips and stumbles as she leads him to Eliza's door.

Sally looks at him long and hard, and at last seems to find resolve. "Knock. I'm not leaving until you go into that room."

Somehow his arm rises and he knocks lightly on the door. Limply he lets his hand return to his side. Sally stands with him, waiting, breaths rising and falling heavily in her chest. He doesn't know if he's breathing at all.

A few moments pass and he's about to leave, but Eliza calls out, "Come in."

Sally turns the knob, pushes the door open, and when Dmitri doesn't move, nudges him forward. Eliza is standing at the narrow window, her back to him, staring out at the courtyard; he can see her in the mid-peripheral vision of his downcast eyes. *Not my Elizabetta. Don't look ... don't look up at her.*

Dmitri focuses on a crack in the stone floor. Sally softly closes the door, shutting him inside the room with Eliza. He's here now, no way to avoid it. He knows she's waiting for him to speak, but he hasn't spoken to anyone in weeks. Feeling gutted, devastated, and ashamed of everything he's done makes it more difficult for him to find words in his mind and push them to his lips.

Dmitri gulps twice, still looking down. "You ... wanted ... to see me?" He doesn't know why he's suddenly breathing so hard, or why his body is trembling.

Eliza turns around to face him. "I owe you an apology. What I did, what I said, was wrong and uncalled for—you didn't deserve that."

She pauses. "It was horrific and shameful, and I'm truly,

deeply sorry for treating you so cruelly, for hurting you. Please ... please, please, Dmitri, find it in your heart to forgive me someday."

That voice ... *My Elizabetta! You've done nothing wrong. There's nothing for me to forgive. I failed you.* He should be begging her forgiveness but can't find the strength or the words to do that. All he wants is the darkness. Somehow the imposter is keeping it away. Still unable to look at her, he simply nods and unconsciously replies in his long-dormant native tongue, "*Blagodarya ti.*" They are the only words that reach his lips—a simple, ridiculous thank you, and he feels foolish for saying them.

Eliza turns back to stare out the window. He remains frozen; she hasn't dismissed him. A couple of minutes pass before she ends the interminable and unbearable silence. "Dmitri, do you recall in Big Sky, when you were sent to break me?"

How can I not? It torments my every hour. The most atrocious deed he's done in his long existence was break her. He will never forget the last time he held her in his arms, trying to keep her pieces together, and failing to stop each one from falling through his fingertips, disappearing forever into the abyss.

Dmitri's throat constricts and he barely manages to force sound from his mouth. "Yes." Chokingly, he admits, "Only I didn't just break you ... I destroyed you." He whispers as an afterthought, "I destroyed me."

Eliza turns to face him, her movement seeming deliberate and slow. She waits. Then she steps forward, stopping about eighteen inches in front of him. He can feel her eyes on him. He sees her hands move slowly, gently reaching for him. When her hands close around his, Dmitri blinks, and blinks again, trying to comprehend this gesture, and the soothing sensation of her touch. Finally he manages to lift his head, and with some effort, his eyes, to her face—throat, chin, lips, nose, eyes—he startles and freezes.

A tender, encouraging smile is on her face. She squeezes his hands, lifting them with hers and holding them to her chest. Her eyes blaze fiercely, passionately. "Dmitri, you didn't destroy me. You ignited me."

To be continued ...

in *Nights of Shadow—Vendetta*

(Read on for a sneak peek)

Coming Fall 2015 ...

Book Two of the *Nights of Shadow* series!

VENDETTA

Prologue

The commotion in the corner of the tavern draws her attention. Sitting there without drinks are nine people talking and arguing. The tall, dark-haired man seated among them glares coldly around the room. "I think we'd best take this elsewhere. We're drawing too much attention here."

His gruff voice fails to quiet their noise. "Enough!" The tall man slams his hand on the table, and they fall silent. "I said, it's time to go."

Nine pairs of angry eyes sweep the room. Without another word, the group rises and leaves the tavern.

A petite woman with black hair waits a moment after they walk out the door, then cautiously steps out of the tavern and follows them. Keeping to the shadows, she trails them to a warehouse near the docks. Quietly slipping inside, she listens, letting the sound of their voices guide her to the back of the warehouse, where they're now seated among crates and shelves of goods. She crouches between the rows of crates to listen, and to her relief their argument continues.

A man is speaking. "I'm telling you, his mind is gone. It was as if he didn't know us, couldn't see us. I don't think he knows himself. We never got one intelligent response from him."

"I still want to know why he's like that," a woman says, sounding concerned.

Another woman adds, "Maria claims Elizabetta drove him to this madness."

The first man confirms it. "I don't blame her ... I'm not happy with her, but I don't blame her. We all know who is ultimately responsible for this. The reason we're discussing this is to decide what we're going to do about it."

The second woman says sadly, "I don't know what anyone can do. Maria says he's so far gone that even Master has stopped tormenting him."

Elizabetta. Maria. Master. The petite woman, hidden within the shadows, raises her eyebrows at the mention of the names. Now she needs confirmation of where their loyalties lie, and she hopes they will provide it. The man paying for her services is offering a handsome bonus if she can report this detail.

The first woman says, "As best we can figure out, it is a combination of the centuries of torture and Elizabetta's not knowing about her past, believing her new life ... new role."

A third woman impatiently asks, "What did she do to him?"

"The rumor is, she threw a tantrum about everything she believes he's done to her."

"I don't care what she did," the first man bellows. "The

point of this meeting is what, if anything, we are going to do about it. If Master has done this to them, what's to stop him from targeting one of us next?"

A third man's words are cautious, measured. "What are you suggesting?"

"I don't know if it's possible to undo the damage done to Dmitri. There may be a chance to restore Elizabetta's memories, if Maria doesn't ally against us." He pauses. "It may be time for us to consider ending Shashenka Belyakov's reign."

The warehouse falls silent for several long seconds and then heatedly erupts into further argument.

Smiling, the petite woman slips out of the warehouse and starts running.

Confirmation.

CHAPTER 1: DMITRI

The Void

The voice is talking again. It is one of two voices he hears, and he's not sure he knows either, but this one is hauntingly familiar and always pulling him away from the darkness. The other voice, the one he hears the most, he assumes is his inner one; his outer voice disappeared, and he hasn't found it within the shadows.

The void is coming to take me.

Someone has found him in the darkness and is lifting him, compelling him to move. He doesn't want to leave, but his body rarely listens to his mind anymore.

The void is taking me.

The next few moments flicker images from outside. The lovely woman with long dark hair is here again. She's talking, but no sound is coming out. Dmitri feels as if he should know her. Sometimes he wishes he could stay ...

The void is my companion, my friend.

A tangle of memories, dreams, and reality melt into the sensation of a woman's arm curled around his side and her breath at his back. Dmitri realizes they are lying on a bed. He should know this touch. Then he remembers it is hers.

Elizabetta.

Suddenly the pain is excruciating. Walls, heavy, thick black walls are rising up, moving in, and surrounding him. The pain is still there, and another set of black walls comes forth, layering upon the first. Then another set of walls, and the pain is less—more walls, too many layers to count, too many to care. There is no pain. There is nothing here.

The void never hurts me. It's safe here. I'm safe.

Millennia pass for Dmitri, and every few hundred years the black walls crumble, revealing a world outside and beyond the secrets of the darkness he lives in. There used to be others here on the outside, but now there's only one. He finds her breathtaking ... heartbreaking. New walls build and the darkness wraps its arms around him again.

Playlist for Nights of Shadow—Artifice

The songs in this playlist fit the themes and scenes of *Nights of Shadow—Artifice*, and some are specific to Dmitri, Elizabetta/Eliza, and Matt. They helped inspire me during the writing of *Artifice*; hopefully they will also help you enjoy a deeper emotional connection to the story and its characters.

YouTube: http://tinyurl.com/o8hceoj

1) "Black Roses" by Candice Night [Eliza's anthem]
2) "My Silver Lining" by First Aid Kit [Dmitri's anthem]
3) "The Forgotten" by Green Day [Dmitri's motivation to bring Elizabetta back]
4) "Don't Let The Sun Go Down On Me" by Elton John [Dmitri's reflections—recalled to Prague]
5) "Rolling in the Deep" by Adele [the standoff and aftermath at McAllister]
6) "Wind is Calling" by Candice Night [Eliza's nagging thoughts about her past]
7) "Decode" by Paramore [Eliza confronts Dmitri at Big Sky]
8) "Possibility" by Lykke Li [Dmitri shatters at Big Sky]
9) "The Spinner's Tale" by Blackmore's Night [Eliza embraces her endless nights of shadow]
10) "Dangerous Smile" by Candice Night [Eliza's determination to destroy Shashenka]

11) "Take Me to Church" by Hozier [Dmitri's desperation in Novgorod]

12) "Wolf" by First Aid Kit [Matt's quest]

13) "I Didn't Mean It" by The Belle Brigade [Dmitri confronts Eliza in London]

14) "Gone Gone Gone" by Candice Night [Eliza's motivation to save Dmitri]

15) "Past The Point Of Rescue" by Hal Ketchum [Dmitri longing for what he's lost with Elizabetta]

16) "Ghost Town" by First Aid Kit [Eliza's growing list of things to make up for someday]

17) "Don't Strike A Match" by Hal Ketchum [Dmitri's silent pleading, trying to hold on]

18) "Now and Then" by Blackmore's Night [Dmitri letting go of Eliza]

19) "My Immortal" by Evanescence [Dmitri haunted by Elizabetta in the void]

About the Author

Lianne Miller grew up in the mountains of southwestern Montana, about two hundred miles northwest of Bozeman. She now lives on the high plains in the northeastern part of the state, where she runs a horse ranch with her husband and an extended family member.

From riding horses to driving a semitruck and owning a small business, Lianne has worn many hats and labels, and she often claims to be a jack-of-all-trades and master of none. Now many of her days are spent writing and bringing to life the stories she began creating while raising her children. Lianne's books delve into judgment, tolerance, prejudice, and acceptance—challenges in both the human and the paranormal worlds. She has chosen *Nights of Shadow—Artifice* as her debut novel, the first in a series.

For news about Lianne's stories and characters or to sign up for email alerts, visit her online world:

Website: www.liannemiller.com
Blog: http://apps.liannemiller.com/Blog
Facebook: www.facebook.com/MillerLianne
Twitter: https://twitter.com/_LianneMiller
YouTube Channel: http://tinyurl.com/owrvqhh

Acknowledgments

To my readers, I humbly thank you for buying this book. Please consider writing a review for this story wherever it was purchased online. I want to hear your thoughts about Eliza, Dmitri, Matt, the Druzhinas, Maria, and yes, even Shashenka, and their shadow realm world. Let me know what made you laugh or cry or made you angry, but most importantly, whether you enjoyed the story.

Special thanks to my beta reader team—Mark, Ruth, Elaine, Abram, Tony, Rose, Tim, Maryann, Kirk, Rachel, Hank, and Lyudmila. Your critical and complimentary input, along with your enthusiasm and encouragement, helped make the final version of this story possible.

My heartfelt thanks goes to my family, for putting up with me when I'm in serious writing mode and for all the times you have pushed me to follow this dream. I couldn't have done this without you.

Lastly, I want to thank my editor, Christina M. Frey of Page Two Editing, for all of her diligent and hard work. I came to you with the desire to put my best work out there, and I believe you have succeeded in helping me accomplish that goal. It has been a pleasure working with you.